December 25, 1994

Dearest Andrew —

Have a marvelous
Christmas and a wonderful
New Year —

All our love —

ROUND THE FIRE STORIES

SIR ARTHUR CONAN DOYLE

ROUND THE FIRE STORIES

First U.S. edition copyright © 1908 by The McClure Company

Printed in the United States of America

Library of Congress Cataloging-in-Publication Data

Doyle, Arthur Conan, Sir, 1859–1930.
    Round the fire stories / Sir Arthur Conan Doyle.
       p.   cm.
    ISBN 0-87701-883-9
    1. Horror tales, English.   I. Title.
PR4622.R68   1991
823'.8—dc20   90-23799
                                               CIP

Illustration and cover design: Alex Laurant
Composition: Walker Graphics

Distributed in Canada by Raincoast Books,
112 East Third Avenue, Vancouver, B.C. V5T 1C8

10   9   8   7   6   5   4   3   2

Chronicle Books
275 Fifth Street
San Francisco, CA 94103

♲ printed on recycled paper

CONTENTS

PREFACE

In a previous volume, *The Green Flag,* I have assembled a number of my stories which deal with warfare or with sport. In the present collection those have been brought together which are concerned with the grotesque and with the terrible—such tales as might well be read "round the fire" upon a winter's night. This would be my ideal atmosphere for such stories, if an author might choose his time and place as an artist does the light and hanging of his picture. However, if they have the good fortune to give pleasure to anyone, at anytime or place, their author will be very satisfied.

Arthur Conan Doyle

Windlesham,
  Crowborough

THE LEATHER FUNNEL

My friend, Lionel Dacre, lived in the Avenue de Wagram, Paris. His house was that small one, with the iron railings and grass plot in front of it, on the left-hand side as you pass down from the Arc de Triomphe. I fancy that it had been there long before the avenue was constructed, for the gray tiles were stained with lichens, and the walls were mildewed and discolored with age. It looked a small house from the street, five windows in front, if I remember right, but it deepened into a single long chamber at the back. It was here that Dacre had that singular library of occult literature, and the fantastic curiosities which served as a hobby for himself, and an amusement for his friends. A wealthy man of refined and eccentric tastes, he had spent much of his life and fortune in gathering together what was said to be a unique private collection of Talmudic, cabalistic, and magical works, many of them of great rarity and value. His tastes leaned toward the marvelous and the monstrous, and I have heard that his experiments in the direction of the unknown have passed all the bounds of civilization and of decorum. To his English friends he never alluded to such matters, and took the tone of the student and virtuoso; but a Frenchman whose tastes were of the same nature has assured me that the worst excesses of the black mass have been perpetrated in that large and lofty hall, which is lined with the shelves of his books, and the cases of his museum.

Dacre's appearance was enough to show that his deep interest in these psychic matters was intellectual rather than spiritual. There was no trace of asceticism upon his heavy face, but there was much mental force in his huge dome-like skull, which curved upward from amongst his thinning locks, like a snow peak above its fringe of fir trees. His knowledge was greater than his wisdom, and his powers were far superior to his character. The small bright eyes, buried deeply in his fleshy face, twinkled with intelligence and an unabated curiosity of life, but they were the eyes of a sensualist and an egotist. Enough of the man, for he is dead now, poor devil, dead at the very time that he had made sure that he had at last discovered the elixir of life. It is not with his complex character that I have to deal, but with the very strange and inexplicable incident which had its rise in my visit to him in the early spring of the year '82.

I had known Dacre in England, for my researches in the Assyrian Room of the British Museum had been conducted at the time when he was endeavoring to establish a mystic and esoteric meaning in the Babylonian tablets, and this community of interests had brought us together. Chance remarks had led to daily conversation, and that to something verging upon friendship. I had promised him that on my next visit to Paris I would call upon him. At the time when I was able to fulfill my compact I was living in a cottage at Fontainebleau, and as the evening trains were inconvenient, he asked me to spend the night in his house.

"I have only that one spare couch," said he, pointing to a broad sofa in his large salon; "I hope that you will manage to be comfortable there."

It was a singular bedroom, with its high walls of brown volumes, but there could be no more agreeable furniture to a bookworm like myself, and there is no scent so pleasant to my nostrils as that faint, subtle reek which comes from an ancient book. I assured him that I could desire no more charming chamber, and no more congenial surroundings.

"If the fittings are neither convenient nor conventional, they are at least costly," said he, looking round at his shelves. "I have expended nearly a quarter of a million of money upon these objects which surround you. Books, weapons, gems, carvings, tapestries, images—there is hardly a thing here which has not its history, and it is generally one worth telling."

He was seated as he spoke at one side of the open fireplace, and I at the other. His reading table was on his right, and the strong lamp above it ringed it with a very vivid circle of golden light. A half-rolled palimpsest lay in the center, and around it were many quaint articles of bric-à-brac. One of these was a large funnel, such as is used for filling wine casks. It appeared to be made of black wood, and to be rimmed with discolored brass.

"That is a curious thing," I remarked. "What is the history of that?"

"Ah!" said he, "it is the very question which I have had occasion to ask myself. I would give a good deal to know. Take it in your hands and examine it."

I did so, and found that what I had imagined to be wood was in reality leather, though age had dried it into an extreme hardness. It was a large funnel, and might hold a quart when full. The brass rim encircled the wide end, but the narrow was also tipped with metal.

"What do you make of it?" asked Dacre.

"I should imagine that it belonged to some vintner or maltster in the middle ages," said I. "I have seen in England leathern drinking flagons of the seventeenth century—'black jacks' as they were called—which were of the same color and hardness as this filler."

"I dare say the date would be about the same," said Dacre, "and no doubt, also, it was used for filling a vessel with liquid. If my suspicions are correct, however, it was a queer vintner who used it, and a very singular cask which was filled. Do you observe nothing strange at the spout end of the funnel."

As I held it to the light I observed that at a spot some five inches above the brass tip the narrow neck of the leather funnel was all haggled and scored, as if someone had notched it round with a blunt knife. Only at that point was there any roughening of the dead black surface.

"Someone has tried to cut off the neck."

"Would you call it a cut?"

"It is torn and lacerated. It must have taken some strength to leave these marks on such tough material, whatever the instrument may have been. But what do you think of it? I can tell that you know more than you say."

Dacre smiled, and his little eyes twinkled with knowledge.

"Have you included the psychology of dreams among your learned studies?" he asked.

"I did not even know that there was such a psychology."

"My dear sir, that shelf above the gem case is filled with volumes, from Albertus Magnus onward, which deal with no other subject. It is a science in itself."

"A science of charlatans."

"The charlatan is always the pioneer. From the astrologer came the astronomer, from the alchemist the chemist, from the mesmerist the experimental psychologist. The quack of yesterday is the professor of tomorrow. Even such subtle and elusive things as dreams will in time be reduced to system and order. When that time comes the researches of our friends in the bookshelf yonder will no longer be the amusement of the mystic, but the foundations of a science."

"Supposing that is so, what has the science of dreams to do with a large black brass-rimmed funnel?"

"I will tell you. You know that I have an agent who is always on the lookout for rarities and curiosities for my collection. Some days ago he heard of a dealer upon one of the Quais who had acquired some old rubbish found in a cupboard in an ancient house at the back of the Rue Mathurin, in the Quartier Latin. The dining room of this old house is decorated with a coat of arms, chevrons, and bars rouge upon a field argent, which prove, upon inquiry, to be the shield of Nicholas de la Reynie, a high official of King Louis XIV. There can be no doubt that the other articles in the cupboard date back to the early days of that king. The inference is, therefore, that they were all the property of this Nicholas de la Reynie, who was, as I understand, the gentleman specially concerned with the maintenance and execution of the Draconic laws of that epoch."

"What then?"

"I would ask you now to take the funnel into your hands once more and to examine the upper brass rim. Can you make out any lettering upon it?"

There were certainly some scratches upon it, almost obliterated by time. The general effect was of several letters, the last of which bore some resemblance to a *B*.

"You make it a *B*?"

"Yes, I do."

"So do I. In fact, I have no doubt whatever that it is a *B*."

"But the nobleman you mentioned would have had *R* for his initial."

Exactly! That's the beauty of it. He owned this curious object, and yet he had someone else's initials upon it. Why did he do this?"

"I can't imagine; can you?"

"Well, I might, perhaps, guess. Do you observe something drawn a little further along the rim?"

"I should say it was a crown."

It is undoubtedly a crown; but if you examine it in a good light, you will convince yourself that it is not an ordinary crown. It is a heraldic crown—a badge of rank, and it consists of an alternation of four pearls and strawberry leaves, the proper badge of a marquis. We may infer, therefore, that the person whose initials end in *B* was entitled to wear that coronet."

"Then this common leather filler belonged to a marquis?"

Dacre gave a peculiar smile.

"Or to some member of the family of a marquis," said he. "So much we have clearly gathered from this engraved rim."

"But what has all this to do with dreams?" I do not know whether it was from a look upon Dacre's face, or from some subtle suggestion in his manner, but a feeling of repulsion, of unreasoning horror, came upon me as I looked at the gnarled old lump of leather.

"I have more than once received important information through my dreams," said my companion, in the didactic manner which he loved to affect. "I make it a rule now when I am in doubt upon any material point to place the article in question beside me as I sleep, and to hope for some enlightenment. The process does not appear to me to be very obscure, though it has not yet received the blessing of orthodox science. According to my theory, any object which has been intimately associated with any supreme paroxysm of human emotion, whether it be joy or pain, will retain a certain atmosphere or association which it is capable of communicating to a sensitive mind. By a sensitive mind I do not mean an abnormal one, but such a trained and educated mind as you or I possess."

"You mean, for example, that if I slept beside that old sword upon the wall, I might dream of some bloody incident in which that very sword took part?"

"An excellent example, for, as a matter of fact, that sword was used in that fashion by me, and I saw in my sleep the death of its owner, who perished in a brisk skirmish, which I have been unable to identify, but which occurred at the time of the wars of the Frondists. If you think of it, some of our popular observances show that the fact has already been recognized by our ancestors, although we, in our wisdom, have classed it among superstitions."

"For example?"

"Well, the placing of the bride's cake beneath the pillow in order that the sleeper may have pleasant dreams. That is one of several instances which you will find set forth in a small brochure which I am myself writing upon the subject. But to come back to the point, I slept one night with this funnel beside me, and I had a dream which certainly throws a curious light upon its use and origin."

"What did you dream?"

"I dreamed—" He paused, and an intent look of interest came over his massive face. "By Jove that's well thought of," said he. "This really will be an exceedingly interesting experiment. You are yourself a psychic subject—with nerves which respond readily to any impression."

"I have never tested myself in that direction."

"Then we shall test you tonight. Might I ask you as a very great favor, when you occupy that couch, tonight, to sleep with this old funnel placed by the side of your pillow?"

The request seemed to me a grotesque one; but I have myself, in my complex nature, a hunger after all which is bizarre and fantastic. I had not the faintest belief in Dacre's theory, nor any hopes for success in such an experiment; yet it amused me that the experiment should be made. Dacre, with great gravity, drew a small stand to the head of my settee, and placed the funnel upon it. Then, after a short conversation, he wished me good-night and left me.

I sat for some little time smoking by the smoldering fire, and turning over in my mind the curious incident which had occurred, and the strange experience which might lie before me. Skeptical as I was, there was something impressive in the assurance of Dacre's manner, and my extraordinary surroundings, the huge room with the strange and often sinister objects which were hung round it, struck solemnity into my soul. Finally I undressed, and, turning out the lamp, I lay down. After long tossing I fell asleep. Let me try to describe as accurately as I can the scene which came to me in my dreams. It stands out now in my memory more clearly than anything which I have seen with my waking eyes.

There was a room which bore the appearance of a vault. Four spandrels from the corners ran up to join a sharp cup-shaped roof. The architecture was rough, but very strong. It was evidently part of a great building.

Three men in black, with curious top-heavy black velvet hats, sat in a line upon a red-carpeted dais. Their faces were very solemn and sad. On the left stood two long-gowned men with portfolios in their hands, which seemed to be stuffed with papers. Upon the right, looking toward me, was a small woman with blond hair and singular light blue eyes— the eyes of a child. She was past her first youth, but could not yet be called middle-aged. Her figure was inclined to stoutness, and her bearing was proud and confident. Her face was pale, but serene. It was a curious face, comely and yet feline, with a subtle suggestion of cruelty about the straight, strong little mouth and chubby jaw. She was draped in some sort of loose white gown. Beside her stood a thin, eager priest, who whispered in her ear, and continually raised a crucifix before her eyes. She turned her head and looked fixedly past the crucifix at the three men in black, who were, I felt, her judges.

As I gazed the three men stood up and said something, but I could distinguish no words, though I was aware that it was the central one who was speaking. They then swept out of the room, followed by the two men with the papers. At the same instant several rough-looking fellows in stout jerkins came bustling in and removed first the red carpet, and then the boards which formed the dais, so as to entirely clear the room. When this screen was removed I saw some singular articles of furniture behind it. One looked like a bed with wooden rollers at each end, and a winch handle to regulate its length. Another was a wooden horse. There were several other curious objects, and a number of swinging cords which played over pulleys. It was not unlike a modern gymnasium.

When the room had been cleared there appeared a new figure upon the scene. This was a tall thin person clad in black, with a gaunt and austere face. The aspect of the man made me shudder. His clothes were all shining with grease and mottled with stains. He bore himself with a slow and impressive dignity, as if he took command of all things from the instant of his entrance. In spite of his rude appearance and sordid dress, it was now *his* business, *his* room, his to command. He carried a coil of light ropes over his left forearm. The lady looked him up and down with a searching glance, but her expression was unchanged. It was confident—even defiant. But it was very different with the priest. His face was ghastly white, and I saw the moisture glisten and run on his high, sloping forehead. He threw up his hands in prayer, and he stooped continually to mutter frantic words in the lady's ear.

The man in black now advanced, and taking one of the cords from his left arm, he bound the woman's hands together. She held them meekly toward him as he did so. Then he took her arm with a rough grip and led her toward the wooden horse, which was little higher than her waist. On to this she was lifted and laid, with her back upon it, and her face to the ceiling, while the priest, quivering with horror, had rushed out of the room. The woman's lips were moving rapidly, and though I could hear nothing, I knew that she was praying. Her feet hung down on either side of the horse, and I saw that the rough varlets in attendance had fastened cords to her ankles and secured the other ends to iron rings in the stone floor.

My heart sank within me as I saw these ominous preparations, and yet I was held by the fascination of horror, and I could not take my eyes from the strange spectacle. A man had entered the room with a bucket of water in either hand. Another followed with a third bucket. They were laid beside the wooden horse. The second man had a wooden dipper—a bowl with a straight handle—in his other hand. This he gave to the man in black. At the same moment one of the varlets approached with a dark object in his hand, which even in my dream filled me with a vague feeling of familiarity. It was a leathern filler. With horrible energy he thrust it—but I could stand no more. My hair stood on end with horror. I writhed, I struggled, I broke through the bonds of sleep, and I burst with a shriek into my own life, and found myself lying shivering with terror in the huge library, with the moonlight flooding through the window and throwing strange silver and black traceries upon the opposite wall. Oh, what a blessed relief to feel that I was back in the nineteenth century—back out of that mediæval vault into a world where men had human hearts within their bosoms. I sat up on my couch, trembling in every limb, my mind divided between thankfulness and horror. To think that such things were ever done—that they *could* be done without God striking the villains dead. Was it all a fantasy, or did it really stand for something which had happened in the black, cruel days of the world's history? I sank my throbbing head upon my shaking hands. And then, suddenly, my heart seemed to stand still in my bosom, and I could not even scream, so great was my terror. Something was advancing toward me through the darkness of the room.

It is a horror coming upon a horror which breaks a man's spirit. I could not reason, I could not pray; I could only sit like a frozen image, and glare at the dark figure which was coming down the great room. And then it moved out into the white lane of moonlight, and I breathed once more. It was Dacre, and his face showed that he was as frightened as myself.

"Was that you? For God's sake what's the matter?" he asked in a husky voice.

"Oh, Dacre, I am glad to see you! I have been down into hell. It was dreadful."

"Then it was you who screamed?"

"I dare say it was."

"It rang through the house. The servants are all terrified." He struck a match and lit the lamp. "I think we may get the fire to burn up again," he added, throwing some logs upon the embers. "Good God, my dear chap, how white you are! You look as if you had seen a ghost."

"So I have—several ghosts."

"The leather funnel has acted, then?"

"I wouldn't sleep near the infernal thing again for all the money you could offer me."

Dacre chuckled.

"I expected that you would have a lively night of it," said he. "You took it out of me in return, for that scream of yours wasn't a very pleasant sound at two in the morning. I suppose from what you say that you have seen the whole dreadful business."

"What dreadful business?"

"The torture of the water—the 'Extraordinary Question,' as it was called in the genial days of 'Le Roi Soleil.' Did you stand it out to the end?"

"No, thank God, I awoke before it really began."

"Ah! it is just as well for you. I held out till the third bucket. Well, it is an old story, and they are all in their graves now anyhow, so what does it matter how they got there. I suppose that you have no idea what it was that you have seen?"

"The torture of some criminal. She must have been a terrible malefactor indeed if her crimes are in proportion to her penalty."

"Well, we have that small consolation," said Dacre, wrapping his dressing gown round him and crouching closer to the fire. "They *were* in proportion to her penalty. That is to say, if I am correct in the lady's identity."

"How could you possibly know her identity?"

For answer Dacre took down an old vellum-covered volume from the shelf.

"Just listen to this," said he; "it is in the French of the seventeenth century, but I will give a rough translation as I go. You will judge for yourself whether I have solved the riddle or not:

The prisoner was brought before the Grand Chambers and Tournelles of Parliament sitting as a court of justice, charged with the murder of Master Dreux d'Aubray, her father, and of her two brothers, MM. d'Aubray, one being civil lieutenant, and the other a counselor of Parliament. In person it seemed hard to believe that she had really done such wicked deeds, for she was of a mild appearance, and of short stature, with a fair skin and blue eyes. Yet the Court, having found her guilty, condemned her to the ordinary and to the extraordinary question in order that she might be forced to name her accomplices, after which she should be carried in a cart to the Place de Grève, there to have her head cut off, her body being afterward burned and her ashes scattered to the winds.

"The date of this entry is July 16, 1676."

"It is interesting," said I, "but not convincing. How do you prove the two women to be the same?"

"I am coming to that. The narrative goes on to tell of the woman's behavior when questioned. 'When the executioner approached her she recognized him by the cords which he held in his hands, and she at once held out her own hands to him, looking at him from head to foot without uttering a word.' How's that?"

"Yes, it was so."

" 'She gazed without wincing upon the wooden horse and rings which had twisted so many limbs and caused so many shrieks of agony. When her eyes fell upon the three pails of water, which were all ready for her, she said with a smile, "All that water must have been brought here for the purpose of drowning me, Monsieur. You have no idea, I trust, of making a person of my small stature swallow it all." ' Shall I read the details of the torture?"

"No, for Heaven's sake, don't."

"Here is a sentence which must surely show you that what is here recorded is the very scene which you have gazed upon tonight: 'The good Abbé Pirot, unable to contemplate the agonies which were suffered by his penitent, had hurried from the room.' Does that convince you?"

"It does entirely. There can be no question that it is indeed the same event. But who, then, is this lady whose appearance was so attractive and whose end was so horrible?"

For answer Dacre came across to me, and placed the small lamp upon the table which stood by my bed. Lifting up the ill-omened filler, he turned the brass rim so that the light fell upon it. Seen in this way the engraving seemed clearer than on the night before.

"We have already agreed that this is the badge of a marquis or of a marquise," said he. "We have also settled that the last letter is *B*."

"It is undoubtedly so."

"I now suggest to you that the other letters from left to right are, *M*, *M*, a small *d*, *A*, a small *d*, and then the final *B*."

"Yes, I am sure that you are right. I can make out the two small *d*'s quite plainly."

"What I have read to you tonight," said Dacre, "is the official record of the trial of Marie Madeleine d'Aubray, Marquis de Brinvilliers, one of the most famous poisoners and murderers of all time."

I sat in silence, overwhelmed at the extraordinary nature of the incident, and at the completeness of the proof with which Dacre had exposed its real meaning. In a vague way I remembered some details of the woman's career, her unbridled debauchery, the cold-blooded and protracted torture of her sick father, the murder of her brothers for motives of petty gain. I recollected also that the bravery of her end had done something to atone for the horror of her life, and that all Paris had sympathized with her last moments, and blessed her as a martyr within a few days of the time when they had cursed her as a murderess. One objection, and one only, occurred to my mind.

"How came her initials and her badge of rank upon the filler. Surely they did not carry their mediæval homage to the nobility to the point of decorating instruments of torture with their titles?

"I was puzzled with the same point," said Dacre, "but it admits of a simple explanation. The case excited extraordinary interest at the time, and nothing could be more natural than that La Reynie, the head of the police, should retain this filler as a grim souvenir. It was not often that a marchioness of France underwent the extraordinary question. That he should engrave her initials upon it for the information of others was surely a very ordinary proceeding upon his part."

"And this?" I asked, pointing to the marks upon the leathern neck.

"She was a cruel tigress," said Dacre, as he turned away. "I think it is evident that like other tigresses her teeth were both strong and sharp."

THE BEETLE HUNTER

A curious experience? said the Doctor. Yes, my friends, I have had one very curious experience. I never expect to have another, for it is against all doctrines of chances that two such events would befall any one man in a single lifetime. You may believe me or not, but the thing happened exactly as I tell it.

I had just become a medical man, but I had not started in practice, and I lived in rooms in Gower Street. The street has been renumbered since then, but it was in the only house which has a bow window, upon the left-hand side as you go down from the Metropolitan Station. A widow named Murchison kept the house at that time, and she had three medical students and one engineer as lodgers. I occupied the top room, which was the cheapest, but cheap as it was it was more than I could afford. My small resources were dwindling away, and every week it became more necessary that I should find something to do. Yet I was very unwilling to go into general practice, for my tastes were all in the direction of science, and especially of zoology, toward which I had always a strong leaning. I had almost given the fight up and resigned myself to being a medical drudge for life, when the turning point of my struggles came in a very extraordinary way.

One morning I had picked up the *Standard* and was glancing over its contents. There was a complete absence of news, and I was about to toss the paper down again, when my eyes were caught by an advertisement at the head of the personal column. It was worded in this way:

> Wanted for one or more days the services of a medical man. It is
> essential that he should be a man of strong physique, of steady
> nerves, and of a resolute nature. Must be an entomologist—co-
> leopterist preferred. Apply, in person, at 77B, Brooke Street. Ap-
> plication must be made before twelve o'clock today.

Now, I have already said that I was devoted to zoology. Of all branches
of zoology, the study of insects was the most attractive to me, and of all
insects beetles were the species with which I was most familiar. Butterfly
collectors are numerous, but beetles are far more varied, and more
accessible in these islands than are butterflies. It was this fact which had
attracted my attention to them, and I had myself made a collection
which numbered some hundred varieties. As to the other requisites of
the advertisement, I knew that my nerves could be depended upon, and
I had won the weight-throwing competition at the inter-hospital sports.
Clearly, I was the very man for the vacancy. Within five minutes of my
having read the advertisement I was in a cab and on my way to Brooke
Street.

As I drove, I kept turning the matter over in my head and trying to
make a guess as to what sort of employment it could be which needed
such curious qualifications. A strong physique, a resolute nature, a medical training, and knowledge of beetles—what connection could there
be between these various requisites? And then there was the disheart-
ening fact that the situation was not a permanent one, but terminable
from day to day, according to the terms of the advertisement. The more
I pondered over it the more unintelligible did it become; but at the end
of my meditations I always came back to the ground fact that, come
what might, I had nothing to lose, that I was completely at the end of
my resources, and that I was ready for any adventure, however desperate, which would put a few honest sovereigns into my pocket. The man
fears to fail who has to pay for his failure, but there was no penalty
which Fortune could exact from me. I was like the gambler with empty
pockets, who is still allowed to try his luck with the others.

No. 77B, Brooke Street, was one of those dingy and yet imposing
houses, dun-colored and flat-faced, with the intensely respectable and
solid air which marks the Georgian builder. As I alighted from the cab,
a young man came out of the door and walked swiftly down the street.
In passing me, I noticed that he cast an inquisitive and somewhat ma-

levolent glance at me, and I took the incident as a good omen, for his appearance was that of a rejected candidate, and if he resented my application it meant that the vacancy was not yet filled up. Full of hope, I ascended the broad steps and rapped with the heavy knocker.

A footman in powder and livery opened the door. Clearly I was in touch with people of wealth and fashion.

"Yes, sir?" said the footman.

"I came in answer to—"

"Quite so, sir," said the footman. "Lord Linchmere will see you at once in the library."

Lord Linchmere! I had vaguely heard the name, but could not for the instant recall anything about him. Following the footman, I was shown into a large, book-lined room in which there was seated behind a writing desk a small man with a pleasant, clean-shaven, mobile face, and long hair shot with gray, brushed back from his forehead. He looked me up and down with a very shrewd, penetrating glance, holding the card which the footman had given him in his right hand. Then he smiled pleasantly, and I felt that externally at any rate I possessed the qualifications which he desired.

"You have come in answer to my advertisement, Dr. Hamilton?" he asked.

"Yes, sir."

"Do you fulfill the conditions which are there laid down?"

"I believe that I do."

"You are a powerful man, or so I should judge from your appearance."

"I think that I am fairly strong."

"And resolute?"

"I believe so."

"Have you ever known what it was to be exposed to imminent danger?"

"No, I don't know that I ever have."

"But you think you would be prompt and cool at such a time?"

"I hope so."

"Well, I believe that you would. I have the more confidence in you because you do not pretend to be certain as to what you would do in a position that was new to you. My impression is that, so far as personal qualities go, you are the very man of whom I am in search. That being settled, we may pass on to the next point."

"Which is?"

"To talk to me about beetles."

I looked across to see if he was joking, but, on the contrary, he was leaning eagerly forward across his desk, and there was an expression something like anxiety in his eyes.

"I am afraid that you do not know about beetles," he cried.

"On the contrary, sir, it is the one scientific subject about which I feel that I really do know something."

"I am overjoyed to hear it. Please talk to me about beetles."

I talked. I do not profess to have said anything original upon the subject, but I gave a short sketch of the characteristics of the beetle, and ran over the more common species, with some allusions to the specimens in my own little collection and to the article upon "Burying Beetles" which I had contributed to the *Journal of Entomological Science*.

"What! Not a collector?" cried Lord Linchmere. "You don't mean that you are yourself a collector?" His eyes danced with pleasure at the thought.

"You are certainly the very man in London for my purpose. I thought that among five millions of people there must be such a man, but the difficulty is to lay one's hands upon him. I have been extraordinarily fortunate in finding you."

He rang a gong upon the table, and the footman entered.

"Ask Lady Rossiter to have the goodness to step this way," said his lordship, and a few moments later the lady was ushered into the room. She was a small, middle-aged woman, very like Lord Linchmere in appearance, with the same quick, alert features and gray-black hair. The expression of anxiety, however, which I had observed upon his face was very much more marked upon hers. Some great grief seemed to have cast its shadow over her features. As Lord Linchmere presented me she turned her face full upon me, and I was shocked to observe a half-healed scar extending for two inches over her right eyebrow. It was partly concealed by plaster, but none the less I could see that it had been a serious wound and not long inflicted.

"Dr. Hamilton is the very man for our purpose, Evelyn," said Lord Linchmere. "He is actually a collector of beetles, and he has written articles upon the subject."

"Really!" said Lady Rossiter. "Then you must have heard of my husband. Every one who knows anything about beetles must have heard of Sir Thomas Rossiter."

For the first time a thin little ray of light began to break into the obscure business. Here, at last, was a connection between these people and beetles. Sir Thomas Rossiter—he was the greatest authority upon the subject in the world. He had made it his lifelong study, and had written a most exhaustive work upon it. I hastened to assure her that I had read and appreciated it.

"Have you met my husband?" she asked.

"No, I have not."

"But you shall," said Lord Linchmere, with decision.

The lady was standing beside the desk, and she put her hand upon his shoulder. It was obvious to me as I saw their faces together that they were brother and sister.

"Are you really prepared for this, Charles? It is noble of you, but you fill me with fears." Her voice quavered with apprehension, and he appeared to me to be equally moved, though he was making strong efforts to conceal his agitation.

"Yes, yes, dear; it is all settled, it is all decided; in fact, there is no other possible way, that I can see."

"There is one obvious way."

"No, no, Evelyn, I shall never abandon you—never. It will come right—depend upon it; it will come right, and surely it looks like the interference of Providence that so perfect an instrument should be put into our hands."

My position was embarrassing, for I felt that for the instant they had forgotten my presence. But Lord Linchmere came back suddenly to me and to my engagement.

"The business for which I want you, Dr. Hamilton, is that you should put yourself absolutely at my disposal. I wish you to come for a short journey with me, to remain always at my side, and to promise to do without question whatever I may ask you, however unreasonable it may appear to you to be."

"That is a good deal to ask," said I.

"Unfortunately I cannot put it more plainly, for I do not myself know what turn matters may take. You may be sure, however, that you will not be asked to do anything which your conscience does not approve; and I promise you that, when all is over, you will be proud to have been concerned in so good a work."

"If it ends happily," said the lady.

"Exactly; if it ends happily," his lordship repeated.

"And terms?" I asked.

"Twenty pounds a day."

I was amazed at the sum, and must have showed my surprise upon my features.

"It is a rare combination of qualities, as must have struck you when you first read the advertisement," said Lord Linchmere; "such varied gifts may well command a high return, and I do not conceal from you that your duties might be arduous or even dangerous. Besides, it is possible that one or two days may bring the matter to an end."

"Please God!" sighed his sister.

"So now, Dr. Hamilton, may I rely upon your aid?"

"Most undoubtedly," said I. "You have only to tell me what my duties are."

"Your first duty will be to return to your home. You will pack up whatever you may need for a short visit to the country. We start together from Paddington Station at 3:40 this afternoon."

"Do we go far?"

"As far as Pangbourne. Meet me at the bookstall at 3:30. I shall have the tickets. Good-bye, Dr. Hamilton! And, by the way, there are two things which I should be very glad if you would bring with you, in case you have them. One is your case for collecting beetles and the other is a stick, and the thicker and heavier the better."

You may imagine that I had plenty to think of from the time that I left Brooke Street until I set out to meet Lord Linchmere at Paddington. The whole fantastic business kept arranging and rearranging itself in kaleidoscopic forms inside my brain, until I had thought out a dozen explanations, each of them more grotesquely improbable than the last. And yet I felt that the truth must be something grotesquely improbable also. At last I gave up all attempts at finding a solution, and contented myself with exactly carrying out the instructions which I had received. With a hand valise, specimen case, and a loaded cane, I was waiting at the Paddington bookstall when Lord Linchmere arrived. He was an even smaller man than I had thought—frail and peaky, with a manner which was more nervous than it had been in the morning. He wore a long, thick traveling ulster, and I observed that he carried a heavy blackthorn cudgel in his hand.

"I have the tickets," said he, leading the way up the platform. "This is our train. I have engaged a carriage, for I am particularly anxious to impress one or two things upon you while we travel down."

And yet all that he had to impress upon me might have been said in a sentence, for it was that I was to remember that I was there as a protection to himself, and that I was not on any consideration to leave him for an instant. This he repeated again and again as our journey drew to a close, with an insistence which showed that his nerves were thoroughly shaken.

"Yes," he said at last, in answer to my looks rather than to my words, "I *am* nervous, Dr. Hamilton. I have always been a timid man, and my timidity depends upon my frail physical health. But my soul is firm, and I can bring myself up to face a danger which a less nervous man might shrink from. What I am doing now is done from no compulsion, but entirely from a sense of duty, and yet it is, beyond doubt, a desperate risk. If things should go wrong, I will have some claims to the title of martyr."

This eternal reading of riddles was too much for me. I felt that I must put a term to it.

"I think it would be very much better, sir, if you were to trust me entirely," said I. "It is impossible for me to act effectively, when I do not know what are the objects which we have in view, or even where we are going."

"Oh, as to where we are going, there need be no mystery about that," said he; "we are going to Delamere Court, the residence of Sir Thomas Rossiter, with whose work you are so conversant. As to the exact object of our visit, I do not know that at this stage of the proceedings anything would be gained, Dr. Hamilton, by my taking you into my complete confidence. I may tell you that we are acting—I say 'we,' because my sister, Lady Rossiter, takes the same view as myself—with the one object of preventing anything in the nature of a family scandal. That being so, you can understand that I am loath to give any explanations which are not absolutely necessary. It would be a different matter, Dr. Hamilton, if I were asking your advice. As matters stand, it is only your active help which I need, and I will indicate to you from time to time how you can best give it."

There was nothing more to be said, and a poor man can put up with a good deal for twenty pounds a day, but I felt none the less than Lord Linchmere was acting rather scurvily toward me. He wished to convert me into a passive tool, like the blackthorn in his hand. With his sensitive disposition I could imagine, however, that scandal would be abhorrent to him, and I realized that he would not take me into his confidence until no other course was open to him. I must trust to my own eyes and ears to solve the mystery, but I had every confidence that I should not trust to them in vain.

Delamere Court lies a good five miles from Pangbourne Station, and we drove for that distance in an open fly. Lord Linchmere sat in deep thought during the time, and he never opened his mouth until we were close to our destination. When he did speak it was to give me a piece of information which surprised me.

"Perhaps you are not aware," said he, "that I am a medical man like yourself?"

"No, sir, I did not know it."

"Yes, I qualified in my younger days, when there were several lives between me and the peerage. I have not had occasion to practice, but I

have found it a useful education, all the same. I never regretted the
years which I devoted to medical study. These are the gates of Delamere
Court."

We had come to two high pillars crowned with heraldic monsters
which flanked the opening of a winding avenue. Over the laurel bushes
and rhododendrons I could see a long, many-gabled mansion, girdled
with ivy, and toned to the warm, cheery, mellow glow of old brickwork.
My eyes were still fixed in admiration upon this delightful house when
my companion plucked nervously at my sleeve.

"Here's Sir Thomas," he whispered. "Please talk beetle all you can."

A tall, thin figure, curiously angular and bony, had emerged through
a gap in the hedge of laurels. In his hand he held a spud, and he wore
gauntleted gardener's gloves. A broad brimmed, gray hat cast his face
into shadow, but it struck me as exceedingly austere, with an ill-nourished beard and harsh, irregular features. The fly pulled up and Lord
Linchmere sprang out.

"My dear Thomas, how are you?" said he, heartily.

But the heartiness was by no means reciprocal. The owner of the
grounds glared at me over his brother-in-law's shoulder, and I caught
broken scraps of sentences—"well-known wishes . . . hatred of
strangers . . . unjustifiable intrusion . . . perfectly inexcusable." Then there
was a muttered explanation, and the two of them came over together to
the side of the fly.

"Let me present you to Sir Thomas Rossiter, Dr. Hamilton," said
Lord Linchmere. "You will find that you have a strong community of
tastes."

I bowed. Sir Thomas stood very stiffly, looking at me severely from
under the broad brim of his hat.

"Lord Linchmere tells me that you know something about beetles,"
said he. "What do you know about beetles?"

"I know what I have learned from your work upon the coleoptera,
Sir Thomas," I answered.

"Give me the names of the better-known species of the British scara-
baei," said he.

I had not expected an examination, but fortunately I was ready for
one. My answers seemed to please him, for his stern features relaxed.

"You appear to have read my book with some profit, sir," said he. "It
is a rare thing for me to meet anyone who takes an intelligent interest in
such matters. People can find time for such trivialities as sport or society,
and yet the beetles are overlooked. I can assure you that the greater part
of the idiots in this part of the country are unaware that I have ever
written a book at all—I, the first man who ever described the true

function of the elytra. I am glad to see you, sir, and I have no doubt that I can show you some specimens which will interest you." He stepped into the fly and drove up with us to the house, expounding to me as we went some recent researches which he had made into the anatomy of the ladybird.

I have said that Sir Thomas Rossiter wore a large hat drawn down over his brows. As he entered the hall he uncovered himself, and I was at once aware of a singular characteristic which the hat had concealed. His forehead, which was naturally high, and higher still on account of receding hair, was in a continual state of movement. Some nervous weakness kept the muscles in a constant spasm, which sometimes produced a mere twitching and sometimes a curious rotary movement unlike anything which I had ever seen before. It was strikingly visible as he turned toward us after entering the study, and seemed the more singular from the contrast with the hard, steady, gray eyes which looked out from underneath those palpitating brows.

"I am sorry," said he, "that Lady Rossiter is not here to help me to welcome you. By the way, Charles, did Evelyn say anything about the date of her return?"

"She wished to stay in town for a few more days," said Lord Linchmere. "You know how ladies' social duties accumulate if they have been for some time in the country. My sister has many old friends in London at present."

"Well, she is her own mistress, and I should not wish to alter her plans, but I shall be glad when I see her again. It is very lonely here without her company."

"I was afraid that you might find it so, and that was partly why I ran down. My young friend, Dr. Hamilton, is so much interested in the subject which you have made your own, that I thought you would not mind his accompanying me."

"I lead a retired life, Dr. Hamilton, and my aversion to strangers grows upon me," said our host. "I have sometimes thought that my nerves are not so good as they were. My travels in search of beetles in my younger days took me into many malarious and unhealthy places. But a brother coleopterist like yourself is always a welcome guest, and I shall be delighted if you will look over my collection, which I think that I may without exaggeration describe as the best in Europe."

And so no doubt it was. He had a huge oaken cabinet arranged in shallow drawers, and here, neatly ticketed and classified, were beetles from every corner of the earth, black, brown, blue, green, and mottled. Every now and then as he swept his hand over the lines and lines of

impaled insects he would catch up some rare specimen, and, handling
it with as much delicacy and reverence as if it were a precious relic, he
would hold forth upon its peculiarities and the circumstances under
which it came into his possession. It was evidently an unusual thing for
him to meet with a sympathetic listener, and he talked and talked until
the spring evening had deepened into night, and the gong announced
that it was time to dress for dinner. All the time Lord Linchmere said
nothing, but he stood at his brother-in-law's elbow, and I caught him
continually shooting curious little, questioning glances into his face.
And his own features expressed some strong emotion, apprehension,
sympathy, expectation: I seemed to read them all. I was sure that Lord
Linchmere was fearing something and awaiting something, but what
that something might be I could not imagine.

The evening passed quietly but pleasantly, and I should have been
entirely at my ease if it had not been for that continual sense of tension
upon the part of Lord Linchmere. As to our host, I found that he
improved upon acquaintance. He spoke constantly with affection of his
absent wife, and also of his little son, who had recently been sent to
school. The house, he said, was not the same without them. If it were
not for his scientific studies, he did not know how he could get through
the days. After dinner we smoked for some time in the billiard room,
and finally went early to bed.

And then it was that, for the first time, the suspicion that Lord
Linchmere was a lunatic crossed my mind. He followed me into my
bedroom, when our host had retired.

"Doctor," said he, speaking in a low, hurried voice, "you must come
with me. You must spend the night in my bedroom."

"What do you mean?"

"I prefer not to explain. But this is part of your duties. My room is
close by, and you can return to your own before the servant calls you in
the morning."

"But why?" I asked.

"Because I am nervous of being alone," said he. "That's the reason,
since you must have a reason."

It seemed rank lunacy, but the argument of those twenty pounds
would overcome many objections. I followed him to his room.

"Well," said I, "there's only room for one in that bed."

"Only one shall occupy it," said he.

"And the other?"

"Must remain, on watch."

"Why?" said I. "One would think you expected to be attacked."

"Perhaps I do."

"In that case, why not lock your door?"

"Perhaps I *want* to be attacked."

It looked more and more like lunacy. However, there was nothing for it but to submit. I shrugged my shoulders and sat down in the armchair beside the empty fireplace.

"I am to remain on watch, then?" said I, ruefully.

"We will divide the night. If you will watch until two, I will watch the remainder."

"Very good."

"Call me at two o'clock, then."

"I will do so."

"Keep your ears open, and if you hear any sounds wake me instantly—instantly, you hear?"

"You can rely upon it." I tried to look as solemn as he did.

"And for God's sake don't go to sleep," said he, and so, taking off only his coat, he threw the coverlet over him and settled down for the night.

It was a melancholy vigil, and made more so by my own sense of its folly. Supposing that by any chance Lord Linchmere had cause to suspect that he was subject to danger in the house of Sir Thomas Rossiter, why on earth could he not lock his door and so protect himself? His own answer that he might wish to be attacked was absurd. Why should he possibly wish to be attacked? And who would wish to attack him? Clearly, Lord Linchmere was suffering from some singular delusion, and the result was that on an imbecile pretext I was to be deprived of my night's rest. Still, however, absurd, I was determined to carry out his injunctions to the letter as long as I was in his employment. I sat therefore beside the empty fireplace, and listened to a sonorous chiming clock somewhere down the passage, which gurgled and struck every quarter of an hour. It was an endless vigil. Save for that single clock, an absolute silence reigned throughout the great house. A small lamp stood on the table at my elbow, throwing a circle of light round my chair, but leaving the corners of the room draped in shadow. On the bed Lord Linchmere was breathing peacefully. I envied him his quiet sleep, and again and again my own eyelids drooped, but every time my sense of duty came to my help, and I sat up, rubbing my eyes and pinching myself with a determination to see my irrational watch to an end.

And I did so. From down the passage came the chimes of two o'clock, and I laid my hand upon the shoulder of the sleeper. Instantly he was sitting up, with an expression of the keenest interest upon his face.

"You have heard something?"

"No, sir. It is two o'clock."

"Very good. I will watch. You can go to sleep."

I lay down under the coverlet as he had done, and was soon unconscious. My last recollection was of that circle of lamplight, and of the
small, hunched-up figure and strained anxious face of Lord Linchmere
in the center of it.

How long I slept I do not know; but I was suddenly aroused by a
sharp tug at my sleeve. The room was in darkness, but a hot smell of oil
told me that the lamp had only that instant been extinguished.

"Quick! Quick!" said Lord Linchmere's voice in my ear.

I sprang out of bed, he still dragging at my arm.

."Over here!" he whispered and pulled me into a corner of the room.
"Hush! Listen!"

In the silence of the night I could distinctly hear that someone was
coming down the corridor. It was a stealthy step, faint and intermittent,
as of a man who paused cautiously after every stride. Sometimes for half
a minute there was no sound, and then came the shuffle and creak which
told of a fresh advance. My companion was trembling with excitement.
His hand which still held my sleeve twitched like a branch in the wind.

"What is it?" I whispered.

"It's he!"

"Sir Thomas?"

"Yes."

"What does he want?"

"Hush! Do nothing until I tell you."

I was conscious now that someone was trying the door. There was the
faintest little rattle from the handle, and then I dimly saw a thin slit of
subdued light. There was a lamp burning somewhere far down the
passage, and it just sufficed to make the outside visible from the darkness of our room. The grayish slit, grew broader and broader, very gradually, very gently, and then outlined against it I saw the dark figure of a
man. He was squat and crouching, with the silhouette of a bulky and mis-
shapen dwarf. Slowly the door swung open with this ominous shape
framed in the center of it. And then, in an instant the crouching figure
shot up, there was a tiger spring across the room, and thud, thud, thud,
came three tremendous blows from some heavy object upon the bed.

I was so paralyzed with amazement that I stood motionless and
staring until I was aroused by a yell for help from my companion. The
open door shed enough light for me to see the outline of things, and
there was little Lord Linchmere with his arms round the neck of his
brother-in-law, holding bravely on to him like a game bullterrier with
his teeth into a gaunt deerhound. The tall, bony man dashed himself
about, writhing round and round to get a grip upon his assailant; but

the other, clutching on from behind, still kept his hold, though his shrill, frightened cries showed how unequal he felt the contest to be. I sprang to the rescue, and the two of us managed to throw Sir Thomas to the ground, though he made his teeth meet in my shoulder. With all my youth and weight and strength, it was a desperate struggle before we could master his frenzied struggles; but at last we secured his arms with the waistcord of the dressing gown which he was wearing. I was holding his legs while Lord Linchmere was endeavoring to relight the lamp, when there came the pattering of many feet in the passage, and the butler and two footmen, who had been alarmed by the cries, rushed into the room. With their aid we had no further difficulty in securing our prisoner, who lay foaming and glaring upon the ground. One glance at his face was enough to prove that he was a dangerous maniac, while the short, heavy hammer which lay beside the bed showed how murderous had been his intentions.

"Do not use any violence!" said Lord Linchmere, as we raised the struggling man to his feet. "He will have a period of stupor after this excitement. I believe that it is coming on already." As he spoke the convulsions became less violent, and the madman's head fell forward upon his breast, as if he were overcome by sleep. We led him down the passage and stretched him upon his own bed, where he lay unconscious, breathing heavily.

"Two of you will watch him," said Lord Linchmere. "And now, Dr. Hamilton, if you will return with me to my room, I will give you the explanation which my horror of scandal has perhaps caused me to delay too long. Come what may, you will never have cause to regret your share in this night's work.

"This case may be made clear in a very few words," he continued, when we were alone. "My poor brother-in-law is one of the best fellows upon earth, a loving husband and an estimable father, but he comes from a stock which is deeply tainted with insanity. He has more than once had homicidal outbreaks, which are the more painful because his inclination is always to attack the very person to whom he is most attached. His son was sent away to school to avoid this danger, and then came an attempt upon my sister, his wife, from which she escaped with injuries that you may have observed when you met her in London. You understand that he knows nothing of the matter when he is in his sound senses, and would ridicule the suggestion that he could under any circumstances injure those whom he loves so dearly. It is often, as you know, a characteristic of such maladies that it is absolutely impossible to convince the man who suffers from them of their existence.

"Our great object was, of course, to get him under restraint before he could stain his hands with blood, but the matter was full of difficulty. He is a recluse in his habits, and would not see any medical man. Besides, it was necessary for our purpose that the medical man should convince himself of his insanity; and he is sane as you or I, save on these very rare occasions. But, fortunately, before he has these attacks, he always shows certain premonitory symptoms, which are providential danger signals, warning us to be upon our guard. The chief of these is that nervous contortion of the forehead which you must have observed. This is a phenomenon which always appears from three to four days before his attacks of frenzy. The moment it showed itself his wife came into town on some pretext, and took refuge in my house in Brooke Street.

"It remained for me to convince a medical man of Sir Thomas's insanity, without which it is impossible to put him where he could do no harm. The first problem was how to get a medical man into his house. I bethought me of his interest in beetles, and his love for anyone who shared his tastes. I advertised, therefore, and was fortunate enough to find in you the very man I wanted. A stout companion was necessary, for I knew that the lunacy could only be proved by a murderous assault, and I had every reason to believe that that assault would be made upon myself, since he had the warmest regard for me in his moments of sanity. I think your intelligence will supply all the rest. I did not know that the attack would come by night, but I thought it very probable, for the crises of such cases usually do occur in the early hours of the morning. I am a very nervous man myself, but I saw no other way in which I could remove this terrible danger from my sister's life. I need not ask you whether you are willing to sign the lunacy papers."

"Undoubtedly. But *two* signatures are necessary."

"You forget that I am myself a holder of a medical degree. I have the papers on a side table here, so if you will be good enough to sign them now, we can have the patient removed in the morning."

So that was my visit to Sir Thomas Rossiter, the famous beetle hunter, and that was also my first step upon the ladder of success, for Lady Rossiter and Lord Linchmere have proved to be stanch friends, and they have never forgotten my association with them in the time of their need. Sir Thomas is out and said to be cured, but I still think that if I spent another night at Delamere Court, I should be inclined to lock my door upon the inside.

THE MAN WITH THE WATCHES

There are many who will still bear in mind the singular circumstances which, under the heading of the Rugby Mystery, filled many columns of the daily Press in the spring of the year 1892. Coming as it did at a period of exceptional dullness, it attracted perhaps rather more attention than it deserved, but it offered to the public that mixture of the whimsical and the tragic which is most stimulating to the popular imagination. Interest dropped, however, when, after weeks of fruitless investigation, it was found that no final explanation of the facts was forthcoming, and the tragedy seemed from that time to the present to have finally taken its place in the dark catalogue of inexplicable and unexpiated crimes. A recent communication (the authenticity of which appears to be above question) has, however, thrown some new and clear light upon the matter. Before laying it before the public it would be as well, perhaps, that I should refresh their memories as to the singular facts upon which this commentary is founded. These facts were briefly as follows:

At five o'clock on the evening of the 18th of March in the year already mentioned a train left Euston Station for Manchester. It was a rainy, squally day, which grew wilder as it progressed, so it was by no means the weather in which anyone would travel who was not driven to do so by necessity. The train, however, is a favorite one among Manchester businessmen who are returning from town, for it does the journey in four hours and twenty minutes, with only three stoppages upon the way.

In spite of the inclement evening it was, therefore, fairly well filled upon the occasion of which I speak. The guard of the train was a tried servant of the company—a man who had worked for twenty-two years without blemish or complaint. His name was John Palmer.

The station clock was upon the stroke of five, and the guard was about to give the customary signal to the engine driver when he observed two belated passengers hurrying down the platform. The one was an exceptionally tall man, dressed in a long black overcoat with Astrakhan collar and cuffs. I have already said that the evening was an inclement one, and the tall traveler had the high, warm collar turned up to protect his throat against the bitter March wind. He appeared, as far as the guard could judge by so hurried an inspection, to be a man between fifty and sixty years of age, who had retained a good deal of the vigor and activity of his youth. In one hand he carried a brown leather Gladstone bag. His companion was a lady, tall and erect, walking with a vigorous step which outpaced the gentleman beside her. She wore a long, fawn-colored dust cloak, a black, close-fitting toque, and a dark veil which concealed the greater part of her face. The two might very well have passed as father and daughter. They walked swiftly down the line of carriages, glancing in at the windows, until the guard, John Palmer, overtook them.

"Now, then, sir, look sharp, the train is going," said he.

"First class," the man answered.

The guard turned the handle of the nearest door. In the carriage, which he had opened, there sat a small man with a cigar in his mouth. His appearance seems to have impressed itself upon the guard's memory, for he was prepared, afterward, to describe or to identify him. He was a man of thirty-four or thirty-five years of age, dressed in some gray material, sharp-nosed, alert, with a ruddy, weather-beaten face, and a small, closely cropped black beard. He glanced up as the door was opened. The tall man paused with his foot upon the step.

"This is a smoking compartment. The lady dislikes smoke," said he, looking round at the guard.

"All right! Here you are, sir!" said John Palmer. He slammed the door of the smoking carriage, opened that of the next one, which was empty, and thrust the two travelers in. At the same moment he sounded his whistle and the wheels of the train began to move. The man with the cigar was at the window of his carriage, and said something to the guard as he rolled past him, but the words were lost in the bustle of the departure. Palmer stepped into the guard's van, as it came up to him, and thought no more of the incident.

Twelve minutes after its departure the train reached Willesden Junction, where it stopped for a very short interval. An examination of the tickets has made it certain that no one either joined or left it at this time, and no passenger was seen to alight upon the platform. At 5:14 the journey to Manchester was resumed, and Rugby was reached at 6:50, the express being five minutes late.

At Rugby the attention of the station officials was drawn to the fact that the door of one of the first-class carriages was open. An examination of that compartment, and of its neighbor, disclosed a remarkable state of affairs.

The smoking carriage in which the short, red-faced man with the black beard had been seen was now empty. Save for a half-smoked cigar, there was no trace whatever of its recent occupant. The door of this carriage was fastened. In the next compartment, to which attention had been originally drawn, there was no sign either of the gentleman with the Astrakhan collar or of the young lady who accompanied him. All three passengers had disappeared. On the other hand, there was found upon the floor of this carriage—the one in which the tall traveler and the lady had been—a young man, fashionably dressed and of elegant appearance. He lay with his knees drawn up, and his head resting against the further door, an elbow upon either seat. A bullet had penetrated his heart and his death must have been instantaneous. No one had seen such a man enter the train, and no railway ticket was found in his pocket, neither were there any markings upon his linen, nor papers nor personal property which might help to identify him. Who he was, whence he had come, and how he had met his end were each as great a mystery as what had occurred to the three people who had started an hour and a half before from Willesden in those two compartments.

I have said that there was no personal property which might help to identify him, but it is true that there was one peculiarity about this unknown young man which was much commented upon at the time. In his pockets were found no fewer than six valuable gold watches, three in the various pockets of his waistcoat, one in his ticket pocket, one in his breast pocket, and one small one in a leather strap and fastened round his left wrist. The obvious explanation that the man was a pickpocket, and that this was his plunder, was discounted by the fact that all six were of American make, and of a type which is rare in England. Three of them bore the mark of the Rochester Watchmaking Company; one was by Mason, of Elmira; one was unmarked; and the small one, which was highly jeweled and ornamented, was from Tiffany, of New York. The other contents of his pocket consisted of an ivory knife with a corkscrew by Rodgers, of Sheffield; a small circular mirror, one inch in diameter; a re-admission slip to the Lyceum theater; a silver box full of vesta matches, and a brown leather cigar case containing two cheroots— also two pounds fourteen shillings in money. It was clear, then, that whatever motives may have led to his death, robbery was not among them. As already mentioned, there were no markings upon the man's linen, which appeared to be new, and no tailor's name upon his coat. In appearance he was young, short, smooth cheeked, and delicately featured. One of his front teeth was conspicuously stopped with gold.

On the discovery of the tragedy an examination was instantly made of the tickets of all passengers, and the number of the passengers themselves was counted. It was found that only three tickets were unaccounted for, corresponding to the three travelers who were missing. The express was then allowed to proceed, but a new guard was sent with it, and John Palmer was detained as a witness at Rugby. The carriage which included the two compartments in question was uncoupled and sidetracked. Then, on the arrival of Inspector Vane, of Scotland Yard, and of Mr. Henderson, a detective in the service of the railway company, an exhaustive inquiry was made into all the circumstances.

That crime had been committed was certain. The bullet, which appeared to have come from a small pistol or revolver, had been fired from some little distance, as there was no scorching of the clothes. No weapon was found in the compartment (which finally disposed of the theory of suicide), nor was there any sign of the brown leather bag which the guard had seen in the hand of the tall gentleman. A lady's parasol was found upon the rack, but no other trace was to be seen of the travelers in either of the sections. Apart from the crime, the question of how or why three passengers (one of them a lady) could get out of the train, and one other get in during the unbroken run between Willesden and Rugby, was one which excited the utmost curiosity among the general public, and gave rise to much speculation in the London Press.

John Palmer, the guard, was able at the inquest to give some evidence which threw a little light upon the matter. There was a spot between Tring and Cheddington, according to his statement, where, on account of some repairs to the line, the train had for a few minutes slowed down to a pace not exceeding eight or ten miles an hour. At that place it might be possible for a man, or even for an exceptionally active woman, to have left the train without serious injury. It was true that a gang of platelayers was there, and that they had seen nothing, but it was their custom to stand in the middle between the metals, and the open carriage door was upon the far side, so that it was conceivable that someone might have alighted unseen, as the darkness would by that time be drawing in. A steep embankment would instantly screen anyone who sprang from the observation of the navvies.

The guard also deposed that there was a good deal of movement upon the platform at Willesden Junction, and that though it was certain that no one had either joined or left the train there, it was still quite possible that some of the passengers might have changed unseen from one compartment to another. It was by no means uncommon for a gentleman to finish his cigar in a smoking carriage and then to change to a clearer atmosphere. Supposing that the man with the black beard had done so at Willesden (and the half-smoked cigar upon the floor seemed to favor the supposition), he would naturally go into the nearest section, which would bring him into the company of the two other actors in this drama. Thus the first stage of the affair might be surmised without any great breach of probability. But what the second stage had been, or how the final one had been arrived at, neither the guard nor the experienced detective officers could suggest.

A careful examination of the line between Willesden and Rugby resulted in one discovery which might or might not have a bearing upon the tragedy. Near Tring, at the very place where the train slowed down, there was found at the bottom of the embankment a small pocket Testament, very shabby and worn. It was printed by the Bible Society of London, and bore an inscription: "From John to Alice. Jan. 13th, 1856," upon the flyleaf. Underneath was written: "James, July 4th, 1859," and beneath that again: "Edward, Nov. 1st, 1869," all the entries being in the same handwriting. This was the only clue, if it could be called a clue, which the police obtained, and the coroner's verdict of "Murder by a person or persons unknown" was the unsatisfactory ending of a singular case. Advertisements, rewards and inquiries proved equally fruitless, and nothing could be found which was solid enough to form the basis for a profitable investigation.

It would be a mistake, however, to suppose that no theories were formed to account for the facts. On the contrary, the Press, both in England and in America, teemed with suggestions and suppositions, most of which were obviously absurd. The fact that the watches were of American make, and some peculiarities in connection with the gold stopping of his front tooth, appeared to indicate that the deceased was a citizen of the United States, though his linen, clothes, and boots were undoubtedly of British manufacture. It was surmised, by some, that he was concealed under the seat, and that, being discovered, he was for some reason, possibly because he had overheard their guilty secrets, put

THE MAN WITH THE WATCHES 31

to death by his fellow passengers. When coupled with generalities as to the ferocity and cunning of anarchical and other secret societies, this theory sounded as plausible as any.

The fact that he should be without a ticket would be consistent with the idea of concealment, and it was well known that women played a prominent part in the Nihilistic propaganda. On the other hand, it was clear from the guard's statement, that the man must have been hidden there *before* the others arrived, and how unlikely the coincidence that conspirators should stray exactly into the very compartment in which a spy was already concealed! Besides, this explanation ignored the man in the smoking carriage, and gave no reason at all for his simultaneous disappearance. The police had little difficulty in showing that such a theory would not cover the facts, but they were unprepared in the absence of evidence to advance any alternative explanation.

There was a letter in the *Daily Gazette*, over the signature of a well-known criminal investigator, which gave rise to considerable discussion at the time. He had formed a hypothesis which had at least ingenuity to recommend it, and I cannot do better than append it in his own words.

"Whatever may be the truth," said he, "it must depend upon some bizarre and rare combination of events, so we need have no hesitation in postulating such events in our explanation. In the absence of data we must abandon the analytic or scientific method of investigation, and must approach it in the synthetic fashion. In a word, instead of taking known events and deducing from them what has occurred, we must build up a fanciful explanation if it will only be consistent with known events. We can then test this explanation by any fresh facts which may arise. If they all fit into their places, the probability is that we are upon the right track, and with each fresh fact this probability increases in a geometrical progression until the evidence becomes final and convincing.

"Now, there is one most remarkable and suggestive fact which has not met with the attention which it deserves. There is a local train running through Harrow and King's Langley, which is timed in such a way that the express must have overtaken it at or about the period when it eased down its speed to eight miles an hour on account of the repairs of the line. The two trains would at that time be traveling in the same direction at a similar rate of speed and upon parallel lines. It is within everyone's experience how, under such circumstances, the occupant of each carriage can see very plainly the passengers in the other carriages opposite to him. The lamps of the express had been lit at Willesden, so that each compartment was brightly illuminated, and most visible to an observer from outside.

"Now, the sequence of events as I reconstruct them would be after this fashion. This young man with the abnormal number of watches was alone in the carriage of the slow train. His ticket, with his papers and gloves and other things, was we will suppose, on the seat beside him. He was probably an American, and also probably a man of weak intellect. The excessive wearing of jewelry is an early symptom in some forms of mania.

"As he sat watching the carriages of the express which were (on account of the state of the line) going at the same pace as himself, he suddenly saw some people in it whom he knew. We will suppose for the sake of our theory that these people were a woman whom he loved and a man whom he hated—and who in return hated him. The young man was excitable and impulsive. He opened the door of his carriage, stepped from the footboard of the local train to the footboard of the express, opened the other door, and made his way into the presence of these two people. The feat (on the supposition that the trains were going at the same pace) is by no means so perilous as it might appear.

"Having now got our young man without his ticket into the carriage in which the elder man and the young woman are traveling, it is not difficult to imagine that a violent scene ensued. It is possible that the pair were also Americans, which is the more probable as the man carried a weapon—an unusual thing in England. If our supposition of incipient mania is correct, the young man is likely to have assaulted the other. As the upshot of the quarrel the elder man shot the intruder, and then made his escape from the carriage, taking the young lady with him. We will suppose that all this happened very rapidly, and that the train was still going at so slow a pace that it was not difficult for them to leave it. A woman might leave a train going at eight miles an hour. As a matter of fact, we know that this woman *did* do so.

"And now we have to fit in the man in the smoking carriage. Presuming that we have, up to this point, reconstructed the tragedy correctly, we shall find nothing in this other man to cause us to reconsider our conclusions. According to my theory, this man saw the young fellow cross from one train to the other, saw him open the door, heard the pistol shot, saw the two fugitives spring out onto the line, realized that murder had been done, and sprang out himself in pursuit. Why he has never been heard of since—whether he met his own death in the pursuit, or whether, as is more likely, he was made to realize that it was not a case for his interference—is a detail which we have at present no means of explaining. I acknowledge that there are some difficulties in the way. At first sight, it might seem improbable that at such a moment a murderer would burden himself in his flight with a brown leather bag. My answer is that he was well aware that if the bag were found his identity would be established. It was absolutely necessary for him to take it with him. My theory stands or falls upon one point, and I call upon the railway company to make strict inquiry as to whether a ticket was found unclaimed in the local train through Harrow and King's Langley upon the 18th of March. If such a ticket were found my case is proved. If not, my theory may still be the correct one, for it is conceivable either that he traveled without a ticket or that his ticket was lost."

To this elaborate and plausible hypothesis the answer of the police and of the company was, first, that no such ticket was found; secondly, that the slow train would never run parallel to the express; and, thirdly, that the local train had been stationary in King's Langley Station when the express, going at fifty miles an hour, had flashed past it. So perished the only satisfying explanation, and five years have elapsed without supplying a new one. Now, at last, there comes a statement which covers all the facts, and which must be regarded as authentic. It took the shape of a letter dated from New York, and addressed to the same criminal investigator whose theory I have quoted. It is given here in extenso, with the exception of the two opening paragraphs, which are personal in their nature:

"You'll excuse me if I'm not very free with names. There's less reason now than there was five years ago when mother was still living. But for all that, I had rather cover up our tracks all I can. But I owe you an explanation, for if your idea of it was wrong, it was a mighty ingenious one all the same. I'll have to go back a little so as you may understand all about it.

"My people came from Bucks, England, and emigrated to the States in the early fifties. They settled in Rochester, in the State of New York, where my father ran a large dry goods store. There were only two sons: myself, James, and my brother, Edward. I was ten years older than my brother, and after my father died I sort of took the place of a father to him, as an elder brother would. He was a bright, spirited boy, and just one of the most beautiful creatures that ever lived. But there was always a soft spot in him, and it was like mold in cheese, for it spread and spread, and nothing that you could do would stop it. Mother saw it just as clearly as I did, but she went on spoiling him all the same, for he had such a way with him that you could refuse him nothing. I did all I could to hold him in, and he hated me for my pains.

"At last he fairly got his head, and nothing that we could do would stop him. He got off into New York, and went rapidly from bad to worse.

At first he was only fast, and then he was criminal; and then, at the end of a year or two, he was one of the most notorious young crooks in the city. He had formed a friendship with Sparrow MacCoy, who was at the head of his profession as a buncosteerer, green goodsman, and general rascal. They took to cardsharping, and frequented some of the best hotels in New York. My brother was an excellent actor (he might have made an honest name for himself if he had chosen), and he would take the parts of a young Englishman of title, of a simple lad from the West, or of a college undergraduate, whichever suited Sparrow MacCoy's purpose. And then one day he dressed himself as a girl, and he carried it off so well, and made himself such a valuable decoy, that it was their favorite game afterward. They had made it right with Tammany and with the police, so it seemed as if nothing could ever stop them, for those were in the days before the Lexow Commission, and if you only had a pull, you could do pretty nearly everything you wanted.

"And nothing would have stopped them if they had only stuck to cards and New York, but they must needs come up Rochester way, and forge a name upon a check. It was my brother that did it, though everyone knew that it was under the influence of Sparrow MacCoy. I bought up that check, and a pretty sum it cost me. Then I went to my brother, laid it before him on the table, and swore to him that I would prosecute if he did not clear out of the country. At first he simply laughed. I could not prosecute, he said, without breaking our mother's heart, and he knew that I would not do that. I made him understand, however, that our mother's heart was being broken in any case, and that I had set firm on the point that I would rather see him in a Rochester jail than in a New York hotel. So at last he gave in, and he made me a solemn promise that he would see Sparrow MacCoy no more, that he would go to Europe, and that he would turn his hand to any honest trade that I helped him to get. I took him down right away to an old family friend, Joe Willson, who is an exporter of American watches and clocks, and I got him to give Edward an agency in London, with a small salary and a 15 percent commission on all business. His manner and appearance were so good that he won the old man over at once, and within a week he was sent off to London with a case full of samples.

"It seemed to me that this business of the check had really given my brother a fright, and that there was some chance of his settling down into an honest line of life. My mother had spoken with him, and what she said had touched him, for she had always been the best of mothers to him, and he had been the great sorrow of her life. But I knew that this man Sparrow MacCoy had a great influence over Edward, and my chance of keeping the lad straight lay in breaking the connection between them. I had a friend in the New York detective force, and through him I kept a watch upon MacCoy. When within a fortnight of my brother's sailing I heard that MacCoy had taken a berth in the *Etruria*, I was as certain as if he had told me that he was going over to England for the purpose of coaxing Edward back again into the ways that he had left. In an instant I had resolved to go also, and to put my influence against MacCoy's. I knew it was a losing fight, but I thought, and my mother thought, that it was my duty. We passed the last night together in prayer for my success, and she gave me her own Testament that my father had given her on the day of their marriage in the Old Country, so that I might always wear it next my heart.

"I was a fellow traveler, on the steamship, with Sparrow MacCoy, and at least I had the satisfaction of spoiling his little game for the voyage. The very first night I went into the smoking room, and found him at the head of a card table, with half-a-dozen young fellows who were carrying their full purses and their empty skulls over to Europe. He was settling down for his harvest, and a rich one it would have been. But I soon changed all that.

" 'Gentlemen,' said I, 'are you aware whom you are playing with?'

" 'What's that to you? You mind your own business!' said he, with an oath.

" 'Who is it, anyway?' asked one of the dudes.

" 'He's Sparrow MacCoy, the most notorious cardsharper in the States.'

"Up he jumped with a bottle in his hand, but he remembered that he was under the flag of the effete Old Country, where law and order run, and Tammany has no pull. Jail and the gallows wait for violence and murder, and there's no slipping out by the back door on board an ocean liner.

" 'Prove your words, you—!' said he.

" 'I will!' said I. 'If you will turn up your right shirtsleeve to the shoulder, I will either prove my words or I will eat them.'

"He turned white and said not a word. You see, I knew something of his ways, and I was aware that part of the mechanism which he and all such sharpers use consists of an elastic down the arm with a clip just above the wrist. It is by means of this clip that they withdraw from their hands the cards which they do not want, while they substitute other cards from another hiding place. I reckoned on it being there, and it was. He cursed me, slunk out of the saloon, and was hardly seen again during the voyage. For once, at any rate, I got level with Mister Sparrow MacCoy.

"But he soon had his revenge upon me, for when it came to influencing my brother he outweighed me every time. Edward had kept himself straight in London for the first few weeks, and had done some business with his American watches, until this villain came across his path once more. I did my best, but the best was little enough. The next thing I heard there had been a scandal at one of the Northumberland Avenue hotels: a traveler had been fleeced of a large sum by two confederate cardsharpers, and the matter was in the hands of Scotland Yard. The first I learned of it was in the evening paper, and I was at once certain that my brother and MacCoy were back at their old games. I hurried at once to Edward's lodgings. They told me that he and a tall gentleman (whom I recognized as MacCoy) had gone off together, and that he had left the lodgings and taken his things with him. The landlady had heard them give several directions to the cabman, ending with Euston Station, and she had accidentally overheard the tall gentleman saying something about Manchester. She believed that that was their destination.

"A glance at the timetable showed me that the most likely train was at five, though there was another at 4:35 which they might have caught. I had only time to get the later one, but found no sign of them either at the depot or in the train. They must have gone on by the earlier one, so I determined to follow them to Manchester and search for them in the hotels there. One last appeal to my brother by all that he owed to my mother might even now be the salvation of him. My nerves were overstrung, and I lit a cigar to steady them. At that moment, just as the train was moving off, the door of my compartment was flung open, and there were MacCoy and my brother on the platform.

"They were both disguised, and with good reason, for they knew that the London police were after them. MacCoy had a great Astrakhan collar drawn up, so that only his eyes and nose were showing. My brother was dressed like a woman, with a black veil half down his face, but of course it did not deceive me for an instant, nor would it have done so even if I had not known that he had often used such a dress before. I started up, and as I did so MacCoy recognized me. He said something, the conductor slammed the door, and they were shown into the next compartment. I tried to stop the train so as to follow them, but the wheels were already moving, and it was too late.

"When we stopped at Willesden, I instantly changed my carriage. It appears that I was not seen to do so, which is not surprising, as the station was crowded with people. MacCoy, of course, was expecting me, and he had spent the time between Euston and Willesden in saying all he could to harden my brother's heart and set him against me. That is what I fancy, for I had never found him so impossible to soften or to move. I tried this way and I tried that; I pictured his future in an English jail; I described the sorrow of his mother when I came back with the news; I said everything to touch his heart, but all to no purpose. He sat there with a fixed sneer upon his handsome face, while every now and then Sparrow MacCoy would throw in a taunt at me or some word of encouragement to hold my brother to his resolutions.

" 'Why don't you run a Sunday school?' he would say to me, and then, in the same breath: 'He thinks you have no will of your own. He thinks you are just the baby brother and that he can lead you where he likes. He's only just finding out that you are a man as well as he.'

"It was those words of his which set me talking bitterly. We had left Willesden, you understand, for all this took some time. My temper got the better of me, and for the first time in my life I let my brother see the rough side of me. Perhaps it would have been better had I done so earlier and more often.

" 'A man!' said I. 'Well, I'm glad to have your friend's assurance of it, for no one would suspect it to see you like a boarding-school missy. I don't suppose in all this country there is a more contemptible-looking creature than you are as you sit there with that Dolly pinafore upon you.' He colored up at that, for he was a vain man, and he winced from ridicule.

" 'It's only a dust cloak,' said he, and he slipped it off. 'One has to throw the coppers off one's scent, and I had no other way to do it.' He took his toque off with the veil attached, and he put both it and the cloak into his brown bag. 'Anyway, I don't need to wear it until the conductor comes round,' said he.

" 'Nor then, either,' said I, and taking the bag I slung it with all my force out of the window. 'Now,' said I, 'you'll never make a Mary Jane of yourself while I can help it. If nothing but that disguise stands between you and a jail, then to jail you shall go.'

"That was the way to manage him. I felt my advantage at once. His supple nature was one which yielded to roughness far more readily than to entreaty. He flushed with shame, and his eyes filled with tears. But MacCoy saw my advantage also, and was determined that I should not pursue it.

" 'He's my pard, and you shall not bully him,' he cried.

" 'He's my brother, and you shall not ruin him,' said I. 'I believe a spell of prison is the very best way of keeping you apart, and you shall have it, or it will be no fault of mine.'

" 'Oh, you would squeal, would you?' he cried, and in an instant he whipped out his revolver. I sprang for his hand, but saw that I was too late, and jumped aside. At the same instant he fired, and the bullet which would have struck me passed through the heart of my unfortunate brother.

"He dropped without a groan upon the floor of the compartment, and MacCoy and I, equally horrified, knelt at each side of him, trying to bring back some signs of life. MacCoy still held the loaded revolver in his hand, but his anger against me and my resentment toward him had both for the moment been swallowed up in this sudden tragedy. It was he who first realized the situation. The train was for some reason going very slowly at the moment and he saw his opportunity for escape. In an instant he had the door open, but I was as quick as he, and jumping upon him the two of us fell off the footboard and rolled in each other's arms down a steep embankment. At the bottom I struck my head against a stone, and I remembered nothing more. When I came to myself I was lying among some low bushes, not far from the railroad track, and somebody was bathing my head with a wet handkerchief. It was Sparrow MacCoy.

" 'I guess I couldn't leave you,' said he. 'I didn't want to have the blood of two of you on my hands in one day. You loved your brother, I've no doubt; but you didn't love him a cent more than I loved him, though you'll say that I took a queer way to show it. Anyhow, it seems a mighty empty world now that he is gone, and I don't care a continental whether you give me over to the hangman or not.'

"He had turned his ankle in the fall, and there we sat, he with his useless foot, and I with my throbbing head, and we talked and talked until gradually my bitterness began to soften and to turn into something like sympathy. What was the use of revenging his death upon a man who was as much stricken by that death as I was? And then, as my wits gradually returned, I began to realize also that I could do nothing against MacCoy which would not recoil upon my mother and myself. How could we convict him without a full account of my brother's career being made public—the very thing which of all others we wished to avoid? It was really as much our interest as his to cover the matter up, and from being an avenger of crime I found myself changed to a conspirator against Justice. The place in which we found ourselves was one of those pheasant preserves which are so common in the Old Country, and as we groped our way through it I found myself consulting the slayer of my brother as to how far it would be possible to hush it up.

"I soon realized from what he said that unless there were some papers of which we knew nothing in my brother's pockets, there was really no possible means by which the police could identify him or learn how he had got there. His ticket was in MacCoy's pocket, and so was the ticket for some baggage which they had left at the depot. Like most Americans, he had found it cheaper and easier to buy an outfit in London than to bring one from New York, so that all his linen and clothes were new and unmarked. The bag, containing the dust cloak, which I had thrown out of the window, may have fallen among some bramble patch where it is still concealed, or may have been carried off by some tramp, or may have come into the possession of the police, who kept the incident to themselves. Anyhow, I have seen nothing about it in the London papers. As to the watches, they were a selection from those which had been intrusted to him for business purposes. It may have been for the same business purposes that he was taking them to Manchester, but—well, it's too late to enter into that.

"I don't blame the police for being at fault. I don't see how it could have been otherwise. There was just one little clue that they might have followed up but it was a small one. I mean that small circular mirror which was found in my brother's pocket. It isn't a very common thing for a young man to carry about with him, is it? But a gambler might have told you what such a mirror may mean to a cardsharper. If you sit back a little from the table, and lay the mirror, face upward, upon your lap, you can see, as you deal, every card that you give to your adversary. It is not hard to say whether you see a man or raise him when you know his cards as well as your own. It was as much a part of a sharper's outfit as the elastic clip upon Sparrow MacCoy's arm. Taking that, in connection with the recent frauds at the hotels, the police might have got hold of one end of the string.

"I don't think there is much more for me to explain. We got to a village called Amersham that night in the character of two gentlemen upon a walking tour, and afterward we made our way quietly to London, whence MacCoy went on to Cairo and I returned to New York. My mother died six months afterward, and I am glad to say that to the day of her death she never knew what happened. She was always under the delusion that Edward was earning an honest living in London, and I never had the heart to tell her the truth. He never wrote; but, then, he never did write at any time, so that made no difference. His name was the last upon her lips.

"There's just one other thing that I have to ask you, sir, and I should take it as a kind return for all this explanation, if you could do it for me. You remember that Testament that was picked up. I always carried it in my inside pocket, and it must have come out in my fall. I value it very highly, for it was the family book with my birth and my brother's marked by my father in the beginning of it. I wish you would apply at the proper place and have it sent to me. It can be of no possible value to anyone else. If you address it to X, Bassano's Library, Broadway, New York, it is sure to come to hand."

THE POT OF CAVIARE

It was the fourth day of the siege. Ammunition and provisions were
both nearing an end. When the Boxer insurrection had suddenly
flamed up, and roared, like a fire in dry grass, across Northern
China, the few scattered Europeans in the outlying provinces had huddled together at the nearest defensible post and had held on for dear
life until rescue came—or until it did not. In the latter case, the less said
about their fate the better. In the former, they came back into the world
of men with that upon their faces which told that they had looked very
closely upon such an end as would ever haunt their dreams.

Ichau was only fifty miles from the coast, and there was a European
squadron in the Gulf of Liantong. Therefore the absurd little garrison,
consisting of native Christians and railway men, with a German officer
to command them and five civilian Europeans to support him, held on
bravely with the conviction that help must soon come sweeping down to
them from the low hills to eastward. The sea was visible from those hills,
and on the sea were their armed countrymen. Surely, then, they could
not feel deserted. With brave hearts they manned the loopholes in the
crumbling brick walls outlining the tiny European quarter, and they
fired away briskly, if ineffectively, at the rapidly advancing sangars of the
Boxers. It was certain that in another day or so they would be at the end
of their resources, but then it was equally certain that in another day or
so they must be relieved. It might be a little sooner or it might be a little
later, but there was no one who ever ventured to hint that the relief

would not arrive in time to pluck them out of the fire. Up to Tuesday night there was no word of discouragement.

It was true that on the Wednesday their robust faith in what was going forward behind those eastern hills had weakened a little. The gray slopes lay bare and unresponsive while the deadly sangars pushed ever nearer, so near that the dreadful faces which shrieked imprecations at them from time to time over the top could be seen in every hideous feature. There was not so much of that now since young Ainslie, of the diplomatic service, with his neat little .303 sporting rifle, had settled down in the squat church tower, and had devoted his days to abating the nuisance. But a silent sangar is an even more impressive thing than a clamorous one, and steadily, irresistibly, inevitably, the lines of brick and rubble drew closer. Soon they would be so near that one rush would assuredly carry the frantic swordsmen over the frail entrenchment. It all seemed very black upon Wednesday evening. Colonel Dresler, the German ex-infantry soldier, went about with an imperturbable face, but a heart of lead. Ralston, of the railway, was up half the night writing farewell letters. Professor Mercer, the old entomologist, was even more silent and grimly thoughtful than ever. Ainslie had lost some of his flippancy. On the whole, the ladies—Miss Sinclair, the nurse of the Scotch Mission, Mrs. Patterson, and her pretty daughter Jessie, were the most composed of the party. Father Pierre of the French Mission was also unaffected, as was natural to one who regarded martyrdom as a glorious crown. The Boxers yelling for his blood beyond the walls disturbed him less than his forced association with the sturdy Scotch Presbyterian presence of Mr. Patterson, with whom for ten years he had wrangled over the souls of the natives. They passed each other now in the corridors as dog passes cat, and each kept a watchful eye upon the other lest even in the trenches he might filch some sheep from the rival fold, whispering heresy in his ear.

But the Wednesday night passed without a crisis, and on the Thursday all was bright once more. It was Ainslie up in the clock tower who had first heard the distant thud of a gun. Then Dresler heard it and within half an hour it was audible to all—that strong iron voice, calling to them from afar and bidding them to be of good cheer, since help was coming. It was clear that the landing party from the squadron was well on its way. It would not arrive an hour too soon. The cartridges were nearly finished. Their half rations of food would soon dwindle to an even more pitiful supply. But what need to worry about that now that relief was assured? There would be no attack that day, as most of the Boxers could be seen streaming off in the direction of the distant firing, and the long lines of sangars were silent and deserted. They were all able, therefore, to assemble at the lunch table, a merry, talkative party, full of that joy of living which sparkles most brightly under the imminent shadow of death.

"The pot of caviare!" cried Ainslie. "Come, Professor, out with the pot of caviare!"

"Potz-tausend! yes," grunted old Dresler. "It is certainly time that we had that famous pot."

The ladies joined in and from all parts of the long, ill-furnished table there came the demand for caviare.

It was a strange time to ask for such a delicacy, but the reason is soon told. Professor Mercer, the old Californian entomologist, had received a jar of caviare in a hamper of goods from San Francisco, arriving a day or two before the outbreak. In the general pooling and distribution of provisions this one dainty and three bottles of Lachryma Christi from the same hamper had been excepted and set aside. By common consent they were to be reserved for the final joyous meal when the end of their peril should be in sight. Even as they sat the thud-thud of the relieving guns came to their ears—more luxurious music to their lunch than the most sybaritic restaurant of London could have supplied. Before evening the relief would certainly be there. Why, then, should their stale bread not be glorified by the treasured caviare?

But the Professor shook his gnarled old head and smiled his inscrutable smile.

"Better wait," said he.

"Wait! Why wait?" cried the company.

"They have still far to come," he answered.

"They will be here for supper at the latest," said Ralston, of the railway—a keen, birdlike man, with bright eyes and long, projecting nose. "They cannot be more than ten miles from us now. If they only did two miles an hour it would make them due at seven."

"There is a battle on the way," remarked the Colonel. "You will grant two hours or three hours for the battle."

"Not half an hour," cried Ainslie. "They will walk through them as if they were not there. What can these rascals with their matchlocks and swords do against modern weapons?"

"It depends on who leads the column of relief," said Dresler. "If they are fortunate enough to have a German officer—"

"An Englishman for my money!" cried Ralston.

"The French commodore is said to be an excellent strategist," remarked Father Pierre.

"I don't see that it matters a toss," cried the exuberant Ainslie. "Mr. Mauser and Mr. Maxim are the two men who will see us through, and with them on our side no leader can go wrong. I tell you they will just brush them aside and walk through them. So now, Professor, come on with that pot of caviare!"

But the old scientist was unconvinced.

"We shall reserve it for supper," said he.

"After all," said Mr. Patterson, in his slow, precise Scottish intonation, "it will be a courtesy to our guests—the officers of the relief—if we have some palatable food to lay before them. I'm in agreement with the Professor that we reserve the caviare for supper."

The argument appealed to their sense of hospitality. There was something pleasantly chivalrous, too, in the idea of keeping their one little delicacy to give a savor to the meal of their preservers. There was no more talk of the caviare.

"By the way, Professor," said Mr. Patterson, "I've only heard today that this is the second time that you have been besieged in this way. I'm sure we should all be very interested to hear some details of your previous experience."

The old man's face set very grimly.

"I was in Sung-tong, in South China, in 'eighty-nine," said he.

"It's a very extraordinary coincidence that you should twice have been in such a perilous situation," said the missionary. "Tell us how you were relieved at Sung-tong."

The shadow deepened upon the weary face.

"We were not relieved," said he.

"What! the place fell?"

"Yes, it fell."

"And you came through alive?"

"I am a doctor as well as an entomologist. They had many wounded; they spared me."

"And the rest?"

"Assez! assez!" cried the little French priest, raising his hand in protest. He had been twenty years in China. The Professor had said nothing, but there was something, some lurking horror, in his dull, gray eyes which had turned the ladies pale.

"I am sorry," said the missionary. "I can see that it is a painful subject. I should not have asked."

"No," the Professor answered, slowly. "It is wiser not to ask. It is better not to speak about such things at all. But surely those guns are very much nearer?"

There could be no doubt of it. After a silence the thud-thud had recommenced with a lively ripple of rifle fire playing all round that deep bass master note. It must be just at the farther side of the nearest hill. They pushed back their chairs and ran out to the ramparts. The silent-footed native servants came in and cleared the scanty remains from the table. But after they had left, the old Professor sat on there, his massive, gray-crowned head leaning upon his hands and the same pensive look of horror in his eyes. Some ghosts may be laid for years, but when they do rise it is not so easy to drive them back to their slumbers. The guns had ceased outside, but he had not observed it, lost as he was in the one supreme and terrible memory of his life.

His thoughts were interrupted at last by the entrance of the Commandant. There was a complacent smile upon his broad German face.

"The Kaiser will be pleased," said he, rubbing his hands. "Yes, certainly it should mean a decoration. 'Defense of Ichau against the Boxers by Colonel Dresler, late Major of the 114th Hanoverian Infantry. Splendid resistance of small garrison against overwhelming odds.' It will certainly appear in the Berlin papers."

"Then you think we are saved?" said the old man, with neither emotion nor exultation in his voice.

The Colonel smiled.

"Why, Professor," said he, "I have seen you more excited on the morning when you brought back *Lepidus Mercerensis* in your collecting box."

"The fly was safe in my collecting box first," the entomologist answered. "I have seen so many strange turns of Fate in my long life that I do not grieve nor do I rejoice until I know that I have cause. But tell me the news."

"Well," said the Colonel, lighting his long pipe, and stretching his gaitered legs in the bamboo chair, "I'll stake my military reputation that all is well. They are advancing swiftly, the firing has died down to show that resistance is at an end, and within an hour we'll see them over the brow. Ainslie is to fire his gun three times from the church tower as a signal, and then we shall make a little sally on our own account."

"And you are waiting for this signal?"

"Yes, we are waiting for Ainslie's shots. I thought I would spend the time with you, for I had something to ask you."

"What was it?"

"Well, you remember your talk about the other siege—the siege of Sung-tong. It interests me very much from a professional point of view. Now that the ladies and civilians are gone you will have no objection to discussing it."

"It is not a pleasant subject."

"No, I dare say not. Mein Gott! it was indeed a tragedy. But you have seen how I have conducted the defense here. Was it wise? Was it good? Was it worthy of the traditions of the German army?"

"I think you could have done no more."

"Thank you. But this other place, was it as ably defended? To me a comparison of this sort is very interesting. Could it have been saved?"

"No; everything possible was done—save only one thing."

"Ah! there was one omission. What was it?"

"No one—above all, no woman—should have been allowed to fall alive into the hands of the Chinese."

The Colonel held out his broad red hand and enfolded the long, white, nervous fingers of the Professor.

"You are right—a thousand times right. But do not think that this has escaped my thoughts. For myself I would die fighting, so would Ralston, so would Ainslie. I have talked to them, and it is settled. But the others, I have spoken with them, but what are you to do? There are the priest, and the missionary, and the women."

"Would they wish to be taken alive?"

"They would not promise to take steps to prevent it. They would not lay hands on their own lives. Their consciences would not permit it. Of course, it is all over now, and we need not speak of such dreadful things. But what would you have done in my place?"

"Kill them."

"Mein Gott! You would murder them?"

"In mercy I would kill them. Man, I have been through it. I have seen the death of the hot eggs; I have seen the death of the boiling kettle; I have seen the women—my God! I wonder that I have ever slept sound again." His usually impassive face was working and quivering with the agony of the remembrance. "I was strapped to a stake with thorns in my eyelids to keep them open, and my grief at their torture was a less thing than my self-reproach when I thought that I could with one tube of tasteless tablets have snatched them at the last instant from the hands of their tormentors. Murder! I am ready to stand at the Divine bar and answer for a thousand murders such as that! Sin! Why, it is such an act as might well cleanse the stain of real sin from the soul. But if, knowing what I do, I should have failed this second time to do it, then by Heaven! there is no hell deep enough or hot enough to receive my guilty craven spirit."

The Colonel rose, and again his hand clasped that of the Professor.

"You speak sense," said he. "You are a brave, strong man, who know your own mind. Yes, by the Lord! you would have been my great help had things gone the other way. I have often thought and wondered in the dark, early hours of the morning, but I did not know how to do it. But we should have heard Ainslie's shots before now, I will go and see."

Again the old scientist sat alone with his thoughts. Finally, as neither the guns of the relieving force nor yet the signal of their approach sounded upon his ears, he rose, and was about to go himself upon the ramparts to make inquiry when the door flew open, and Colonel Dresler staggered into the room. His face was of a ghastly yellow-white, and his chest heaved like that of a man exhausted with running. There was brandy on the side table, and he gulped down a glassful. Then he dropped heavily into a chair.

"Well," said the Professor, coldly, "they are not coming?"

"No, they cannot come."

There was silence for a minute or more, the two men staring blankly at each other.

"Do they all know?"

"No one knows but me."

"How did you learn?"

"I was at the wall near the postern gate—the little wooden gate that opens on the rose garden. I saw something crawling among the bushes. There was a knocking at the door. I opened it. It was a Christian Tartar, badly cut about with swords. He had come from the battle. Commodore Wyndham, the Englishman, had sent him. The relieving force had been checked. They had shot away most of their ammunition. They had entrenched themselves and sent back to the ships for more. Three days must pass before they could come. That was all. Mein Gott! it was enough."

The Professor bent his shaggy gray brows.

"Where is the man?" he asked.

"He is dead. He died of loss of blood. His body lies at the postern gate."

"And no one saw him?"

"Not to speak to."

"Oh! they did see him, then?"

"Ainslie must have seen him from the church tower. He must know that I have had tidings. He will want to know what they are. If I tell him they must all know."

"How long can we hold out?"

"An hour or two at the most."

"Is that absolutely certain?"

"I pledge my credit as a soldier upon it."

"Then we must fall?"

"Yes, we must fall."

"There is no hope for us?"

"None."

The door flew open and young Ainslie rushed in. Behind him crowded Ralston, Patterson, and a crowd of white men and of native Christians.

"You've had news, Colonel?"

Professor Mercer pushed to the front.

"Colonel Dresler has just been telling me. It is all right. They have halted, but will be here in the early morning. There is no longer any danger."

A cheer broke from the group in the doorway. Everyone was laughing and shaking hands.

"But suppose they rush us before tomorrow morning?" cried Ralston, in a petulant voice. "What infernal fools these fellows are not to push on! Lazy devils, they should be court-martialed, every man of them."

"It's all safe," said Ainslie. "These fellows have had a bad knock. We can see their wounded being carried by the hundred over the hill. They must have lost heavily. They won't attack before morning."

"No, no," said the Colonel; "it is certain that they won't attack before morning. None the less, get back to your posts. We must give no point away." He left the room with the rest, but as he did so he looked back, and his eyes for an instant met those of the old Professor. "I leave it in your hands," was the message which he flashed. A stern set smile was his answer.

The afternoon wore way without the Boxers making their last attack. To Colonel Dresler it was clear that the unwonted stillness meant only that they were reassembling their forces from their fight with the relief column, and were gathering themselves for the inevitable and final rush. To all the others it appeared that the siege was indeed over, and that the assailants had been crippled by the losses which they had already sustained. It was a joyous and noisy party, therefore, which met at the supper table, when the three bottles of Lachryma Christi were uncorked and the famous pot of caviare was finally opened. It was a large jar, and though each had a tablespoonful of the delicacy, it was by no means exhausted. Ralston, who was an epicure, had a double allowance. He pecked away at it like a hungry bird. Ainslie, too, had a second helping. The Professor took a large spoonful himself, and Colonel Dresler, watching him narrowly, did the same. The ladies ate freely, save only pretty Miss Patterson, who disliked the salty, pungent taste. In spite of the hospitable entreaties of the Professor, her portion lay hardly touched at the side of her plate.

"You don't like my little delicacy. It is a disappointment to me when I had kept it for your pleasure," said the old man. "I beg that you will eat the caviare."

"I have never tasted it before. No doubt I should like it in time."

"Well, you must make a beginning. Why not start to educate your taste now? Do, please!"

Pretty Jessie Patterson's bright face shone with her sunny, boyish smile.

"Why, how earnest you are!" she laughed. "I had no idea you were so polite, Professor Mercer. Even if I do not eat it I am just as grateful."

"You are foolish not to eat it," said the Professor, with such intensity that the smile died from her face and her eyes reflected the earnestness of his own. "I tell you it is foolish not to eat caviare tonight."

"But why—why?" she asked.

"Because you have it on your plate. Because it is sinful to waste it."

"There! there!" said stout Mrs. Patterson, leaning across. "Don't trouble her any more. I can see that she does not like it. But it shall not be wasted." She passed the blade of her knife under it, and scraped it from Jessie's plate on to her own. "Now it won't be wasted. Your mind will be at ease, Professor."

But it did not seem at ease. On the contrary, his face was agitated like that of a man who encounters an unexpected and formidable obstacle. He was lost in thought.

The conversation buzzed cheerily. Everyone was full of his future plans.

"No, no, there is no holiday for me," said Father Pierre. "We priests don't get holidays. Now that the mission and school are formed I am to leave it to Father Amiel, and to push westward to found another."

"You are leaving?" said Mr. Patterson. "You don't mean that you are going away from Ichau?"

Father Pierre shook his venerable head in waggish reproof. "You must not look so pleased, Mr. Patterson."

"Well, well, our views are very different," said the Presbyterian, "but there is no personal feeling towards you, Father Pierre. At the same time, how any reasonable educated man at this time of the world's history can teach these poor benighted heathen that—"

A general buzz of remonstrance silenced the theology.

"What will you do yourself, Mr. Patterson?" asked someone.

"Well, I'll take three months in Edinburgh to attend the annual meeting. You'll be glad to do some shopping in Princes Street, I'm thinking, Mary. And you, Jessie, you'll see some folk your own age. Then we can come back in the fall, when your nerves have had a rest."

"Indeed, we shall all need it," said Miss Sinclair, the mission nurse. "You know, this long strain takes me in the strangest way. At the present moment, I can hear such a buzzing in my ears."

"Well, that's funny, for it's just the same with me," cried Ainslie. "An absurd up-and-down buzzing, as if a drunken bluebottle were trying experiments on his register. As you say, it must be due to nervous strain. For my part I am going back to Peking, and I hope I may get some promotion over this affair. I can get good polo here, and that's as fine a change of thought as I know. How about you, Ralston?"

"Oh, I don't know. I've hardly had time to think. I want to have a real good sunny, bright holiday and forget it all. It was funny to see all the letters in my room. It looked so black on Wednesday night that I had settled up my affairs and written to all my friends. I don't quite know how they were to be delivered, but I trusted to luck. I think I will keep those papers as a souvenir. They will always remind me of how close a shave we have had."

"Yes, I would keep them," said Dresler.

His voice was so deep and solemn that every eye was turned upon him.

"What is it, Colonel? You seem in the blues tonight." It was Ainslie who spoke.

"No, no; I am very contented."

"Well, so you should be when you see success in sight. I am sure we are all indebted to you for your science and skill. I don't think we could have held the place without you. Ladies and gentlemen, I ask you to drink the health of Colonel Dresler, of the Imperial German army. Er soll leben—hoch!"

They all stood up and raised their glasses to the soldier, with smiles and bows.

His pale face flushed with professional pride.

"I have always kept my books with me. I have forgotten nothing," said he. "I do not think that more could be done. If things had gone wrong with us and the place had fallen you would, I am sure, have freed me from any blame or responsibility." He looked wistfully round him.

"I'm voicing the sentiments of this company, Colonel Dresler," said the Scotch minister, "when I say—but, Lord save us! what's amiss with Mr. Ralston?"

He had dropped his face upon his folded arms and was placidly sleeping.

"Don't mind him," said the Professor, hurriedly. "We are all in the stage of reaction now. I have no doubt that we are all liable to collapse. It is only tonight that we shall feel what we have gone through."

"I'm sure I can fully sympathize with him," said Mrs. Patterson. "I don't know when I have been more sleepy. I can hardly hold my own head up." She cuddled back in her chair and shut her eyes.

"Well, I've never known Mary do that before," cried her husband, laughing heartily. "Gone to sleep over her supper! What ever will she think when we tell her of it afterward? But the air does seem hot and heavy. I can certainly excuse anyone who falls asleep tonight. I think that I shall turn in early myself."

Ainslie was in a talkative, excited mood. He was on his feet once more with his glass in his hand.

"I think that we ought to have one drink all together, and then sing 'Auld Lang Syne,' " said he, smiling round at the company. "For a week we have all pulled in the same boat, and we've got to know each other as people never do in the quiet days of peace. We've learned to appreciate each other and we've learned to appreciate each other's nations. There's the Colonel here stands for Germany. And Father Pierre is for France. Then there's the Professor for America. Ralston and I are Britishers. Then there's the ladies, God bless 'em! They have been angels of mercy and compassion all through the siege. I think we should drink to the health of the ladies. Wonderful thing—the quiet courage, the patience, the—what shall I say—the fortitude, the—the—by George, look at the Colonel! He's gone to sleep, too—most infernal sleepy weather." His glass crashed down upon the table, and he sank back, mumbling and muttering, into his seat. Miss Sinclair, the pale mission nurse, had dropped off also. She lay like a broken lily across the arm of her chair. Mr. Patterson looked round him and sprang to his feet. He passed his hand over his flushed forehead.

"This isn't natural, Jessie," he cried. "Why are they all asleep? There's Father Pierre—he's off too. Jessie, Jessie, your mother is cold. Is it sleep? Is it death? Open the windows! Help! help! help!" He staggered to his feet and rushed to the windows, but midway his head spun round, his knees sank under him, and he pitched forward upon his face.

The young girl had also sprung to her feet. She looked round her with horror-stricken eyes at her prostrate father and the silent ring of figures.

"Professor Mercer! What is it? What is it?" she cried. "Oh, my God, they are dying! They are dead!"

The old man had raised himself by a supreme effort of his will, though the darkness was already gathering thickly round him.

"My dear young lady," he said, stuttering and stumbling over the words, "we would have spared you this. It would have been painless to mind and body. It was cyanide. I had it in the caviare. But you would not have it."

"Great Heaven!" She shrank away from him with dilated eyes. "Oh, you monster! You monster! You have poisoned them!"

"No, no! I saved them. You don't know the Chinese. They are horrible. In another hour we should all have been in their hands. Take it now, child." Even as he spoke, a burst of firing broke out under the very windows of the room. "Hark! There they are! Quick, dear, quick, you may cheat them yet!" But his words fell upon deaf ears, for the girl had sunk back senseless in her chair. The old man stood listening for an instant to the firing outside. But what was that? Merciful Father, what was that? Was he going mad? Was it the effect of the drug? Surely it was a European cheer? Yes, there were sharp orders in English. There was the shouting of sailors. He could no longer doubt it. By some miracle the relief had come after all. He threw his long arms upward in his despair. "What have I done? Oh, good Lord, what *have* I done?" he cried.

It was Commodore Wyndham himself who was the first, after his desperate and successful night attack, to burst into that terrible supper room. Round the table sat the white and silent company. Only in the young girl who moaned and faintly stirred was any sign of life to be seen. And yet there was one in the circle who had the energy for a last supreme duty. The Commodore, standing stupefied at the door, saw a gray head slowly lifted from the table, and the tall form of the Professor staggered for an instant to its feet.

"Take care of the caviare! For God's sake, don't touch the caviare!" he croaked.

Then he sank back once more and the circle of death was complete.

THE JAPANNED BOX

It *was* a curious thing, said the private tutor; one of those grotesque and whimsical incidents which occur to one as one goes through life. I lost the best situation which I am ever likely to have through it. But I am glad that I went to Thorpe Place, for I gained—well, as I tell you the story you will learn what I gained.

I don't know whether you are familiar with that part of the Midlands which is drained by the Avon. It is the most English part of England. Shakespeare, the flower of the whole race, was born right in the middle of it. It is a land of rolling pastures, rising in higher folds to the westward, until they swell into the Malvern Hills. There are no towns, but numerous villages, each with its gray Norman church. You have left the brick of the southern and eastern counties behind you, and everything is stone—stone for the walls, and lichened slabs of stone for the roofs. It is all grim and solid and massive, as befits the heart of a great nation.

It was in the middle of this country, not very far from Evesham, that Sir John Bollamore lived in the old ancestral home of Thorpe Place, and thither it was that I came to teach his two little sons. Sir John was a widower—his wife had died three years before—and he had been left with these two lads aged eight and ten, and one dear little girl of seven. Miss Witherton, who is now my wife, was governess to this little girl. I was tutor to the two boys. Could there be a more obvious prelude to an engagement? She governs me now, and I tutor two little boys of our own. But, there—I have already revealed what it was which I gained in Thorpe Place!

It was a very, very old house, incredibly old—pre-Norman, some of it—and the Bollamores claimed to have lived in that situation since long before the Conquest. It struck a chill to my heart when first I came there, those enormously thick gray walls, the rude crumbling stones, the smell as from a sick animal which exhaled from the rotting plaster of the aged building. But the modern wing was bright and the garden was well kept. No house could be dismal which had a pretty girl inside it and such a show of roses in front.

Apart from a very complete staff of servants there were only four of us in the household. These were Miss Witherton, who was at that time four-and-twenty and as pretty—well, as pretty as Mrs. Colmore is now—myself, Frank Colmore, aged thirty, Mrs. Stevens, the housekeeper, a dry, silent woman, and Mr. Richards, a tall, military-looking man, who acted as steward to the Bollamore estates. We four always had our meals together, but Sir John had his usually alone in the library. Sometimes he joined us at dinner, but on the whole we were just as glad when he did not.

For he was a very formidable person. Imagine a man six foot three inches in height, majestically built, with a high-nosed, aristocratic face, brindled hair, shaggy eyebrows, a small, pointed Mephistophelian beard, and lines upon his brow and round his eyes as deep as if they had been carved with a penknife. He had gray eyes, weary, hopeless-looking eyes, proud and yet pathetic, eyes which claimed your pity and yet dared you to show it. His back was rounded with study, but otherwise he was as fine a looking man of his age—five-and-fifty perhaps—as any woman would wish to look upon.

But his presence was not a cheerful one. He was always courteous, always refined, but singularly silent and retiring. I have never lived so long with any man and known so little of him. If he were indoors he spent his time either in his own small study in the Eastern Tower, or in the library in the modern wing. So regular was his routine that one could always say at any hour exactly where he would be. Twice in the day he would visit his study, once after breakfast, and once about ten at night. You might set your watch by the slam of the heavy door. For the rest of the day he would be in his library—save that for an hour or two in the afternoon he would take a walk or a ride, which was solitary like the rest of his existence. He loved his children, and was keenly interested in the progress of their studies, but they were a little awed by the silent, shaggy-browed figure, and they avoided him as much as they could. Indeed, we all did that.

It was some time before I came to know anything about the circumstances of Sir John Bollamore's life, for Mrs. Stevens, the housekeeper, and Mr. Richards, the land steward, were too loyal to talk easily of their employer's affairs. As to the governess, she knew no more than I did, and our common interest was one of the causes which drew us together. At last, however, an incident occurred which led to a closer acquaintance with Mr. Richards and a fuller knowledge of the life of the man whom I served.

The immediate cause of this was no less than the falling of Master Percy, the youngest of my pupils, into the millrace, with imminent danger both to his life and to mine, since I had to risk myself in order to save him. Dripping and exhausted—for I was far more spent than the child—I was making for my room when Sir John, who had heard the hubbub, opened the door of his little study and asked me what was the matter. I told him of the accident, but assured him that his child was in no danger, while he listened with a rugged, immobile face, which expressed in its intense eyes and tightened lips all the emotion which he tried to conceal.

"One moment! Step in here! Let me have the details!" said he, turning back through the open door.

And so I found myself within that little sanctum, inside which, as I afterward learned, no other foot had for three years been set save that of the old servant who cleaned it out. It was a round room, conforming to the shape of the tower in which it was situated, with a low ceiling, a single narrow, ivy-wreathed window, and the simplest of furniture. An old carpet, a single chair, a deal table, and a small shelf of books made up the whole contents. On the table stood a full-length photograph of a woman—I took no particular notice of the features, but I remember that a certain gracious gentleness was the prevailing impression. Beside it were a large black japanned box and one or two bundles of letters or papers fastened together with elastic bands.

Our interview was a short one, for Sir John Bollamore perceived that I was soaked, and that I should change without delay. The incident led, however, to an instructive talk with Richards, the agent, who had never penetrated into the chamber which chance had opened to me. That very afternoon he came to me, all curiosity, and walked up and down the garden path with me, while my two charges played tennis upon the lawn beside us.

"You hardly realize the exception which has been made in your favor," said he. "That room has been kept such a mystery, and Sir John's visits to it have been so regular and consistent, that an almost superstitious feeling has arisen about it in the household. I assure you that if I were to repeat to you the tales which are flying about, tales of mysterious visitors there, and of voices overheard by the servants, you might suspect that Sir John had relapsed into his old ways."

"Why do you say relapsed?" I asked.

He looked at me in surprise.

"Is it possible," said he, "that Sir John Bollamore's previous history is unknown to you?"

"Absolutely."

"You astound me. I thought that every man in England knew something of his antecedents. I should not mention the matter if it were not that you are now one of ourselves, and that the facts might come to your ears in some harsher form if I were silent upon them. I always took it for granted that you knew that you were in the service of 'Devil' Bollamore."

"But why 'Devil'?" I asked.

"Ah, you are young and the world moves fast, but twenty years ago the name of 'Devil' Bollamore was one of the best known in London. He was the leader of the fastest set, bruiser, driver, gambler, drunkard—a survival of the old type, and as bad as the worst of them."

I stared at him in amazement.

"What!" I cried, "that quiet, studious, sad-faced man?"

"The greatest rip and debauchee in England! All between ourselves, Colmore. But you understand now what I mean when I say that a woman's voice in his room might even now give rise to suspicions."

"But what can have changed him so?"

"Little Beryl Clare, when she took the risk of becoming his wife. That was the turning point. He had got so far that his own fast set had thrown him over. There is a world of difference, you know, between a man who drinks and a drunkard. They all drink, but they taboo a drunkard. He had become a slave to it—hopeless and helpless. Then she stepped in, saw the possibilities of a fine man in the wreck, took her chance in marrying him, though she might have had the pick of a dozen, and, by devoting her life to it, brought him back to manhood and decency. You have observed that no liquor is ever kept in the house. There never has been any since her foot crossed its threshold. A drop of it would be like blood to a tiger even now."

"Then her influence still holds him?"

"That is the wonder of it. When she died three years ago, we all expected and feared that he would fall back into his old ways. She feared it herself, and the thought gave a terror to death, for she was like a guardian angel to that man, and lived only for the one purpose. By the way, did you see a black japanned box in his room?"

"Yes."

"I fancy it contains her letters. If ever he has occasion to be away, if only for a single night, he invariably, takes his black japanned box with him. Well, well, Colmore, perhaps I have told you rather more than I should, but I shall expect you to reciprocate if anything of interest should come to your knowledge." I could see that the worthy man was consumed with curiosity and just a little piqued that I, the newcomer, should have been the first to penetrate into the untrodden chamber. But the fact raised me in his esteem, and from that time onward I found myself upon more confidential terms with him.

And now the silent and majestic figure of my employer became an object of greater interest to me. I began to understand that strangely human look in his eyes, those deep lines upon his careworn face. He was a man who was fighting a ceaseless battle, holding at arm's length, from morning till night, a horrible adversary, who was forever trying to close with him—an adversary which would destroy him body and soul could it but fix its claws once more upon him. As I watched the grim, round-backed figure pacing the corridor or walking in the garden, this imminent danger seemed to take bodily shape, and I could almost fancy that I saw this most loathsome and dangerous of all the fiends crouching closely in his very shadow, like a half-cowed beast which slinks beside its keeper, ready at any unguarded moment to spring at his throat. And the dead woman, the woman who had spent her life in warding off this danger, took shape also to my imagination, and I saw her as a shadowy but beautiful presence which intervened forever with arms uplifted to screen the man whom she loved.

In some subtle way he divined the sympathy which I had for him, and he showed in his own silent fashion that he appreciated it. He even invited me once to share his afternoon walk, and although no word passed between us on this occasion, it was a mark of confidence which he had never shown to anyone before. He asked me also to index his library (it was one of the best private libraries in England), and I spent many hours in the evening in his presence, if not in his society, he reading at his desk and I sitting in a recess by the window reducing to order the chaos which existed among his books. In spite of these close relations I was never again asked to enter the chamber in the turret.

And then came my revulsion of feeling. A single incident changed all my sympathy to loathing, and made me realize that my employer still remained all that he had ever been, with the additional vice of hypocrisy. What happened was as follows.

One evening Miss Witherton had gone down to Broadway, the neighboring village, to sing at a concert for some charity, and I, according to my promise, had walked over to escort her back. The drive sweeps round under the eastern turret, and I observed as I passed that the light was lit in the circular room. It was a summer evening, and the window, which was a little higher than our heads, was open. We were, as it happened, engrossed in our own conversation at the moment, and we had paused upon the lawn which skirts the old turret, when suddenly something broke in upon our talk and turned our thoughts away from our own affairs.

It was a voice—the voice undoubtedly of a woman. It was low—so low that it was only in that still night air that we could have heard it, but, hushed as it was, there was no mistaking its feminine timber. It spoke hurriedly, gaspingly for a few sentences, and then was silent—a piteous, breathless, imploring sort of voice. Miss Witherton and I stood for an instant staring at each other. Then we walked quickly in the direction of the hall door.

"It came through the window," I said.

"We must not play the part of eavesdroppers," she answered. "We must forget that we have ever heard it."

There was an absence of surprise in her manner which suggested a new idea to me.

"You have heard it before," I cried.

"I could not help it. My own room is higher up on the same turret. It has happened frequently."

"Who can the woman be?"

"I have no idea. I had rather not discuss it."

Her voice was enough to show me what she thought. But granting that our employer led a double and dubious life, who could she be, this mysterious woman who kept him company in the old tower? I knew from my own inspection how bleak and bare a room it was. She certainly did not live there. But in that case where did she come from? It could not be anyone of the household. They were all under the vigilant eyes of Mrs. Stevens. The visitor must come from without. But how?

And then suddenly I remembered how ancient this building was, and how probable that some mediæval passage existed in it. There is hardly an old castle without one. The mysterious room was the basement of the turret, so that if there was anything of the sort it would open through the floor. There were numerous cottages in the immediate vicinity. The other end of the secret passage might lie among some tangle of bramble in the neighboring copse. I said nothing to anyone, but I felt that the secret of my employer lay within my power.

And the more convinced I was of this the more I marveled at the manner in which he concealed his true nature. Often as I watched his austere figure, I asked myself if it were indeed possible that such a man should be living this double life, and I tried to persuade myself that my suspicions might after all prove to be ill-founded. But there was the female voice, there was the secret nightly rendezvous in the turret chamber—how could such facts admit of an innocent interpretation? I conceived a horror of the man, I was filled with loathing at his deep, consistent hypocrisy.

Only once during all those months did I ever see him without that sad but impassive mask which he usually presented toward his fellow man. For an instant I caught a glimpse of those volcanic fires which he had damped down so long. The occasion was an unworthy one, for the object of his wrath was none other than the aged charwoman whom I have already mentioned as being the one person who was allowed within his mysterious chamber. I was passing the corridor which led to the turret—for my own room lay in that direction—when I heard a sudden, startled scream, and merged in it the husky, growling note of a man who is inarticulate with passion. It was the snarl of a furious wild beast. Then I heard his voice thrilling with anger. "You would dare!" he cried. "You would dare to disobey my directions!" An instant later the charwoman passed me, flying down the passage, white faced and tremulous, while the terrible voice thundered behind her. "Go to Mrs. Stevens for your money! Never set foot in Thorpe Place again!" Consumed with curiosity, I could not help following the woman, and found her round the corner leaning against the wall and palpitating like a frightened rabbit.

"What is the matter, Mrs. Brown?" I asked.

"It's master!" she gasped. "Oh 'ow 'e frightened me! If you had seen 'is eyes, Mr. Colmore, sir. I thought 'e would 'ave been the death of me."

"But what had you done?"

"Done, sir! Nothing. At least nothing to make so much of. Just laid my 'and on that black box of 'is—'adn't even opened it, when in 'e came and you 'eard the way 'e went on. I've lost my place, and glad I am of it, for I would never trust myself within reach of 'im again."

So it was the japanned box which was the cause of this outburst—the box from which he would never permit himself to be separated. What was the connection, or was there any connection between this and the secret visits of the lady whose voice I had overheard? Sir John Bollamore's wrath was enduring as well as fiery, for from that day Mrs. Brown, the charwoman, vanished from our ken, and Thorpe Place knew her no more.

And now I wish to tell you the singular chance which solved all these strange questions and put my employer's secret in my possession. The story may leave you with some lingering doubt as to whether my curiosity did not get the better of my honor, and whether I did not condescend to play the spy. If you choose to think so I cannot help it, but can only assure you that, improbable as it may appear, the matter came about exactly as I describe it.

The first stage in this dénouement was that the small room on the turret became uninhabitable. This occurred through the fall of the worm-eaten oaken beam which supported the ceiling. Rotten with age, it snapped in the middle one morning, and brought down a quantity of plaster with it. Fortunately Sir John was not in the room at the time. His precious box was rescued from amongst the débris and brought into the library, where, henceforward, it was locked within his bureau. Sir John took no steps to repair the damage, and I never had an opportunity of searching for that secret passage, the existence of which I had surmised. As to the lady, I had thought that this would have brought her visits to an end, had I not one evening heard Mr. Richards asking Mrs. Stevens who the woman was whom he had overheard talking to Sir John in the library. I could not catch her reply, but I saw from her manner that it was not the first time that she had had to answer or avoid the same question.

"You've heard the voice, Colmore?" said the agent.

I confessed that I had.

"And what do *you* think of it?"

I shrugged my shoulders, and remarked that it was no business of mine.

"Come, come, you are just as curious as any of us. Is it a woman or not?"

"It is certainly a woman."

"Which room did you hear it from?"

"From the turret room, before the ceiling fell."

"But I heard it from the library only last night. I passed the doors as I was going to bed, and I heard something wailing and praying just as plainly as I hear you. It may be a woman—"

"Why, what else *could* it be?"

He looked at me hard.

"There are more things in heaven and earth," said he. "If it is a woman, how does she get there?"

"I don't know."

"No, nor I. But if it is the other thing—but there, for a practical businessman at the end of the nineteenth century this is rather a ridiculous line of conversation." He turned away, but I saw that he felt even more than he had said. To all the old ghost stories of Thorpe Place a new one was being added before our very eyes. It may by this time have taken its permanent place, for though an explanation came to me, it never reached the others.

And my explanation came in this way. I had suffered a sleepless night from neuralgia, and about midday I had taken a heavy dose of chlorodyne to alleviate the pain. At that time I was finishing the indexing of Sir John Bollamore's library, and it was my custom to work there from five till seven. On this particular day I struggled against the double effect of my bad night and the narcotic. I have already mentioned that there was a recess in the library, and in this it was my habit to work. I settled down steadily, to my task, but my weariness overcame me and, falling back upon the settee, I dropped into a heavy sleep.

How long I slept I do not know, but it was quite dark when I awoke. Confused by the chlorodyne which I had taken, I lay motionless in a semiconscious state. The great room with its high walls covered with books loomed darkly all around me. A dim radiance from the moonlight came through the farther window, and against this lighter background I saw that Sir John Bollamore was sitting at his study table. His well-set head and clearly cut profile were sharply outlined against the glimmering square behind him. He bent as I watched him, and I heard the sharp turning of a key and the rasping of metal upon metal. As if in a dream I was vaguely conscious that this was the japanned box which stood in front of him, and that he had drawn something out of it, something squat and uncouth, which now lay before him upon the table. I never realized—it never occurred to my bemuddled and torpid brain that I was intruding upon his privacy, that he imagined himself to be alone in the room. And then, just as it rushed upon my horrified perceptions, and I had half risen to announce my presence, I heard a strange, crisp, metallic clicking, and then the voice.

Yes it was a woman's voice; there could not be a doubt of it. But a voice so charged with entreaty and with yearning love, that it will ring forever in my ears. It came with a curious faraway tinkle, but every word was clear, though faint—very faint, for they were the last words of a dying woman.

"I am not really gone, John," said the thin, gasping voice. "I am here at your elbow, and shall be until we meet once more. I die happy to think that morning and night you will hear my voice. Oh, John, be strong, be strong, until we meet again."

I say that I had risen in order to announce my presence, but I could not do so while the voice was sounding. I could only remain half lying, half sitting, paralyzed, astounded, listening to those yearning distant musical words. And he—he was so absorbed that even if I had spoken he might not have heard me. But with the silence of the voice came my half-articulated apologies and explanations. He sprang across the room, switched on the electric light, and in its white glare I saw him, his eyes gleaming with anger, his face twisted with passion, as the hapless charwoman may have seen him weeks before.

"Mr. Colmore!" he cried. "You here! What is the meaning of this, sir?"

With halting words I explained it all, my neuralgia, the narcotic, my luckless sleep and singular awakening. As he listened the glow of anger faded from his face, and the sad, impassive mask closed once more over his features.

"My secret is yours, Mr. Colmore," said he. "I have only myself to blame for relaxing my precautions. Half confidences are worse than no confidences, and so you may know all since you know so much. The story may go where you will when I have passed away, but until then I rely upon your sense of honor that no human soul shall hear it from your lips. I am proud still—God help me!—or, at least, I am proud enough to resent that pity which this story would draw upon me. I have smiled at envy, and disregarded hatred, but pity is more than I can tolerate.

"You have heard the source from which the voice comes—that voice which has, as I understand, excited so much curiosity in my household. I am aware of the rumors to which it has given rise. These speculations whether scandalous or superstitious, are such as I can disregard and forgive. What I should never forgive would be a disloyal spying and eavesdropping in order to satisfy an illicit curiosity. But of that, Mr. Colmore, I acquit you.

"When I was a young man, sir, many years younger than you now, I was launched upon town without a friend or adviser, and with a purse which brought only too many false friends and false advisers to my side. I drank deeply of the wine of life—if there is a man living who has

drank more deeply he is not a man whom I envy. My purse suffered, my
character suffered, my constitution suffered, stimulants became a necessity to me, I was a creature from whom my memory recoils. And it
was at that time, the time of my blackest degradation, that God sent into
my life the gentlest, sweetest spirit that ever descended as a ministering
angel from above. She loved me, broken as I was, loved me, and spent
her life in making a man once more of that which had degraded itself
to the level of the beasts.

"But a fell disease struck her, and she withered away before my eyes.
In the hour of her agony it was never of herself, of her own sufferings
and her own death that she thought. It was all of me. The one pang
which her fate brought to her was the fear that when her influence was
removed I should revert to that which I had been. It was in vain that I
made oath to her that no drop of wine would ever cross my lips. She
knew only too well the hold that the devil had upon me—she who had
striven so to loosen it—and it haunted her night and day the thought
that my soul might again be within his grip.

"It was from some friend's gossip of the sick room that she heard of
this invention—this phonograph—and with the quick insight of a loving
woman she saw how she might use it for her ends. She sent me to
London to procure the best which money could buy. With her dying
breath she gasped into it the words which have held me straight ever
since. Lonely and broken, what else have I in all the world, to uphold
me? But it is enough. Please God, I shall face her without shame when
He is pleased to reunite us! That is my secret, Mr. Colmore, and whilst
I live I leave it in your keeping."

THE BLACK DOCTOR

Bishop's Crossing is a small village lying ten miles in a south-westerly direction from Liverpool. Here in the early seventies there settled a doctor named Aloysius Lana. Nothing was known locally either of his antecedents or of the reasons which had prompted him to come to this Lancashire hamlet. Two facts only were certain about him: the one that he had gained his medical qualification with some distinction at Glasgow; the other that he came undoubtedly of a tropical race, and was so dark that he might almost have had a strain of the Indian in his composition. His predominant features were, however, European, and he possessed a stately courtesy and carriage which suggested a Spanish extraction. A swarthy skin, raven-black hair, and dark, sparkling eyes under a pair of heavily-tufted brows made a strange contrast to the flaxen or chestnut rustics of England, and the newcomer was soon known as "The Black Doctor of Bishop's Crossing." At first it was a term of ridicule and reproach; as the years went on it became a title of honor which was familiar to the whole countryside, and extended far beyond the narrow confines of the village.

For the newcomer proved himself to be a capable surgeon and an accomplished physician. The practice of that district had been in the hands of Edward Rowe, the son of Sir William Rowe, the Liverpool consultant, but he had not inherited the talents of his father, and Dr. Lana, with his advantages of presence and of manner, soon beat him out of the field. Dr. Lana's social success was as rapid as his professional. A remarkable surgical cure in the case of the Hon. James Lowry, the second son of Lord Belton, was the means of introducing him to county society, where he became a favorite through the charm of his conversation and the elegance of his manners. An absence of antecedents and of relatives is sometimes an aid rather than an impediment to social advancement, and the distinguished individuality of the handsome doctor was its own recommendation.

His patients had one fault—and one fault only—to find with him. He appeared to be a confirmed bachelor. This was the more remarkable since the house which he occupied was a large one, and it was known that his success in practice had enabled him to save considerable sums. At first the local matchmakers were continually coupling his name with one or other of the eligible ladies, but as years passed and Dr. Lana remained unmarried, it came to be generally understood that for some reason he must remain a bachelor. Some even went so far as to assert that he was already married, and that it was in order to escape the consequence of an early misalliance that he had buried himself at Bishop's Crossing. And then, just as the matchmakers had finally given him up in despair, his engagement was suddenly announced to Miss Frances Morton, of Leigh Hall.

Miss Morton was a young lady who was well known upon the countryside, her father, James Haldane Morton, having been the Squire of Bishop's Crossing. Both her parents were, however, dead, and she lived with her only brother, Arthur Morton, who had inherited the family estate. In person Miss Morton was tall and stately, and she was famous for her quick, impetuous nature and for her strength of character. She met Dr. Lana at a garden party, and a friendship, which quickly ripened into love, sprang up between them. Nothing could exceed their devotion to each other. There was some discrepancy in age, he being thirty-seven, and she twenty-four; but, save in that respect, there was no possible objection to be found with the match. The engagement was in February, and it was arranged that the marriage should take place in August.

Upon the 3rd of June Dr. Lana received a letter from abroad. In a small village the postmaster is also in a position to be the gossip-master, and Mr. Bankley, of Bishop's Crossing, had many of the secrets of his neighbors in his possession. Of this particular letter he remarked only that it was in a curious envelope, that it was in a man's handwriting, that the postscript was Buenos Ayres, and the stamp of the Argentine Republic. It was the first letter which he had ever known Dr. Lana to have from abroad, and this was the reason why his attention was particularly called to it before he handed it to the local postman. It was delivered by the evening delivery of that date.

Next morning—that is, upon the 4th of June—Dr. Lana called upon Miss Morton, and a long interview followed, from which he was observed to return in a state of great agitation. Miss Morton remained in her room all that day, and her maid found her several times in tears. In the course of a week it was an open secret to the whole village that the engagement was at an end, that Dr. Lana had behaved shamefully to the young lady, and that Arthur Morton, her brother, was talking of horsewhipping him. In what particular respect the doctor had behaved badly was unknown—some surmised one thing and some another; but it was observed, and taken as the obvious sign of a guilty conscience, that he would go for miles round rather than pass the windows of Leigh Hall, and that he gave up attending morning service upon Sundays where he might have met the young lady. There was an advertisement also in the *Lancet* as to the sale of a practice which mentioned no names, but which was thought by some to refer to Bishop's Crossing, and to mean that Dr. Lana was thinking of abandoning the scene of his success. Such was the position of affairs when, upon the evening of Monday, June 21st, there came a fresh development which changed what had been a mere village scandal into a tragedy which arrested the attention of the whole nation. Some detail is necessary to cause the facts of that evening to present their full significance.

The sole occupants of the doctor's house were his housekeeper, an elderly and most respectable woman, named Martha Woods, and a young servant—Mary Pilling. The coachman and the surgery boy slept out. It was the custom of the doctor to sit at night in his study, which was next the surgery in the wing of the house which was farthest from the servants' quarters. This side of the house had a door of its own for the convenience of patients, so that it was possible for the doctor to admit and receive a visitor there without the knowledge of anyone. As a matter of fact, when patients came late it was quite usual for him to let them in and out by the surgery entrance, for the maid and the housekeeper were in the habit of retiring early.

On this particular night Martha Woods went into the doctor's study at half past nine, and found him writing at his desk. She bade him goodnight, sent the maid to bed, and then occupied herself until a quarter to eleven in household matters. It was striking eleven upon the hall clock when she went to her own room. She had been there about a quarter of an hour or twenty minutes when she heard a cry or call, which appeared to come from within the house. She waited some time, but it was not repeated. Much alarmed, for the sound was loud and urgent, she put on a dressing gown, and ran at the top of her speed to the doctor's study.

"Who's there?" cried a voice, as she tapped at the door.

"I am here, sir—Mrs. Woods."

"I beg that you will leave me in peace. Go back to your room this instant!" cried the voice, which was, to the best of her belief, that of her master. The tone was so harsh and so unlike her master's usual manner, that she was surprised and hurt.

"I thought I heard you calling, sir," she explained, but no answer was given to her. Mrs. Woods looked at the clock as she returned to her room, and it was then half past eleven.

At some period between eleven and twelve (she could not be positive as to the exact hour) a patient called upon the doctor and was unable to get any reply from him. This late visitor was Mrs. Madding, the wife of the village grocer, who was dangerously ill of typhoid fever. Dr. Lana had asked her to look in the last thing and let him know how her husband was progressing. She observed that the light was burning in the study, but having knocked several times at the surgery door without response, she concluded that the doctor had been called out, and so returned home.

There is a short, winding drive with a lamp at the end of it leading down from the house to the road. As Mrs. Madding emerged from the gate a man was coming along the footpath. Thinking that it might be Dr. Lana returning from some professional visit, she waited for him, and was surprised to see that it was Mr. Arthur Morton, the young squire. In the light of the lamp she observed that his manner was excited, and that he carried in his hand a heavy hunting crop. He was turning in at the gate when she addressed him.

"The doctor is not in, sir," said she.

"How do you know that?" he asked, harshly.

"I have been to the surgery door, sir."

"I see a light," said the young squire, looking up the drive. "That is in his study, is it not?"

"Yes, sir; but I am sure that he is out."

"Well, he must come in again," said young Morton, and passed through the gate while Mrs. Madding went upon her homeward way.

At three o'clock that morning her husband suffered a sharp relapse, and she was so alarmed by his symptoms that she determined to call the doctor without delay. As she passed through the gate she was surprised to see someone lurking among the laurel bushes. It was certainly a man, and to the best of her belief Mr. Arthur Morton. Preoccupied with her own troubles, she gave no particular attention to the incident, but hurried on upon her errand.

When she reached the house she perceived to her surprise that the light was still burning in the study. She therefore tapped at the surgery door. There was no answer. She repeated the knocking several times without effect. It appeared to her to be unlikely that the doctor would either go to bed or go out leaving so brilliant a light behind him, and it struck Mrs. Madding that it was possible that he might have dropped asleep in his chair. She tapped at the study window, therefore, but without result. Then, finding that there was an opening between the curtain and the woodwork, she looked through.

The small room was brilliantly lighted from a large lamp on the central table, which was littered with the doctor's books and instruments. No one was visible, nor did she see anything unusual, except that in the further shadow thrown by the table a dingy white glove was lying upon the carpet. And then suddenly, as her eyes became more accustomed to the light, a boot emerged from the other end of the shadow, and she realized, with a thrill of horror, that what she had taken to be a glove was the hand of a man, who was prostrate upon the floor. Understanding that something terrible had occurred, she rang at the front door, roused Mrs. Woods, the housekeeper, and the two women made their way into the study, having first dispatched the maidservant to the police station.

At the side of the table, away from the window, Dr. Lana was discovered stretched upon his back and quite dead. It was evident that he had been subjected to violence, for one of his eyes was blackened, and there were marks of bruises about his face and neck. A slight thickening and swelling of his features appeared to suggest that the cause of his death had been strangulation. He was dressed in his usual professional clothes, but wore cloth slippers, the soles of which were perfecty clean. The carpet was marked all over, especially on the side of the door with traces of dirty boots, which were presumably left by the murderer. It was evident that someone had entered by the surgery door, had killed the doctor, and had then made his escape unseen. That the assailant was a man was certain, from the size of the footprints and from the nature of the injuries. But beyond that point the police found it very difficult to go.

There were no signs of robbery, and the doctor's gold watch was safe in his pocket. He kept a heavy cashbox in the room, and this was discovered to be locked but empty. Mrs. Woods had an impression that a large sum was usually kept there, but the doctor had paid a heavy corn bill in cash only that very day, and it was conjectured that it was to this and not to a robber that the emptiness of the box was due. One thing in the room was missing—but that one thing was suggestive. The portrait of Miss Morton, which had always stood upon the side table, had been taken from its frame, and carried off. Mrs. Woods had observed it there when she waited upon her employer that evening, and now it was gone. On the other hand, there was picked up from the floor a green eye-patch, which the housekeeper could not remember to have seen before. Such a patch might, however, be in the possession of a doctor, and there was nothing to indicate that it was in any way connected with the crime.

Suspicion could only turn in one direction, and Arthur Morton, the young squire, was immediately arrested. The evidence against him was circumstantial, but damning. He was devoted to his sister, and it was shown that since the rupture between her and Dr. Lana he had been heard again and again to express himself in the most vindictive terms toward her former lover. He had, as stated, been seen somewhere about eleven o'clock entering the doctor's drive with a hunting crop in his hand. He had then, according to the theory of the police, broken in upon the doctor, whose exclamation of fear or of anger had been loud enough to attract the attention of Mrs. Woods. When Mrs. Woods descended, Dr. Lana had made up his mind to talk it over with his visitor, and had, therefore, sent his housekeeper back to her room. This conversation had lasted a long time, had become more and more fiery, and had ended by a personal struggle, in which the doctor lost his life. The fact, revealed by a postmortem, that his heart was much diseased—an ailment quite unsuspected during his life—would make it possible that death might in his case ensue from injuries which would not be fatal to a healthy man. Arthur Morton had then removed his sister's photograph, and had made his way homeward, stepping aside into the laurel bushes to avoid Mrs. Madding at the gate. This was the theory of the prosecution, and the case which they presented was a formidable one.

On the other hand, there were some strong points for the defense. Morton was high-spirited and impetuous, like his sister, but he was respected and liked by everyone, and his frank and honest nature seemed to be incapable of such a crime. His own explanation was that he was anxious to have a conversation with Dr. Lana about some urgent family matters (from first to last he refused even to mention the name of his sister). He did not attempt to deny that this conversation would probably have been of an unpleasant nature. He had heard from a patient that the doctor was out, and he therefore waited until about three in the morning for his return, but as he had seen nothing of him up to that hour, he had given it up and had returned home. As to his death, he knew no more about it than the constable who arrested him. He had formerly been an intimate friend of the deceased man; but circumstances, which he would prefer not to mention, had brought about a change in his sentiments.

There were several facts which supported his innocence. It was certain that Dr. Lana was alive and in his study at half past eleven o'clock. Mrs. Woods was prepared to swear that it was at that hour that she had heard his voice. The friends of the prisoner contended that it was probable that at that time Dr. Lana was not alone. The sound which had originally attracted the attention of the housekeeper, and her master's unusual impatience that she should leave him in peace, seemed to point to that. If that were so, then it appeared to be probable that he had met his end between the moment when the housekeeper heard his voice and the time when Mrs. Madding made her first call and found it impossible to attract his attention. But if this were the time of his death, then it was certain that Mr. Arthur Morton could not be guilty, as it was *after* this that she had met the young squire at the gate.

If this hypothesis were correct, and someone was with Dr. Lana before Mrs. Madding met Mr. Arthur Morton, then who was this someone, and what motives had he for wishing evil to the doctor? It was universally admitted that if the friends of the accused could throw light upon this, they would have gone a long way toward establishing his innocence. But in the meanwhile it was open to the public to say—as they did say—that there was no proof that anyone had been there at all except the young squire; while, on the other hand, there was ample proof that his motives in going were of a sinister kind. When Mrs. Madding called the doctor might have retired to his room, or he might, as she thought at the time, have gone out and returned afterward to find Mr. Arthur Morton waiting for him. Some of the supporters of the accused laid stress upon the fact that the photograph of his sister Frances, which had been removed from the doctor's room, had not been found in her brother's possession. This argument, however, did not count for much, as he had ample time before his arrest to burn it or to destroy it. As to the only positive evidence in the case—the muddy footmarks upon the floor—they were so blurred by the softness of the carpet that it was impossible to make any trustworthy deduction from them. The most that could be said was that their appearance was not inconsistent with the theory that they were made by the accused, and it was further shown that his boots were very muddy upon that night. There had been a heavy shower in the afternoon, and all boots were probably in the same condition.

Such is a bald statement of the singular and romantic series of events which centered public attention upon this Lancashire tragedy. The unknown origin of the doctor, his curious and distinguished personality, the position of the man who was accused of the murder, and the love affair which had preceded the crime, all combined to make the affair one of those dramas which absorb the whole interest of a nation. Throughout the three kingdoms men discussed the case of the Black Doctor of Bishop's Crossing, and many were the theories put forward to explain the facts; but it may safely be said that among them all there was not one which prepared the minds of the public for the extraordinary sequel, which caused so much excitement upon the first day of the trial, and came to a climax upon the second. The long files of the *Lancaster Weekly* with their report of the case lie before me as I write, but I must content myself with a synopsis of the case up to the point when, upon the evening of the first day, the evidence of Miss Frances Morton threw a singular light upon the case.

Mr. Porlock Carr, the counsel for the prosecution, had marshaled his facts with his usual skill, and as the day wore on, it became more and more evident how difficult was the task which Mr. Humphrey, who had been retained for the defense, had before him. Several witnesses were put up to swear to the intemperate expressions which the young squire had been heard to utter about the doctor, and the fiery manner in which he resented the alleged ill-treatment of his sister. Mrs. Madding repeated her evidence as to the visit which had been paid late at night by the prisoner to the deceased, and it was shown by another witness that the prisoner was aware that the doctor was in the habit of sitting up alone in this isolated wing of the house, and that he had chosen this very late hour to call because he knew that his victim would then be at his mercy. A servant at the squire's house was compelled to admit that he had heard his master return about three that morning, which corroborated Mrs. Madding's statement that she had seen him among the laurel bushes near the gate upon the occasion of her second visit. The muddy boots and an alleged similarity in the footprints were duly dwelt upon, and it was felt when the case for the prosecution had been presented that, however circumstantial it might be, it was none the less so complete and so convincing, that the fate of the prisoner was sealed, unless something quite unexpected should be disclosed by the defense. It was three o'clock when the prosecution closed. At half past four, when the Court rose, a new and unlooked for development had occurred. I extract the incident, or part of it, from the journal which I have already mentioned, omitting the preliminary observations of the counsel.

"Considerable sensation was caused in the crowded court when the first witness called for the defense proved to be Miss Frances Morton, the sister of the prisoner. Our readers will remember that the young lady had been engaged to Dr. Lana, and that it was his anger over the sudden termination of this engagement which was thought to have driven her brother to the perpetration of this crime. Miss Morton had not, however, been directly implicated in the case in any way, either at the inquest or at the police court proceedings, and her appearance as the leading witness for the defense came as a surprise upon the public.

"Miss Frances Morton, who was a tall and handsome brunette, gave her evidence in a low but clear voice, though it was evident throughout that she was suffering from extreme emotion. She alluded to her engagement to the doctor, touched briefly upon its termination, which was due, she said, to personal matters connected with his family, and surprised the Court by asserting that she had always considered her brother's resentment to be unreasonable and intemperate. In answer to a direct question from her counsel, she replied that she did not feel that she had any grievance whatever against Dr. Lana, and that in her opinion he had acted in a perfectly honorable manner. Her brother, on an insufficient knowledge of the facts, had taken another view, and she was compelled to acknowledge that, in spite of her entreaties, he had uttered threats of personal violence against the doctor, and had, upon the evening of the tragedy, announced his intention of 'having it out with him.' She had done her best to bring him to a more reasonable frame of mind, but he was very headstrong where his emotions or prejudices were concerned.

"Up to this point the young lady's evidence had appeared to make against the prisoner rather than in his favor. The questions of her counsel, however, soon put a very different light upon the matter, and disclosed an unexpected line of defense.

Mr. Humphrey: Do you believe your brother to be guilty of this crime?

The Judge: I cannot permit that question, Mr. Humphrey. We are here to decide upon questions of fact—not of belief.

Mr. Humphrey: Do you know that your brother is not guilty of the death of Doctor Lana?

Miss Morton: Yes.

Mr. Humphrey: How do you know it?

Miss Morton: Because Dr. Lana is not dead.

"There followed a prolonged sensation in court, which interrupted the cross-examination of the witness.

Mr. Humphrey: And how do you know, Miss Morton, that Dr. Lana is not dead?

Miss Morton: Because I have received a letter from him since the date of his supposed death.

Mr. Humphrey: Have you this letter?

Miss Morton: Yes, but I should prefer not to show it.

Mr. Humphrey: Have you the envelope?

Miss Morton: Yes, it is here.

Mr. Humphrey: What is the postmark?

Miss Morton: Liverpool.

Mr. Humphrey: And the date?

Miss Morton: June the 22nd.

Mr. Humphrey: That being the day after his alleged death. Are you prepared to swear to this handwriting, Miss Morton?

Miss Morton: Certainly.

Mr. Humphrey: I am prepared to call six other witnesses, my lord, to testify that this letter is in the writing of Doctor Lana.

The Judge: Then you must call them tomorrow.

Mr. Porlock Carr (counsel for the prosecution): In the meantime, my lord, we claim possession of this document, so that we may obtain expert evidence as to how far it is an imitation of the handwriting of the gentleman whom we still confidently assert to be deceased. I need not point out that the theory so unexpectedly sprung upon us may prove to be a very obvious device adopted by the friends of the prisoner in order to divert this inquiry. I would draw attention to the fact that the young lady must, according to her own account, have possessed this letter during the proceedings at the inquest and at the police court. She desires us to believe that she permitted these to proceed, although she held in her pocket evidence which would at any moment have brought them to an end.

Mr. Humphrey: Can you explain this, Miss Morton?

Miss Morton: Dr. Lana desired his secret to be preserved.

Mr. Porlock Carr: Then why have you made this public?

Miss Morton: To save my brother.

"A murmur of sympathy broke out in court, which was instantly suppressed by the Judge.

The Judge: Admitting this line of defense, it lies with you, Mr.

Humphrey, to throw a light upon who this man is whose body has been recognized by so many friends and patients of Dr. Lana as being that of the doctor himself.

A Juryman: Has anyone up to now expressed any doubt about the matter?

Mr. Porlock Carr: Not to my knowledge.

Mr. Humphrey: We hope to make the matter clear.

The Judge: Then the Court adjourns until tomorrow.

"This new development of the case excited the utmost interest among the general public. Press comment was prevented by the fact that the trial was still undecided, but the question was everywhere argued as to how far there could be truth in Miss Morton's declaration, and how far it might be a daring ruse for the purpose of saving her brother. The obvious dilemma in which the missing doctor stood was that if by any extraordinary chance he was not dead, then he must be held responsible for the death of this unknown man, who resembled him so exactly, and who was found in his study. This letter which Miss Morton refused to produce was possibly a confession of guilt, and she might find herself in the terrible position of only being able to save her brother from the gallows by the sacrifice of her former lover. The court next morning was crammed to overflowing, and a murmur of excitement passed over it when Mr. Humphrey was observed to enter in a state of emotion, which even his trained nerves could not conceal, and to confer with the opposing counsel. A few hurried words—words which left a look of amazement upon Mr. Porlock Carr's face—passed between them, and then the counsel for the defense, addressing the judge, announced that, with the consent of the prosecution, the young lady who had given evidence upon the sitting before would not be recalled.

The Judge: But you appear, Mr. Humphrey, to have left matters in a very unsatisfactory state.

Mr. Humphrey: Perhaps, my lord, my next witness may help to clear them up.

The Judge: Then call your next witness.

Mr. Humphrey: I call Dr. Aloysius Lana.

"The learned counsel has made many telling remarks in his day, but he has certainly never produced such a sensation with so short a sentence. The Court was simply stunned with amazement as the very man whose fate had been the subject of so much contention appeared bodily before them in the witness-box. Those among the spectators who had known him at Bishop's Crossing saw him now, gaunt and thin, with deep lines of care upon his face. But in spite of his melancholy bearing and despondent expression, there were few who could say that they had ever seen a man of more distinguished presence. Bowing to the judge, he asked if he might be allowed to make a statement, and having been duly informed that whatever he said might be used against him, he bowed once more, and proceeded:

"My wish," said he, "is to hold nothing back, but to tell with perfect frankness all that occurred upon the night of the 21st of June. Had I known that the innocent had suffered, and that so much trouble had been brought upon those whom I love best in the world, I should have come forward long ago; but there were reasons which prevented these things from coming to my ears. It was my desire that an unhappy man should vanish from the world which had known him, but I had not foreseen that others would be affected by my actions. Let me to the best of my ability repair the evil which I have done.

"To anyone who is acquainted with the history of the Argentine Republic the name of Lana is well known. My father, who came of the best blood of old Spain, filled all the highest offices of the State, and would have been President but for his death in the riots of San Juan. A brilliant career might have been open to my twin brother Ernest and myself had it not been for financial losses which made it necessary that we should earn our own living. I apologize, sir, if these details appear to be irrelevant, but they are a necessary introduction to that which is to follow.

"I had, as I have said, a twin brother named Ernest, whose resemblance to me was so great that even when we were together people could see no difference between us. Down to the smallest detail we were exactly the same. As we grew older this likeness became less marked because our expression was not the same, but with our features in repose the points of difference were very slight.

"It does not become me to say too much of one who is dead, the more so as he is my only brother, but I leave his character to those who knew him best. I will only say—for I *have* to say it—that in my early manhood I conceived a horror of him, and that I had good reason for the aversion which filled me. My own reputation suffered from his actions for our close resemblance caused me to be credited with many of them. Eventually, in a peculiarly disgraceful business, he contrived to throw the whole odium upon me in such a way that I was forced to leave the Argentine forever, and to seek a career in Europe. The freedom from his hated presence more than compensated me for the loss of my native land. I had enough money to defray my medical studies at Glasgow, and I finally settled in practice at Bishop's Crossing, in the firm conviction that in that remote Lancashire hamlet I should never hear of him again.

"For years my hopes were fulfilled, and then at last he discovered me. Some Liverpool man who visited Buenos Ayres put him upon my track. He had lost all his money, and he thought that he would come over and share mine. Knowing my horror of him, he rightly thought that I would be willing to buy him off. I received a letter from him saying that he was coming. It was at a crisis in my own affairs, and his arrival might conceivably bring trouble, and even disgrace, upon some whom I was especially bound to shield from anything of the kind. I took steps to insure that any evil which might come should fall on me only, and that"—here he turned and looked at the prisoner—"was the cause of conduct upon my part which has been too harshly judged. My only motive was to screen those who were dear to me from any possible connection with scandal or disgrace. That scandal and disgrace would come with my brother was only to say that what had been would be again.

"My brother arrived himself one night not very long after my receipt of the letter. I was sitting in my study after the servants had gone to bed, when I heard a footstep upon the gravel outside, and an instant later I saw his face looking in at me through the window. He was a clean-shaven man like myself, and the resemblance between us was still so great that, for an instant, I thought it was my own reflection in the glass. He had a dark patch over his eye, but our features were absolutely the same. Then he smiled in a sardonic way which had been a trick of his from his boyhood, and I knew that he was the same brother who had driven me from my native land, and brought disgrace upon what had been an honorable name. I went to the door and I admitted him. That would be about ten o'clock that night.

"When he came into the glare of the lamp, I saw at once that he had fallen upon very evil days. He had walked from Liverpool, and he was tired and ill. I was quite shocked by the expression upon his face. My medical knowledge told me that there was some serious internal malady. He had been drinking also, and his face was bruised as the result of a scuffle which he had had with some sailors. It was to cover his injured eye that he wore this patch, which he removed when he entered the room. He was himself dressed in a pea jacket and flannel shirt, and his feet were bursting through his boots. But his poverty had only made him more savagely vindictive toward me. His hatred rose to the height of a mania. I had been rolling in money in England, according to his account, while he had been starving in South America. I cannot describe to you the threats which he uttered or the insults which he poured upon me. My impression is, that hardships and debauchery had unhinged his reason. He paced about the room like a wild beast, demanding drink, demanding money, and all in the foulest language. I am a hot-tempered man, but I thank God that I am able to say that I remained master of myself, and that I never raised a hand against him. My coolness only irritated him the more. He raved, he cursed, he shook his fists in my face, and then suddenly a horrible spasm passed over his features, he clapped his hand to his side, and with a loud cry he fell in a heap at my feet. I raised him up and stretched him upon the sofa, but no answer came to my exclamations, and the hand which I held in mine was cold and clammy. His diseased heart had broken down. His own violence had killed him.

"For a long time I sat as if I were in some dreadful dream, staring at the body of my brother. I was aroused by the knocking of Mrs. Woods, who had been disturbed by that dying cry. I sent her away to bed. Shortly afterward a patient tapped at the surgery door, but as I took no notice, he or she went off again. Slowly and gradually as I sat there a plan was forming itself in my head in the curious automatic way in which plans do form. When I rose from my chair my future movements were finally decided upon without my having been conscious of any process of thought. It was an instinct which irresistibly inclined me toward one course.

"Ever since that change in my affairs to which I have alluded, Bishop's Crossing had become hateful to me. My plans of life had been ruined, and I had met with hasty judgments and unkind treatment where I had expected sympathy. It is true that any danger of scandal from my brother had passed away with his life; but still, I was sore about the past, and felt that things could never be as they had been. It may be that I was unduly sensitive, and that I had not made sufficient allowance for others, but my feelings were as I describe. Any chance of getting away from Bishop's Crossing and of everyone in it would be most welcome to me. And here was such a chance as I could never have dared to hope for, a chance which would enable me to make a clean break with the past.

"There was this dead man lying upon the sofa, so like me that save for some little thickness and coarseness of the features there was no difference at all. No one had seen him come and no one would miss him. We were both clean-shaven, and his hair was about the same length as my own. If I changed clothes with him, then Dr. Aloysius Lana would be found lying dead in his study, and there would be an end of an unfortunate fellow, and of a blighted career. There was plenty of ready money in the room, and this I could carry away with me to help me to start once more in some other land. In my brother's clothes I could walk by night unobserved as far as Liverpool, and in that great seaport I would soon find some means of leaving the country. After my lost hopes, the humblest existence where I was unknown was far preferable in my estimation to a practice, however successful, in Bishop's Crossing, where at any moment I might come face to face with those whom I should wish, if it were possible, to forget. I determined to effect the change.

"And I did so. I will not go into particulars, for the recollection is as painful as the experience; but in an hour my brother lay, dressed down to the smallest detail in my clothes, while I slunk out by the surgery door, and taking the back path which led across some fields, I started off to make the best of my way to Liverpool, where I arrived the same night. My bag of money and a certain portrait were all I carried out of the house, and I left behind me in my hurry the shade which my brother had been wearing over his eye. Everything else of his I took with me.

"I give you my word, sir, that never for one instant did the idea occur to me that people might think that I had been murdered, nor did I imagine that anyone might be caused serious danger through this stratagem by which I endeavored to gain a fresh start in the world. On the contrary, it was the thought of relieving others from the burden of my presence which was always uppermost in my mind. A sailing vessel was leaving Liverpool that very day for Corunna, and in this I took my passage, thinking that the voyage would give me time to recover my balance, and to consider the future. But before I left my resolution softened. I bethought me that there was one person in the world to whom I would not cause an hour of sadness. She would mourn me in her heart, however harsh and unsympathetic her relatives might be. She understood and appreciated the motives upon which I had acted, and if the rest of her family condemned me, she, at least, would not forget. And so I sent her a note under the seal of secrecy to save her from a baseless grief. If under the pressure of events she broke that seal, she has my entire sympathy and forgiveness.

"It was only last night that I returned to England, and during all this time I have heard nothing of the sensation which my supposed death had caused, nor of the accusation that Mr. Arthur Morton had been concerned in it. It was in a late evening paper that I read an account of the proceedings of yesterday, and I have come this morning as fast as an express train could bring me to testify to the truth."

Such was the remarkable statement of Dr. Aloysius Lana which brought the trial to a sudden termination. A subsequent investigation corroborated it to the extent of finding out the vessel in which his brother Ernest Lana had come over from South America. The ship's doctor was able to testify that he had complained of a weak heart during the voyage, and that his symptoms were consistent with such a death as was described.

As to Dr. Aloysius Lana, he returned to the village from which he had made so dramatic a disappearance, and a complete reconciliation was effected between him and the young squire, the latter having acknowledged that he had entirely misunderstood the other's motives in withdrawing from his engagement. That another reconciliation followed may be judged from a notice extracted from a prominent column in the *Morning Post*:

A marriage was solemnized upon September 19th, by the Rev. Stephen Johnson, at the parish church of Bishop's Crossing, between Aloysius Xavier Lana, son of Don Alfredo Lana, formerly Foreign Minister of the Argentine Republic, and Frances Morton, only daughter of the late James Morton, J.P., of Leigh Hall, Bishop's Crossing, Lancashire.

PLAYING WITH FIRE

I cannot pretend to say what occurred on the 14th of April last at No. 17, Badderly Gardens. Put down in black and white, my surmise might seem too crude, too grotesque, for serious consideration. And yet that something did occur, and that it was of a nature which will leave its mark upon every one of us for the rest of our lives, is as certain as the unanimous testimony of five witnesses can make it. I will not enter into any argument or speculation. I will only give a plain statement, which will be submitted to John Moir, Harvey Deacon, and Mrs. Delamere, and withheld from publication unless they are prepared to corroborate every detail. I cannot obtain the sanction of Paul Le Duc, for he appears to have left the country.

It was John Moir (the well-known senior partner of Moir, Moir, and Sanderson), who had originally turned our attention to occult subjects. He had, like many very hard and practical men of business, a mystic side to his nature, which had led him to the examination, and eventually to the acceptance, of those elusive phenomena which are grouped together with much that is foolish, and much that is fraudulent, under the common heading of spiritualism. His researches, which had begun with an open mind, ended unhappily in dogma, and he became as positive and fanatical as any other bigot. He represented in our little group the body of men who have turned these singular phenomena into a new religion.

Mrs. Delamere, our medium, was his sister, the wife of Delamere, the rising sculptor. Our experience had shown us that to work on these subjects without a medium was as futile as for an astronomer to make observations without a telescope. On the other hand, the introduction of a paid medium was hateful to all of us. Was it not obvious that he or she would feel bound to return some result for money received, and that the temptation to fraud would be an overpowering one? No phenomena could be relied upon which were produced at a guinea an hour. But, fortunately, Moir had discovered that his sister was mediumistic— in other words, that she was a battery of that animal magnetic force which is the only form of energy which is subtle enough to be acted upon from the spiritual plane as well as from our own material one. Of course, when I say this, I do not mean to beg the question; but I am simply indicating the theories upon which we were ourselves, rightly, or wrongly, explaining what we saw. The lady came, not altogether with the approval of her husband, and though she never gave indications of any very great psychic force, we were able, at least, to obtain those usual phenomena of message-tilting which are at the same time so puerile and so inexplicable. Every Sunday evening we met in Harvey Deacon's studio at Badderly Gardens, the next house to the corner of Merton Park Road.

Harvey Deacon's imaginative work in art would prepare anyone to find that he was an ardent lover of everything which was *outré* and sensational. A certain picturesqueness in the study of the occult had been the quality which had originally attracted him to it, but his attention was speedily arrested by some of those phenomena to which I have referred, and he was coming rapidly to the conclusion that what he had looked upon as an amusing romance and an after-dinner entertainment was really a very formidable reality. He is a man with a remarkably clear and logical brain—a true descendant of his ancestor, the well-known Scotch professor—and he represented in our small circle the critical element, the man who has no prejudices, is prepared to follow facts as far as he can see them, and refuses to theorize in advance of his data. His caution annoyed Moir as much as the latter's robust faith amused Deacon, but each in his own way was equally keen upon the matter.

And I? What am I to say that I represented? I was not the devotee. I was not the scientific critic. Perhaps the best that I can claim for myself is that I was the dilettante man about town, anxious to be in the swim of every fresh movement, thankful for any new sensation which would take me out of myself and open up fresh possibilities of existence. I am not an enthusiast myself, but I like the company of those who are. Moir's talk, which made me feel as if we had a private passkey through the door of death, filled me with a vague contentment. The soothing atmosphere of the séance with the darkened lights was delightful to me. In a word, the thing amused me, and so I was there.

It was, as I have said, upon the 14th of April last that the very singular event which I am about to put upon record took place. I was the first of the men to arrive at the studio, but Mrs. Delamere was already there, having had afternoon tea with Mrs. Harvey Deacon. The two ladies and Deacon himself were standing in front of an unfinished picture of his upon the easel. I am not an expert in art, and I have never professed to understand what Harvey Deacon meant by his pictures; but I could see in this instance that it was all very clever and imaginative, fairies and animals and allegorical figures of all sorts. The ladies were loud in their praises, and indeed the color effect was a remarkable one.

"What do you think of it, Markham?" he asked.

"Well, it's above me," said I. "These beasts—what are they?"

"Mythical monsters, imaginary creatures, heraldic emblems—a sort of weird, bizarre procession of them."

"With a white horse in front!"

"It's not a horse," said he, rather testily—which was surprising, for he was a very good-humored fellow as a rule, and hardly ever took himself seriously.

"What is it, then?"

"Can't you see the horn in front? It's a unicorn. I told you they were heraldic beasts. Can't you recognize one?"

"Very sorry, Deacon," said I, for he really seemed to be annoyed.

He laughed at his own irritation.

"Excuse me, Markham!" said he; "the fact is that I have had an awful job over the beast. All day I have been painting him in and painting him out, and trying to imagine what a real live, ramping unicorn would look like. At last I got him, as I hoped; so when you failed to recognize it, it took me on the raw."

"Why, of course it's a unicorn," said I, for he was evidently depressed at my obtuseness. "I can see the horn quite plainly, but I never saw a unicorn except beside the Royal Arms, and so I never thought of the creature. And these others are griffins and cockatrices, and dragons of sorts?"

"Yes, I had no difficulty with them. It was the unicorn which bothered me. However, there's an end of it until tomorrow." He turned the picture round upon the easel, and we all chatted about other subjects.

Moir was late that evening, and when he did arrive he brought with him, rather to our surprise, a small, stout Frenchman, whom he introduced as Monsieur Paul Le Duc. I say to our surprise, for we held a theory that any intrusion into our spiritual circle deranged the conditions, and introduced an element of suspicion. We knew that we could trust each other, but all our results were vitiated by the presence of an outsider. However, Moir soon reconciled us to the innovation. Monsieur Paul Le Duc was a famous student of occultism, a seer, a medium, and a mystic. He was traveling in England with a letter of introduction to Moir from the President of the Parisian brothers of the Rosy Cross. What more natural than that he should bring him to our little séance, or that we should feel honored by his presence?

He was, as I have said, a small, stout man, undistinguished in appearance, with a broad, smooth, clean-shaven face, remarkable only for a pair of large, brown velvety eyes, staring vaguely out in front of him. He was well dressed, with the manners of a gentleman, and his curious little turns of English speech set the ladies smiling. Mrs. Deacon had a prejudice against our researches and left the room, upon which we lowered the lights, as was our custom, and drew up our chairs to the square mahogany table which stood in the center of the studio. The light was subdued, but sufficient to allow us to see each other quite plainly. I remember that I could even observe the curious, podgy little square-topped hands which the Frenchman laid upon the table.

"What a fun!" said he. "It is many years since I have sat in this fashion, and it is to me amusing. Madame is medium. Does madame make the trance?"

"Well, hardly that," said Mrs. Delamere. "But I am always conscious of extreme sleepiness."

"It is the first stage. Then you encourage it, and there comes the trance. When the trance comes, then out jumps your little spirit and in jumps another little spirit, and so you have direct talking or writing. You leave your machine to be worked by another. *Hein?* But what have unicorns to do with it?"

Harvey Deacon started in his chair. The Frenchman was moving his head slowly round and staring into the shadows which draped the walls.

"What a fun!" said he. "Always unicorns. Who has been thinking so hard upon a subject so bizarre?"

"This is wonderful!" cried Deacon. "I have been trying to paint one all day. But how could you know it?"

"You have been thinking of them in this room."

"Certainly."

"But thoughts are things, my friend. When you imagine a thing you make a thing. You did not know it, *hein?* But I can see your unicorns because it is not only with my eye that I can see."

"Do you mean to say that I create a thing which has never existed by merely thinking of it?"

"But certainly. It is the fact which lies under all other facts. That is why an evil thought is also a danger."

"They are, I suppose, upon the astral plane?" said Moir.

"Ah, well, these are but words, my friends. They are there—somewhere—everywhere—I cannot tell myself. I see them. I could not touch them."

"You could not make us *see* them."

"It is to materialize them. Hold! It is an experiment. But the power is wanting. Let us see what power we have, and then arrange what we shall do. May I place you as I should wish?"

"You evidently know a great deal more about it than we do," said Harvey Deacon; "I wish that you would take complete control."

"It may be that the conditions are not good. But we will try what we can do. Madame will sit where she is, I next, and this gentleman beside me. Meester Moir will sit next to madame, because it is well to have blacks and blondes in turn. So! And now with your permission I will turn the lights all out."

"What is the advantage of the dark?" I asked.

"Because the force with which we deal is a vibration of ether and so also is light. We have the wires all for ourselves now—*hein?* You will not be frightened in the darkness, madame? What a fun is such a séance!"

At first the darkness appeared to be absolutely pitchy, but in a few minutes our eyes became so far accustomed to it that we could just make out each other's presence—very dimly and vaguely, it is true. I could see nothing else in the room—only the black loom of the motionless figures. We were all taking the matter much more seriously than we had ever done before.

"You will place your hands in front. It is hopeless that we touch, since we are so few round so large a table. You will compose yourself, madame, and if sleep should come to you you will not fight against it. And now we sit in silence and we expect—*hein?*"

So we sat in silence and expected, staring out into the blackness in front of us. A clock ticked in the passage. A dog barked intermittently far away. Once or twice a cab rattled past in the street, and the gleam of its lamps through the chink in the curtains was a cheerful break in that gloomy vigil. I felt those physical symptoms with which previous séances had made me familiar—the coldness of the feet, the tingling in the hands, the glow of the palms, the feeling of a cold wind upon the back. Strange little shooting pains came in my forearms, especially as it seemed to me in my left one, which was nearest to our visitor—due no doubt to disturbance of the vascular system, but worthy of some attention all the same. At the same time I was conscious of a strained feeling of expectancy which was almost painful. From the rigid, absolute silence of my companions I gathered that their nerves were as tense as my own.

And then suddenly a sound came out of the darkness—a low, sibilant sound, the quick, thin breathing of a woman. Quicker and thinner yet it came, as between clenched teeth, to end in a loud gasp with a dull rustle of cloth.

"What's that? Is all right?" someone asked in the darkness.

"Yes, all is right," said the Frenchman. "It is madame. She is in her trance. Now, gentlemen, if you will wait quiet you will see something I think which will interest you much."

Still the ticking in the hall. Still the breathing, deeper and fuller now, from the medium. Still the occasional flash, more welcome than ever, of the passing lights of the hansoms. What a gap we were bridging, the half-raised veil of the eternal on the one side and the cabs of London on the other. The table was throbbing with a mighty pulse. It swayed steadily, rhythmically, with an easy swooping, scooping motion under our fingers. Sharp little raps and cracks came from its substance, file-firing, volley-firing, the sounds of a fagot burning briskly on a frosty night.

"There is much power," said the Frenchman. "See it on the table!"

I had thought it was some delusion of my own, but all could see it now. There was a greenish-yellow phosphorescent light—or I should say a luminous vapor rather than a light—which lay over the surface of the table. It rolled and wreathed and undulated in dim glimmering folds, turning and swirling like clouds of smoke. I could see the white, square-ended hands of the French medium in this baleful light.

"What a fun!" he cried. "It is splendid!"

"Shall we call the alphabet?" asked Moir.

"But no—for we can do much better," said our visitor. "It is but a clumsy thing to tilt the table for every letter of the alphabet, and with such a medium as madame we should do better than that."

"Yes, you will do better," said a voice.

"Who was that? Who spoke? Was that you, Markham?"

"No, I did not speak."

"It was madame who spoke."

"But it was not her voice."

"Is that you, Mrs. Delamere?"

"It is not the medium, but it is the power which uses the organs of the medium," said the strange, deep voice.

"Where is Mrs. Delamere? It will not hurt her, I trust."

"The medium is happy in another plane of existence. She has taken my place, as I have taken hers."

"Who are you?"

"It cannot matter to you who I am. I am one who has lived as you are living, and who has died as you will die."

We heard the creak and grate of a cab pulling up next door. There was an argument about the fare, and the cabman grumbled hoarsely down the street. The green-yellow cloud still swirled faintly over the table, dull elsewhere, but glowing into a dim luminosity in the direction of the medium. It seemed to be piling itself up in front of her. A sense of fear and cold struck into my heart. It seemed to me that lightly and flippantly we had approached the most real and august of sacraments, that communion with the dead of which the fathers of the Church had spoken.

"Don't you think we are going too far? Should we not break up this séance?" I cried.

But the others were all earnest to see the end of it. They laughed at my scruples.

"All the powers are made for use," said Harvey Deacon. "If we *can* do this, we *should* do this. Every new departure of knowledge has been called unlawful in its inception. It is right and proper that we should inquire into the nature of death."

"It is right and proper," said the voice.

"There, what more could you ask?" cried Moir, who was much excited. "Let us have a test. Will you give us a test that you are really there?"

"What test do you demand?"

"Well, now—I have some coins in my pocket. Will you tell me how many?"

"We come back in the hope of teaching and of elevating, and not to guess childish riddles."

"Ha, ha, Meester Moir, you catch it that time," cried the Frenchman. "But surely this is very good sense what the Control is saying."

"It is a religion, not a game," said the cold, hard voice.

"Exactly—the very view I take of it," cried Moir. "I am sure I am very sorry if I have asked a foolish question. You will not tell me who you are?"

"What does it matter?"

"Have you been a spirit long?"

"Yes."

"How long?"

"We cannot reckon time as you do. Our conditions are different."

"Are you happy?"

"Yes."

"You would not wish to come back to life?"

"No—certainly not."

"Are you busy?"

"We could not be happy if we were not busy."

"What do you do?"

"I have said that the conditions are entirely different."

"Can you give us no idea of your work?"

"We labor for our own improvement and for the advancement of others."

"Do you like coming here tonight?"

"I am glad to come if I can do any good by coming."

"Then to do good is your object?"

"It is the object of all life on every plane."

"You see, Markham, that should answer your scruples."

It did, for my doubts had passed and only interest remained.

"Have you pain in your life?" I asked.

"No, pain is a thing of the body."

"Have you mental pain?"

"Yes, one may always be sad or anxious."

"Do you meet the friends whom you have known on earth?"

"Some of them."

"Why only some of them?"

"Only those who are sympathetic."

"Do husbands meet wives?"

"Those who have truly loved."

"And the others?"

"They are nothing to each other."

"There must be a spiritual connection?"

"Of course."

"Is what we are doing right?"

"If done in the right spirit."

"What is the wrong spirit?"

"Curiosity and levity."

"May harm come of that?"

"Very serious harm."

"What sort of harm?"

"You may call up forces over which you have no control."

"Evil forces?"

"Undeveloped forces."

"You say they are dangerous. Dangerous to body or mind?"

"Sometimes to both."

There was a pause, and the blackness seemed to grow blacker still, while the yellow-green fog swirled and smoked upon the table.

"Any questions you would like to ask, Moir?" said Harvey Deacon.

"Only this—do you pray in your world?"

"One should pray in every world."

"Why?"

"Because it is the acknowledgment of forces outside ourselves."

"What religion do you hold over there?"

"We differ exactly as you do."

"You have no certain knowledge?"

"We have only faith."

"These questions of religion," said the Frenchman, "they are of interest to you serious English people, but they are not so much fun. It seems to me that with this power here we might be able to have some great experience—*hein?* Something of which we could talk."

"But nothing could be more interesting than this," said Moir.

"Well, if you think so, that is very well," the Frenchman answered, peevishly. "For my part, it seems to me that I have heard all this before, and that tonight I should weesh to try some experiment with all this force which is given to us. But if you have other questions, then ask them, and when you are finish we can try something more."

But the spell was broken. We asked and asked, but the medium sat silent in her chair. Only her deep, regular breathing showed that she was there. The mist still swirled upon the table.

"You have disturbed the harmony. She will not answer."

"But we have learned already all that she can tell—*hein?* For my part I wish to see something that I have never seen before."

"What then?"

"You will let me try?"

"What would you do?"

"I have said to you that thoughts are things. Now I wish to *prove* it to you, and to show you that which is only a thought. Yes, yes, I can do it and you will see. Now I ask you only to sit still and say nothing, and keep ever your hands quiet upon the table."

The room was blacker and more silent than ever. The same feeling of apprehension which had lain heavily upon me at the beginning of the séance was back at my heart once more. The roots of my hair were tingling.

"It is working! It is working!" cried the Frenchman, and there was a crack in his voice as he spoke which told me that he also was strung to his tightest.

The luminous fog drifted slowly off the table, and wavered and flickered across the room. There in the farther and darkest corner it gathered and glowed, hardening down into a shining core—a strange, shifty, luminous, but non-illuminating patch of radiance, bright itself and yet throwing no rays into the darkness. It had changed from a greenish-yellow to a dusky sullen red. Then round this center there coiled a dark, smoky substance, thickening, hardening, growing denser and blacker. And then the light went out, smothered in that which had grown round it.

"It has gone."

"Hush—there's something in the room."

We heard it in the corner where the light had been, something which breathed deeply and fidgeted in the darkness.

"What is it? Le Duc, what have you done?"

"It is all right. No harm will come." The Frenchman's voice was treble with agitation.

"Good heavens, Moir, there's a large animal in the room. Here it is, close by my chair! Go away! Go away!"

It was Harvey Deacon's voice, and then came the sound of a blow upon some hard object. And then . . . And then . . . how can I tell you what happened then?

Some huge thing hurtled against us in the darkness, rearing, stamping, smashing, springing, snorting. The table was splintered. We were scattered in every direction. It clattered and scrambled amongst us, rushing with horrible energy from one corner of the room to another. We were all screaming with fear, grovelling upon our hands and knees to get away from it. Something trod upon my left hand, and I felt the bones splinter under the weight.

"A light! A light!" someone yelled.

"Moir, you have matches, matches!"

"No, I have none. Deacon, where are the matches? For God's sake, the matches!"

"I can't find them. Here, you Frenchman, stop it!"

"It is beyond me. Oh, *mon Dieu*, I cannot stop it. The door! Where is the door?"

My hand, by good luck, lit upon the handle as I groped about in the darkness. The hard-breathing, snorting, rushing creature tore past me and butted with a fearful crash against the oaken partition. The instant that it had passed I turned the handle, and next moment we were all outside and the door shut behind us. From within came a horrible crashing and rending and stamping.

"What is it? In Heaven's name, what is it?"

"A horse. I saw it when the door opened. But Mrs. Delamere—?"

"We must fetch her out. Come on, Markham; the longer we wait the less we shall like it."

He flung open the door and we rushed in. She was there on the ground amidst the splinters of her chair. We seized her and dragged her swiftly out, and as we gained the door I looked over my shoulder into the darkness. There were two strange eyes glowing at us, a rattle of hoofs, and I had just time to slam the door when there came a crash upon it which split it from top to bottom.

"It's coming through! It's coming!"

"Run, run for your lives!" cried the Frenchman.

Another crash, and something shot through the riven door. It was a long white spike, gleaming in the lamplight. For a moment it shone before us, and then with a snap it disappeared again.

"Quick! Quick! This way!" Harvey Deacon shouted. "Carry her in! Here! Quick!"

We had taken refuge in the dining room, and shut the heavy oak door. We laid the senseless woman upon the sofa, and as we did so, Moir, the hard man of business, drooped and fainted across the hearthrug. Harvey Deacon was as white as a corpse, jerking and twitching like an epileptic. With a crash we heard the studio door fly to pieces, and the snorting and stamping were in the passage, up and down, up and down, shaking the house with their fury. The Frenchman had sunk his face on his hands, and sobbed like a frightened child.

"What shall we do?" I shook him roughly by the shoulder. "Is a gun any use?"

"No, no. The power will pass. Then it will end."

"You might have killed us all—you unspeakable fool—with your infernal experiments."

"I did not know. How could I tell that it would be frightened? It is mad with terror. It was his fault. He struck it."

Harvey Deacon sprang up. "Good heavens!" he cried.

A terrible scream sounded through the house.

"It's my wife! Here, I'm going out. If it's the Evil One himself I am going out!"

He had thrown open the door and rushed out into the passage. At the end of it, at the foot of the stairs, Mrs. Deacon was lying senseless, struck down by the sight which she had seen. But there was nothing else.

With eyes of horror we looked about us, but all was perfectly quiet and still. I approached the black square of the studio door, expecting with every slow step that some atrocious shape would hurl itself out of it. But nothing came, and all was silent inside the room. Peeping and peering, our hearts in our mouths, we came to the very threshold, and stared into the darkness. There was still no sound, but in one direction there was also no darkness. A luminous, glowing cloud, with an incandescent center, hovered in the corner of the room. Slowly it dimmed and faded, growing thinner and fainter, until at last the same dense, velvety blackness filled the whole studio. And with the last flickering gleam of that baleful light the Frenchman broke into a shout of joy.

"What a fun!" he cried. "No one is hurt, and only the door broken, and the ladies frightened. But, my friends, we have done what has never been done before."

"And as far as I can help it," said Harvey Deacon, "it will certainly never be done again."

And that was what befell on the 14th of April last at No. 17, Badderly Gardens. I began by saying that it would seem too grotesque to dogmatize as to what it was which actually did occur; but I give my impressions, *our* impressions (since they are corroborated by Harvey Deacon and John Moir), for what they are worth. You may if it pleases you imagine that we were the victims of an elaborate and extraordinary hoax. Or you may think with us that we underwent a very real and a very terrible experience. Or perhaps you may know more than we do of such occult matters, and can inform us of some similar occurrence. In this latter case a letter to William Markham, 146M, The Albany, would help to throw a light upon that which is very dark to us.

THE JEW'S BREASTPLATE

My particular friend Ward Mortimer was one of the best men of his day at everything connected with Oriental archæology. He had written largely upon the subject, he had lived two years in a tomb at Thebes, while he excavated in the Valley of the Kings, and finally he had created a considerable sensation by his exhumation of the alleged mummy of Cleopatra in the inner room of the Temple of Horus, at Philæ. With such a record at the age of thirty-one, it was felt that a considerable career lay before him, and no one was surprised when he was elected to the curatorship of the Belmore Street Museum, which carries with it the lectureship at the Oriental College, and an income which has sunk with the fall in land, but which still remains at that ideal sum which is large enough to encourage an investigator, but not so large as to enervate him.

There was only one reason which made Ward Mortimer's position a little difficult at the Belmore Street Museum, and that was the extreme eminence of the man whom he had to succeed. Professor Andreas was a profound scholar and a man of European reputation. His lectures were frequented by students from every part of the world, and his admirable management of the collection intrusted to his care was a commonplace in all learned societies. There was, therefore, considerable surprise when, at the age of fifty-five, he suddenly resigned his position and retired from those duties which had been both his livelihood and his pleasure. He and his daughter left the comfortable suite of rooms which had formed his official residence in connection with the museum, and my friend, Mortimer, who was a bachelor, took up his quarters there.

On hearing of Mortimer's appointment Professor Andreas had written him a very kindly and flattering congratulatory letter. I was actually present at their first meeting, and I went with Mortimer round the museum when the Professor showed us the admirable collection which he had cherished so long. The Professor's beautiful daughter and a young man, Captain Wilson, who was, as I understood, soon to be her husband, accompanied us in our inspection. There were fifteen rooms, but the Babylonian, the Syrian, and the central hall, which contained the Jewish and Egyptian collection, were the finest of all. Professor Andreas was a quiet, dry, elderly man, with a clean-shaven face and an impassive manner, but his dark eyes sparkled and his features quickened into enthusiastic life as he pointed out to us the rarity and the beauty of some of his specimens. His hand lingered so fondly over them, that one could read his pride in them and the grief in his heart now that they were passing from his care into that of another.

He had shown us in turn his mummies, his papyri, his rare scarabs, his inscriptions, his Jewish relics, and his duplication of the famous seven-branched candlestick of the Temple, which was brought to Rome by Titus, and which is supposed by some to be lying at this instant in the bed of the Tiber. Then he approached a case which stood in the very center of the hall, and he looked down through the glass with reverence in his attitude and manner.

"This is no novelty to an expert like yourself, Mr. Mortimer," said he, "but I dare say that your friend Mr. Jackson will be interested to see it."

Leaning over the case I saw an object, some five inches square, which consisted of twelve precious stones in a framework of gold, with golden hooks at two of the corners. The stones were all varying in sort and color, but they were of the same size. Their shapes, arrangement, and gradation of tint made me think of a box of watercolor paints. Each stone had some hieroglyphic scratched upon its surface.

"You have heard, Mr. Jackson, of the urim and thummim?"

I had heard the term, but my idea of its meaning was exceedingly vague.

"The urim and thummim was a name given to the jeweled plate which lay upon the breast of the high priest of the Jews. They had a very special feeling of reverence for it—something of the feeling which an ancient Roman might have for the Sibylline books in the Capitol. There are, as you see, twelve magnificent stones, inscribed with mystical

characters. Counting from the left-hand top corner, the stones are carnelian, peridot, emerald, ruby, lapis lazuli, onyx, sapphire, agate, ame-
thyst, topaz, beryl, and jasper."

I was amazed at the variety and beauty of the stones.

"Has the breastplate any particular history?" I asked.

"It is of great age and of immense value," said Professor Andreas.
"Without being able to make an absolute assertion, we have many reasons to think that it is possible that it may be the original urim and
thummim of Solomon's Temple. There is certainly nothing so fine in
any collection in Europe. My friend, Captain Wilson here, is a practical
authority upon precious stones, and he would tell you how pure these
are."

Captain Wilson, a man with a dark, hard, incisive face, was standing
beside his fiancée at the other side of the case.

"Yes," said he, curtly, " I have never seen finer stones."

"And the goldwork is also worthy of attention. The ancients excelled
in—" He was apparently about to indicate the setting of the stones,
when Captain Wilson interrupted him.

"You will see a finer example of their goldwork in this candlestick,"
said he, turning to another table, and we all joined him in his admiration
of its embossed stem and delicately ornamented branches. Altogether it
was an interesting and a novel experience to have objects of such rarity
explained by so great an expert; and when, finally, Professor Andreas
finished our inspection by formally handing over the precious collection
to the care of my friend, I could not help pitying him and envying his
successor whose life was to pass in so pleasant a duty. Within a week
Ward Mortimer was duly installed in his new set of rooms, and had
become the autocrat of the Belmore Street Museum.

About a fortnight afterward my friend gave a small dinner to half-a-
dozen bachelor friends to celebrate his promotion. When his guests were
departing he pulled my sleeve and signaled to me that he wished me to
remain.

"You have only a few hundred yards to go," said he—I was living in
chambers in the Albany. "You may as well stay and have a quiet cigar
with me. I very much want your advice."

I relapsed into an armchair and lit one of his excellent Matronas.
When he had returned from seeing the last of his guests out, he drew a
letter from his dress jacket and sat down opposite to me.

"This is an anonymous letter which I received this morning," said he.
"I want to read it to you and to have your advice."

"You are very welcome to it for what it is worth."

"This is how the note runs: 'Sir,—I should strongly advise you to keep a very careful watch over the many valuable things which are committed to your charge. I do not think that the present system of a single watchman is sufficient. Be upon your guard, or an irreparable misfortune may occur.' "

"Is that all?"

"Yes, that is all."

"Well," said I, "it is at least obvious that it was written by one of the limited number of people who are aware that you have only one watchman at night."

Ward Mortimer handed me the note, with a curious smile. "Have you an eye for handwriting?" said he. "Now, look at this!" He put another letter in front of me. "Look at the *c* in 'congratulate' and the *c* in 'committed.' Look at the capital *I*. Look at the trick of putting in a dash instead of a stop!"

"They are undoubtedly from the same hand—with some attempt at disguise in the case of this first one."

"The second," said Ward Mortimer, "is the letter of congratulation which was written to me by Professor Andreas upon my obtaining my appointment."

I stared at him in amazement. Then I turned over the letter in my hand, and there, sure enough, was "Martin Andreas" signed upon the other side. There could be no doubt, in the mind of anyone who had the slightest knowledge of the science of graphology, that the Professor had written an anonymous letter warning his successor against thieves. It was inexplicable, but it was certain.

"Why should he do it?" I asked.

"Precisely what I should wish to ask you. If he had any such misgivings, why could he not come and tell me direct?"

"Will you speak to him about it?"

"There again I am in doubt. He might choose to deny that he wrote it."

"At any rate," said I, "this warning is meant in a friendly spirit, and I should certainly act upon it. Are the present precautions enough to insure you against robbery?"

"I should have thought so. The public are only admitted from ten till five, and there is a guardian to every two rooms. He stands at the door between them and so commands them both."

"But at night?"

"When the public are gone, we at once put up the great iron shutters, which are absolutely burglarproof. The watchman is a capable fellow.

He sits in the lodge, but he walks round every three hours. We keep one electric light burning in each room all night."

"It is difficult to suggest anything more—short of keeping your day watchers all night."

"We could not afford that."

"At least, I should communicate with the police, and have a special constable put on outside in Belmore Street," said I. "As to the letter, if the writer wishes to be anonymous, I think he has a right to remain so. We must trust to the future to show some reason for the curious course which he has adopted."

So we dismissed the subject, but all that night after my return to my chambers I was puzzling my brain as to what possible motive Professor Andreas could have for writing an anonymous warning letter to his successor—for that the writing was his was as certain to me as if I had seen him actually doing it. He foresaw some danger to the collection. Was it because he foresaw it that he abandoned his charge of it? But if so, why should he hesitate to warn Mortimer in his own name? I puzzled and puzzled until at last I fell into a troubled sleep, which carried me beyond my usual hour of rising.

I was aroused in a singular and effective method, for about nine o'clock my friend Mortimer rushed into my room with an expression of consternation upon his face. He was usually one of the most tidy men of my acquaintance, but now his collar was undone at one end, his tie was flying, and his hat at the back of his head. I read his whole story in his frantic eyes.

"The museum has been robbed!" I cried, springing up in bed.

"I fear so! Those jewels! The jewels of the urim and thummim!" he gasped, for he was out of breath with running. "I'm going on to the police station. Come to the museum as soon as you can, Jackson! Good-bye!" He rushed distractedly out of the room, and I heard him clatter down the stairs.

I was not long in following his directions, but I found when I arrived that he had already returned with a police inspector, and another elderly gentleman, who proved to be Mr. Purvis, one of the partners of Morson and Company, the well-known diamond merchants. As an expert in stones he was always prepared to advise the police. They were grouped round the case in which the breastplate of the Jewish priest had been exposed. The plate had been taken out and laid upon the glass top of the case, and the three heads were bent over it.

"It is obvious that it has been tampered with," said Mortimer. "It caught my eye the moment that I passed through the room this morning. I examined it yesterday evening, so that it is certain that this has happened during the night."

It was, as he had said, obvious that someone had been at work upon it. The settings of the uppermost row of four stones—the carnelian, peridot, emerald, and ruby—were rough and jagged as if someone had scraped all round them. The stones were in their places, but the beautiful goldwork which we had admired only a few days before had been very clumsily pulled about.

"It looks to me," said the police inspector, "as if someone had been trying to take out the stones."

"My fear is," said Mortimer, "that he not only tried, but succeeded. I believe these four stones to be skillful imitations which have been put in the place of the originals."

The same suspicion had evidently been in the mind of the expert, for he had been carefully examining the four stones with the aid of a lens. He now submitted them to several tests, and finally turned cheerfully to Mortimer.

"I congratulate you, sir," said he, heartily. "I will pledge my reputation that all four of these stones are genuine, and of a most unusual degree of purity."

The color began to come back to my poor friend's frightened face, and he drew a long breath of relief.

"Thank God!" he cried. "Then what in the world did the thief want?"

"Probably he meant to take the stones, but was interrupted."

"In that case one would expect him to take them out one at a time, but the setting of each of these has been loosened, and yet the stones are all here."

"It is certainly most extraordinary," said the inspector. "I never remember a case like it. Let us see the watchman."

The commissionaire was called—a soldierly, honest-faced man, who seemed as concerned as Ward Mortimer at the incident.

"No, sir, I never heard a sound," he answered, in reply to the questions of the inspector. "I made my rounds four times, as usual, but I saw nothing suspicious. I've been in my position ten years, but nothing of the kind has ever occurred before."

"No thief could have come through the windows?"

"Impossible, sir."

"Or passed you at the door?"

"No, sir; I never left my post except when I walked my rounds."

"What other openings are there in the museum?"

"There is the door into Mr. Ward Mortimer's private rooms."

"That is locked at night," my friend explained, "and in order to reach it anyone from the street would have to open the outside door as well."

"Your servants?"

"Their quarters are entirely separate."

"Well, well," said the inspector, "this is certainly very obscure. However, there has been no harm done, according to Mr. Purvis."

"I will swear that those stones are genuine."

"So that the case appears to be merely one of malicious damage. But nonetheless, I should be very glad to go carefully round the premises, and to see if we find any trace to show us who your visitor may have been."

His investigation, which lasted all the morning, was careful and intelligent, but it led in the end to nothing. He pointed out to us that there were two possible entrances to the museum which we had not considered. The one was from the cellars by a trapdoor opening in the passage. The other through a skylight from the lumber room, overlooking that very chamber to which the intruder had penetrated. As neither the cellar nor the lumber room could be entered unless the thief was already within the locked doors, the matter was not of any practical importance, and the dust of cellar and attic assured us that no one had used either one or the other. Finally, we ended as we began, without the slightest clue as to how, why, or by whom the setting of these four jewels had been tampered with.

There remained one course for Mortimer to take, and he took it. Leaving the police to continue their fruitless researches, he asked me to accompany him that afternoon in a visit to Professor Andreas. He took with him the two letters, and it was his intention to openly tax his predecessor with having written the anonymous warning, and to ask him to explain the fact that he should have anticipated so exactly that which had actually occurred. The Professor was living in a small villa in Upper Norwood, but we were informed by the servant that he was away from home. Seeing our disappointment, she asked us if we should like to see Miss Andreas, and showed us into the modest drawing room.

I have mentioned incidentally that the Professor's daughter was a very beautiful girl. She was a blonde, tall and graceful, with a skin of that delicate tint which the French call "mat," the color of old ivory or the lighter petals of the sulphur rose. I was shocked, however, as she entered the room to see how much she had changed in the last fortnight. Her young face was haggard and her bright eyes heavy with trouble.

"Father has gone to Scotland," she said. "He seems to be tired, and has had a good deal to worry him. He only left us yesterday."

"You look a little tired yourself, Miss Andreas," said my friend.

"I have been so anxious about father."

"Can you give me his Scotch address?"

"Yes, he is with his brother, the Rev. David Andreas, 1, Arran Villas, Ardrossan."

Ward Mortimer made a note of the address, and we left without saying anything as to the object of our visit. We found ourselves in Belmore Street in the evening in exactly the same position in which we had been in the morning. Our only clue was the Professor's letter, and my friend had made up his mind to start for Ardrossan next day, and to get to the bottom of the anonymous letter, when a new development came to alter our plans.

Very early on the following morning I was aroused from my sleep by a tap upon my bedroom door. It was a messenger with a note from Mortimer.

"Do come round," it said; "the matter is becoming more and more extraordinary."

When I obeyed his summons I found him pacing excitedly up and down the central room, while the old soldier who guarded the premises stood with military stiffness in a corner.

"My dear Jackson," he cried, "I am so delighted that you have come, for this is a most inexplicable business."

"What has happened, then?"

He waved his hand towards the case which contained the breastplate.

"Look at it," said he.

I did so, and could not restrain a cry of surprise. The setting of the middle row of precious stones had been profaned in the same manner as the upper ones. Of the twelve jewels, eight had been now tampered with in this singular fashion. The setting of the lower four was neat and smooth. The others jagged and irregular.

"Have the stones been altered?" I asked.

"No, I am certain that these upper four are the same which the expert pronounced to be genuine, for I observed yesterday that little discoloration on the edge of the emerald. Since they have not extracted the upper stones, there is no reason to think the lower have been transposed. You say that you heard nothing, Simpson?"

"No, sir," the commissionaire answered. "But when I made my round after daylight I had a special look at these stones, and I saw at once that someone had been meddling with them. Then I called you, sir, and told you. I was backwards and forwards all the night, and I never saw a soul or heard a sound."

"Come up and have some breakfast with me," said Mortimer, and he took me into his own chambers.

"Now, what *do* you think of this, Jackson?" he asked.

"It is the most objectless, futile, idiotic business that ever I heard of. It can only be the work of a monomaniac."

"Can you put forward any theory?"

A curious idea came into my head. "This object is a Jewish relic of great antiquity and sanctity," said I. "How about the anti-Semitic movement? Could one conceive that a fanatic of that way of thinking might desecrate—"

"No, no, no!" cried Mortimer. "That will never do! Such a man might push his lunacy to the length of destroying a Jewish relic, but why on earth should he nibble round every stone so carefully that he can only do four stones in a night? We must have a better solution than that, and we must find it for ourselves, for I do not think that our inspector is likely to help us. First of all, what do you think of Simpson, the porter?"

"Have you any reason to suspect him?"

"Only that he is the one person on the premises."

"But why should he indulge in such wanton destruction? Nothing has been taken away. He has no motive."

"Mania?"

"No, I will swear to his sanity."

"Have you any other theory?"

"Well, yourself, for example. You are not a somnambulist, by any chance?"

"Nothing of the sort, I assure you."

"Then I give it up."

"But I don't—and I have a plan by which we will make it all clear."

"To visit Professor Andreas ?"

"No, we shall find our solution nearer than Scotland. I will tell you what we shall do. You know that skylight which overlooks the central hall? We will leave the electric lights in the hall, and we will keep watch in the lumber room, you and I, and solve the mystery for ourselves. If our mysterious visitor is doing four stones at a time, he has four still to do, and there is every reason to think that he will return tonight and complete the job."

"Excellent!" I cried.

"We will keep our own secret, and say nothing either to the police or to Simpson. Will you join me?"

"With the utmost pleasure," said I; and so it was agreed.

It was ten o'clock that night when I returned to the Belmore Street Museum. Mortimer was, as I could see, in a state of suppressed nervous excitement, but it was still too early to begin our vigil, so we remained for an hour or so in his chambers, discussing all the possibilities of the singular business which we had met to solve. At last the roaring stream of hansom cabs and the rush of hurrying feet became lower and more intermittent as the pleasure-seekers passed on their way to their stations or their homes. It was nearly twelve when Mortimer led the way to the lumber room which overlooked the central hall of the museum.

He had visited it during the day, and had spread some sacking so that we could lie at our ease, and look straight down into the museum. The skylight was of unfrosted glass, but was so covered with dust that it would be impossible for anyone looking up from below to detect that he was overlooked. We cleared a small piece at each corner, which gave us a complete view of the room beneath us. In the cold white light of the electric lamps everything stood out hard and clear, and I could see the smallest detail of the contents of the various cases.

Such a vigil is an excellent lesson, since one has no choice but to look hard at those objects which we usually pass with such halfhearted interest. Through my little peephole I employed the hours in studying every specimen, from the huge mummy case which leaned against the wall to those very jewels which had brought us there, gleaming and sparkling in their glass case immediately beneath us. There was much precious goldwork and many valuable stones scattered through the numerous cases, but those wonderful twelve which made up the urim and thummim glowed and burned with a radiance which far eclipsed the others. I studied in turn the tomb pictures of Sicara, the friezes from Karnak, the statues of Memphis, and the inscriptions of Thebes, but my eyes would always come back to that wonderful Jewish relic, and my mind to the singular mystery which surrounded it. I was lost in the thought of it when my companion suddenly drew his breath sharply in, and seized my arm in a convulsive grip. At the same instant I saw what it was which had excited him.

I have said that against the wall—on the right-hand side of the doorway (the right-hand side as we looked at it, but the left as one entered)—there stood a large mummy case. To our unutterable amazement it was slowly opening. Gradually, gradually the lid was swinging back, and the black slit which marked the opening was becoming wider and wider. So gently and carefully was it done that the movement was almost imperceptible. Then, as we breathlessly watched it, a white thin hand appeared at the opening, pushing back the painted lid, then another hand, and finally a face—a face which was familiar to us both, that of Professor Andreas. Stealthily he slunk out of the mummy case, like a fox stealing from its burrow, his head turning incessantly to left and to right, stepping, then pausing, then stepping again, the very image of craft and of caution. Once some sound in the street struck him motionless, and he stood listening with his ear turned, ready to dart back to the shelter behind him. Then he crept onwards again upon tiptoe, very, very softly and slowly, until he had reached the case in the center of the room. There he took a bunch of keys from his pocket, unlocked the case, took out the Jewish breastplate, and, laying it upon the glass in front of him, began to work upon it with some sort of small, glistening tool. He was so directly underneath us that his bent head covered his work, but we could guess from the movement of his hand that he was engaged in finishing the strange disfigurement which he had begun.

I could realize from the heavy breathing of my companion, and the twitchings of the hand which still clutched my wrist, the furious indignation which filled his heart as he saw this vandalism in the quarter of all others where he could least have expected it. He, the very man who a fortnight before had reverently bent over this unique relic, and who had impressed its antiquity and its sanctity upon us, was now engaged in this outrageous profanation. It was impossible, unthinkable—and yet there, in the white glare of the electric light beneath us, was that dark figure with the bent, gray head, and the twitching elbow. What inhuman hypocrisy, what hateful depth of malice against his successor must underlie these sinister nocturnal labors. It was painful to think of and dreadful to watch. Even I, who had none of the acute feelings of a virtuoso, could not bear to look on and see this deliberate mutilation of so ancient a relic. It was a relief to me when my companion tugged at my sleeve as a signal that I was to follow him as he softly crept out of the room. It was not until we were within his own quarters that he opened his lips, and then I saw by his agitated face how deep was his consternation.

"The abominable Goth!" he cried. "Could you have believed it?"

"It is amazing."

"He is a villain or a lunatic—one or the other. We shall very soon see which. Come with me, Jackson, and we shall get to the bottom of this black business."

A door opened out of the passage which was the private entrance from his rooms into the museum. This he opened softly with his key, having first kicked off his shoes, an example which I followed. We crept together through room after room, until the large hall lay before us, with that dark figure still stooping and working at the central case. With an advance as cautious as his own we closed in upon him, but softly as we went we could not take him entirely unawares. We were still a dozen yards from him when he looked round with a start, and uttering a husky cry of terror, ran frantically down the museum.

"Simpson! Simpson!" roared Mortimer, and far away down the vista of electric lighted doors we saw the stiff figure of the old soldier suddenly appear. Professor Andreas saw him also, and stopped running, with a gesture of despair. At the same instant we each laid a hand upon his shoulder.

"Yes, yes, gentlemen," he panted, "I will come with you. To your room, Mr. Ward Mortimer, if you please! I feel that I owe you an explanation."

My companion's indignation was so great that I could see that he dared not trust himself to reply. We walked on each side of the old Professor, the astonished commissionaire bringing up the rear. When we reached the violated case, Mortimer stopped and examined the breastplate. Already one of the stones of the lower row had had its setting turned back in the same manner as the others. My friend held it up and glanced furiously at his prisoner.

"How could you!" he cried. "How could you!"

"It is horrible—horrible!" said the Professor. "I don't wonder at your feelings. Take me to your room."

"But this shall not be left exposed!" cried Mortimer. He picked the breastplate up and carried it tenderly in his hand, while I walked beside the Professor, like a policeman with a malefactor. We passed into Mortimer's chambers, leaving the amazed old soldier to understand matters as best he could. The Professor sat down in Mortimer's armchair and turned so ghastly a color that for the instant all our resentment was changed to concern. A stiff glass of brandy brought the life back to him once more.

"There, I am better now!" said he. "These last few days have been too much for me. I am convinced that I could not stand it any longer. It is a nightmare—a horrible nightmare—that I should be arrested as a burglar in what has been for so long my own museum. And yet I cannot blame you. You could not have done otherwise. My hope always was that I should get it all over before I was detected. This would have been my last night's work."

"How did you get in?" asked Mortimer.

"By taking a very great liberty with your private door. But the object justified it. The object justified everything. You will not be angry when you know everything—at least, you will not be angry with me. I had a key to your side door and also to the museum door. I did not give them up when I left. And so you see it was not difficult for me to let myself into the museum. I used to come in early before the crowd had cleared from the street. Then I hid myself in the mummy case, and took refuge there whenever Simpson came round. I could always hear him coming. I used to leave in the same way I came."

"You ran a risk."

"I had to."

"But why? What on earth was your object—*you* to do a thing like that!" Mortimer pointed reproachfully at the plate which lay before him on the table.

"I could devise no other means. I thought and thought, but there was no alternative except a hideous public scandal, and a private sorrow which would have clouded our lives. I acted for the best, incredible as it may seem to you, and I only ask your attention to enable me to prove it."

"I will hear what you have to say before I take any further steps," said Mortimer, grimly.

"I am determined to hold back nothing, and to take you both completely into my confidence. I will have it your own generosity how far you will use the facts with which I supply you."

"We have the essential facts already."

"And yet you understand nothing. Let me go back to what passed a few weeks ago, and I will make it all clear to you. Believe me that what I say is the absolute and exact truth.

"You have met the person who calls himself Captain Wilson. I say 'calls himself' because I have reason now to believe that it is not his correct name. It would take me too long if I were to describe all the means by which he obtained an introduction to me and ingratiated himself into my friendship and the affection of my daughter. He brought letters from foreign colleagues which compelled me to show him some attention. And then, by his own attainments, which are considerable, he succeeded in making himself a very welcome visitor at my rooms. When I learned that my daughter's affections had been gained by him, I may have thought it premature, but I certainly was not surprised, for he had a charm of manner and of conversation which would have made him conspicuous in any society.

"He was much interested in Oriental antiquities, and his knowledge of the subject justified his interest. Often when he spent the evening with us he would ask permission to go down into the museum and have an opportunity of privately inspecting the various specimens. You can imagine that I, as enthusiast, was in sympathy with such a request, and that I felt no surprise at the constancy of his visits. After his actual engagement to Elise there was hardly an evening which he did not pass with us, and an hour or two were generally devoted to the museum. He had the free run of the place, and when I have been away for the evening I had no objection to his doing whatever he wished here. This state of things was only terminated by the fact of my resignation of my official duties and my retirement to Norwood, where I hoped to have the leisure to write a considerable work which I had planned.

"It was immediately after this—within a week or so—that I first realized the true nature and character of the man whom I had so imprudently introduced into my family. This discovery came to me through letters from my friends abroad, which showed me that his introductions to me had been forgeries. Aghast at the revelation, I asked myself what motive this man could originally have had in practicing this elaborate deception upon me. I was too poor a man for any fortune hunter to have marked me down. Why, then, had he come? I remembered that some of the most precious gems in Europe had been under my charge, and I remembered also the ingenious excuses by which this man had made himself familiar with the cases in which they were kept. He was a rascal who was planning some gigantic robbery. How could I, without striking my own daughter, who was infatuated about him, prevent him from carrying out any plan which he might have formed? My device was a clumsy one, and yet I could think of nothing more effective. If I had written a letter under my own name, you would naturally have turned to me for details which I did wish to give. I resorted to an anonymous letter begging you to be upon your guard.

"I may tell you that my change from Belmore Street to Norwood had not affected the visits of this man, who had, I believe, a real and over-powering affection for my daughter. As to her, I could not have believed that any woman could be so completely under the influence of a man as she was. His stronger nature seemed to entirely dominate her. I had not realized how far this was the case, or the extent of the confidence which existed between them until that very evening when his true character for the first time was made clear to me. I had given orders that when he called he should be shown into my study instead of to the drawing room. There I told him bluntly that I knew all about him, that I had taken steps to defeat his designs, and that neither I nor my daughter desired ever to see him again. I added that I thanked God that I had found him out before he had time to harm those precious objects which it had been the work of my lifetime to protect.

"He was certainly a man of iron nerve. He took my remarks without a sign either of surprise or of defiance, but listened gravely and attentively until I had finished. Then he walked across the room without a word and struck the bell.

" 'Ask Miss Andreas to be so kind as to step this way,' said he to the servant.

"My daughter entered, and the man closed the door behind her. Then he took her hand in his.

" 'Elise,' said he, 'your father has just discovered that I am a villain. He knows now what you knew before.'

"She stood in silence, listening.

" 'He says that we are to part forever,' said he.

"She did not withdraw her hand.

" 'Will you be true to me, or will you remove the last good influence which is ever likely to come into my life?'

" 'John,' she cried, passionately, 'I will never abandon you! Never, never, not if the whole world were against you.'

"In vain I argued and pleaded with her. It was absolutely useless. Her whole life was bound up in this man before me. My daughter, gentlemen, is all that I have left to love, and it filled me with agony when I saw how powerless I was to save her from her ruin. My helplessness seemed to touch this man who was the cause of my trouble.

" 'It may not be as bad as you think, sir,' said he, in his quiet, inflexible way. 'I love Elise with a love which is strong enough to rescue even one who has such a record as I have. It was but yesterday that I promised her that never again in my whole life would I do a thing of which she should be ashamed. I have made up my mind to it, and never yet did I make up my mind to a thing which I did not do.'

"He spoke with an air which carried conviction with it. As he concluded he put his hand into his pocket and he drew out a small cardboard box.

" 'I am about to give you a proof of my determination,' said he. 'This, Elise, shall be the first-fruits of your redeeming influence over me. You are right, sir, in thinking that I had designs upon the jewels in your possession. Such ventures have had a charm for me, which depended as much upon the risk run as upon the value of the prize. Those famous antique stones of the Jewish priest were a challenge to my daring and ingenuity. I determined to get them.'

" 'I guessed as much.'

" 'There was only one thing that you did not guess.'

" 'And what is that?'

" 'That I got them. They are in this box.'

"He opened the box, and tilted out the contents upon the corner of my desk. My hair rose and my flesh grew cold as I looked. There were twelve magnificent square stones engraved with mystical characters. There could be no doubt that they were the jewels of the urim and thummim.

" 'Good God!' I cried. 'How have you escaped discovery?'

"By the substitution of twelve others, made especially to my order, in which the originals are so carefully imitated that I defy the eye to detect the difference.'

" 'Then the present stones are false?' I cried.

" 'They have been for some weeks.'

"We all stood in silence, my daughter white with emotion, but still holding this man by the hand.

" 'You see what I am capable of, Elise,' said he.

" 'I see that you are capable of repentance and restitution,' she answered.

" 'Yes, thanks to your influence! I leave the stones in your hands, sir. Do what you like about it. But remember that whatever you do against me, is done against the future husband of your only daughter. You will hear from me soon again, Elise. It is the last time that I will ever cause pain to your tender heart,' and with these words he left both the room and the house.

"My position was a dreadful one. Here I was with these precious relics in my possession, and how could I return them without a scandal and an exposure? I knew the depth of my daughter's nature too well to suppose that I would ever be able to detach her from this man now that she had entirely given him her heart. I was not even sure how far it was right to detach her if she had such an ameliorating influence over him. How could I expose him without injuring her—and how far was I justified in exposing him when he had voluntarily put himself into my power? I thought and thought, until at last I formed a resolution which may seem to you to be a foolish one, and yet, if I had to do it again, I believe it would be the best course open to me.

"My idea was to return the stones without anyone being the wiser. With my keys I could get into the museum at any time, and I was confident that I could avoid Simpson, whose hours and methods were familiar to me. I determined to take no one into my confidence—not even my daughter—whom I told that I was about to visit my brother in

Scotland. I wanted a free hand for a few nights, without inquiry as to my comings and goings. To this end I took a room in Harding Street that very night, with an intimation that I was a Pressman, and that I should keep very late hours.

"That night I made my way into the museum, and I replaced four of the stones. It was hard work, and took me all night. When Simpson came round I always heard his footsteps, and concealed myself in the mummy case. I had some knowledge of goldwork, but was far less skillful than the thief had been. He had replaced the setting so exactly that I defy anyone to see the difference. My work was rude and clumsy. However, I hoped that the plate might not be carefully examined, or the roughness of the setting observed until my task was done. Next night I replaced four more stones. And tonight I should have finished my task had it not been for the unfortunate circumstance which has caused me to reveal so much which I should have wished to keep concealed. I appeal to you, gentlemen, to your sense of honor and of compassion, whether what I have told you should go any further or not. My own happiness, my daughter's future, the hopes of this man's regeneration, all depend upon your decision."

"Which is," said my friend, "that all is well that ends well, and that the whole matter ends here and at once. Tomorrow the loose settings shall be tightened by an expert goldsmith, and so passes the greatest danger to which, since the destruction of the Temple, the urim and thummim have been exposed. Here is my hand, Professor Andreas, and I can only hope that under such difficult circumstances I should have carried myself as unselfishly and as well."

Just one footnote to this narrative. Within a month Elise Andreas was married to a man whose name, had I the indiscretion to mention it, would appeal to my readers as one who is now widely and deservedly honored. But if the truth were known, that honor is due not to him but to the gentle girl who plucked him back when he had gone so far down that dark road along which few return.

THE LOST SPECIAL

The confession of Herbert de Lernac, now lying under sentence of death at Marseilles, has thrown light upon one of the most inexplicable crimes of the century—an incident which is, I believe, absolutely unprecedented in the criminal annals of any country. Although there is a reluctance to discuss the matter in official circles, and little information has been given to the Press, there are still indications that the statement of this archcriminal is corroborated by the facts, and that we have at last found a solution for a most astounding business. As the matter is eight years old, and as its importance was somewhat obscured by a political crisis which was engaging the public attention at the time, it may be as well to state the facts as far as we have been able to ascertain them. They are collated from the Liverpool papers of that date, from the proceedings at the inquest upon John Slater, the engine driver, and from the records of the London and West Coast Railway Company, which have been courteously put at my disposal. Briefly, they are as follows:

On the 3rd of June, 1890, a gentleman who gave his name as Monsieur Louis Caratal desired an interview with Mr. James Bland, the superintendent of the London and West Coast Central Station in Liverpool. He was a small man, middle-aged and dark, with a stoop which was so marked that it suggested some deformity of the spine. He was accompanied by a friend, a man of imposing physique, whose deferential manner and constant attention showed that his position was one of dependence. This friend or companion, whose name did not transpire, was certainly a foreigner, and probably, from his swarthy complexion, either a Spaniard or a South American. One peculiarity was observed in him. He carried in his left hand a small black leather dispatch box, and it was noticed by a sharp-eyed clerk in the central office that this box was fastened to his wrist by a strap. No importance was attached to the fact at the time, but subsequent events endowed it with some significance. Monsieur Caratal was shown up to Mr. Bland's office, while his companion remained outside.

Monsieur Caratal's business was quickly dispatched. He had arrived that afternoon from Central America. Affairs of the utmost importance demanded that he should be in Paris without the loss of an unnecessary hour. He had missed the London express. A special must be provided. Money was of no importance. Time was everything. If the company would speed him on his way, they might make their own terms.

Mr. Bland struck the electric bell, summoned Mr. Potter Hood, the traffic manager, and had the matter arranged in five minutes. The train would start in three quarters of an hour. It would take that time to insure that the line should be clear. The powerful engine called Rochdale (No. 247 on the company's register) was attached to two carriages, with a guard's van behind. The first carriage was solely for the purpose of decreasing the inconvenience arising from the oscillation. The second was divided, as usual, into four compartments, a first-class, a first-class smoking, a second-class, and a second-class smoking. The first compartment, which was nearest to the engine, was the one allotted to the travelers. The other three were empty. The guard of the special train was James McPherson, who had been some years in the service of the company. The stoker, William Smith, was a new hand.

Monsieur Caratal, upon leaving the superintendent's office, rejoined his companion, and both of them manifested extreme impatience to be off. Having paid the money asked, which amounted to fifty pounds five shillings, at the usual special rate of five shillings a mile, they demanded to be shown the carriage, and at once took their seats in it, although they were assured that the better part of an hour must elapse before the line could be cleared. In the meantime a singular coincidence had occurred in the office which Monsieur Caratal had just quitted.

A request for a special is not very uncommon circumstance in a rich commercial center, but that two should be required upon the same afternoon was most unusual. It so happened, however, that Mr. Bland had hardly dismissed the first traveler before a second entered with a similar request. This was a Mr. Horace Moore, a gentlemanly man of military appearance, who alleged that the sudden serious illness of his wife in London made it absolutely imperative that he should not lose an instant in starting upon the journey. His distress and anxiety were so evident that Mr. Bland did all that was possible to meet his wishes. A second special was out of the question, as the ordinary local service was already somewhat deranged by the first. There was the alternative, however, that Mr. Moore should share the expense of Monsieur Caratal's train, and should travel in the other empty first-class compartment, if Monsieur Caratal objected to having him in the one which he occupied. It was difficult to see any objection to such an arrangement, and yet Monsieur Caratal, upon the suggestion being made to him by Mr. Potter Hood, absolutely refused to consider it for an instant. The train was his, he said, and he would insist upon the exclusive use of it. All argument failed to overcome his ungracious objections, and finally the plan had to be abandoned. Mr. Horace Moore left the station in great distress, after learning that his only course was to take the ordinary slow train which leaves Liverpool at six o'clock. At four thirty-one exactly by the station clock the special train containing the crippled Monsieur Caratal and his gigantic companion steamed out of the Liverpool station. The line was at that time clear, and there should have been no stoppage before Manchester.

The trains of the London and West Coast Railway run over the lines of another company as far as this town, which should have been reached by the special rather before six o'clock. At a quarter after six considerable surprise and some consternation were caused amongst the officials at Liverpool by the receipt of a telegram from Manchester to say that it had not yet arrived. An inquiry directed to St. Helens, which is a third of the way between the two cities, elicited the following reply:

"To James Bland, Superintendent, Central L. & W. C., Liverpool: Special passed here at 4:52, well up to time.—Dowser, St. Helens."

This telegram was received at 6:40. At 6:50 a second message was received from Manchester:

"No sign of special as advised by you."

And then ten minutes later a third, more bewildering:

"Presume some mistake as to proposed running of special. Local train from St. Helens timed to follow it has just arrived and has seen nothing of it. Kindly wire advices.—Manchester."

The matter was assuming a most amazing aspect, although in some respects the last telegram was a relief to the authorities at Liverpool. If an accident had occurred to the special, it seemed hardly possible that the local train could have passed down the same line without observing it. And yet, what was the alternative? Where could the train be? Had it possibly been sidetracked for some reason in order to allow the slower train to go past? Such an explanation was possible if some small repair had to be effected. A telegram was dispatched to each of the stations between St. Helens and Manchester, and the superintendent and traffic manager waited in the utmost suspense at the instrument for the series of replies which would enable them to say for certain what had become of the missing train. The answers came back in the order of questions, which was the order of the stations beginning at the St. Helens end:

"Special passed here 5 o'clock.—Collins Green."

"Special passed here 6 past 5.—Earlestown."

"Special passed here 5:10.—Newton."

"Special passed here 5:20.—Kenyon Junction."

"No special train has passed here.—Barton Moss."

The two officials stared at each other in amazement.

"This is unique in my thirty years of experience," said Mr. Bland.

"Absolutely unprecedented and inexplicable, sir. The special has gone wrong between Kenyon Junction and Barton Moss."

"And yet there is no siding, so far as my memory serves me, between the two stations. The special must have run off the metals."

"But how could the four-fifty parliamentary pass over the same line without observing it?"

"There's no alternative, Mr. Hood. It *must* be so. Possibly the local train may have observed something which may throw some light upon the matter. We will wire to Manchester for more information, and to Kenyon Junction with instructions that the line be examined instantly as far as Barton Moss."

The answer from Manchester came within a few minutes.

"No news of missing special. Driver and guard of slow train positive no accident between Kenyon Junction and Barton Moss. Line quite clear, and no sign of anything unusual.—Manchester."

"That driver and guard will have to go," said Mr. Bland, grimly. "There has been a wreck and they have missed it. The special has obviously run off the metals without disturbing the line—how it could have done so passes my comprehension—but so it must be, and we shall have a wire from Kenyon or Barton Moss presently to say that they have found her at the bottom of an embankment."

But Mr. Bland's prophecy was not destined to be fulfilled. Half an hour passed, and then there arrived the following message from the stationmaster of Kenyon Junction:

"There are no traces of the missing special. It is quite certain that she passed here, and that she did not arrive at Barton Moss. We have detached engine from goods train, and I have myself ridden down the line, but all is clear, and there is no sign of any accident."

Mr. Bland tore his hair in his perplexity.

"This is rank lunacy, Hood!" he cried. "Does a train vanish into thin air in England in broad daylight? The thing is preposterous. An engine, a tender, two carriages, a van, five human beings—and all lost on a straight line of railway! Unless we get something positive within the next hour I'll take Inspector Collins and go down myself."

And then at last something positive did occur. It took the shape of another telegram from Kenyon Junction.

"Regret to report that the dead body of John Slater, driver of the special train, has just been found among the gorse bushes at a point two and a quarter miles from the Junction. Had fallen from his engine, pitched down the embankment, and rolled among bushes. Injuries to his head, from the fall, appear to be cause of death. Ground has now been carefully examined, and there is no trace of the missing train."

The country was, as has already been stated, in the throes of a political crisis, and the attention of the public was further distracted by the important and sensational developments in Paris, where a huge scandal threatened to destroy the Government and to wreck the reputations of many of the leading men in France. The papers were full of these events, and the singular disappearance of the special train attracted less attention than would have been the case in more peaceful times. The grotesque nature of the event helped to detract from its importance, for the papers were disinclined to believe the facts as reported to them. More than one of the London journals treated the matter as an ingenious hoax, until the coroner's inquest upon the unfortunate driver (an inquest which elicited nothing of importance) convinced them of the tragedy of the incident.

Mr. Bland, accompanied by Inspector Collins, the senior detective officer in the service of the company, went down to Kenyon Junction the same evening, and their research lasted throughout the following day, but was attended with purely negative results. Not only was no trace found of the missing train, but no conjecture could be put forward which could possibly explain the facts. At the same time, Inspector Collins's official report (which lies before me as I write) served to show that the possibilities were more numerous than might have been expected.

"In the stretch of railway between these two points," said he, "the country is dotted with ironworks and collieries. Of these, some are being worked and some have been abandoned. There are no fewer than twelve which have small gauge lines which run trolley cars down to the main line. These can, of course, be disregarded. Besides these, however, there are seven which have or have had proper lines running down and connecting with points to the main line, so as to convey their produce from the mouth of the mine to the great centers of distribution. In every case these lines are only a few miles in length. Out of the seven, four belong to collieries which are worked out, or at least to shafts which are no longer used. These are the Redgauntlet, Hero, Slough of Despond, and Heartease mines, the latter having ten years ago been one of the principle mines in Lancashire. These four side lines may be eliminated from our inquiry, for, to prevent possible accidents, the rails nearest to the main line have been taken up, and there is no longer any connection. There remains three other side lines leading

(*a*) To the Carnstock Iron Works;
(*b*) To the Big Ben Colliery;
(*c*) To the Perseverance Colliery.

Of these the Big Ben line is not more than a quarter of a mile long, and ends at a dead wall of coal waiting removal from the mouth of the mine. Nothing had been seen or heard there of any special. The Carnstock Iron Works line was blocked all day upon the 3rd of June by sixteen truckloads of hematite. It is a single line, and nothing could have passed. As to the Perseverance line, it is a large double line, which does a considerable traffic, for the output of the mine is very large. On the 3rd of June this traffic proceeded as usual; hundreds of men, including a gang of railway platelayers, were working along the two miles and a quarter which constitute the total length of the line, and it is inconceivable that an unexpected train could have come down there without attracting universal attention. It may be remarked in conclusion that this branch line is nearer to St. Helens than the point at which the engine driver was discovered, so that we have every reason to believe that the train was past that point before misfortune overtook her.

"As to John Slater, there is no clue to be gathered from his appearance or injuries. We can only say that, so far as we can see, he met his end by falling off his engine, though why he fell, or what became of the engine after his fall, is a question upon which I do not feel qualified to offer an opinion." In conclusion, the inspector offered his resignation to the Board, being much nettled by an accusation of incompetence in the London papers.

A month elapsed, during which both the police and the company prosecuted their inquiries without the slightest success. A reward was offered and a pardon promised in case of crime, but they were both unclaimed. Every day the public opened their papers with the conviction that so grotesque a mystery would at last be solved, but week after week passed by, and a solution remained as far off as ever. In broad daylight, upon a June afternoon in the most thickly inhabited portion of England, a train with its occupants had disappeared as completely as if some master of subtle chemistry had volatilized it into gas. Indeed, among the various conjectures which were put forward in the public Press there were some which seriously asserted that supernatural, or, at least, preternatural, agencies had been at work, and that the deformed Monsieur Caratal was probably a person who was better known under a less polite name. Others fixed upon his swarthy companion as being the author of the mischief, but what it was exactly which he had done could never be clearly formulated in words.

Amongst the many suggestions put forward by various newspapers or private individuals, there were one or two which were feasible enough to attract the attention of the public. One which appeared in the *Times*, over the signature of an amateur reasoner of some celebrity at that date, attempted to deal with the matter in a critical and semi-scientific manner. An extract must suffice, although the curious can see the whole letter in the issue of the 3rd of July.

"It is one of the elementary principles of practical reasoning," he remarked, "that when the impossible has been eliminated the residuum, *however improbable*, must contain the truth. It is certain that the train left Kenyon Junction. It is certain that it did not reach Barton Moss. It is in the highest degree unlikely, but still possible, that it may have taken one of the seven available side lines. It is obviously impossible for a train to run where there are no rails, and therefore we may reduce our improbables to the three open lines, namely, the Carnstock Iron Works, the Big Ben, and the Perseverance. Is there a secret society of colliers, an English *camorra*, which is capable of destroying both train and passengers? It is improbable, but it is not impossible. I confess that I am unable to suggest any other solution. I should certainly advise the company to direct all their energies towards the observation of those three lines, and of the workmen at the end of them. A careful supervision of the pawnbrokers' shops of the district might possibly bring some suggestive facts to light."

The suggestion, coming from a recognized authority upon such matters, created considerable interest, and a fierce opposition from those who considered such a statement to be a preposterous libel upon an honest and deserving set of men. The only answer to this criticism was a challenge to the objectors to lay any more feasible explanation before the public. In reply to this two others were forthcoming (*Times*, July 7th and 9th). The first suggested that the train might have run off the metals and be lying submerged in the Lancashire and Staffordshire Canal, which runs parallel to the railway for some hundreds of yards. This suggestion was thrown out of court by the published depth of the canal, which was entirely insufficient to conceal so large an object. The second correspondent wrote calling attention to the bag which appeared to be the sole luggage which the travelers had brought with them, and suggesting that some novel explosive of immense and pulverizing power might have been concealed in it. The obvious absurdity, however, of supposing that the whole train might be blown to dust while the metals remained uninjured reduced any such explanation to a farce. The investigation had drifted into this hopeless position when a new and most unexpected incident occurred.

This was nothing less than the receipt by Mrs. McPherson of a letter from her husband, James McPherson, who had been the guard of the missing train. The letter, which was dated July 5th, 1890, was posted from New York, and came to hand upon July 14th. Some doubts were expressed as to its genuine character, but Mrs. McPherson was positive as to the writing, and the fact that it contained a remittance of a hundred dollars in five-dollar notes was enough in itself to discount the idea of a hoax. No address was given in the letter, which ran in this way:

> MY DEAR WIFE,
>
> I have been thinking a great deal, and I find it very hard to give you up. The same with Lizzie. I try to fight against it, but it will always come back to me. I send you some money which will change into twenty English pounds. This should be enough to bring both Lizzie and you across the Atlantic, and you will find the Hamburg boats which stop at Southampton very good boats, and cheaper than Liverpool. If you could come here and stop at the Johnston House I would try and send you word how to meet, but things are very difficult with me at present, and I am not very happy, finding it hard to give you both up. So no more at present, from your loving husband,
>
> JAMES MCPHERSON.

For a time it was confidently anticipated that this letter would lead to the clearing up of the whole matter, the more so as it was ascertained that a passenger who bore a close resemblance to the missing guard had traveled from Southampton under the name of Summers in the Hamburg and New York liner *Vistula*, which started upon the 7th of June. Mrs. McPherson and her sister Lizzie Dolton went across to New York as directed, and stayed for three weeks at the Johnston House, without hearing anything from the missing man. It is probable that some injudicious comments in the Press may have warned him that the police were using them as a bait. However this may be, it is certain that he neither wrote nor came, and the women were eventually compelled to return to Liverpool.

And so the matter stood, and has continued to stand up to the present year of 1898. Incredible as it may seem, nothing has transpired during these eight years which has shed the least light upon the extraordinary disappearance of the special train which contained Monsieur Caratal and his companion. Careful inquiries into the antecedents of the two travelers have only established the fact that Monsieur Caratal was well known as a financier and political agent in Central America, and that during his voyage to Europe he had betrayed extraordinary anxiety to reach Paris. His companion, whose name was entered upon the passenger lists as Eduardo Gomez, was a man whose record was a violent one, and whose reputation was that of a bravo and a bully. There was evidence to show, however, that he was honestly devoted to the interests of Monsieur Caratal, and that the latter, being a man of puny physique, employed the other as a guard and protector. It may be added that no information came from Paris as to what the objects of Monsieur Caratal's hurried journey may have been. This comprises all the facts of the case up to the publication in the Marseilles papers of the recent confession of Herbert de Lernac, now under sentence of death for the murder of a merchant named Bonvalot. This statement may be literally translated as follows:

"It is not out of mere pride or boasting that I give this information, for, if that were my object, I could tell a dozen actions of mine which are quite as splendid; but I do it in order that certain gentlemen in Paris may understand that I, who am able here to tell about the fate of Monsieur Caratal, can also tell in whose interest and at whose request the deed was done, unless the reprieve which I am awaiting comes to me very quickly. Take warning, Messieurs, before it is too late! You know Herbert de Lernac, and you are aware that his deeds are as ready as his words. Hasten then, or you are lost!

"At present I shall mention no names—if you only heard the names, what would you not think!—but I shall merely tell you how cleverly I did it. I was true to my employers then, and no doubt they will be true to me now. I hope so, and until I am convinced that they have betrayed me, these names, which would convulse Europe, shall not be divulged. But on that day . . . well, I say no more!

"In a word, then, there was a famous trial in Paris, in the year 1890, in connection with a monstrous scandal in politics and finance. How monstrous that scandal was can never be known save by such confidential agents as myself. The honor and careers of many of the chief men in France were at stake. You have seen a group of ninepins standing, all so rigid, and prim, and unbending. Then there comes the ball from far away and pop, pop, pop—there are your ninepins on the floor. Well, imagine some of the greatest men in France as these ninepins, and then this Monsieur Caratal was the ball which could be seen coming from far away. If he arrived, then it was pop, pop, pop for all of them. It was determined that he should not arrive.

"I do not accuse them all of being conscious of what was to happen. There were, as I have said, great financial as well as political interests at stake, and a syndicate was formed to manage the business. Some subscribed to the syndicate who hardly understood what were its objects. But others understood very well, and they can rely upon it that I have not forgotten their names. They had ample warning that Monsieur Caratal was coming long before he left South America, and they knew that the evidence which he held would certainly mean ruin to all of them. The syndicate had the command of an unlimited amount of money—absolutely unlimited, you understand. They looked round for an agent who was capable of wielding this gigantic power. The man chose must be inventive, resolute, adaptive—a man in a million. They chose Herbert de Lernac, and I admit that they were right.

"My duties were to choose my subordinates, to use freely the power which money gives, and to make certain that Monsieur Caratal should never arrive in Paris. With characteristic energy I set about my commission within an hour of receiving my instructions, and the steps which I took were the very best for the purpose which could possibly be devised.

"A man whom I could trust was dispatched instantly to South America to travel home with Monsieur Caratal. Had he arrived in time the ship would never have reached Liverpool; but, alas, it had already started before my agent could reach it. I fitted out a small armed brig to intercept it, but again I was unfortunate. Like all great organizers I was, however, prepared for failure, and had a series of alternatives prepared, one or the other of which must succeed. You must not underrate the difficulties of my undertaking, or imagine that a mere commonplace assassination would meet the case. We must destroy not only Monsieur Caratal, but Monsieur Caratal's documents, and Monsieur Caratal's companions also, if we had reason to believe that he had communicated his secrets to them. And you must remember that they were on the alert, and keenly suspicious of any such attempt. It was a task which was in every way worthy of me, for I am always most masterful where another would be appalled.

"I was all ready for Monsieur Caratal's reception in Liverpool, and I was the more eager because I had reason to believe that he had made arrangements by which he would have a considerable guard from the moment that he arrived in London. Anything which was to be done must be done between the moment of his setting foot upon the Liverpool quay and that of his arrival at the London and West Coast terminus in London. We prepared six plans, each more elaborate than the last; which plan would be used would depend upon his own movements. Do what he would, we were ready for him. If he had stayed in Liverpool, we were ready. If he took an ordinary train, an express, or a special, all was ready. Everything had been foreseen and provided for.

"You may imagine that I could not do all this myself. What could I know of the English railway lines? But money can procure willing agents all the world over, and I soon had one of the acutest brains in England to assist me. I will mention no names, but it would be unjust to claim all the credit for myself. My English ally was worthy of such an alliance. He knew the London and West Coast line thoroughly, and he had the command of a band of workers who were trustworthy and intelligent. The idea was his, and my own judgment was only required in the details. We bought over several officials, amongst whom the most important was James McPherson, whom we had ascertained to be the guard most likely to be employed upon a special train. Smith, the stoker, was also in our employ. John Slater, the engine driver, had been approached, but had been found to be obstinate and dangerous, so we desisted. We had no certainty that Monsieur Caratal would take a special, but we thought it very probable, for it was of the utmost importance to him that he should reach Paris without delay. It was for this contingency, therefore, that we made special preparations—preparations which were complete down to the last detail long before his steamer had sighted the shores of England. You will be amused to learn that there was one of my agents in the pilot boat which brought that steamer to its moorings.

"The moment that Caratal arrived in Liverpool we knew that he suspected danger and was on his guard. He had brought with him as an escort a dangerous fellow, named Gomez, a man who carried weapons, and was prepared to use them. This fellow carried Caratal's confidential papers for him, and was ready to protect either them or his master. The probability was that Caratal had taken him into his counsels, and that to remove Caratal without removing Gomez would be a mere waste of energy. It was necessary that they should be involved in a common fate, and our plans to that end were much facilitated by their request for a special train. On that special train you will understand that two out of the three servants of the company were really in our employ, at a price which would make them independent for a lifetime. I do not go so far as to say that the English are more honest than any other nation, but I have found them more expensive to buy.

"I have already spoken of my English agent—who is a man with a considerable future before him, unless some complaint of the throat carries him off before his time. He had charge of all arrangements at Liverpool, whilst I was stationed at the inn at Kenyon, where I awaited a cipher signal to act. When the special was arranged for, my agent instantly telegraphed to me and warned me how soon I should have everything ready. He himself under the name of Horace Moore applied immediately for a special also, in the hope that he would be sent down with Monsieur Caratal, which might under certain circumstances have been helpful to us. If, for example, our great *coup* had failed, it would then have become the duty of my agent to have shot them both and destroyed their papers. Caratal was on his guard, however, and refused to admit any other traveler. My agent then left the station, returned by another entrance, entered the guard's van on the side farthest from the platform, and traveled down with McPherson the guard.

"In the meantime you will be interested to know what my movements were. Everything had been prepared for days before, and only the finishing touches were needed. The side line which we had chosen had once joined the main line, but it had been disconnected. We had only to replace a few rails to connect it once more. These rails had been laid down as far as could be done without danger of attracting attention, and now it was merely a case of completing a juncture with the line, and arranging the points as they had been before. The sleepers had never been removed, and the rails, fishplates, and rivets were all ready, for we had taken them from a siding on the abandoned portion of the line. With my small but competent band of workers, we had everything ready long before the special arrived. When it did arrive, it ran off upon the small side line so easily that the jolting of the points appears to have been entirely unnoticed by the two travelers.

"Our plan had been that Smith the stoker should chloroform John Slater the driver, so that he should vanish with the others. In this respect, and in this respect only, our plans miscarried—I except the

criminal folly of McPherson in writing home to his wife. Our stoker did
his business so clumsily that Slater in his struggles fell off the engine,
and though fortune was with us so far that he broke his neck in the fall,
still he remained as a blot upon that which would otherwise have been
one of those complete masterpieces which are only to be contemplated
in silent admiration. The criminal expert will find in John Slater the
one flaw in all our admirable combinations. A man who has had as many
triumphs as I can afford to be frank, and I therefore lay my finger upon
John Slater, and I proclaim him to be a flaw.

"But now I have got our special train upon the small line two kilo-
meters, or rather more than one mile, in length, which leads, or rather
used to lead, to the abandoned Heartsease mine, once one of the largest
coal mines in England. You will ask how it is that no one saw the train
upon this unused line. I answer that along its entire length it runs
through a deep cutting, and that, unless someone had been on the edge
of that cutting, he could not have seen it. There *was* someone on the
edge of that cutting. I was there. And now I will tell you what I saw.

"My assistant had remained at the points in order that he might
superintend the switching off of the train. He had four armed men with
him, so that if the train ran off the line—we thought it probable, because the points were very rusty—we might still have resources to fall
back upon. Having once seen it safely on the side line, he handed over
the responsibility to me. I was waiting at a point which overlooks the
mouth of the mine, and I was also armed, as were my two companions.
Come what might, you see, I was always ready.

"The moment that the train was fairly on the side line, Smith, the
stoker, slowed down the engine, and then, having turned it on to the
fullest speed again, he and McPherson, with my English lieutenant,
sprang off before it was too late. It may be that it was this slowing down
which first attracted the attention of the travelers, but the train was
running at full speed again before their heads appeared at the open
window. It makes me smile to think how bewildered they must have
been. Picture to yourself your own feelings if, on looking out of your
luxurious carriage, you suddenly perceived that the lines upon which
you ran were rusted and corroded, red and yellow with disuse and
decay! What a catch must have come in their breath as in a second it
flashed upon them that it was not Manchester but Death which was
waiting for them at the end of that sinister line. But the train was
running with frantic speed, rolling and rocking over the rotten line,
while the wheels made a frightful screaming sound upon the rusted
surface. I was close to them, and could see their faces. Caratal was

praying, I think—there was something like a rosary dangling out of his hand. The other roared like a bull who smells the blood of the slaughterhouse. He saw us standing on the bank, and he beckoned to us like a madman. Then he tore at his wrist and threw his dispatch box out of the window in our direction. Of course, his meaning was obvious. Here was the evidence, and they would promise to be silent if their lives were spared. It would have been very agreeable if we could have done so, but business is business. Besides, the train was now as much beyond our control as theirs.

"He ceased howling when the train rattled round the curve and they saw the black mouth of the mine yawning before them. We had removed the boards which had covered it, and we had cleared the square entrance. The rails had formerly run very close to the shaft for the convenience of loading the coal, and we had only to add two or three lengths of rail in order to lead to the very brink of the shaft. In fact, as the lengths would not quite fit, our line projected about three feet over the edge. We saw the two heads at the window: Caratal below, Gomez above; but they had both been struck silent by what they saw. And yet they could not withdraw their heads. The sight seemed to have paralyzed them.

"I had wondered how the train running at a great speed would take the pit into which I had guided it, and I was much interested in watching it. One of my colleagues thought that it would actually jump it, and indeed it was not very far from doing so. Fortunately, however, it fell short, and the buffers of the engine struck the other lip of the shaft with a tremendous crash. The funnel flew off into the air. The tender, carriages, and van were all smashed up into one jumble, which, with the remains of the engine, choked for a minute or so the mouth of the pit. Then something gave way in the middle, and the whole mass of green iron, smoking coals, brass fittings, wheels, woodwork, and cushions all crumbled together and crashed down into the mine. We heard the rattle, rattle, rattle, as the débris struck against the walls, and then quite a long time afterwards there came a deep roar as the remains of the train struck the bottom. The boiler may have burst, for a sharp crash came after the roar, and then a dense cloud of steam and smoke swirled up out of the black depths, falling in a spray as thick as rain all round us. Then the vapor shredded off into thin wisps, which floated away in the summer sunshine, and all was quiet again in the Heartsease mine.

"And now, having carried out our plans so successfully, it only remained to leave no trace behind us. Our little band of workers at the other end had already ripped up the rails and disconnected the side line, replacing everything as it had been before. We were equally busy at the mine. The funnel and other fragments were thrown in, the shaft was planked over as it used to be, and the lines which led to it were torn up and taken away. Then, without flurry, but without delay, we all made our way out of the country, most of us to Paris, my English colleague to Manchester, and McPherson to Southampton, whence he emigrated to America. Let the English papers of that date tell how thoroughly we had done our work, and how completely we had thrown the cleverest of their detectives off our track.

"You will remember that Gomez threw his bag of papers out of the window, and I need not say that I secured that bag and brought them to my employers. It may interest my employers now, however, to learn that out of that bag I took one or two little papers as a souvenir of the occasion. I have no wish to publish these papers; but, still, it is every man for himself in this world, and what else can I do if my friends will not come to my aid when I want them? Messieurs,.you may believe that Herbert de Lernac is quite as formidable when he is against you as when he is with you, and that he is not a man to go to the guillotine until he has seen that everyone of you is en route for New Caledonia. For your own sake, if not for mine, make haste, Monsieur de ——, and General ——, and Baron —— (you can fill up the blanks for yourselves as you read this). I promise you that in the next edition there will be no blanks to fill.

"P. S.—As I look over my statement there is only one omission which I can see. It concerns the unfortunate man McPherson, who was foolish enough to write to his wife and to make an appointment with her in New York. It can be imagined that when interests like ours were at stake, we could not leave them to the chance of whether a man in that class of life would or would not give away his secrets to a woman. Having once broken his oath by writing to his wife, we could not trust him any more. We took steps therefore to insure that he should not see his wife. I have sometimes thought that it would be a kindness to write to her and to assure her that there is no impediment to her marrying again."

THE CLUBFOOTED GROCER

My uncle, Mr. Stephen Maple, had been at the same time the most successful and the least respectable of our family, so that we hardly knew whether to take credit for his wealth or to feel ashamed of his position. He had, as a matter of fact, established a large grocery in Stepney which did a curious mixed business, not always, as we had heard, of a very savory character, with the riverside and seafaring people. He was ship's chandler, provision merchant, and, if rumor spoke truly, some other things as well. Such a trade, however lucrative, had its drawbacks, as was evident when, after twenty years of prosperity, he was savagely assaulted by one of his customers and left for dead, with three smashed ribs and a broken leg, which mended so badly that it remained forever three inches shorter than the other. This incident seemed, not unnaturally, to disgust him with his surroundings, for, after the trial, in which his assailant was condemned to fifteen years' penal servitude, he retired from his business and settled in a lonely part of the North of England, whence, until that morning, we had never once heard of him—not even at the death of my father, who was his only brother.

My mother read his letter aloud to me: "If your son is with you, Ellen, and if he is as stout a lad as he promised for when last I heard from you, then send him up to me by the first train after this comes to hand. He will find that to serve me will pay him better than the engineering, and if I pass away (though, thank God, there is no reason to complain as to my health) you will see that I have not forgotten my brother's son. Congleton is the station, and then a drive of four miles to Greta House, where I am now living. I will send a trap to meet the seven o'clock train, for it is the only one which stops here. Mind that you send him, Ellen, for I have very strong reasons for wishing him to be with me. Let bygones be bygones if there has been anything between us in the past. If you should fail me now you will live to regret it."

We were seated at either side of the breakfast table, looking blankly at each other and wondering what this might mean, when there came a ring at the bell, and the maid walked in with a telegram. It was from Uncle Stephen.

"On no account let John get out at Congleton," said the message. "He will find trap waiting seven o'clock evening train Stedding Bridge, one station further down line. Let him drive not me, but Garth Farm House— six miles. There will receive instructions. Do not fail; only you to look to."

"That is true enough," said my mother. "As far as I know, your uncle has not a friend in the world, nor has he ever deserved one. He has always been a hard man in his dealings, and he held back his money from your father at a time when a few pounds would have saved him from ruin. Why should I send my only son to serve him now?"

But my own inclinations were all for the adventure.

"If I have him for a friend, he can help me in my profession," I argued, taking my mother upon her weakest side.

"I have never known him to help anyone yet," said she, bitterly. "And why all this mystery about getting out at a distant station and driving to the wrong address? He has got himself into some trouble and he wishes us to get him out of it. When he has used us he will throw us aside as he has done before. Your father might have been living now if he had only helped him."

But at last my arguments prevailed, for, as I pointed out, we had much to gain and little to lose, and why should we, the poorest members of a family, go out of our way to offend the rich one? My bag was packed and my cab at the door, when there came a second telegram.

"Good shooting. Let John bring gun. Remember Stedding Bridge, not Congleton." And so, with a gun case added to my luggage and some surprise at my uncle's insistence, I started off upon my adventure.

The journey lies over the main Northern Railway as far as the station of Carnfield, where one changes for the little branch line which winds over the fells. In all England there is no harsher or more impressive scenery. For two hours I passed through desolate rolling plains, rising at places into low, stone-littered hills, with long, straight outcrops of jagged rock showing upon their surface. Here and there little gray-roofed, gray-walled cottages huddled into villages, but for many miles at a time no house was visible nor any sign of life save the scattered sheep which wandered over the mountain sides. It was a depressing country, and my heart grew heavier and heavier as I neared my journey's end, until at last the train pulled up at the little village of Stedding Bridge, where my uncle had told me to alight. A single ramshackle trap, with a country lout to drive it, was waiting at the station.

"Is this Mr. Stephen Maple's?" I asked.

The fellow looked at me with eyes which were full of suspicion. "What is your name?" he asked, speaking a dialect which I will not attempt to reproduce.

"John Maple."

"Anything to prove it?"

I half raised my hand, for my temper is none of the best, and then I reflected that the fellow was probably only carrying out the directions of my uncle. For answer I pointed to my name printed upon my gun case.

"Yes, yes, that is right. It's John Maple sure enough!" said he, slowly spelling it out. "Get in, maister, for we have a bit of a drive before us."

The road, white and shining, like all the roads in that limestone country, ran in long sweeps over the fells, with low walls of loose stone upon either side of it. The huge moors, mottled with sheep and with boulders, rolled away in gradually ascending curves to the misty skyline. In one place a fall of the land gave a glimpse of a gray angle of distant sea. Bleak and sad and stern were all my surroundings, and I felt, under their influence, that this curious mission of mine was a more serious thing than it had appeared when viewed from London. This sudden call for help from an uncle whom I had never seen, and of whom I had heard little that was good, the urgency of it, his reference to my physical powers, the excuse by which he had ensured that I should bring a weapon, all hung together and pointed to some vague but sinister meaning. Things which appeared to be impossible in Kensington became very probable upon these wild and isolated hillsides. At last, oppressed with my own dark thoughts, I turned to my companion with the intention of asking some questions about my uncle, but the expression upon his face drove the idea from my head.

He was not looking at his old, unclipped chestnut horse, nor at the road along which he was driving, but his face was turned in my direction, and he was staring past me with an expression of curiosity and, as

I thought, of apprehension. He raised the whip to lash the horse, and then dropped it again, as if convinced that it was useless. At the same time, following the direction of his gaze, I saw what it was which had excited him.

A man was running across the moor. He ran clumsily, stumbling and slipping among the stones; but the road curved, and it was easy for him to cut us off. As we came up to the spot for which he had been making, he scrambled over the stone wall and stood waiting, with the evening sun shining on his brown, clean-shaven face. He was a burly fellow, and in bad condition, for he stood with his hand on his ribs panting and blowing after his short run. As we drove up I saw the glint of earrings in his ears.

"Say, mate, where are you bound for?" he asked, in a rough but good-humored fashion.

"Farmer Purcell's, at the Garth Farm," said the driver.

"Sorry to stop you," cried the other, standing aside; "I thought as I would hail you as you passed, for if so be as you had been going my way I should have made bold to ask you for a passage."

His excuse was an absurd one, since it was evident that our little trap was as full as it could be, but my driver did not seem disposed to argue. He drove on without a word, and, looking back, I could see the stranger sitting by the roadside and cramming tobacco into his pipe.

"A sailor," said I.

"Yes, maister. We're not more than a few miles from Morecambe Bay," the driver remarked.

"You seemed frightened of him," I observed.

"Did I?" said he, drily; and then, after a long pause, "Maybe I was." As to his reasons for fear, I could get nothing from him, and though I asked him many questions he was so stupid, or else so clever, that I could learn nothing from his replies. I observed, however, that from time to time he swept the moors with a troubled eye, but their huge brown expanse was unbroken by any moving figure. At last in a sort of cleft in the hills in front of us I saw a long, low-lying farm building, the center of all those scattered flocks.

"Garth Farm," said my driver. "There is Farmer Purcell himself," he added, as a man strolled out of the porch and stood waiting for our arrival. He advanced as I descended from the trap, a hard, weather-worn fellow with light blue eyes, and hair and beard like sun-bleached grass. In his expression I read the same surly ill will which I had already observed in my driver. Their malevolence could not be directed towards a complete stranger like myself, and so I began to suspect that my uncle was no more popular on the north-country fells than he had been in Stepney Highway.

"You're to stay here until nightfall. That's Mr. Stephen Maple's wish," said he, curtly. "You can have some tea and bacon if you like. It's the best we can give you."

I was very hungry, and accepted the hospitality in spite of the churlish tone in which it was offered. The farmer's wife and his two daughters came into the sitting room during the meal, and I was aware of a certain curiosity with which they regarded me. It may have been that a young man was a rarity in this wilderness, or it may be that my attempts at conversation won their good will, but they all three showed a kindliness in their manner. It was getting dark, so I remarked that it was time for me to be pushing on to Greta House.

"You've made up your mind to go, then?" said the older woman.

"Certainly. I have come all the way from London,"

"There's no one hindering you from going back there."

"But I have come to see Mr. Maple, my uncle."

"Oh, well, no one can stop you if you want to go on," said the woman, and became silent as her husband entered the room.

With every fresh incident I felt that I was moving in an atmosphere of mystery and peril, and yet it was all so intangible and so vague that I could not guess where my danger lay. I should have asked the farmer's wife point-blank, but her surly husband seemed to divine the sympathy which she felt for me, and never again left us together. "It's time you were going, mister," said he at last, as his wife lit the lamp upon the table.

"Is the trap ready?"

"You'll need no trap. You'll walk," said he.

"How shall I know the way?"

"William will go with you."

William was the youth who had driven me up from the station. He was waiting at the door, and he shouldered my gun case and bag. I stayed behind to thank the farmer for his hospitality, but he would have none of it. "I ask no thanks from Mr. Stephen Maple nor any friend of his," said he, bluntly. "I am paid for what I do. If I was not paid I would not do it. Go your way, young man, and say no more." He turned rudely on his heel and reentered his house, slamming the door behind him.

It was quite dark outside, with heavy black clouds drifting slowly across the sky. Once clear of the farm inclosure and out on the moor I should have been hopelessly lost if it had not been for my guide, who walked in front of me along narrow sheep tracks which were quite invisible to me. Every now and then, without seeing anything, we heard the clumsy scuffling of the creatures in the darkness. At first my guide walked swiftly and carelessly, but gradually his pace slowed down, until at last he was going very slowly and stealthily, like one who walks light-footed amid imminent menace. This vague, inexplicable sense of danger in the midst of the loneliness of that vast moor was more daunting than any evident peril could be, and I had begun to press him as to what it was that he feared, when suddenly he stopped and dragged me down among some gorse bushes which lined the path. His tug at my coat was so strenuous and imperative that I realized that the danger was a pressing one, and in an instant I was squatting down beside him as still as the bushes which shadowed us. It was so dark there that I could not even see the lad beside me.

It was a warm night, and a hot wind puffed in our faces. Suddenly in this wind there came something homely and familiar—the smell of burning tobacco. And then a face, illuminated by the glowing bowl of a pipe, came floating towards us. The man was all in shadow, but just that one dim halo of light with the face which filled it, brighter below and shading away into darkness above, stood out against the universal blackness. A thin, hungry face, thickly freckled with yellow over the cheek bones, blue, watery eyes, an ill-nourished, light-colored mustache, a peaked yachting cap—that was all that I saw. He passed us, looking vacantly in front of him, and we heard the steps dying away along the path.

"Who was it ?" I asked, as we rose to our feet.

"I don't know."

The fellow's continual profession of ignorance made me angry.

"Why should you hide yourself, then?" I asked, sharply.

"Because Maister Maple told me. He said that I were to meet no one. If I met anyone I should get no pay."

"You met that sailor on the road?"

"Yes, and I think he was one of them."

"One of whom?"

"One of the folk that have come on the fells. They are watchin' Greta House, and Maister Maple is afeard of them. That's why he wanted us to keep clear of them, and that's why I've been a-trying to dodge 'em."

Here was something definite at last. Some body of men were threatening my uncle. The sailor was one of them. The man with the peaked cap—probably a sailor also—was another. I bethought me of Stepney Highway and of the murderous assault made upon my uncle there.

Things were fitting themselves into a connected shape in my mind when a light twinkled over the fell, and my guide informed me that it was Greta. The place lay in a dip among the moors, so that one was very near it before one saw it. A short walk brought us up to the door.

I could see little of the building save that the lamp which shone through a small latticed window showed me dimly that it was both long and lofty. The low door under an overhanging lintel was loosely fitted, and light was bursting out on each side of it. The inmates of this lonely house appeared to be keenly on their guard, for they had heard our footsteps, and we were challenged before we reached the door.

"Who is there?" cried a deep-booming voice, and urgently, "Who is it, I say?"

"It's me, Maister Maple. I have brought the gentleman."

There was a sharp click, and a small wooden shutter flew open in the door. The gleam of a lantern shone upon us for a few seconds. Then the shutter closed again; with a great rasping of locks and clattering of bars, the door was opened, and I saw my uncle standing framed in that vivid yellow square cut out of the darkness.

He was a small, thick man, with a great rounded, bald head and one thin border of gingery curls. It was a fine head, the head of a thinker, but his large white face was heavy and commonplace, with a broad, loose-lipped mouth and two hanging dewlaps on either side of it. His eyes were small and restless, and his light-colored lashes were continually moving. My mother had said once that they reminded her of the legs of a woodlouse, and I saw at the first glance what she meant. I heard also that in Stepney he had learned the language of his customers, and I blushed for our kinship as I listened to his villainous accent. "So, nephew," said he, holding out his hand. "Come in, come in, man, quick, and don't leave the door open. Your mother said you were grown a big lad, and, my word, she 'as a right to say so. 'Ere's a 'alf-crown for you, William, and you can go back again. Put the things down. 'Ere, Enoch, take Mr. John's things, and see that 'is supper is on the table."

As my uncle, after fastening the door, turned to show me into the sitting room, I became aware of his most striking peculiarity. The injuries which he had received some years ago had, as I have already remarked, left one leg several inches shorter than the other. To atone for this he wore one of those enormous wooden soles to his boots which are prescribed by surgeons in such cases. He walked without a limp, but his tread on the stone flooring made a curious clack-click, clack-click, as the wood and the leather alternated. Whenever he moved it was to the rhythm of this singular castanet.

The great kitchen, with its huge fireplace and carved settle corners, showed that this dwelling was an old-time farmhouse. On one side of the room a line of boxes stood all corded and packed. The furniture was scant and plain, but on a trestle table in the center some supper, cold meat, bread, and a jug of beer was laid for me. An elderly man-servant, as manifest a Cockney as his master, waited upon me, while my uncle, sitting in a corner, asked me many questions as to my mother and myself. When my meal was finished he ordered his man Enoch to unpack my gun. I observed that two other guns, old rusted weapons, were leaning against the wall beside the window.

"It's the window I'm afraid of," said my uncle, in the deep, reverberant voice which contrasted oddly with his plump little figure. "The door's safe against anything short of dynamite, but the window's a terror. Hi! hi!" he yelled, "don't walk across the light! You can duck when you pass the lattice."

"For fear of being seen?" I asked.

"For fear of bein' shot, my lad. That's the trouble. Now, come an' sit beside me on the trestle 'ere, and I'll tell you all about it, for I can see that you are the right sort and can be trusted."

His flattery was clumsy and halting, and it was evident that he was very eager to conciliate me. I sat down beside him, and he drew a folded paper from his pocket. It was a *Western Morning News*, and the date was ten days before. The passage over which he pressed a long, black nail was concerned with the release from Dartmoor of a convict named Elias, whose term of sentence had been remitted on account of his defense of a warder who had been attacked in the quarries. The whole account was only a few lines long.

"Who is he, then?" I asked.

My uncle cocked his distorted foot into the air. "That's 'is mark!" said he. " 'E was doin' time for that. Now 'e's out an' after me again."

"But why should he be after you?"

"Because 'e wants to kill me. Because 'e'll never rest, the worrying devil, until 'e's 'as 'ad 'is revenge on me. It's this way, nephew! I've no secrets from you. 'E thinks I've wronged 'im. For argument's sake we'll suppose I 'ave wronged 'im. And now 'im and 'is friends are after me."

"Who are his friends?"

My uncle's boom sank suddenly to a frightened whisper. "Sailors!" said he. "I knew they would come when I saw that 'ere paper and two days ago I looked through that window and three of them was standin' lookin' at the 'ouse. It was after that that I wrote to your mother. They've marked me down, and they're waitin' for 'im."

"But why not send for the police?"

My uncle's eyes avoided mine.

"Police are no use," said he. "It's you that can help me."

"What can I do?"

"I'll tell you. I'm going to move. That's what all these boxes are for. Everything will soon be packed and ready. I 'ave friends at Leeds, and I shall be safer there. Not safe, mind you, but safer. I start tomorrow evening, and if you will stand by me until then I will make it worth your while. There's only Enoch and me to do everything, but we shall 'ave it all ready, I promise you, by tomorrow evening. The cart will be round then, and you and me and Enoch and the boy William can guard the things as far as Congleton station. Did you see anything of them on the fells?"

"Yes," said I; "a sailor stopped us on the way."

"Ah, I knew they were watching us. That was why I asked you to get out at the wrong station and to drive to Purcell's instead of comin' 'ere. We are blockaded—that's the word."

"And there was another," said I, "a man with a pipe."

"What was 'e like?"

"Thin face, freckles, a peaked—"

My uncle gave a hoarse scream.

"That's 'im! that's 'im! 'e's come! God be merciful to me, a sinner!" He went click-clacking about the room with his great foot like one distracted. There was something piteous and baby-like in that big bald head, and for the first time I felt a gush of pity for him.

"Come, uncle," said I, "you are living in a civilized land. There is a law that will bring these gentry to order. Let me drive over to the county police station tomorrow morning and I'll soon set things right."

But he shook his head at me.

" 'E's cunning and 'e's cruel," said he. "I can't draw a breath without thinking of him, cos 'e buckled up three of my ribs. 'E'll kill me this time, sure. There's only one chance. We must leave what we 'ave not packed, and we must be off first thing tomorrow mornin'. Great God, what's that!"

A tremendous knock upon the door had reverberated through the house and then another and another. An iron fist seemed to be beating upon it. My uncle collapsed into his chair. I seized a gun and ran to the door.

"Who's there?" I shouted.

There was no answer.

I opened the shutter and looked out.

No one was there.

And then suddenly I saw that a long slip of paper was protruding through the slit of the door. I held it to the light. In rude but vigorous handwriting the message ran:

"Put them out on the doorstep and save your skin."

"What do they want?" I asked, as I read him the message.

"What they'll never 'ave! No, by the Lord, never!" he cried, with a fine burst of spirit. "'Ere, Enoch! Enoch!"

The old fellow came running to the call.

"Enoch, I've been a good master to you all my life, and it's your turn now. Will you take a risk for me?"

I thought better of my uncle when I saw how readily the man consented. Whomever else he had wronged, this one at least seemed to love him.

"Put your cloak on and your 'at, Enoch, and out with you by the back door. You know the way across the moor to the Purcells'. Tell them that I must 'ave the cart first thing in the mornin', and that Purcell must come with the shepherd as well. We must get clear of this or we are done. First thing in the mornin', Enoch, and ten pound for the job. Keep the black cloak on and move slow, and they will never see you. We'll keep the 'ouse till you come back."

It was a job for a brave man to venture out into the vague and invisible dangers of the fell, but the old servant took it as the most ordinary of messages. Picking his long, black cloak and his soft hat from the hook behind the door, he was ready on the instant. We extinguished the small lamp in the back passage, softly unbarred the back door, slipped him out, and barred it up again. Looking through the small hall window, I saw his black garments merge instantly into the night.

"It is but a few hours before the light comes, nephew," said my uncle, after he had tried all the bolts and bars. "You shall never regret this night's work. If we come through safely it will be the making of you. Stand by me till mornin', and I stand by you while there's breath in my body. The cart will be 'ere by five. What isn't ready we can afford to leave be'ind. We've only to load up and make for the early train at Congleton."

"Will they let us pass?"

"In broad daylight they dare not stop us. There will be six of us, if they all come, and three guns. We can fight our way through. Where can they get guns, common, wandering seamen? A pistol or two at the most. If we can keep them out for a few hours we are safe. Enoch must be 'alfway to Purcell's by now."

"But what do these sailors want?" I repeated. "You say yourself that you wronged them."

A look of mulish obstinacy came over his large, white face.

"Don't ask questions, nephew, and just do what I ask you," said he. "Enoch won't come back. 'E'll just bide there and come with the cart. 'Ark, what is that?"

A distant cry rang from out of the darkness, and then another one, short and sharp like the wail of the curlew.

"It's Enoch!" said my uncle, gripping my arm. "They're killin' poor old Enoch."

The cry came again, much nearer, and I heard the sound of hurrying steps and a shrill call for help.

"They are after 'im!" cried my uncle, rushing to the front door. He picked up the lantern and flashed it through the little shutter. Up the yellow funnel of light a man was running frantically, his head bowed and a black cloak fluttering behind him. The moor seemed to be alive with dim pursuers.

"The bolt! The bolt!" gasped my uncle. He pushed it back whilst I turned the key, and we swung the door open to admit the fugitive. He dashed in and turned at once with a long yell of triumph. "Come on, lads! Tumble up, all hands, tumble up! Smartly there, all of you!"

It was so quickly and neatly done that we were taken by storm before we knew that we were attacked. The passage was full of rushing sailors. I slipped out of the clutch of one and ran for my gun, but it was only to crash down onto the stone floor an instant later with two of them holding on to me. They were so deft and quick that my hands were lashed together even while I struggled, and I was dragged into the settle corner, unhurt but very sore in spirit at the cunning with which our defences had been forced and the ease with which we had been over-come. They had not even troubled to bind my uncle, but he had been pushed into his chair, and the guns had been taken away. He sat with a very white face, his homely figure and absurd row of curls looking curiously out of place among the wild figures who surrounded him.

There were six of them, all evidently sailors. One I recognized as the man with the earrings whom I had already met upon the road that evening. They were all fine, weather-bronzed bewhiskered fellows. In the midst of them, leaning against the table, was the freckled man who had passed me on the moor. The great black cloak which poor Enoch had taken out with him was still hanging from his shoulders. He was of a very different type from the others—crafty, cruel, dangerous, with sly, thoughtful eyes which gloated over my uncle. They suddenly turned themselves upon me and I never knew how one's skin can creep at a man's glance before.

"Who are you?" he asked. "Speak out, or we'll find a way to make you."

"I am Mr. Stephen Maple's nephew, come to visit him."

"You are, are you? Well, I wish you joy of your uncle and of your visit too. Quick's the word, lads, for we must be aboard before morning. What shall we do with the old 'un?"

"Trice him up Yankee fashion and give him six dozen," said one of the seamen.

"D'you hear, you cursed Cockney thief? We'll beat the life out of you if you don't give back what you've stolen. Where are they? I know you never parted with them."

My uncle pursed up his lips and shook his head, with a face in which his fear and his obstinacy contended.

"Won't tell, won't you? We'll see about that! Get him ready, Jim!"

One of the seamen seized my uncle, and pulled his coat and shirt over his shoulders. He sat lumped in his chair, his body all creased into white rolls which shivered with cold and with terror.

"Up with him to those hooks."

There were rows of them along the walls where the smoked meat used to be hung. The seamen tied my uncle by the wrists to two of these. Then one of them undid his leather belt.

"The buckle end, Jim," said the captain. "Give him the buckle."

"You cowards," I cried; "to beat an old man!"

"We'll beat a young one next," said he, with a malevolent glance at my corner. "Now, Jim, cut a wad out of him!"

"Give him one more chance!" cried one of the seamen.

"Aye, aye," growled one or two others. "Give the swab a chance!"

"If you turn soft, you may give them up forever," said the captain. "One thing or the other! You must lash it out of him; or you may give up what you took such pains to win and what would make you gentlemen for life—every man of you. There's nothing else for it. Which shall it be?"

"Let him have it," they cried, savagely.

"Then stand clear!" The buckle of the man's belt whined savagely as he whirled it over his shoulder.

But my uncle cried out before the blow fell.

"I can't stand it!" he cried. "Let me down!"

"Where are they, then?"

"I'll show you if you'll let me down."

They cast off the handkerchiefs and he pulled his coat over his fat, round shoulders. The seamen stood round him, the most intense curiosity and excitement upon their swarthy faces.

"No gammon!" cried the man with the freckles. "We'll kill you joint by joint if you try to fool us. Now then! Where are they?"

"In my bedroom."

"Where is that?"

"The room above."

"Whereabouts?"

"In the corner of the oak ark by the bed."

The seamen all rushed to the stair, but the captain called them back.

"We don't leave this cunning old fox behind us. Ha, your face drops at that, does it? By the Lord, I believe you are trying to slip your anchor. Here, lads, make him fast and take him along!"

With a confused trampling of feet they rushed up the stairs, dragging my uncle in the midst of them. For an instant I was alone. My hands were tied, but not my feet. If I could find my way across the moor I might rouse the police and intercept these rascals before they could reach the sea. For a moment I hesitated as to whether I should leave my uncle alone in such a plight. But I should be of more service to him—or, at the worst, to his property—if I went than if I stayed. I rushed to the hall door, and as I reached it I heard a yell above my head, a shattering, splintering noise, and then amid a chorus of shouts a huge weight fell with a horrible thud at my very feet. Never while I live will that squelching thud pass out of my ears. And there, just in front of me, in the lane of light cast by the open door, lay my unhappy uncle, his bald head twisted onto one shoulder, like the wrung neck of a chicken. It needed but a glance to see that his spine was broken and that he was dead.

The gang of seamen had rushed downstairs so quickly that they were clustered at the door and crowding all round me almost as soon I had realized what had occurred.

"It's no doing of ours, mate," said one of them to me. "He hove himself through the window, and that's the truth. Don't you put it down to us."

"He thought he could get to windward of us if once he was out in the dark, you see," said another. "But he came head foremost and broke his bloomin' neck."

"And a blessed good job, too!" cried the chief, with a savage oath. "I'd have done it for him if he hadn't took the lead. Don't make any mistake, my lads, this is murder, and we're all in it, together. There's only one way out of it, and that is to hang together, unless, as the saying goes, you mean to hang apart. There's only one witness—"

He looked at me with his malicious little eyes, and I saw that he had something that gleamed—either a knife or a revolver—in the breast of his pea jacket. Two of the men slipped between us.

"Stow that, Captain Elias," said one of them. "If this old man met his end it is through no fault of ours. The worst we ever meant him was to take some of the skin off his back. But as to this young fellow, we have no quarrel with him—"

"You fool, you may have no quarrel with him, but he has his quarrel with you. He'll swear your life away if you don't silence his tongue. It's his life or ours, and don't you make any mistake."

"Aye, aye, the skipper has the longest head of any of us. Better do what he tells you," cried another.

But my champion, who was the fellow with the earrings, covered me with his own broad chest and swore roundly that no one should lay a finger on me. The others were equally divided, and my fate might have been the cause of a quarrel between them when suddenly the captain gave a cry of delight and amazement which was taken up by the whole gang. I followed their eyes and outstretched fingers, and this was what I saw.

My uncle was lying with his legs outstretched, and the clubfoot was that which was farthest from us. All round this foot a dozen brilliant objects were twinkling and flashing in the yellow light which streamed from the open door. The captain caught up the lantern and held it to the place. The huge sole of his boot had been shattered in the fall, and it was clear now that it had been a hollow box in which he stowed his valuables, for the path was all sprinkled with precious stones. Three which I saw were of an unusual size, and as many as forty, I should think, of fair value. The seamen had cast themselves down and were greedily gathering them up, when my friend with the earrings plucked me by the sleeve.

"Here's your chance, mate," he whispered. "Off you go before worse comes of it."

It was a timely hint, and it did not take me long to act upon it. A few cautious steps and I had passed unobserved beyond the circle of light. Then I set off running, falling and rising and falling again, for no one who has not tried it can tell how hard it is to run over uneven ground with hands which are fastened together. I ran and ran, until for want of breath I could no longer put one foot before the other. But I need not have hurried so, for when I had gone a long way I stopped at last to breathe, and, looking back, I could still see the gleam of the lantern far away, and the outline of the seamen who squatted round it. Then at last this single point of light went suddenly out, and the whole great moor was left in the thickest darkness.

So deftly was I tied, that it took me a long half hour and a broken tooth before I got my hands free. My idea was to make my way across to the Purcells' farm, but north was the same as south under that pitchy sky, and for hours I wandered among the rustling, scuttling sheep without any certainty as to where I was going. When at last there came a glimmer in the east, and the undulating fells, gray with the morning mist, rolled once more to the horizon, I recognized that I was close by Purcell's farm, and there a little in front of me I was startled to see another man walking in the same direction. At first I approached him warily, but before I overtook him I knew by the bent back and tottering step that it was Enoch, the old servant, and right glad i was to see that he was living. He had been knocked down, beaten, and his cloak and hat taken away by these ruffians, and all night he had wandered in the darkness, like myself, in search of help. He burst into tears when I told him of his master's death, and sat hiccoughing with the hard, dry sobs of an old man among the stones upon the moor.

"It's the men of the *Black Mogul*," he said. "Yes, yes, I knew that they would be the end of 'im."

"Who are they?" I asked.

"Well, well, you are one of 'is own folk," said he. " 'E 'as passed away; yes, yes, it is all over and done. I can tell you about it, no man better, but mum's the word with old Enoch unless master wants 'im to speak. But his own nephew who came to 'elp 'im in the hour of need—yes, yes, Mister John, you ought to know.

"It was like this, sir. Your uncle 'ad 'is grocer's business at Stepney, but 'e 'ad another business also. 'E would buy as well as sell, and when 'e bought 'e never asked no questions where the stuff came from. Why should 'e? It wasn't no business of 'is, was it? If folk brought him a stone or a silver plate, what was it to 'im where they got it? That's good sense, and it ought to be good law, as I 'old. Any'ow, it was good enough for us at Stepney.

"Well, there was a steamer came from South Africa what foundered at sea. At least, they say so, and Lloyd's paid the money. She 'ad some very fine diamonds invoiced as being aboard of 'er. Soon after there came the brig *Black Mogul* into the port o' London, with 'er papers all right as 'avin' cleared from Port Elizabeth with a cargo of 'ides. The captain, which 'is name was Elias, 'e came to see the master, and what d'you think that 'e 'ad to sell? Why, sir, as I'm a livin' sinner 'e 'ad a packet of diamonds for all the world just the same as what was lost out o' that there African steamer. 'Ow did 'e get them? I don't know. Master didn't know. 'E didn't seek to know either. The captain 'e was anxious for reasons of 'is own to get them safe, so 'e gave them to master, same as you might put a thing in a bank. But master 'e'd 'ad time to get fond of them, and 'e wasn't over satisfied as to where the *Black Mogul* 'ad been tradin', or where her captain 'ad got the stones, so when 'e come back for them the master 'e said as 'e thought they were best in 'is own 'ands. Mind I don't 'old with it myself, but that was what the master said to Captain Elias in the little back parlor at Stepney. That was 'ow 'e got 'is leg broke and three of his ribs.

"So the captain got jugged for that, and the master, when 'e was able to get about, thought that 'e would 'ave peace for fifteen years, and 'e came away from London because 'e was afraid of the sailor men; but, at the end of five years, the captain was out and after 'im, with as many of 'is crew as 'e could gather. Send for the perlice, you says! Well, there are two sides to that, and the master 'e wasn't much more fond of the perlice than Elias was. But they fair 'emmed master in, as you 'ave seen for yourself, and they bested 'im at last, and the loneliness that 'e thought would be 'is safety 'as proved 'is ruin. Well, well, 'e was 'ard to many, but a good master to me, and it's long before I come on such another."

One word in conclusion. A strange cutter, which had been hanging about the coast, was seen to beat down the Irish Sea that morning, and it is conjectured that Elias and his men were on board of it. At any rate, nothing has been heard of them since. It was shown at the inquest that my uncle had lived in a sordid fashion for years, and he left little behind him. The mere knowledge that he possessed this treasure, which he carried about with him in so extraordinary a fashion, had appeared to be the joy of his life, and he had never, as far as we could learn, tried to realize any of his diamonds. So his disreputable name when living was not atoned for by any posthumous benevolence, and the family, equally scandalized by his life and by his death, have finally buried all memory of the clubfooted grocer of Stepney.

THE SEALED ROOM

A solicitor of an active habit and athletic tastes who is compelled by his hopes of business to remain within the four walls of his office from ten till five must take what exercise he can in the evenings. Hence it was that I was in the habit of indulging in very long nocturnal excursions, in which I sought the heights of Hampstead and Highgate in order to cleanse my system from the impure air of Abchurch Lane. It was in the course of one of these aimless rambles that I first met Felix Stanniford, and so led up to what has been the most extraordinary adventure of my lifetime.

One evening—it was in April or early May of the year 1894—I made my way to the extreme northern fringe of London, and was walking down one of those fine avenues of high brick villas which the huge city is for ever pushing farther and farther out into the country. It was a fine, clear spring night, the moon was shining out of an unclouded sky, and I, having already left many miles behind me, was inclined to walk slowly and look about me. In this contemplative mood, my attention was arrested by one of the houses which I was passing.

It was a very large building, standing in its own grounds, a little back from the road. It was modern in appearance, and yet it was far less so than its neighbors, all of which were crudely and painfully new. Their symmetrical line was broken by the gap caused by the laurel-studded lawn, with the great, dark, gloomy house looming at the back of it.

Evidently it had been the country retreat of some wealthy merchant, built perhaps when the nearest street was a mile off, and now gradually overtaken and surrounded by the red brick tentacles of the London octopus. The next stage, I reflected, would be its digestion and absorption, so that the cheap builder might rear a dozen eighty-pound-a-year villas upon the garden frontage. And then, as all this passed vaguely, through my mind, an incident occurred which brought my thoughts into quite another channel.

A four-wheeled cab, that opprobrium of London, was coming jolting and creaking in one direction, while in the other there was a yellow glare from the lamp of a cyclist. They were the only moving objects in the whole long, moonlit road, and yet they crashed into each other with that malignant accuracy which brings two ocean liners together in the broad waste of the Atlantic. It was the cyclist's fault. He tried to cross in front of the cab, miscalculated his distance, and was knocked sprawling by the horse's shoulder. He rose, snarling; the cabman back at him, and then, realizing that his number had not yet been taken, lashed his horse and lumbered off. The cyclist caught at the handles of his prostrate machine, and then suddenly sat down with a groan. "Oh, Lord!" he said.

I ran across the road to his side. "Any harm done?" I asked.

"It's my ankle," said he. "Only a twist, I think; but it's pretty painful. Just give me your hand, will you?"

He lay in the yellow circle of the cycle lamp, and I noted as I helped him to his feet that he was a gentlemanly young fellow, with a slight dark mustache and large, brown eyes, sensitive and nervous in appearance, with indications of weak health upon his sunken cheeks. Work or worry had left its traces upon his thin, yellow face. He stood up when I pulled his hand, but he held one foot in the air, and he groaned as he moved it.

"I can't put it to the ground," said he.

"Where do you live?"

"Here." He nodded his head towards the big, dark house in the garden. "I was cutting across to the gate when that confounded cab ran into me. Could you help me so far?"

It was easily done. I put his cycle inside the gate, and then I supported him down the drive, and up the steps to the hall door. There was not a light anywhere, and the place was as black and silent as if no one had ever lived in it.

"That will do. Thank you very much," said he, fumbling with his key in the lock.

"No, you must allow me to see you safe."

He made some feeble, petulant protest, and then realized that he could really do nothing without me. The door had opened into a pitch-dark hall. He lurched forward, with my hand still on his arm.

"This door to the right," said he, feeling about in the darkness.

I opened the door, and at the same moment he managed to strike a light. There was a lamp upon the table, and we lit it between us. "Now, I'm all right. You can leave me now! Good-bye!" said he, and with the words he sat down in the armchair and fainted dead away.

It was a queer position for me. The fellow looked so ghastly, that really I was not sure that he was not dead. Presently his lips quivered and his breast heaved, but his eyes were two white slits and his color was horrible. The responsibility was more than I could stand. I pulled at the bell rope, and heard the bell ringing furiously far away. But no one came in response. The bell tinkled away into silence which no murmur or movement came to break. I waited, and rang again, with the same result. There must be someone about. This young gentleman could not live all alone in that huge house. His people ought to know of his condition. If they would not answer the bell, I must hunt them out myself. I seized the lamp and rushed from the room.

What I saw outside amazed me. The hall was empty. The stairs were bare, and yellow with dust. There were three doors opening into spacious rooms, and each was uncarpeted and undraped, save for the gray webs which drooped from the cornice, and rosettes of lichen which had formed upon the walls. My feet reverberated in those empty and silent chambers. Then I wandered on down the passage, with the idea that the kitchens, at least, might be tenanted. Some caretaker might lurk in some secluded room. No, they were all equally desolate. Despairing of finding any help, I ran down another corridor, and came on something which surprised me more than ever.

The passage ended in a large, brown door, and the door had a seal of red wax the size of a five-shilling piece over the keyhole. This seal gave me the impression of having been there for a long time, for it was dusty and discolored. I was still staring at it, and wondering what that door might conceal, when I heard a voice calling behind me, and, running back, found my young man sitting up in his chair and very much astonished at finding himself in darkness.

"Why on earth did you take the lamp away?" he asked.

"I was looking for assistance."

"You might look for some time," said he. "I am alone in the house."

"Awkward if you get an illness."

"It was foolish of me to faint. I inherit a weak heart from my mother, and pain or emotion has that effect upon me. It will carry me off someday, as it did her. You're not a doctor, are you?"

"No, a lawyer. Frank Alder is my name."

"Mine is Felix Stanniford. Funny that I should meet a lawyer, for my friend, Mr. Perceval, was saying that we should need one soon."

"Very happy, I am sure."

"Well, that will depend upon him, you know. Did you say that you had run with that lamp all over the ground floor?"

"Yes."

"*All* over it?" he asked, with emphasis, and he looked at me very hard.

"I think so. I kept on hoping that I should find someone."

"Did you enter all the rooms?" he asked, with the same intent gaze.

"Well, all that I could enter."

"Oh, then you *did* notice it!" said he, and he shrugged his shoulders with the air of a man who makes the best of a bad job.

"Notice what?"

"Why, the door with the seal on it."

"Yes, I did."

"Weren't you curious to know what was in it?"

"Well, it did strike me as unusual."

"Do you think you could go on living alone in this house, year after year, just longing all the time to know what is at the other side of that door, and yet not looking?"

"Do you mean to say," I cried, "that you don't know yourself?"

"No more than you do."

"Then why don't you look?"

"I mustn't," said he.

He spoke in a constrained way, and I saw that I had blundered on to some delicate ground. I don't know that I am more inquisitive than my neighbors, but there certainly was something in the situation which appealed very strongly to my curiosity. However, my last excuse for remaining in the house was gone now that my companion had recovered his senses. I rose to go.

"Are you in a hurry?" he asked.

"No; I have nothing to do."

"Well, I should be very glad if you would stay with me a little. The fact is that I live a very retired and secluded life here. I don't suppose there is a man in London who leads such a life as I do. It is quite unusual for me to have anyone to talk with."

I looked round at the little room, scantily furnished, with a sofa bed at one side. Then I thought of the great, bare house, and the sinister door with the discolored red seal upon it. There was something queer and grotesque in the situation, which made me long to know a little more. Perhaps I should, if I waited. I told him that I should be very happy.

"You will find the spirits and a siphon upon the side table. You must forgive me if I cannot act as host, but I can't get across the room. Those are cigars in the tray there. I'll take one myself, I think. And so you are a solicitor, Mr. Alder?"

"Yes."

"And I am nothing. I am that most helpless of living creatures, the son of a millionaire. I was brought up with the expectation of great wealth; and here I am, a poor man, without any profession at all. And then, on the top of it all, I am left with this great mansion on my hands, which I cannot possibly keep up. Isn't it an absurd situation? For me to use this as my dwelling is like a coster drawing his barrow with a thoroughbred. A donkey would be more useful to him, and a cottage to me."

"But why not sell the house?" I asked.

"I mustn't."

"Let it, then?"

"No, I musn't do that either."

I looked puzzled, and my companion smiled.

"I'll tell you how it is, if it won't bore you," said he.

"On the contrary, I should be exceedingly interested."

"I think, after your kind attention to me, I cannot do less than relieve any curiosity that you may feel. You must know that my father was Stanislaus Stanniford, the banker."

Stanniford, the banker! I remembered the name at once. His flight from the country some seven years before had been one of the scandals and sensations of the time.

"I see that you remember," said my companion. "My poor father left the country to avoid numerous friends, whose savings he had invested in an unsuccessful speculation. He was a nervous, sensitive man, and the responsibility quite upset his reason. He had committed no legal offence. It was purely a matter of sentiment. He would not even face his own family, and he died among strangers without ever letting us know where he was."

"He died?" said I.

"We could not prove his death, but we know that it must be so, because the speculations came right again, and so there was no reason why he should not look any man in the face. He would have returned if he were alive. But he must have died in the last two years."

"Why in the last two years?"

"Because we heard from him two years ago."

"Did he not tell you then where he was living?"

"The letter came from Paris, but no address was given. It was when my poor mother died. He wrote to me then, with some instructions and some advice, and I have never heard from him since."

"Had you heard before?"

"Oh, yes, we had heard before, and that's where our mystery of the sealed door, upon which you stumbled tonight, has its origin. Pass me that desk, if you please. Here I have my father's letters, and you are the first man except Mr. Perceval who has seen them."

"Who is Mr. Perceval, may I ask ?"

"He was my father's confidential clerk, and he has continued to be the friend and adviser of my mother and then of myself. I don't know what we should have done without Perceval. He saw the letters, but no one else. This is the first one, which came on the very day when my father fled, seven years ago. Read it to yourself."

This is the letter which I read:

MY EVER DEAREST WIFE,

Since Sir William told me how weak your heart is, and how harmful any shock might be, I have never talked about my business affairs to you. The time has come when at all risks I can no longer refrain from telling you that things have been going badly with me. This will cause me to leave you for a little time, but it is with the absolute assurance that we shall see each other very soon. On this you can thoroughly rely. Our parting is only for a very short time, my own darling, so don't let it fret you, and above all don't let it impair your health, for that is what I want above all things to avoid.

Now, I have a request to make, and I implore you by all that binds us together to fulfill it exactly as I tell you. There are some things which I do not wish to be seen by anyone in my darkroom — the room which I use for photographic purposes at the end of the garden passage. To prevent any painful thoughts, I may assure you once for all, dear, that it is nothing of which I need be ashamed. But still I do not wish you or Felix to enter that room. It is locked, and I implore you when you receive this to at once place a seal over the lock, and leave it so. Do not sell or let the house, for in either case my secret will be discovered. As long as you or Felix are in the house, I know that you will comply with my wishes. When Felix is twenty-one he may enter the room—not before.

And now, good-bye, my own best of wives. During our short

separation you can consult Mr. Perceval on any matters which may
arise. He has my complete confidence. I hate to leave Felix and
you—even for a time—but there is really no choice.

Ever and always your loving husband,
STANISLAUS STANNIFORD.

June 4th, 1887.

"These are very private family matters for me to inflict upon you,"
said my companion, apologetically. "You must look upon it as done in
your professional capacity. I have wanted to speak about it for years."

"I am honored by your confidence," I answered, "and exceedingly
interested by the facts."

"My father was a man who was noted for his almost morbid love of
truth. He was always pedantically accurate. When he said, therefore,
that he hoped to see my mother very soon, and when he said that he
had nothing to be ashamed of in that darkroom, you may rely upon it
that he meant it."

"Then what can it be?" I ejaculated.

"Neither my mother nor I could imagine. We carried out his wishes
to the letter, and placed the seal upon the door; there it has been ever
since. My mother lived for five years after my father's disappearance,
although at the time all the doctors said that she could not survive long.
Her heart was terribly diseased. During the first few months she had
two letters from my father. Both had the Paris postmark, but no address.
They were short and to the same effect: that they would soon be reunited, and that she should not fret. Then there was a silence, which
lasted until her death; and then came a letter to me of so private a
nature that I cannot show it to you, begging me never to think evil of
him, giving me much good advice, and saying that the sealing of the
room was of less importance now than during the lifetime of my mother,
but that the opening might still cause pain to others, and that, therefore,
he thought it best that it should be postponed until my twenty-first year,
for the lapse of time would make things easier. In the meantime, he
committed the care of the room to me; so now you can understand how
it is that, although I am a very poor man, I can neither let nor sell this
great house."

"You could mortgage it."

"My father had already done so."

"It is a most singular state of affairs."

"My mother and I were gradually compelled to sell the furniture and to dismiss the servants, until now, as you see, I am living unattended in a single room. But I have only two more months."

"What do you mean?"

"Why, that in two months I come of age. The first thing that I do will be to open that door; the second, to get rid of the house."

"Why should your father have continued to stay away when these investments had recovered themselves?"

"He must be dead."

"You say that he had not committed any legal offence when he fled the country?"

"None."

"Why should he not take your mother with him?"

"I do not know."

"Why should he conceal his address?"

"I do not know."

"Why should he allow your mother to die and be buried without coming back?"

"I do not know."

"My dear sir," said I, "if I may speak with the frankness of a professional adviser, I should say that it is very clear that your father had the strongest reasons for keeping out of the country, and that, if nothing has been proved against him, he at least thought that something might be, and refused to put himself within the power of the law. Surely that must be obvious, for in what other possible way can the facts be explained?"

My companion did not take my suggestion in good part.

"You had not the advantage of knowing my father, Mr. Alder," he said, coldly. "I was only a boy when he left us, but I shall always look upon him as my ideal man. His only fault was that he was too sensitive and too unselfish. That anyone should lose money through him would cut him to the heart. His sense of honor was most acute, and any theory of his disappearance which conflicts with that is a mistaken one."

It pleased me to hear the lad speak out so roundly, and yet I knew that the facts were against him, and that he was incapable of taking an unprejudiced view of the situation.

"I only speak as an outsider," said I. "And now I must leave you, for I have a long walk before me. Your story has interested me so much that I should be glad if you could let me know the sequel."

"Leave me your card," said he; and so, having bade him "Good-night," I left him.

I heard nothing more of the matter for some time, and had almost feared that it would prove to be one of those fleeting experiences which drift away from our direct observation and end only in a hope or a suspicion. One afternoon, however, a card bearing the name of Mr. J. H. Perceval was brought up to my office in Abchurch Lane, and its bearer, a small dry, bright-eyed fellow of fifty, was ushered in by the clerk.

"I believe, sir," said he, "that my name has been mentioned to you by my young friend, Mr. Felix Stanniford?"

"Of course," I answered, "I remember."

"He spoke to you, I understand, about the circumstances in connection with the disappearance of my former employer, Mr. Stanislaus Stanniford, and the existence of a sealed room in his former residence."

"He did."

"'And you expressed an interest in the matter."

"It interested me extremely."

"You are aware that we hold Mr. Stanniford's permission to open the door on the twenty-first birthday of his son?"

"I remember."

"The twenty-first birthday is today."

"Have you opened it?" I asked, eagerly.

"Not yet, sir," said he, gravely. "I have reason to believe that it would be well to have witnesses present when that door is opened. You are a lawyer, and you are acquainted with the facts. Will you be present on the occasion?"

"Most certainly."

"You are employed during the day, and so am I. Shall we meet at nine o'clock at the house?"

"I will come with pleasure."

"Then you will find us waiting for you. Good-bye, for the present." He bowed solemnly, and took his leave.

I kept my appointment that evening, with a brain which was weary with fruitless attempts to think out some plausible explanation of the mystery which we were about to solve. Mr. Perceval and my young acquaintance were waiting for me in the little room. I was not surprised to see the young man looking pale and nervous, but I was rather astonished to find the dry little city man in a state of intense, though partially suppressed, excitement. His cheeks were flushed, his hands twitching, and he could not stand still for an instant.

Stanniford greeted me warmly, and thanked me many times for having come. "And now, Perceval," said he to his companion, "I suppose there is no obstacle to our putting the thing through without delay? I shall be glad to get it over."

The banker's clerk took up the lamp and led the way. But he paused in the passage outside the door, and his hand was shaking, so that the light flickered up and down the high, bare walls.

"Mr. Stanniford," said he, in a cracking voice, "I hope you will prepare yourself in case any shock should be awaiting you when that seal is removed and the door is opened."

"What could there be, Perceval? You are trying to frighten me."

"No, Mr. Stanniford; but I should wish you to be ready . . . to be braced up . . . not to allow yourself. . . ." He had to lick his dry lips between every jerky sentence, and I suddenly realized, as clearly as if he had told me, that he knew what was behind that closed door, and that it *was* something terrible. "Here are the keys, Mr. Stanniford, but remember my warning!"

He had a bunch of assorted keys in his hand, and the young man snatched them from him. Then he thrust a knife under the discolored red seal and jerked it off. The lamp was rattling and shaking in Perceval's hands, so I took it from him and held it near the keyhole, while Stanniford tried key after key. At last one turned in the lock, the door flew open, he took one step into the room, and then, with a horrible cry, the young man fell senseless at our feet.

If I had not given heed to the clerk's warning, and braced myself for a shock, I should certainly have dropped the lamp. The room, windowless and bare, was fitted up as a photographic laboratory, with a tap and sink at the side of it. A shelf of bottles and measures stood at one side, and a peculiar, heavy smell, partly chemical, partly animal, filled the air. A single table and chair were in front of us, and at this, with his back turned towards us, a man was seated in the act of writing. His outline and attitude were as natural as life; but as the light fell upon him, it made my hair rise to see that the nape of his neck was black and wrinkled, and no thicker than my wrist. Dust lay upon him—thick, yellow dust—upon his hair, his shoulders, his shriveled, lemon-colored hands. His head had fallen forward upon his breast. His pen still rested upon a discolored sheet of paper.

"My poor master! My poor, poor master!" cried the clerk, and the tears were running down his cheeks.

"What!" I cried, "Mr. Stanislaus Stanniford!"

"Here he has sat for seven years. Oh, why would he do it? I begged him, I implored him, I went on my knees to him, but he would have his way. You see the key on the table. He had locked the door upon the inside. And he has written something. We must take it."

"Yes, yes, take it, and for God's sake, let us get out of this," I cried;

"the air is poisonous. Come, Stanniford, come!" Taking an arm each, we half led and half carried the terrified man back to his own room.

"It was my father!" he cried, as he recovered his consciousness. "He is sitting there dead in his chair. You knew it, Perceval! This was what you meant when you warned me."

"Yes, I knew it, Mr. Stanniford. I have acted for the best all long, but my position has been a terribly difficult one. For seven years I have known that your father was dead in that room."

"You knew it, and never told us!"

"Don't be harsh with me, Mr. Stanniford, sir! Make allowance for a man who has had a hard part to play."

"My head is swimming round. I cannot grasp it!" He staggered up, and helped himself from the brandy bottle. "These letters to my mother and to myself—were they forgeries?"

"No, sir; your father wrote them and addressed them, and left them in my keeping to be posted. I have followed his instructions to the very letter in all things. He was my master, and I have obeyed him."

The brandy had steadied the young man's shaken nerves. "Tell me about it. I can stand it now," said he.

"Well, Mr. Stanniford, you know that at one time there came a period of great trouble upon your father, and he thought that many poor people were about to lose their savings through his fault. He was a man who was so tenderhearted that he could not bear the thought. It worried him and tormented him, until he determined to end his life. Oh, Mr. Stanniford, if you knew how I have prayed him and wrestled with him over it, you would never blame me! And he in turn prayed me as no man has ever prayed me before. He had made up his mind, and he would do it in any case, he said; but it rested with me whether his death should be happy and easy or whether it should be most miserable. I read in his eyes that he meant what he said. And at last I yielded to his prayers, and I consented to do his will.

"What was troubling him was this. He had been told by the first doctor in London that his wife's heart would fail at the slightest shock. He had a horror of accelerating her end, and yet his own existence had become unendurable to him. How could he end himself without injuring her?

"You know now the course that he took. He wrote the letter which she received. There was nothing in it which was not literally true. When he spoke of seeing her again so soon, he was referring to her own approaching death, which he had been assured could not be delayed more than a very few months. So convinced was he of this, that he only left two letters to be forwarded at intervals after his death. She lived five years, and I had no letters to send.

"He left another letter with me to be sent to you, sir, upon the occasion of the death of your mother. I posted all these in Paris to sustain the idea of his being abroad. It was his wish that I should say nothing, and I have said nothing. I have been a faithful servant. Seven years after his death, he thought no doubt that the shock to the feelings of his surviving friends would be lessened. He was always considerate for others."

There was silence for some time. It was broken by young Stanniford.

"I cannot blame you, Perceval. You have spared my mother a shock, which would certainly have broken her heart. What is that paper?"

"It is what your father was writing, sir. Shall I read it to you?"

"Do so."

" 'I have taken the poison, and I feel it working in my veins. It is strange, but not painful. When these words are read I shall, if my wishes have been faithfully carried out, have been dead many years. Surely no one who has lost money through me will still bear me animosity. And you, Felix, you will forgive me this family scandal. May God find rest for a sorely wearied spirit!' "

"Amen !" we cried, all three.

THE BRAZILIAN CAT

It is hard luck on a young fellow to have expensive tastes, great expectations, aristocratic connections, but no actual money in his pocket, and no profession by which he may earn any. The fact was that my father, a good, sanguine, easy-going man, had such confidence in the wealth and benevolence of his bachelor elder brother, Lord Southerton, that he took it for granted that I, his only son, would never be called upon to earn a living for myself. He imagined that if there were not a vacancy for me on the great Southerton Estates, at least there would be found some post in that diplomatic service which still remains the special preserve of our privileged classes. He died too early to realize how false his calculations had been. Neither my uncle nor the State took the slightest notice of me, or showed any interest in my career. An occasional brace of pheasants, or basket of hares, was all that ever reached me to remind me that I was heir to Otwell House and one of the richest estates in the country. In the meantime, I found myself a bachelor and man about town, living in a suite of apartments in Grosvenor Mansions, with no occupation save that of pigeon shooting and polo playing at Hurlingham. Month by month I realized that it was more and more difficult to get the brokers to renew my bills, or to cash any further post-obits upon an unentailed property. Ruin lay right across my path, and every day I saw it clearer, nearer, and more absolutely unavoidable.

What made me feel my own poverty the more was that, apart from the great wealth of Lord Southerton, all my other relations were fairly well-to-do. The nearest of these was Everard King, my father's nephew and my own first cousin, who had spent an adventurous life in Brazil, and had now returned to this country to settle down on his fortune. We never knew how he made his money, but he appeared to have plenty of it, for he bought the estate of Graylands, near Clipton-on-the-Marsh, in Suffolk. For the first year of his residence in England he took no more notice of me than my miserly uncle; but at last one summer morning, to my very great relief and joy, I received a letter asking me to come down that very day and spend a short visit at Graylands Court. I was expecting a rather long visit to Bankruptcy Court at the time, and this interruption seemed almost providential. If I could only get on terms with this unknown relative of mine, I might pull through yet. For the family credit he could not let me go entirely to the wall. I ordered my valet to pack my valise, and I set off the same evening for Clipton-on-the-Marsh.

After changing at Ipswich, a little local train deposited me at a small, deserted station lying amidst a rolling grassy country, with a sluggish and winding river curving in and out amidst the valleys, between high, silted banks, which showed that we were within reach of the tide. No carriage was awaiting me (I found afterwards that my telegram had been delayed), so I hired a dogcart at the local inn. The driver, an excellent fellow, was full of my relative's praises, and I learned from him that Mr. Everard King was already a name to conjure with in that part of the country. He had entertained the schoolchildren, he had thrown his grounds open to visitors, he had subscribed to charities—in short, his benevolence had been so universal that my driver could only account for it on the supposition that he had Parliamentary ambitions.

My attention was drawn away from my driver's panegyric by the appearance of a very beautiful bird which settled on a telegraph post beside the road. At first I thought that it was a jay, but it was larger, with a brighter plumage. The driver accounted for its presence at once by saying that it belonged to the very man whom we were about to visit. It seems that the acclimatization of foreign creatures was one of his hobbies, and that he had brought with him from Brazil a number of birds and beasts which he was endeavoring to rear in England. When once we had passed the gates of Graylands Park we had ample evidence of this taste of his. Some small spotted deer, a curious wild pig known, I believe, as a peccary, a gorgeously feathered oriole, some sort of armadillo, and a singular lumbering intoed beast like a very fat badger, were among the creatures which I observed as we drove along the winding avenue.

Mr. Everard King, my unknown cousin, was standing in person upon the steps of his house, for he had seen us in the distance, and guessed that it was I. His appearance was very homely and benevolent, short and stout, forty-five years old perhaps, with a round, good-humored face, burned brown with the tropical sun, and shot with a thousand wrinkles. He wore white linen clothes, in true planter style, with a cigar between his lips, and a large Panama hat upon the back of his head. It was such a figure as one associates with a verandahed bungalow, and it looked curiously out of place in front of this broad, stone English mansion, with its solid wings and its Palladio pillars before the doorway.

"My dear!" he cried, glancing over his shoulder; "my dear, here is our guest! Welcome, welcome to Graylands! I am delighted to make your acquaintance, Cousin Marshall, and I take it as a great compliment that you should honor this sleepy little country place with your presence."

Nothing could be more hearty than his manner, and he set me at my ease in an instant. But it needed all his cordiality to atone for the frigidity and even rudeness of his wife, a tall, haggard woman, who came forward at his summons. She was, I believe, of Brazilian extraction, though she spoke excellent English, and I excused her manners on the score of her ignorance of our customs. She did not attempt to conceal, however, either then or afterwards, that I was no very welcome visitor at Graylands Court. Her actual words were, as a rule, courteous, but she was the possessor of a pair of particularly expressive dark eyes, and I read in them very clearly from the first that she heartily wished me back in London once more.

However, my debts were too pressing and my designs upon my wealthy relative were too vital for me to allow them to be upset by the ill-temper of his wife, so I disregarded her coldness and reciprocated the extreme cordiality of his welcome. No pains had been spared by him to make me comfortable. My room was a charming one. He implored me to tell him anything which could add to my happiness. It was on the tip of my tongue to inform him that a blank cheque would materially help towards that end, but I felt that it might be premature in the present state of our acquaintance. The dinner was excellent, and as we sat together afterwards over his Havanas and coffee, which latter he told me was specially prepared upon his own plantation, it seemed to me that all my driver's eulogies were justified, and that I had never met a more large-hearted and hospitable man.

But, in spite of his cheery good nature, he was a man with a strong will and a fiery temper of his own. Of this I had an example upon the following morning. The curious aversion which Mrs. Everard King had conceived towards me was so strong, that her manner at breakfast was almost offensive. But her meaning became unmistakable when her husband had quitted the room.

"The best train in the day is at twelve fifteen," said she.

"But I was not thinking of going today," I answered, frankly—perhaps even defiantly, for I was determined not to be driven out by this woman.

"Oh, if it rests with you—" said she, and stopped, with a most insolent expression in her eyes.

"I am sure," I answered, "that Mr. Everard King would tell me if I were outstaying my welcome."

"What's this? What's this?" said a voice, and there he was in the room. He had overheard my last words, and a glance at our faces had told him the rest. In an instant his chubby, cheery face set into an expression of absolute ferocity.

"Might I trouble you to walk outside, Marshall," said he. (I may mention that my own name is Marshall King.)

He closed the door behind me, and then, for an instant, I heard him talking in a low voice of concentrated passion to his wife. This gross breach of hospitality had evidently hit upon his tenderest point. I am no eavesdropper, so I walked out onto the lawn. Presently I heard a hurried step behind me, and there was the lady, her face pale with excitement, and her eyes red with tears.

"My husband has asked me to apologize to you, Mr. Marshall King," said she, standing with downcast eyes before me.

"Please do not say another word, Mrs. King."

Her dark eyes suddenly blazed out at me.

"You fool!" she hissed, with frantic vehemence, and turning on her heel swept back to the house.

The insult was so outrageous, so insufferable, that I could only stand staring after her in bewilderment. I was still there when my host joined me. He was his cheery, chubby self once more.

"I hope that my wife has apologized for her foolish remarks," said he.

"Oh, yes—yes, certainly!"

He put his hand through my arm and walked with me up and down the lawn.

"You must not take it seriously," said he. "It would grieve me inexpressibly if you curtailed your visit by one hour. The fact is—there is no reason why there should be any concealment between relatives that my poor dear wife is incredibly jealous. She hates that anyone—male or female—should for an instant come between us. Her ideal is a desert island and an eternal tête-à-tête. That gives you the clue to her actions, which are, I confess, upon this particular point, not very far removed from mania. Tell me that you will think no more of it."

"No, no; certainly not."

"Then light this cigar and come round with me and see my little menagerie."

The whole afternoon was occupied by this inspection, which included all the birds, beasts, and even reptiles which he had imported. Some were free, some in cages, a few actually in the house. He spoke with enthusiasm of his successes and his failures, his births and his deaths, and he would cry out in his delight, like a schoolboy, when, as we walked, some gaudy bird would flutter up from the grass, or some curious beast slink into the cover. Finally he led me down a corridor which extended from one wing of the house. At the end of this there was a heavy door with a sliding shutter in it, and beside it there projected from the wall an iron handle attached to a wheel and a drum. A line of stout bars extended across the passage.

"I am about to show you the jewel of my collection," said he. "There is only one other specimen in Europe, now that the Rotterdam cub is dead. It is a Brazilian cat."

"But how does that differ from any other cat?"

"You will soon see that," said he, laughing. "Will you kindly draw that shutter and look through?"

I did so, and found that I was gazing into a large, empty room, with stone flags, and small, barred windows upon the farther wall.

In the center of this room, lying in the middle of a golden patch of sunlight, there was stretched a huge creature, as large as a tiger, but as black and sleek as ebony. It was simply a very enormous and very well-kept black cat, and it cuddled up and basked in that yellow pool of light exactly as a cat would do. It was so graceful, so sinewy, and so gently and smoothly diabolical, that I could not take my eyes from the opening.

"Isn't he splendid?" said my host, enthusiastically.

"Glorious! I never saw such a noble creature."

"Some people call it a black puma, but really it is not a puma at all. That fellow is nearly eleven feet from tail to tip. Four years ago he was a little ball of black fluff, with two yellow eyes staring out of it. He was sold me as a new-born cub up in the wild country at the headwaters of the Rio Negro. They speared his mother to death after she had killed a dozen of them."

"They are ferocious, then?"

"The most absolutely treacherous and bloodthirsty creatures upon earth. You talk about a Brazilian cat to an up-country Indian, and see him get the jumps. They prefer humans to game. This fellow has never tasted living blood yet, but when he does he will be a terror. At present he won't stand anyone but me in his den. Even Baldwin, the groom, dare not go near him. As to me, I am his mother and father in one."

As he spoke he suddenly, to my astonishment, opened the door and slipped in, closing it instantly behind him. At the sound of his voice the huge, lithe creature rose, yawned, and rubbed its round, black head affectionately against his side, while he patted and fondled it.

"Now, Tommy, into your cage!" said he.

The monstrous cat walked over to one side of the room and coiled itself up under a grating. Everard King came out, and taking the iron handle which I have mentioned, he began to turn it. As he did so the line of bars in the corridor began to pass through a slot in the wall and closed up the front of this grating, so as to make an effective cage. When it was in position he opened the door once more and invited me into the room, which was heavy with the pungent, musty smell peculiar to the great carnivora.

"That's how we work it," said he. "We give him the run of the room for exercise, and then at night we put him in his cage. You can let him out by turning the handle from the passage, or you can, as you have seen, coop him up in the same way. No, no, you should not do that!"

I had put my hand between the bars to pat the glossy, heaving flank. He pulled it back, with a serious face.

"I assure you that he is not safe. Don't imagine that because I can take liberties with him anyone else can. He is very exclusive in his friends—aren't you, Tommy? Ah, he hears his lunch coming to him! Don't you, boy?"

A step sounded in the stone-flagged passage, and the creature had sprung to his feet, and was pacing up and down the narrow cage, his yellow eyes gleaming, and his scarlet tongue rippling and quivering over the white line of his jagged teeth. A groom entered with a coarse joint upon a tray and thrust it through the bars to him. He pounced lightly upon it, carried it off to the corner, and there, holding it between his paws, tore and wrenched at it, raising his bloody muzzle every now and then to look at us. It was a malignant and yet fascinating sight.

"You can't wonder that I am fond of him, can you?" said my host, as we left the room, "especially when you consider that I have had the rearing of him. It was no joke bringing him over from the center of South America; but here he is safe and sound—and, as I have said, far the most perfect specimen in Europe. The people at the Zoo are dying to have him, but I really can't part with him. Now, I think that I have inflicted my hobby upon you long enough, so we cannot do better than follow Tommy's example, and go to our lunch."

My South American relative was so engrossed by his grounds and their curious occupants, that I hardly gave him credit at first for having any interests outside them. That he had some, and pressing ones, was soon borne in upon me by the number of telegrams which he received. They arrived at all hours, and were always opened by him with the utmost eagerness and anxiety upon his face. Sometimes I imagined that it must be the turf, and sometimes the Stock Exchange, but certainly he had some very urgent business going forward which was not transacted upon the Downs of Suffolk. During the six days of my visit he had never fewer than three or four telegrams a day, and sometimes as many as seven or eight.

I had occupied these six days so well, that by the end of them I had succeeded in getting upon the most cordial terms with my cousin. Every night we had sat up late in the billiard room, he telling me the most extraordinary stories of his adventures in America—stories so desperate and reckless, that I could hardly associate them with the brown little chubby man before me. In return, I ventured upon some of my own reminiscences of London life, which interested him so much, that he vowed he would come up to Grosvenor Mansions and stay with me. He was anxious to see the faster side of city life, and certainly, though I say it, he could not have chosen a more competent guide. It was not until the last day of my visit that I ventured to approach that which was on my mind. I told him frankly about my pecuniary difficulties and my impending ruin, and I asked his advice—though I hoped for something more solid. He listened attentively, puffing hard at his cigar.

"But surely," said he, "you are the heir of our relative, Lord Southerton?"

"I have every reason to believe so, but he would never make me any allowance."

"No, no, I have heard of his miserly ways. My poor Marshall, your position has been a very hard one. By the way, have you heard any news of Lord Southerton's health lately?"

"He has always been in a critical condition ever since my childhood."

"Exactly—a creaking hinge, if ever there was one. Your inheritance may be a long way off. Dear me, how awkwardly situated you are!"

"I had some hopes, sir, that you, knowing all the facts, might be inclined to advance—"

"Don't say another word, my dear boy," he cried, with the utmost cordiality; "we shall talk it over tonight, and I give you my word that whatever is in my power shall be done."

I was not sorry that my visit was drawing to a close, for it is unpleasant to feel that there is one person in the house who eagerly desires your departure. Mrs. King's sallow face and forbidding eyes had become more and more hateful to me. She was no longer actively rude—her fear of her husband prevented her—but she pushed her insane jealousy to the extent of ignoring me, never addressing me, and in every way making my stay at Graylands as uncomfortable as she could. So offensive was her manner during that last day that I should certainly have left had it not been for that interview with my host in the evening which would, and I hoped, retrieve my broken fortunes.

It was very late when it occurred, for my relative, who had been receiving even more telegrams than usual during the day, went off to his study after dinner, and only emerged when the household had retired to bed. I heard him go round locking the doors, as his custom was of a night, and finally he joined me in the billiard room. His stout figure was wrapped in a dressing gown, and he wore a pair of red Turkish slippers without any heels. Settling down into an armchair, he brewed himself a glass of grog, in which I could not help noticing that the whisky considerably predominated over the water.

"My word!" said he, "what a night!"

It was, indeed. The wind was howling and screaming round the house, and the latticed windows rattled and shook as if they were coming in. The glow of the yellow lamps and the flavor of our cigars seemed the brighter and more fragrant for the contrast.

"Now, my boy," said my host, "we have the house and the night to ourselves. Let me have an idea of how your affairs stand, and I will see what can be done to set them in order. I wish to hear every detail."

Thus encouraged, I entered into a long exposition, in which all my tradesmen and creditors, from my landlord to my valet, figured in turn. I had notes in my pocketbook, and I marshaled my facts, and gave, I flatter myself, a very business-like statement of my own unbusiness-like ways and lamentable position. I was depressed, however, to notice that my companion's eyes were vacant and his attention elsewhere. When he did occasionally throw out a remark, it was so entirely perfunctory and pointless that I was sure he had not in the least followed my remarks. Every now and then he roused himself and put on some show of interest, asking me to repeat or to explain more fully, but it was always to sink once more into the same brown study. At last he rose and threw the end of his cigar into the grate.

"I'll tell you what, my boy," said he. "I never had a head for figures, so you will excuse me. You must jot it all down upon paper, and let me have a note of the amount. I'll understand it when I see it in black and white."

The proposal was encouraging. I promised to do so.

"And now it's time we were in bed. By Jove, there's one o'clock striking in the hall."

The tinging of the chiming clock broke through the deep roar of the gale. The wind was sweeping past with the rush of a great river.

"I must see my cat before I go to bed," said my host. "A high wind excites him. Will you come?"

"Certainly," said I.

"Then tread softly and don't speak, for everyone is asleep."

We passed quietly down the lamp-lit Persian-rugged hall, and through the door at the farther end. All was dark in the stone corridor, but a stable lantern hung on a hook, and my host took it down and lit it. There was no grating visible in the passage, so I knew that the beast was in its cage.

"Come in!" said my relative, and opened the door.

A deep growling as we entered showed that the storm had really excited the creature. In the flickering light of the lantern, we saw it, a huge black mass, coiled in the corner of its den and throwing a squat, uncouth shadow upon the whitewashed wall. Its tail switched angrily among the straw.

"Poor Tommy is not in the best of tempers," said Everard King, holding up the lantern and looking in at him. "What a black devil he looks, doesn't he? I must give him a little supper to put him in a better humor. Would you mind holding the lantern for a moment?"

I took it from his hand and he stepped to the door.

"His larder is just outside here," said he. "You will excuse me for an instant, won't you?" He passed out, and the door shut with a sharp metallic click behind him.

That hard crisp sound made my heart stand still. A sudden wave of terror passed over me. A vague perception of some monstrous treachery turned me cold. I sprang to the door, but there was no handle upon the inner side.

"Here," I cried. "Let me out!"

"All right! Don't make a row!" said my host from the passage. "You've got the light all right."

"Yes, but I don't care about being locked in alone like this."

"Don't you?" I heard his hearty, chuckling laugh. "You won't be alone long."

"Let me out, sir!" I repeated angrily. "I tell you I don't allow practical jokes of this sort."

"Practical is the word," said he, with another hateful chuckle. And then suddenly I heard, amidst the roar of the storm, the creak and whine of the winch handle turning, and the rattle of the grating as it passed through the slot. Great God, he was letting loose the Brazilian cat!

In the light of the lantern I saw the bars sliding slowly before me. Already there was an opening a foot wide at the farther end. With a scream I seized the last bar with my hands and pulled with the strength of a madman. I *was* a madman with rage and horror. For a minute or more I held the thing motionless. I knew that he was straining with all his force upon the handle, and that the leverage was sure to overcome me. I gave inch by inch, my feet sliding along the stones, and all the time I begged and prayed this inhuman monster to save me from this horrible death. I conjured him by his kinship. I reminded him that I was his guest; I begged to know what harm I had ever done him. His only answers were the tugs and jerks upon the handle, each of which, in spite of all my struggles, pulled another bar through the opening. Clinging and clutching, I was dragged across the whole front of the cage, until at last, with aching wrists and lacerated fingers, I gave up the hopeless struggle. The grating clanged back as I released it, and an instant later I heard the shuffle of the Turkish slippers in the passage, and the slam of the distant door. Then everything was silent.

The creature had never moved during this time. He lay still in the corner, and his tail had ceased switching. This apparition of a man adhering to his bars and dragged screaming across him had apparently filled him with amazement. I saw his great eyes staring steadily at me. I had dropped the lantern when I seized the bars, but it still burned upon the floor, and I made a movement to grasp it, with some idea that its light might protect me. But the instant I moved, the beast gave a deep and menacing growl. I stopped and stood still, quivering with fear in every limb. The cat (if one may call so fearful a creature by so homely a name) was not more than ten feet from me. The eyes glimmered like two discs of phosphorus in the darkness. They appalled and yet fascinated me. I could not take my own eyes from them. Nature plays strange tricks with us at such moments of intensity, and those glimmery lights waxed and waned with a steady rise and fall. Sometimes they seemed to be tiny points of extreme brilliancy—little electric sparks in the black obscurity—then they would widen and widen until all that corner of the room was filled with their shifting and sinister light. And then suddenly they went out altogether.

The beast had closed its eyes. I do not know whether there may be any truth in the old idea of the dominance of the human gaze, or whether the huge cat was simply drowsy, but the fact remains that, far from showing any symptom of attacking me, it simply rested its sleek, black head upon its huge forepaws and seemed to sleep. I stood, fearing to move lest I should rouse it into malignant life once more. But at least I was able to think clearly now that the baleful eyes were off me. Here I was shut up for the night with the ferocious beast. My own instincts, to say nothing of the words of the plausible villain who laid this trap for me, warned me that the animal was as savage as its master. How could I stave it off until morning? The door was hopeless, and so were the narrow, barred windows. There was no shelter anywhere in the bare, stone-flagged room. To cry for assistance was absurd. I knew that this den was an outhouse, and that the corridor which connected it with the house was at least a hundred feet long. Besides, with that gale thundering outside, my cries were not likely to be heard. I had only my own courage and my own wits to trust to.

And then, with a fresh wave of horror, my eyes fell upon the lantern. The candle had burned low, and was already beginning to gutter. In ten minutes it would be out. I had only ten minutes then in which to do something, for I felt that if I were once left in the dark with that fearful beast I should be incapable of action. The very thought of it paralyzed me. I cast my despairing eyes round this chamber of death, and they rested upon one spot which seemed to promise—I will not say safety, but less immediate and imminent danger than the open floor.

I have said that the cage had a top as well as a front, and this top was left standing when the front was wound through the slot in the wall. It consisted of bars at a few inches' interval, with stout wire netting between, and it rested upon a strong stanchion at each end. It stood now as a great barred canopy over the crouching figure in the corner. The space between this iron shelf and the roof may have been from two to three feet. If I could only get there, squeezed in between bars and ceiling, I should have only one vulnerable side. I should be safe from below, from behind, and from each side. Only on the open face of it could I be attacked. There, it is true, I had no protection whatever; but, at least, I should be out of the brute's path when he began to pace about his den. He would have to come out of his way to reach me. It was now or never, for if once the light were out it would be impossible. With a gulp in my throat I sprang up, seized the iron edge of the top, and swung myself panting onto it. I writhed in face downwards, and found myself looking straight into the terrible eyes and yawning jaws of the cat. Its fetid breath came up into my face like the steam from some foul pot.

It appeared, however, to be rather curious than angry. With a sleek ripple of its long, black back it rose, stretched itself, and then rearing itself on its hind legs, with one forepaw against the wall, it raised the other, and drew its claws across the wire meshes beneath me. One sharp, white hook tore through my trousers—for I may mention that I was still in evening dress—and dug a furrow in my knee. It was not meant as an attack, but rather as an experiment, for upon my giving a sharp cry of pain he dropped down again, and springing lightly into the room, he began walking swiftly round it, looking up every now and again in my direction. For my part I shuffled backwards until I lay with my back against the wall, screwing myself into the smallest space possible. The farther I got the more difficult it was for him to attack me.

He seemed more excited now that he had begun to move about, and he ran swiftly and noiselessly round and round the den, passing continually underneath the iron couch upon which I lay. It was wonderful to see so great a bulk passing like a shadow, with hardly the softest thudding of velvety pads. The candle was burning low—so low that I could hardly see the creature. And then, with a last flare and splutter it went out altogether. I was alone with the cat in the dark!

It helps one to face a danger when one knows that one has done all that possibly can be done. There is nothing for it then but to quietly await the result. In this case, there was no chance of safety anywhere except the precise spot where I was. I stretched myself out, therefore, and lay silently, almost breathlessly, hoping that the beast might forget my presence if I did nothing to remind him. I reckoned that it must already be two o'clock. At four it would be full dawn. I had not more than two hours to wait for daylight.

Outside, the storm was still raging, and the rain lashed continually against the little windows. Inside, the poisonous and fetid air was overpowering. I could neither hear nor see the cat. I tried to think about other things—but only one had power enough to draw my mind from my terrible position. That was the contemplation of my cousin's villainy, his unparalleled hypocrisy, his malignant hatred of me. Beneath that cheerful face there lurked the spirit of a mediæval assassin. And as I thought of it I saw more clearly how cunningly the thing had been arranged. He had apparently gone to bed with the others. No doubt he had his witnesses to prove it. Then, unknown to them, he had slipped down, had lured me into this den and abandoned me. His story would be so simple. He had left me to finish my cigar in the billiard room. I had gone down my own account to have a last look at the cat. I had entered the room without observing that the cage was opened, and I had been caught. How could such a crime be brought home to him? Suspicion, perhaps—but proof, never!

How slowly those dreadful two hours went by! Once I heard a low, rasping sound, which I took to be the creature licking its own fur. Several times those greenish eyes gleamed at me through the darkness, but never in a fixed stare, and my hopes grew stronger that my presence had been forgotten or ignored. At last the least faint glimmer of light came through the windows—I first dimly saw them as two gray squares upon the black wall, then gray turned to white, and I could see my terrible companion once more. And he, alas, could see me!

It was evident to me at once that he was in a much more dangerous and aggressive mood than when I had seen him last. The cold of the morning had irritated him, and he was hungry as well. With a continual growl he paced swiftly up and down the side of the room which was farthest from my refuge, his whiskers bristling angrily and his tail switching and lashing. As he turned at the corners his savage eyes always looked upwards at me with a dreadful menace. I knew then that he meant to kill me. Yet I found myself even at that moment admiring the sinuous grace of the devilish thing, its long, undulating, rippling movements, the gloss of its beautiful flanks, the vivid, palpitating scarlet of the glistening tongue which hung from the jet-black muzzle. And all the time that deep, threatening growl was rising and rising in an unbroken crescendo. I knew that the crisis was at hand.

It was a miserable hour to meet such a death—so cold, so comfortless, shivering in my light dress clothes upon this gridiron of torment upon which I was stretched. I tried to brace myself to it, to raise my soul above it, and at the same time, with the lucidity which comes to a perfectly desperate man, I cast round for some possible means of escape. One thing was clear to me. If that front of the cage was only back in its position once more, I could find a sure refuge behind it. Could I possibly pull it back? I hardly dared to move for fear of bringing the creature upon me. Slowly, very slowly, I put my hand forward until it grasped the edge of the front, the final bar which protruded through the wall. To my surprise it came quite easily to my jerk. Of course the difficulty of drawing it out arose from the fact that I was clinging to it. I pulled again, and three inches of it came through. It ran apparently on wheels. I pulled again . . . and then the cat sprang.

It was so quick, so sudden, that I never saw it happen. I simply heard the savage snarl, and in an instant afterwards the blazing yellow eyes, the flattened black head with its red tongue and flashing teeth, were within reach of me. The impact of the creature shook the bars upon which I lay, until I thought (as far as I could think of anything at such a moment) that they were coming down. The cat swayed there for an instant, the head and front paws quite close to me, the hind paws clawing to find a grip upon the edge of the grating. I heard the claws rasping as they clung to the wire netting, and the breath of the beast made me sick. But its bound had been miscalculated. It could not retain its position. Slowly, grinning with rage and scratching madly at the bars, it swung backwards and dropped heavily upon the floor. With a growl it instantly faced round to me and crouched for another spring.

I knew that the next few moments would decide my fate. The creature had learned by experience. It would not miscalculate again. I must act promptly, fearlessly, if I were to have a chance for life. In an instant I had formed my plan. Pulling off my dress coat, I threw it down over the head of the beast. At the same moment I dropped over the edge, seized the end of the front grating, and pulled it frantically out of the wall.

It came more easily than I could have expected. I rushed across the room, bearing it with me; but, as I rushed, the accident of my position put me upon the outer side. Had it been the other way, I might have come off scathless. As it was, there was a moment's pause as I stopped it and tried to pass in through the opening which I had left. That moment was enough to give time to the creature to toss off the coat with which I had blinded him and to spring upon me. I hurled myself through the gap and pulled the rails to behind me, but he seized my leg before I could entirely withdraw it. One stroke of that huge paw tore off my calf as a shaving of wood curls off before a plane. The next moment, bleeding and fainting, I was lying among the foul straw with a line of friendly bars between me and the creature which ramped so frantically against them.

Too wounded to move, and too faint to be conscious of fear, I could only lie, more dead than alive, and watch it. It pressed its broad, black chest against the bars and angled for me with its crooked paws as I have seen a kitten do before a mousetrap. It ripped my clothes, but, stretch as it would, it could not quite reach me. I have heard of the curious numbing effect produced by wounds from the great carnivora, and now I was destined to experience it, for I had lost all sense of personality, and was as interested in the cat's failure or success as if it were some game which I was watching. And then gradually my mind drifted away into strange, vague dreams, always with that black face and red tongue coming back into them, and so I lost myself in the nirvana of delirium, the blessed relief of those who are too sorely tried.

Tracing the course of events afterwards, I conclude that I must have been insensible for about two hours. What roused me to consciousness once more was that sharp metallic click which had been the precursor of my terrible experience. It was the shooting back of the spring lock. Then, before my senses were clear enough to entirely apprehend what they saw, I was aware of the round, benevolent face of my cousin peering in through the opened door. What he saw evidently amazed him. There was the cat crouching on the floor. I was stretched upon my back in my shirtsleeves within the cage, my trousers torn to ribbons and a great pool of blood all round me. I can see his amazed face now, with the morning sunlight upon it. He peered at me, and peered again. Then he closed the door behind him, and advanced to the cage to see if I were really dead.

I cannot undertake to say what happened. I was not in a fit state to witness or to chronicle such events. I can only say that I was suddenly conscious that his face was away from me—that he was looking towards the animal.

"Good old Tommy!" he cried. "Good old Tommy!"

Then he came near the bars, with his back still towards me.

"Down, you stupid beast!" he roared. "Down, sir! Don't you know your master?"

Suddenly even in my bemuddled brain a remembrance came of those words of his when he had said that the taste of blood would turn the cat into a fiend. My blood had done it, but he was to pay the price.

"Get away!" he screamed. "Get away, you devil! Baldwin! Baldwin! Oh, my God!"

And then I heard him fall, and rise, and fall again, with a sound like the ripping of sacking. His screams grew fainter until they were lost in the worrying snarl. And then, after I thought that he was dead, I saw, as in a nightmare, a blinded, tattered, blood-soaked figure running wildly round the room—and that was the last glimpse which I had of him before I fainted once again.

I was many months in my recovery—in fact, I cannot say that I have ever recovered, for to the end of my days I shall carry a stick as a sign of my night with the Brazilian cat. Baldwin, the groom, and the other servants could not tell what had occurred when, drawn by the death cries of their master, they found me behind the bars, and his remains— or what they afterwards discovered to be his remains—in the clutch of the creature which he had reared. They stalled him off with hot irons, and afterwards shot him through the loophole of the door before they could finally extricate me. I was carried to my bedroom, and there, under the roof of my would-be murderer, I remained between life and death for several weeks. They had sent for a surgeon from Clipton and a nurse from London, and in a month I was able to be carried to the station, and so conveyed back once more to Grosvenor Mansions.

I have one remembrance of that illness, which might have been part of the ever-changing panorama conjured up by a delirious brain were it not so definitely fixed in my memory. One night, when the nurse was absent, the door of my chamber opened, and a tall woman in blackest mourning slipped into the room. She came across to me, and as she bent her sallow face I saw by the faint gleam of the night-light that it was the Brazilian woman whom my cousin had married. She stared intently into my face, and her expression was more kindly than I had ever seen it.

"Are you conscious?" she asked.

I feebly nodded—for I was still very weak.

"Well, then, I only wished to say to you that you have yourself to blame. Did I not do all I could for you? From the beginning I tried to drive you from the house. By every means, short of betraying my husband, I tried to save you from him. I knew that he had a reason for bringing you here. I knew that he would never let you get away again. No one knew him as I knew him, who had suffered from him so often. I did not dare to tell you all this. He would have killed me. But I did my best for you. As things have turned out, you have been the best friend that I have ever had. You have set me free, and I fancied that nothing but death would do that. I am sorry if you are hurt, but I cannot reproach myself. I told you that you were a fool—and a fool you have been." She crept out of the room, the bitter, singular woman, and I was never destined to see her again. With what remained from her husband's property she went back to her native land, and I have heard that she afterwards took the veil at Pernambuco.

It was not until I had been back in London for some time that the doctors pronounced me to be well enough to do business. It was not a very welcome permission to me, for I feared that it would be the signal for an inrush of creditors; but it was Summers, my lawyer, who first took advantage of it.

"I am very glad to see that your lordship is so much better," said he. "I have been waiting a long time to offer my congratulations."

"What do you mean, Summers? This is no time for joking."

"I mean what I say," he answered. "You have been Lord Southerton for the last six weeks, but we feared that it would retard your recovery if you were to learn it."

Lord Southerton! One of the richest peers in England! I could not believe my ears. And then suddenly I thought of the time which had elapsed, and how it coincided with my injuries.

"Then Lord Southerton must have died about the same time that I was hurt?"

"His death occurred upon that very day." Summers looked hard at me as I spoke, and I am convinced—for he was a very shrewd fellow—that he had guessed the true state of the case. He paused for a moment as if awaiting a confidence from me, but I could not see what was to be gained by exposing such a family scandal.

"Yes, a very curious coincidence," he continued, with the same knowing look. "Of course, you are aware that your cousin Everard King was the next heir to the estates. Now, if it had been you instead of him who had been torn to pieces by this tiger, or whatever it was, then of course he would have been Lord Southerton at the present moment."

"No doubt," said I.

"And he took such an interest in it," said Summers. "I happen to know that the late Lord Southerton's valet was in his pay, and that he used to have telegrams from him every few hours to tell him how he was getting on. That would be about the time when you were down there. Was it not strange that he should wish to be so well informed, since he knew that he was not the direct heir?"

"Very strange," said I. "And now, Summers, if you will bring me my bills and a new cheque-book, we will begin to get things into order."

THE USHER OF LEA HOUSE SCHOOL

Mr. Lumsden, the senior partner of Lumsden and Westmacott, the well-known scholastic and clerical agents, was a small, dapper man, with a sharp, abrupt manner, a critical eye, and an incisive way of speaking.

"Your name, sir?" said he, sitting pen in hand with his long, red-lined folio in front of him.

"Harold Weld."

"Oxford or Cambridge?"

"Cambridge."

"Honors?"

"No, sir."

"Athlete?"

"Nothing remarkable, I am afraid."

"Not a Blue?"

"Oh, no."

Mr. Lumsden shook his head despondently and shrugged his shoulders in a way which sent my hopes down to zero. "There is a very keen competition for masterships, Mr. Weld," said he. "The vacancies are few and the applicants innumerable. A first-class athlete, oar, or cricketer, or a man who has passed very high in his examinations, can usually find a vacancy—I might say always in the case of the cricketer. But the average man—if you will excuse the description, Mr. Weld—has a very great difficulty, almost an insurmountable difficulty. We have already more than a hundred such names upon our lists, and if you think it worthwhile our adding yours, I dare say that in the course of some years we may possibly be able to find you some opening which—"

He paused on account of a knock at the door. It was a clerk with a note. Mr. Lumsden broke the seal and read it.

"Why, Mr. Weld," said he, "this is really rather an interesting coincidence. I understand you to say that Latin and English are your subjects, and that you would prefer for a time to accept a place in an elementary establishment, where you would have time for private study?"

"Quite so."

"This note contains a request from an old client of ours, Dr. Phelps McCarthy, of Willow Lea House Academy, West Hampstead, that I should at once send him a young man who should be qualified to teach Latin and English to a small class of boys under fourteen years of age. His vacancy appears to be the very one which you are looking for. The terms are not munificent—sixty pounds, board, lodging, and washing—but the work is not onerous, and you would have the evenings to yourself."

"That would do," I cried, with all the eagerness of the man who sees work at last after weary months of seeking.

"I don't know that it is quite fair to these gentlemen whose names have been so long upon our list," said Mr. Lumsden, glancing down at his open ledger. "But the coincidence is so striking that I feel we must really give you the refusal of it."

"Then I accept it, sir, and I am much obliged to you."

"There is one small provision in Dr. McCarthy's letter. He stipulates that the applicant must be a man with an imperturbably good temper."

"I am the very man," said I, with conviction.

"Well," said Mr. Lumsden, with some hesitation, "I hope that your temper is really as good as you say, for I rather fancy that you may need it."

"I presume that every elementary schoolmaster does."

"Yes, sir, but it is only fair to you to warn you that there may be some especially trying circumstances in this particular situation. Dr. Phelps McCarthy does not make such a condition without some very good and pressing reason."

There was a certain solemnity in his speech which struck a chill in the delight with which I had welcomed this providential vacancy.

"May I ask the nature of these circumstances?" I asked.

"We endeavor to hold the balance equally between our clients, and to be perfectly frank with all of them. If I knew of objections to you I should certainly communicate them to Dr. McCarthy, and so I have no hesitation in doing as much for you. I find," he continued, glancing over the pages of his ledger, "that within the last twelve months we have supplied no fewer than seven Latin masters to Willow Lea House Academy, four of them having left so abruptly as to forfeit their month's salary, and none of them having stayed more than eight weeks."

"And the other masters? Have they stayed?"

"There is only one other residential master, and he appears to be unchanged. You can understand, Mr. Weld," continued the agent, closing both the ledger and the interview, "that such rapid changes are not desirable from a master's point of view, whatever may be said for them by an agent working on commission. I have no idea why these gentlemen have resigned their situations so early. I can only give you the facts, and advise you to see Dr. McCarthy at once and to form your own conclusions."

Great is the power of the man who has nothing to lose, and it was therefore with perfect serenity, but with a good deal of curiosity, that I rang early that afternoon the heavy wrought-iron bell of the Willow Lea House Academy. The building was a massive pile, square and ugly, standing in its own extensive grounds, with a broad carriage sweep curving up to it from the road. It stood high, and commanded a view on the one side of the gray roofs and bristling spires of Northern London, and on the other of the well-wooded and beautiful country which fringes the great city. The door was opened by a boy in buttons, and I was shown into a well-appointed study, where the principal of the academy presently joined me.

The warnings and insinuations of the agent had prepared me to meet a choleric and overbearing person—one whose manner was an insupportable provocation to those who worked under him. Anything further from the reality cannot be imagined. He was a frail, gentle creature, clean-shaven and round-shouldered, with a bearing which was so courteous that it became almost deprecating. His bushy hair was thickly shot with gray, and his age I should imagine to verge upon sixty. His voice was low and suave, and he walked with a certain mincing delicacy of manner. His whole appearance was that of a kindly scholar, who was more at home among his books than in the practical affairs of the world.

"I am sure that we shall be very happy to have your assistance, Mr. Weld," said he, after a few professional questions. "Mr. Percival Manners left me yesterday, and I should be glad if you could take over his duties tomorrow."

"May I ask if that is Mr. Percival Manners of Selwyn?" I asked.

"Precisely. Did you know him?"

"Yes, he is a friend of mine."

"An excellent teacher, but a little hasty in his disposition. It was his only fault. Now, in your case, Mr. Weld, is your own temper under good control? Supposing for argument's sake that I were to so far forget myself as to be rude to you or to speak roughly or to jar your feelings in any way, could you rely upon yourself to control your emotions?"

I smiled at the idea of this courteous, little, mincing creature ruffling my nerves.

"I think that I could answer for it, sir," said I.

"Quarrels are very painful to me," said he. "I wish everyone to live in harmony under my roof. I will not deny Mr. Percival Manners had provocation, but I wish to find a man who can raise himself above provocation, and sacrifice his own feelings for the sake of peace and concord."

"I will do my best, sir."

"You cannot say more, Mr. Weld. In that case I shall expect you tonight, if you can get your things ready so soon."

I not only succeeded in getting my things ready, but I found time to call at the Benedict Club in Piccadilly, where I knew that I should find Manners if he were still in town. There he was sure enough in the smoking room, and I questioned him, over a cigarette, as to his reasons for throwing up his recent situation.

"You don't tell me that you are going to Dr. Phelps McCarthy's Academy?" he cried, staring at me in surprise. "My dear chap, it's no use. You can't possibly remain there."

"But I saw him, and he seemed the most courtly, inoffensive fellow. I never met a man with more gentle manners."

"He! oh, he's all right. There's no vice in him. Have you seen Theophilus St. James?"

"I have never heard the name. Who is he?"

"Your colleague. The other master."

"No, I have not seen him."

"*He's* the terror. If you can stand him, you have either the spirit of a perfect Christian or else you have no spirit at all. A more perfect bounder never bounded."

"But why does McCarthy stand it?"

My friend looked at me significantly through his cigarette smoke, and shrugged his shoulders.

"You will form your own conclusions about that. Mine were formed very soon, and I never found occasion to alter them."

"It would help me very much if you would tell me them."

"When you see a man in his own house allowing his business to be ruined, his comfort destroyed, and his authority defied by another man in a subordinate position, and calmly submitting to it without so much as a word of protest, what conclusion do you come to?"

"That the one has a hold over the other."

Percival Manners nodded his head.

"There you are! You've hit it first barrel. It seems to me that there's no other explanation which will cover the facts. At some period in his life the little Doctor has gone astray. *Humanum est errare.* I have even done it myself. But this was something serious, and the other man got a hold of it and has never let go. That's the truth. Blackmail is at the bottom of it. But he had no hold over me, and there was no reason why I should stand his insolence, so I came away—and I very much expect to see you do the same."

For some time he talked over the matter, but he always came to the same conclusion—that I should not retain my new situation very long.

It was with no very pleasant feelings after this preparation that I found myself face to face with the very man of whom I had received so evil an account. Dr. McCarthy introduced us to each other in his study on the evening of that same day immediately after my arrival at the school.

"This is your new colleague, Mr. St. James," said he, in his genial, courteous fashion. "I trust that you will mutually agree, and that I shall find nothing but good feeling and sympathy beneath this roof."

I shared the good Doctor's hope, but my expectations of it were not increased by the appearance of my *confrère*. He was a young, bullnecked fellow about thirty years of age, dark eyed and black haired, with an exceedingly vigorous physique. I have never seen a more strongly built man, though he tended to run to fat in a way which showed that he was in the worst of training. His face was coarse, swollen, and brutal with a pair of small black eyes deeply sunken in his head. His heavy jowl, his projecting ears, and his thick bandy legs all went to make up a personality which was as formidable as it was repellent.

"I hear you've never been out before," said he, in a rude, brusque fashion. "Well, it's a poor life: hard work and starvation pay, as you'll find out for yourself."

"But it has some compensations," said the principal. "Surely you will allow that, Mr. St. James?"

"Has it? I never could find them. What do you call compensations?"

"Even to be in the continual presence of youth is a privilege. It has the effect of keeping youth in one's own soul, for one reflects something of their high spirits and their keen enjoyment of life."

"Little beasts!" cried my colleague.

"Come, come, Mr. St. James, you are too hard upon them."

"I hate the sight of them! If I could put them and their blessed copybooks and lexicons and slates into one bonfire I'd do it tonight."

"This is Mr. St. James's way of talking," said the principal, smiling nervously as he glanced at me. "You must not take him too seriously. Now, Mr. Weld, you know where your room is, and no doubt you have your own little arrangements to make. The sooner you make them the sooner you will feel yourself at home."

It seemed to me that he was only too anxious to remove me at once from the influence of this extraordinary colleague, and I was glad to go, for the conversation had become embarrassing.

And so began an epoch which always seems to me as I look back to it to be the most singular in all my experience. The school was in many ways an excellent one. Dr. Phelps McCarthy was an ideal principal. His methods were modern and rational. The management was all that could be desired. And yet in the middle of this well-ordered machine there intruded the incongruous and impossible Mr. St. James, throwing everything into confusion. His duties were to teach English and mathematics, and how he acquitted himself of them I do not know, as our classes were held in separate rooms. I can answer for it, however, that the boys feared him and loathed him, and I know that they had good reason to do so, for frequently my own teaching was interrupted by his bellowings of anger, and even by the sound of his blows. Dr. McCarthy spent most of his time in his class, but it was, I suspect, to watch over the master rather than the boys, and to try to moderate his ferocious temper when it threatened to become dangerous.

It was in his bearing to the headmaster, however, that my colleague's conduct was most outrageous. The first conversation which I have recorded proved to be typical of their intercourse. He domineered over him openly and brutally. I have heard him contradict him roughly before the whole school. At no time would he show him any mark of respect, and my temper often rose within me when I saw the quiet acquiescence of the old Doctor, and his patient tolerance of his monstrous treatment. And yet the sight of it surrounded the principal also with a certain vague horror in my mind, for supposing my friend's theory to be correct—and I could devise no better one—how black must have been the story, which could be held over his head by this man and, by fear of its publicity, force him to undergo such humiliations. This quiet, gentle Doctor might be a profound hypocrite, a criminal, a forger possibly, or a poisoner. Only such a secret as this could account for the complete power which the young man held over him. Why else should he admit so hateful a presence into his house and so harmful an influence into his school? Why should he submit to degradations which could not be witnessed, far less endured, without indignation?

And yet, if it were so, I was forced to confess that my principal carried it off with extraordinary duplicity. Never by word or sign did he show that the young man's presence was distasteful to him. I have seen him look pained, it is true, after some peculiarly outrageous exhibition, but he gave me the impression that it was always on account of the scholars or of me, never on account of himself. He spoke to and of St. James in an indulgent fashion, smiling gently at what made my blood boil within me. In his way of looking at him and addressing him, one could see no trace of resentment, but rather a sort of timid and deprecating goodwill. His company he certainly courted, and they spent many hours together in the study and the garden.

As to my own relations with Theophilus St. James, I made up my mind from the beginning that I should keep my temper with him, and to that resolution I steadfastly adhered. If Dr. McCarthy chose to permit this disrespect, and to condone these outrages, it was his affair and not mine. It was evident that his one wish was that there should be peace between us, and I felt that I could help him best by respecting this desire. My easiest way to do so was to avoid my colleague, and this I did to the best of my ability. When we were thrown together I was quiet, polite, and reserved. He, on his part, showed me no ill will, but met me rather with a coarse joviality, and a rough familiarity which he meant to be ingratiating. He was insistent in his attempts to get me into his room at night, for the purpose of playing euchre and of drinking.

"Old McCarthy doesn't mind," said he. "Don't you be afraid of him. We'll do what we like, and I'll answer for it that he won't object." Once only I went, and when I left, after a dull and gross evening, my host was stretched dead drunk upon the sofa. After that I gave the excuse of a course of study, and spent my spare hours alone in my own room.

One point upon which I was anxious to gain information was as to how long these proceedings had been going on. When did St. James assert his hold over Dr. McCarthy? From neither of them could I learn how long my colleague had been in his present situation. One or two leading questions upon my part were eluded or ignored in a manner so marked that it was easy to see that they were both of them as eager to conceal the point as I was to know it. But at last one evening I had the chance of a chat with Mrs. Carter, the matron—for the Doctor was a widower—and from her I got the information which I wanted. It needed no questioning to get at her knowledge, for she was so full of indignation that she shook with passion as she spoke of it, and raised her hands into the air in the earnestness of her denunciation, as she described the grievances which she had against my colleague.

"It was three years ago, Mr. Weld, that he first darkened this door-step," she cried. "Three bitter years they have been to me. The school had fifty boys then. Now it has twenty-two. That's what he has done for us in three years. In another three there won't be one. And the Doctor, that angel of patience, you see how he treats him, though he is not fit to lace his boots for him. If it wasn't for the Doctor, you may be sure that I wouldn't stay an hour under the same roof with such a man, and so I told him to his own face, Mr. Weld. If the Doctor would only pack him about his business—but I know that I am saying more than I should!" She stopped herself with an effort, and spoke no more upon the subject. She had remembered that I was almost a stranger in the school, and she feared that she had been indiscreet.

There were one or two very singular points about my colleague. The chief one was that he rarely took any exercise. There was a playing field within the college grounds, and that was his farthest point. If the boys went out, it was I or Dr. McCarthy who accompanied them. St. James gave as a reason for this that he had injured his knee some years before, and that walking was painful to him. For my own part I put it down to pure laziness upon his part, for he was of an obese, heavy temperament. Twice however I saw him from my window stealing out of the grounds late at night, and the second time I watched him return in the gray of the morning and slink in through an open window. These furtive excursions were never alluded to, but they exposed the hollowness of his story about his knee, and they increased the dislike and distrust which I had of the man. His nature seemed to be vicious to the core.

Another point, small but suggestive, was that he hardly ever during the months that I was at Willow Lea House received any letters, and on those few occasions they were obviously tradesmen's bills. I am an early riser, and used every morning to pick my own correspondence out of the bundle upon the hall table. I could judge therefore how few were ever there for Mr. Theophilus St. James. There seemed to me to be something peculiarly ominous in this. What sort of a man could he be who during thirty years of life had never made a single friend, high or low, who cared to continue to keep in touch with him? And yet the sinister fact remained that the headmaster not only tolerated, but was even intimate with him. More than once on entering a room I have found them talking confidentially together, and they would walk arm in arm in deep conversation up and down the garden paths. So curious did I become to know what the tie was which bound them, that I found it gradually push out my other interests and become the main purpose of my life. In school and out of school, at meals and at play, I was perpetually engaged in watching Dr. Phelps McCarthy and Mr. Theophilus St. James, and in endeavoring to solve the mystery which surrounded them.

But, unfortunately, my curiosity was a little too open. I had not the art to conceal the suspicions which I felt about the relations which existed between these two men and the nature of the hold which the one appeared to have over the other. It may have been my manner of watching them, it may have been some indiscreet question, but it is certain that I showed too clearly what I felt. One night I was conscious that the eyes of Theophilus St. James were fixed upon me in a surly and menacing stare. I had a foreboding of evil, and I was not surprised when Dr. McCarthy called me next morning into his study.

"I am very sorry, Mr. Weld," said he, "but I am afraid that I shall be compelled to dispense with your services."

"Perhaps you would give me some reason for dismissing me," I answered, for I was conscious of having done my duties to the best of my power, and knew well that only one reason could be given.

"I have no fault to find with you," said he, and the color came to his cheeks.

"You send me away at the suggestion of my colleague."

His eyes turned away from mine.

"We will not discuss the question, Mr. Weld. It is impossible for me to discuss it. In justice to you, I will give you the strongest recommendation for your next situation. I can say no more. I hope that you will continue your duties here until you have found a place elsewhere."

My whole soul rose against the injustice of it, and yet I had no appeal and no redress. I could only bow and leave the room, with a bitter sense of ill-usage at my heart.

My first instinct was to pack my boxes and leave the house. But the headmaster had given me permission to remain until I had found another situation. I was sure that St. James desired me to go, and that was a strong reason why I should stay. If my presence annoyed him, I should give him as much of it as I could. I had begun to hate him and to long to have my revenge upon him. If he had a hold over our principal, might not I in turn obtain one over him? It was a sign of weakness that he should be so afraid of my curiosity. He would not resent it so much if he had not something to fear from it. I entered my name once more upon the books of the agents, but meanwhile I continued to fulfill my duties at Willow Lea House, and so it came about that I was present at the dénouement of this singular situation.

During that week—for it was only a week before the crisis came—I was in the habit of going down each evening, after the work of the day was done, to inquire about my new arrangements. One night, it was a cold and windy evening in March, I had just stepped out from the hall door when a strange sight met my eyes. A man was crouching before one of the windows of the house. His knees were bent and his eyes were fixed upon the small line of light between the curtain and the sash. The window threw a square of brightness in front of it, and in the middle of this the dark shadow of this ominous visitor showed clear and hard. It was but for an instant that I saw him, for he glanced up and was off in a moment through the shrubbery. I could hear the patter of his feet as he ran down the road until it died away in the distance.

It was evidently my duty to turn back and to tell Dr. McCarthy what I had seen. I found him in his study. I had expected him to be disturbed at such an incident, but I was not prepared for the state of panic into which he fell. He leaned back in his chair, white and gasping, like one who has received a mortal blow.

"Which window, Mr. Weld?" he asked, wiping his forehead. "Which window was it?"

"The next to the dining room—Mr. St. James's window."

"Dear me! Dear me! This is, indeed, unfortunate! A man looking through Mr. St. James's window!" He wrung his hands like a man who is at his wits' end what to do.

"I shall be passing the police station, sir. Would you wish me to mention the matter?"

"No, no," he cried, suddenly, mastering his extreme agitation; "I have no doubt that it was some poor tramp who intended to beg. I attach no importance to the incident—none at all. Don't let me detain you, Mr. Weld, if you wish to go out."

I left him sitting in his study with reassuring words upon his lips, but with horror upon his face. My heart was heavy for my little employer as

I started off once more for town. As I looked back from the gate at the square of light which marked the window of my colleague, I suddenly saw the black outline of Dr. McCarthy's figure passing against the lamp. He had hastened from his study then to tell St. James what he had heard. What was the meaning of it all, this atmosphere of mystery, this inexplicable terror, these confidences between two such dissimilar men? I thought and thought as I walked, but do what I would I could not hit upon any adequate conclusion. I little knew how near I was to the solution of the problem.

It was very late—nearly twelve o'clock—when I returned, and the lights were all out save one in the Doctor's study. The black, gloomy house loomed before me as I walked up the drive, its somber bulk broken only by the glimmering point of brightness. I let myself in with my latchkey, and was about to enter my own room when my attention was arrested by a short, sharp cry like that of a man in pain. I stood and listened, my hand upon the handle of my door.

All was silent in the house save for a distant murmur of voices which came, I knew, from the Doctor's room. I stole quietly down the corridor in that direction. The sound resolved itself now into two voices, the rough bullying tones of St. James and the lower tone of the Doctor, the one apparently insisting and the other arguing and pleading. Four thin lines of light in the blackness showed me the door of the Doctor's room, and step by step I drew nearer to it in the darkness. St. James's voice within rose louder and louder, and his words now came plainly to my ear.

"I'll have every pound of it. If you won't give it me I'll take it. Do you hear?"

Dr. McCarthy's reply was inaudible, but the angry voice broke in again.

"Leave you destitute! I leave you this little gold mine of a school, and that's enough for one old man, is it not? How am I to set up in Australia without money? Answer me that!"

Again the Doctor said something in a soothing voice, but his answer only roused his companion to a higher pitch of fury.

"Done for me? What have you ever done for me except what you couldn't help doing? It was for your good name, not for my safety, that you cared. But enough cackle! I must get on my way before morning. Will you open your safe or will you not?"

"Oh, James, how can you use me so?" cried a wailing voice, and then there came a sudden little scream of pain. At the sound of that helpless appeal from brutal violence I lost for once that temper upon which I had prided myself. Every bit of manhood in me cried out against any further neutrality. With my walking cane in my hand I rushed into the study. As I did so I was conscious that the hall-door bell was violently ringing.

"You villain!" I cried, "let him go!"

The two men were standing in front of a small safe, which stood against one wall of the Doctor's room. St. James held the old man by the wrist, and he had twisted his arm round in order to force him to produce the key. My little headmaster, white but resolute, was struggling furiously in the grip of the burly athlete. The bully glared over his shoulder at me with a mixture of fury and terror upon his brutal features. Then, realizing that I was alone, he dropped his victim and made for me with a horrible curse.

"You infernal spy!" he cried. "I'll do for you anyhow before I leave."

I am not a very strong man, and I realized that I was helpless if once at close quarters. Twice I cut at him with my stick, but he rushed in at me with a murderous growl, and seized me by the throat with both his muscular hands. I fell backwards and he on the top of me, with a grip which was squeezing the life from me. I was conscious of his malignant yellow-tinged eyes within a few inches of my own, and then with a beating of pulses in my head and a singing in my ears, my senses slipped away from me. But even in that supreme moment I was aware that the doorbell was still violently ringing.

When I came to myself, I was lying upon the sofa in Dr. McCarthy's study, and the Doctor himself was seated beside me. He appeared to be watching me intently and anxiously, for as I opened my eyes and looked about me he gave a great cry of relief. "Thank God!" he cried. " Thank God!"

"Where is he?" I asked, looking round the room. As I did so, I became aware that the furniture was scattered in every direction, and that there were traces of an even more violent struggle than that in which I had been engaged.

The Doctor sank his face between his hands.

"They have him," he groaned. "After these years of trial they have him again. But how thankful I am that he has not for a second time stained his hands in blood."

As the Doctor spoke I became aware that a man in the braided jacket of an inspector of police was standing in the doorway.

"Yes, sir," he remarked, "You have had a pretty narrow escape. If we had not got in when we did, you would not be here to tell the tale. I don't know that I ever saw anyone much nearer to the undertaker."

I sat up with my hands to my throbbing head.

"Dr. McCarthy," said I, "this is all a mystery to me. I should be glad if you could explain to me who this man is, and why you have tolerated him so long in your house."

"I owe you an explanation, Mr. Weld—and the more so since you have, in so chivalrous a fashion, almost sacrificed your life in my defense. There is no reason now for secrecy. In a word, Mr. Weld, this unhappy man's real name is James McCarthy, and he is my only son."

"Your son?"

"Alas, yes. What sin have I ever committed that I should have such a punishment? He has made my whole life a misery from the first years of his boyhood. Violent, headstrong, selfish, unprincipled, he has always been the same. At eighteen he was a criminal. At twenty, in a paroxysm of passion, he took the life of a boon companion and was tried for murder. He only just escaped the gallows, and he was condemned to penal servitude. Three years ago he succeeded in escaping, and managed, in face of a thousand obstacles, to reach my house in London. My wife's heart had been broken by his condemnation, and as he had succeeded in getting a suit of ordinary clothes, there was no one here to recognize him. For months he lay concealed in the attics until the first search of the police should be over. Then I gave him employment here, as you have seen, though by his rough and overbearing manners he made my own life miserable, and that of his fellow masters unbearable. You have been with us for four months, Mr. Weld, but no other master endured him so long. I apologize now for all you have had to submit to, but I ask you what else could I do? For his dead mother's sake I could not let harm come to him as long as it was in my power to fend it off. Only under my roof could he find a refuge—the only spot in all the world—and how could I keep him here without its exciting remark unless I gave him some occupation? I made him English master therefore, and in that capacity I have protected him here for three years. You have no doubt observed that he never during the daytime went beyond the college grounds. You now understand the reason. But when tonight you came to me with your report of a man who was looking through his window, I understood that his retreat was at last discovered. I besought him to fly at once, but he had been drinking, the unhappy fellow, and my words fell upon deaf ears. When at last he made up his mind to go he wished to take from me in his flight every shilling which I possessed. It was your entrance which saved me from him, while the police in turn arrived only just in time to rescue you. I have made myself amenable to the law by harboring an escaped prisoner, and remain here in the custody of the inspector, but a prison has no terrors for me after what I have endured in this house during the last three years."

"It seems to me, Doctor," said the inspector, "that, if you have broken the law, you have had quite enough punishment already."

"God knows I have!" cried Dr. McCarthy, and sank his haggard face upon his hands.

THE BROWN HAND

Everyone knows that Sir Dominick Holden, the famous Indian surgeon, made me his heir, and that his death changed me in an hour from a hard-working and impecunious medical man to a well-to-do landed proprietor. Many know also that there were at least five people between the inheritance and me, and that Sir Dominick's selection appeared to be altogether arbitrary and whimsical. I can assure them, however, that they are quite mistaken, and that although I only knew Sir Dominick in the closing years of his life, there were none the less very real reasons why he should show his goodwill towards me. As a matter of fact, though I say it myself, no man ever did more for another than I did for my Indian uncle. I cannot expect the story to be believed, but it is so singular that I should feel that it was a breach of duty if I did not put it upon record—so here it is, and your belief or incredulity is your own affair.

Sir Dominick Holden, C.B., K.C.S.I., and I don't know what besides, was the most distinguished Indian surgeon of his day. In the Army originally, he afterwards settled down into civil practice in Bombay, and visited as a consultant every part of India. His name is best remembered in connection with the Oriental Hospital, which he founded and supported. The time came, however, when his iron constitution began to show signs of the long strain to which he had subjected it, and his brother practitioners (who were not, perhaps, entirely disinterested upon the point) were unanimous in recommending him to return to England.

He held on so long as he could, but at last he developed nervous symptoms of a very pronounced character, and so came back, a broken man, to his native county of Wiltshire. He bought a considerable estate with an ancient manor house upon the edge of Salisbury Plain, and devoted his old age to the study of Comparative Pathology, which had been his learned hobby all his life, and in which he was a foremost authority.

We of the family were, as may be imagined, much excited by the news of the return of this rich and childless uncle to England. On his part, although by no means exuberant in his hospitality, he showed some sense of his duty to his relations, and each of us in turn had an invitation to visit him. From the accounts of my cousins it appeared to be a melancholy business, and it was with mixed feelings that I at last received my own summons to appear at Rodenhurst. My wife was so carefully excluded in the invitation that my first impulse was to refuse it, but the interests of the children had to be considered, and so, with her consent, I set out one October afternoon upon my visit to Wiltshire, with little thought of what that visit was to entail.

My uncle's estate was situated where the arable land of the plains begins to swell upwards into the rounded chalk hills which are characteristic of the county. As I drove from Dinton Station in the waning light of that autumn day, I was impressed by the weird nature of the scenery. The few scattered cottages of the peasants were so dwarfed by the huge evidences of prehistoric life, that the present appeared to be a dream and the past to be the obtrusive and masterful reality. The road wound through the valleys, formed by a succession of grassy hills, and the summit of each was cut and carved into the most elaborate fortifications, some circular and some square, but all on a scale which has defied the winds and the rains of many centuries. Some call them Roman and some British, but their true origin and the reasons for this particular tract of country being so interlaced with entrenchments have never been finally made clear. Here and there on the long, smooth, olive-colored slopes there rose small rounded barrows or tumuli. Beneath them lie the cremated ashes of the race which cut so deeply into the hills, but their graves tell us nothing save that a jar full of dust represents the man who once labored under the sun.

It was through this weird country that I approached my uncle's residence of Rodenhurst, and the house was, as I found, in due keeping with its surroundings. Two broken and weather-stained pillars, each surmounted by a mutilated heraldic emblem, flanked the entrance to a neglected drive. A cold wind whistled through the elms which lined it, and the air was full of the drifting leaves. At the far end, under the gloomy arch of trees, a single yellow lamp burned steadily. In the dim half-light of the coming night I saw a long, low building stretching out two irregular wings, with deep eaves, a sloping gambrel roof, and walls which were crisscrossed with timber balks in the fashion of the Tudors. The cheery light of a fire flickered in the broad, latticed window to the left of the low-porched door, and this, as it proved, marked the study of my uncle, for it was thither that I was led by his butler in order to make my host's acquaintance.

He was cowering over his fire, for the moist chill of an English autumn had set him shivering. His lamp was unlit, and I only saw the red glow of the embers beating upon a huge, craggy face, with a Red Indian nose and cheek, and deep furrows and seams from eye to chin, the sinister marks of hidden volcanic fires. He sprang up at my entrance with something of an old-world courtesy and welcomed me warmly to Rodenhurst. At the same time I was conscious, as the lamp was carried in, that it was a very critical pair of light blue eyes which looked out at me from under shaggy eyebrows, like scouts beneath a bush, and that this outlandish uncle of mine was carefully reading off my character with all the ease of a practiced observer and an experienced man of the world.

For my part I looked at him, and looked again, for I had never seen a man whose appearance was more fitted to hold one's attention. His figure was the framework of a giant, but he had fallen away until his coat dangled straight down in a shocking fashion from a pair of broad and bony shoulders. All his limbs were huge and yet emaciated, and I could not take my gaze from his knobby wrists, and long, gnarled hands. But his eyes—those peering light blue eyes—they were the most arrestive of any of his peculiarities. It was not their color alone, nor was it the ambush of hair in which they lurked; but it was the expression which I read in them. For the appearance and bearing of the man were masterful, and one expected a certain corresponding arrogance in his eyes, but instead of that I read the look which tells of a spirit cowed and crushed, the furtive, expectant look of the dog whose master has taken the whip from the rack. I formed my own medical diagnosis upon one glance at those critical and yet appealing eyes. I believed that he was stricken with some mortal ailment, that he knew himself to be exposed to sudden death, and that he lived in terror of it. Such was my judgment—a false one, as the event showed; but I mention it that it may help you to realize the look which I read in his eyes.

My uncle's welcome was, as I have said, a courteous one, and in an hour or so I found myself seated between him and his wife at a comfortable dinner, with curious pungent delicacies upon the table, and a stealthy, quick-eyed Oriental waiter behind his chair. The old couple had come round to that tragic imitation of the dawn of life when husband and wife, having lost or scattered all those who were their intimates, find themselves face to face and alone once more, their work done, and the end nearing fast. Those who have reached that stage in sweetness and love, who can change their winter into a gentle Indian summer, have come as victors through the ordeal of life. Lady Holden was a small, alert woman, with a kindly eye, and her expression as she glanced at him was a certificate of character to her husband. And yet, though I read a mutual love in their glances, I read also a mutual horror, and recognized in her face some reflection of that stealthy fear which I detected in his. Their talk was sometimes merry and sometimes sad, but there was a forced note in their merriment and a naturalness in their sadness which told me that a heavy heart beat upon either side of me.

We were sitting over our first glass of wine, and the servants had left the room, when the conversation took a turn which produced a remarkable effect upon my host and hostess. I cannot recall what it was which started the topic of the supernatural, but it ended in my showing them that the abnormal in psychical experiences was a subject to which I had, like many neurologists, devoted a great deal of attention. I concluded by narrating my experiences when, as a member of the Psychical Research Society, I had formed one of a committee of three who spent the night in a haunted house. Our adventures were neither exciting nor convincing, but, such as it was, the story appeared to interest my auditors in a remarkable degree. They listened with an eager silence, and I caught a look of intelligence between them which I could not understand. Lady Holden immediately afterwards rose and left the room.

Sir Dominick pushed the cigar box over to me, and we smoked for some little time in silence. That huge bony hand of his was twitching as he raised it with his cheroot to his lips, and I felt that the man's nerves were vibrating like fiddle strings. My instincts told me that he was on the verge of some intimate confidence, and I feared to speak lest I should interrupt it. At last he turned towards me with a spasmodic gesture like a man who throws his last scruple to the winds.

"From the little that I have seen of you it appears to me, Dr. Hardacre," said he, "that you are the very man I have wanted to meet."

"I am delighted to hear it, sir."

"Your head seems to be cool and steady. You will acquit me of any desire to flatter you, for the circumstances are too serious to permit of insincerities. You have some special knowledge upon these subjects, and you evidently view them from that philosophical standpoint which robs them of all vulgar terror. I presume that the sight of an apparition would not seriously discompose you?"

"I think not, sir."

"Would even interest you, perhaps?"

"Most intensely."

"As a psychical observer, you would probably investigate it in as impersonal a fashion as an astronomer investigates a wandering comet?"

"Precisely."

He gave a heavy sigh.

"Believe me, Dr. Hardacre, there was a time when I could have spoken as you do now. My nerve was a byword in India. Even the Mutiny never shook it for an instant. And yet you see what I am reduced to— the most timorous man, perhaps, in all this county of Wiltshire. Do not speak too bravely upon this subject, or you may find yourself subjected to as long-drawn a test as I am—a test which can only end in the madhouse or the grave."

I waited patiently until he should see fit to go farther in his confidence. His preamble had, I need not say, filled me with interest and expectation.

"For some years, Dr. Hardacre," he continued, "'my life and that of my wife have been made miserable by a cause which is so grotesque that it borders upon the ludicrous. And yet familiarity has never made it more easy to bear—on the contrary, as time passes my nerves become more worn and shattered by the constant attrition. If you have no physical fears, Dr. Hardacre, I should very much value your opinion upon this phenomenon which troubles us so."

"For what it is worth my opinion is entirely at your service. May I ask the nature of the phenomenon?"

"I think that your experiences will have a higher evidential value if you are not told in advance what you may expect to encounter. You are yourself aware of the quibbles of unconscious cerebration and subjective impressions with which a scientific sceptic may throw a doubt upon your statement. It would be as well to guard against them in advance."

"What shall I do, then?"

"I will tell you. Would you mind following me this way?" He led me out of the dining room and down a long passage until we came to a terminal door. Inside there was a large bare room fitted as a laboratory, with numerous scientific instruments and bottles. A shelf ran along one side, upon which there stood a long line of glass jars containing pathological and anatomical specimens.

"You see that I still dabble in some of my old studies" said Sir Dominick. "These jars are the remains of what was once a most excellent collection, but unfortunately I lost the greater part of them when my house was burned down in Bombay in '92. It was a most unfortunate affair for me—in more ways than one. I had examples of many rare conditions, and my splenic collection was probably unique. These are the survivors."

I glanced over them, and saw that they really were of a very great value and rarity from a pathological point of view: bloated organs, gaping cysts, distorted bones, odious parasites—a singular exhibition of the products of India.

"There is, as you see, a small settee here," said my host. "It was far from our intention to offer a guest so meager an accommodation, but since affairs have taken this turn, it would be a great kindness upon your part if you would consent to spend the night in this apartment. I beg that you will not hesitate to let me know if the idea should be at all repugnant to you."

"On the contrary," I said, "it is most acceptable."

"My own room is the second on the left, so that if you should feel that you are in need of company a call would always bring me to your side."

"I trust that I shall not be compelled to disturb you."

"It is unlikely that I shall be asleep. I do not sleep much. Do not hesitate to summon me."

And so with this agreement we joined Lady Holden in the drawing room and talked of lighter things.

It was no affectation upon my part to say that the prospect of my night's adventure was an agreeable one. I have no pretense to greater physical courage than my neighbors, but familiarity with a subject robs it of those vague and undefined terrors which are the most appalling to the imaginative mind. The human brain is capable of only one strong emotion at a time, and if it be filled with curiosity or scientific enthusiasm, there is no room for fear. It is true that I had my uncle's assurance that he had himself originally taken this point of view, but I reflected that the breakdown of his nervous system might be due to his forty years in India as much as to any psychical experiences which had befallen him. I at least was sound in nerve and brain, and it was with something of the pleasurable thrill of anticipation with which the sportsman takes his position beside the haunt of his game that I shut the laboratory door behind me, and partially undressing, lay down upon the rug-covered settee.

It was not an ideal atmosphere for a bedroom. The air was heavy with many chemical odors, that of methylated spirit predominating. Nor were the decorations of my chamber very sedative. The odious line of glass jars with their relics of disease and suffering stretched in front of my very eyes. There was no blind to the window, and a three-quarter moon streamed its white light into the room, tracing a silver square with filigree lattices upon the opposite wall. When I had extinguished my candle this one bright patch in the midst of the general gloom had certainly an eerie and discomposing aspect. A rigid and absolute silence reigned throughout the old house, so that the low swish of the branches in the garden came softly and soothingly to my ears. It may have been the hypnotic lullaby of this gentle susurrus, or it may have been the result of my tiring day, but after many dozings and many efforts to regain my clearness of perception, I fell at last into a deep and dreamless sleep.

I was awakened by some sound in the room, and I instantly raised myself upon my elbow on the couch. Some hours had passed, for the square patch upon the wall had slid downwards and sideways until it lay obliquely at the end of my bed. The rest of the room was in deep shadow. At first I could see nothing; presently, as my eyes became accustomed to the faint light, I was aware, with a thrill which all my scientific absorption could not entirely prevent, that something was moving slowly along the line of the wall. A gentle, shuffling sound, as of soft slippers, came to my ears, and I dimly discerned a human figure walking stealthily from the direction of the door. As it emerged into the patch of moonlight I saw very clearly what it was and how it was employed. It was a man, short and squat, dressed in some sort of dark gray gown, which hung straight from his shoulders to his feet. The moon shone upon the side of his face, and I saw that it was chocolate brown in color, with a ball of black hair like a woman's at the back of his head. He walked slowly, and his eyes were cast upwards towards the line of bottles which contained those gruesome remnants of humanity. He seemed to examine each jar with attention, and then to pass on to the next. When he had come to the end of the line, immediately opposite my bed, he stopped, faced me, threw up his hands with a gesture of despair, and vanished from my sight.

I have said that he threw up his hands, but I should have said his arms, for as he assumed that attitude of despair. I observed a singular peculiarity about his appearance. He had only one hand! As the sleeves drooped down from the upflung arms I saw the left plainly, but the right ended in a knobby and unsightly stump. In every other way his appearance was so natural, and I had both seen and heard him so clearly, that I could easily have believed that he was an Indian servant of Sir Dominick's who had come into my room in search of something. It was only his sudden disappearance which suggested anything more sinister to me. As it was I sprang from my couch, lit a candle, and examined the whole room carefully. There were no signs of my visitor, and I was forced to conclude that there had really been something outside the normal laws of Nature in his appearance. I lay awake for the remainder of the night, but nothing else occurred to disturb me.

I am an early riser, but my uncle was an even earlier one, for I found him pacing up and down the lawn at the side of the house. He ran towards me in his eagerness when he saw me come out from the door.

"Well, well!" he cried. "Did you see him?"

"An Indian with one hand?"

"Precisely."

"Yes, I saw him"—and I told him all that occurred. When I had finished, he led the way into his study.

"We have a little time before breakfast," said he. "It will suffice to give you an explanation of this extraordinary affair—so far as I can explain that which is essentially inexplicable. In the first place, when I tell you that for four years I have never passed one single night, either in Bombay, aboard ship, or here in England without my sleep being broken by this fellow, you will understand why it is that I am a wreck of my former self. His programme is always the same. He appears by my bedside, shakes me roughly by the shoulder, passes from my room into the laboratory, walks slowly along the line of my bottles, and then vanishes. For more than a thousand times he has gone through the same routine."

"What does he want?"

"He wants his hand."

"His hand?"

"Yes, it came about in this way. I was summoned to Peshawur for a consultation some ten years ago, and while there I was asked to look at the hand of a native who was passing through with an Afghan caravan. The fellow came from some mountain tribe living away at the back of beyond somewhere on the other side of Kaffiristan. He talked a bastard Pushtoo, and it was all I could do to understand him. He was suffering from a soft sarcomatous swelling of one of the metacarpal joints, and I made him realize that it was only by losing his hand that he could hope to save his life. After much persuasion he consented to the operation, and he asked me, when it was over, what fee I demanded. The poor fellow was almost a beggar, so that the idea of a fee was absurd, but I answered in jest that my fee should be his hand, and that I proposed to add it to my pathological collection.

"To my surprise he demurred very much to the suggestion, and he explained that according to his religion it was an all-important matter that the body should be reunited after death, and so make a perfect dwelling for the spirit. The belief is, of course, an old one, and the mummies of the Egyptians arose from an analogous superstition. I answered him that his hand was already off, and asked him how he intended to preserve it. He replied that he would pickle it in salt and carry it about with him. I suggested that it might be safer in my keeping than in his, and that I had better means than salt for preserving it. On realizing that I really intended to carefully keep it, his opposition vanished instantly. 'But remember, sahib,' said he, 'I shall want it back when I am dead.' I laughed at the remark, and so the matter ended. I returned to my practice, and he no doubt in the course of time was able to continue his journey to Afghanistan.

"Well, as I told you last night, I had a bad fire in my house at Bombay. Half of it was burned down, and, among other things, my pathological collection was largely destroyed. What you see are the poor remains of it. The hand of the hillman went with the rest, but I gave the matter no particular thought at the time. That was six years ago.

"Four years ago—two years after the fire—I was awakened one night by a furious tugging at my sleeve. I sat up under the impression that my favorite mastiff was trying to arouse me. Instead of this, I saw my Indian patient of long ago, dressed in the long gray gown which was the badge of his people. He was holding up his stump and looking reproachfully at me. He then went over to my bottles, which at the time I kept in my room, and he examined them carefully, after which he gave a gesture of anger and vanished. I realized that he had just died, and that he had come to claim my promise that I should keep his limb in safety for him.

"Well, there you have it all, Dr. Hardacre. Every night at the same hour for four years this performance has been repeated. It is a simple thing in itself, but it has worn me out like water dropping on a stone. It has brought a vile insomnia with it, for I cannot sleep now for the expectation of his coming. It has poisoned my old age and that of my wife, who has been the sharer in this great trouble. But there is the breakfast gong, and she will be waiting impatiently to know how it fared with you last night. We are both much indebted to you for your gallantry, for it takes something from the weight of our misfortune when we share it, even for a single night, with a friend, and it reassures us as to our sanity, which we are sometimes driven to question."

This was the curious narrative which Sir Dominick confided to me— a story which to many would have appeared to be a grotesque impossibility, but which, after my experience of the night before, and my previous knowledge of such things, I was prepared to accept as an absolute fact. I thought deeply over the matter, and brought the whole range of my reading and experience to bear upon it. After breakfast, I surprised my host and hostess by announcing that I was returning to London by the next train.

"My dear doctor," cried Sir Dominick in great distress, "you make me feel that I have been guilty of a gross breach of hospitality in intruding this unfortunate matter upon you. I should have borne my own burden."

"It is, indeed, that matter which is taking me to London," I answered; "but you are mistaken, I assure you, if you think that my experience of last night was an unpleasant one to me. On the contrary, I am about to ask your permission to return in the evening and spend one more night in your laboratory. I am very eager to see this visitor once again."

My uncle was exceedingly anxious to know what I was about to do, but my fears of raising false hopes prevented me from telling him. I was back in my own consulting room a little after luncheon, and was confirming my memory of a passage in a recent book upon occultism which had arrested my attention when I read it.

"In the case of earthbound spirits," said my authority, "some one dominant idea obsessing them at the hour of death is sufficient to hold them to this material world. They are the amphibia of this life and of the next, capable of passing from one to the other as the turtle passes from land to water. The causes which may bind a soul so strongly to a life which its body has abandoned are any violent emotion. Avarice, revenge, anxiety, love, and pity have all been known to have this effect. As a rule it springs from some unfulfilled wish, and when the wish has been fulfilled the material bond relaxes. There are many cases upon record which show the singular persistence of these visitors, and also their disappearance when their wishes have been fulfilled, or in some cases when a reasonable compromise has been effected."

"*A reasonable compromise effected*"—those were the words which I had brooded over all the morning, and which I now verified in the original. No actual atonement could be made here—but a reasonable compromise! I made my way as fast as a train could take me to the Shadwell Seamen's Hospital, where my old friend Jack Hewett was house surgeon. Without explaining the situation I made him understand exactly what it was that I wanted.

"A brown man's hand!" said he, in amazement. "What in the world do you want that for?"

"Never mind. I'll tell you some day. I know that your wards are full of Indians."

"I should think so. But a hand—" He thought a little and then struck a bell.

"Travers," said he to a student dresser, "what became of the hands of the Lascar which we took off yesterday? I mean the fellow from the East India Dock who got caught in the steam winch."

"They are in the postmortem room, sir."

"Just pack one of them in antiseptics and give it to Dr. Hardacre."

And so I found myself back at Rodenhurst before dinner with this curious outcome of my day in town. I still said nothing to Sir Dominick, but I slept that night in the laboratory, and I placed the Lascar's hand in one of the glass jars at the end of my couch.

So interested was I in the result of my experiment that sleep was out of the question. I sat with a shaded lamp beside me and waited patiently for my visitor. This time I saw him clearly from the first. He appeared beside the door, nebulous for an instant, and then hardening into as distinct an outline as any living man. The slippers beneath his gray gown were red and heelless, which accounted for the low, shuffling sound which he made as he walked. As on the previous night he passed slowly along the line of bottles until he paused before that which contained the hand. He reached up to it, his whole figure quivering with expectation, took it down, examined it eagerly, and then, with a face which was convulsed with fury and disappointment, he hurled it down on the floor. There was a crash which resounded through the house, and when I looked up the mutilated Indian had disappeared. A moment later my door flew open and Sir Dominick rushed in.

"You are not hurt?" he cried.

"No—but deeply disappointed."

He looked in astonishment at the splinters of glass, and the brown hand lying upon the floor.

"Good God!" he cried. "What is this?"

I told him my idea and its wretched sequel. He listened intently, but shook his head.

"It was well thought of," said he, "but I fear that there is no such easy end to my sufferings. But one thing I now insist upon. It is that you shall never again upon any pretext occupy this room. My fears that something might have happened to you—when I heard that crash—have been the most acute of all the agonies which I have undergone. I will not expose myself to a repetition of it."

He allowed me, however, to spend the remainder of that night where
I was, and I lay there worrying over the problem and lamenting my own
failure. With the first light of morning there was the Lascar's hand still
lying upon the floor to remind me of my fiasco. I lay looking at it—and
as I lay suddenly an idea flew like a bullet through my head and brought
me quivering with excitement out of my couch. I raised the grim relic
from where it had fallen. Yes, it was indeed so. The hand was the *left*
hand of the Lascar.

By the first train I was on my way to town, and hurried at once to the
Seamen's Hospital. I remembered that both hands of the Lascar had
been amputated, but I was terrified lest the precious organ which I was
in search of might have been already consumed in the crematory. My
suspense was soon ended. It had still been preserved in the postmortem
room. And so I returned to Rodenhurst in the evening with my mission
accomplished and the material for a fresh experiment.

But Sir Dominick Holden would not hear of my occupying the laboratory again. To all my entreaties he turned a deaf ear. It offended his
sense of hospitality, and he could no longer permit it. I left the hand,
therefore, as I had done its fellow the night before, and I occupied a
comfortable bedroom in another portion of the house, some distance
from the scene of my adventures. But in spite of that my sleep was not
destined to be uninterrupted. In the dead of night my host burst into
my room, a lamp in his hand. His huge gaunt figure was enveloped in a
loose dressing gown, and his whole appearance might certainly have
seemed more formidable to a weak-nerved man than that of the Indian
of the night before. But it was not his entrance so much as his expression
which amazed me. He had turned suddenly younger by twenty years at
the least. His eyes were shining, his features radiant, and he waved one
hand in triumph over his head. I sat up astounded, staring sleepily at
this extraordinary visitor. But his words soon drove the sleep from my
eyes.

"We have done it! We have succeeded!" he shouted. My dear Hardacre, how can I ever in this world repay you?"

"You don't mean to say that it is all right?"

"Indeed I do. I was sure that you would not mind being awakened to
hear such blessed news."

"Mind! I should think not indeed. But is it really certain?"

"I have no doubt whatever upon the point. I owe you such a debt, my
dear nephew, as I have never owed a man before, and never expected
to. What can I possibly do for you that is commensurate? Providence
must have sent you to my rescue. You have saved both my reason and

my life, for another six months of this must have seen me either in a cell or a coffin. And my wife—it was wearing her out before my eyes. Never could I have believed that any human being could have lifted this burden off me." He seized my hand and wrung it in his bony grip.

"It was only an experiment—a forlorn hope—but I am delighted from my heart that it has succeeded. But how do you know that it is all right? Have you seen something?"

He seated himself at the foot of my bed.

"I have seen enough," said he. "It satisfies me that I shall be troubled no more. What has passed is easily told. You know that at a certain hour this creature always comes to me. Tonight he arrived at the usual time, and aroused me with even more violence than is his custom. I can only surmise that his disappointment of last night increased the bitterness of his anger against me. He looked angrily at me, and then went on his usual round. But in a few minutes I saw him, for the first time since this persecution began, return to my chamber. He was smiling. I saw the gleam of his white teeth through the dim light. He stood facing me at the end of my bed, and three times he made the low Eastern salaam which is their solemn leave-taking. And the third time that he bowed he raised his arms over his head, and I saw his *two* hands outstretched in the air. So he vanished, and, as I believe, forever."

So that is the curious experience which won me the affection and the gratitude of my celebrated uncle, the famous Indian surgeon. His anticipations were realized, and never again was he disturbed by the visits of the restless hillman in search of his lost member. Sir Dominick and Lady Holden spent a very happy old age, unclouded, so far as I know, by any trouble, and they finally died during the great influenza epidemic within a few weeks of each other. In his lifetime he always turned to me for advice in everything which concerned that English life of which he knew so little; and I aided him also in the purchase and development of his estates. It was no great surprise to me, therefore, that I found myself eventually promoted over the heads of five exasperated cousins, and changed in a single day from a hard-working country doctor into the head of an important Wiltshire family. I at least have reason to bless the memory of the man with the brown hand, and the day when I was fortunate enough to relieve Rodenhurst of his unwelcome presence.

THE FIEND OF THE COOPERAGE

It was no easy matter to bring the *Gamecock* up to the island, for the river had swept down so much silt that the banks extended for many miles out into the Atlantic. The coast was hardly to be seen when the first white curl of the breakers warned us of our danger, and from there onwards we made our way very carefully under mainsail and jib, keeping the broken water well to the left, as is indicated on the chart. More than once her bottom touched the sand (we were drawing something under six feet at the time), but we had always way enough and luck enough to carry us through. Finally, the water shoaled very rapidly, but they had sent a canoe from the factory, and the Krooboy pilot brought us within two hundred yards of the island. Here we dropped our anchor, for the gestures of the negro indicated that we could not hope to get any farther. The blue of the sea had changed to the brown of the river, and even under the shelter of the island the current was singing and swirling round our bows. The stream appeared to be in spate, for it was over the roots of the palm trees, and everywhere upon its muddy, greasy surface we could see logs of wood and débris of all sorts which had been carried down by the flood.

When I had assured myself that we swung securely at our moorings, I thought it best to begin watering at once, for the place looked as if it reeked with fever. The heavy river, the muddy, shining banks, the bright poisonous green of the jungle, the moist steam in the air, they were all so many danger signals to one who could read them. I sent the longboat off, therefore, with two large hogsheads, which should be sufficient to last us until we made St. Paul de Loanda. For my own part I took the dinghy and rowed for the island, for I could see the Union Jack fluttering above the palms to mark the position of Armitage and Wilson's trading station.

When I had cleared the grove, I could see the place, a long, low, whitewashed building, with a deep verandah in front, and an immense pile of palm oil barrels heaped upon either flank of it. A row of surf boats and canoes lay along the beach, and a single small jetty projected into the river. Two men in white suits with red cummerbunds round their waists were waiting upon the end of it to receive me. One was a large portly fellow with a grayish beard. The other was slender and tall, with a pale, pinched face, which was half-concealed by a great mushroom-shaped hat.

"Very glad to see you," said the latter, cordially. "I am Walker, the agent of Armitage and Wilson. Let me introduce Dr. Severall of the same company. It is not often we see a private yacht in these parts."

"She's the *Gamecock*," I explained. "I'm owner and captain—Meldrum is the name."

"Exploring?" he asked.

"I'm a lepidopterist—a butterfly catcher. I've been doing the west coast from Senegal downwards."

"Good sport?" asked the doctor, turning a slow, yellow-shot eye upon me.

"I have forty cases full. We came in here to water, and also to see what you have in my line."

These introductions and explanations had filled up the time whilst my two Krooboys were making the dinghy fast. Then I walked down the jetty with one of my new acquaintances upon either side, each plying me with questions, for they had seen no white man for months.

"What do we do?" said the Doctor, when I had begun asking questions in my turn. "Our business keeps us pretty busy, and in our leisure time we talk politics."

"Yes, by the special mercy of Providence Severall is a rank Radical and I am a good stiff Unionist, and we talk Home Rule for two solid hours every evening."

"And drink quinine cocktails," said the Doctor. "We're both pretty well salted now, but our normal temperature was about 103 last year. I shouldn't, as an impartial adviser, recommend you to stay here very long unless you are collecting bacilli as well as butterflies. The mouth of the Ogowai River will never develop into a health resort."

There is nothing finer than the way in which these outlying pickets of civilization distill a grim humor out of their desolate situation, and turn not only a bold, but a laughing face upon the chances which their lives may bring. Everywhere from Sierra Leone downwards I had found the same reeking swamps, the same isolated fever-racked communities and the same bad jokes. There is something approaching to the divine in that power of man to rise above his conditions and to use his mind for the purpose of mocking at the miseries of his body.

"Dinner will be ready in about half an hour, Captain Meldrum," said the Doctor. "Walker has gone in to see about it; he's the housekeeper this week. Meanwhile, if you like, we'll stroll round and I'll show you the sights of the island."

The sun had already sunk beneath the line of palm trees, and the great arch of the heaven above our head was like the inside of a huge shell, shimmering with dainty pinks and delicate iridescence. No one who has not lived in a land where the weight and heat of a napkin become intolerable upon the knees can imagine the blessed relief which the coolness of evening brings along with it. In this sweeter and purer air the Doctor and I walked round the little island, he pointing out the stores, and explaining the routine of his work.

"There's a certain romance about the place," said he, in answer to some remark of mine about the dullness of their lives. "We are living here just upon the edge of the great unknown. Up there," he continued, pointing to the northeast, "Du Chaillu penetrated, and found the home of the gorilla. That is the Gaboon country—the land of the great apes. In this direction," pointing to the southeast, "no one has been very far. The land which is drained by this river is practically unknown to Europeans. Every log which is carried past us by the current has come from an undiscovered country. I've often wished that I was a better botanist when I have seen the singular orchids and curious-looking plants which have been cast up on the eastern end of the island."

The place which the Doctor indicated was a sloping brown beach, freely littered with the flotsam of the stream. At each end was a curved point, like a little natural breakwater, so that a small shallow bay was left between. This was full of floating vegetation, with a single huge splintered tree lying stranded in the middle of it, the current rippling against its high black aside.

"These are all from up-country," said the Doctor. "They get caught in our little bay, and then when some extra freshet comes they are washed out again and carried out to sea."

"What is the tree?" I asked.

"Oh, some kind of teak I should imagine, but pretty rotten by the look of it. We get all sorts of big hardwood trees floating past here, to say nothing of the palms. Just come in here, will you?"

He led the way into a long building with an immense quantity of barrel staves and iron hoops littered about in it.

"This is our cooperage," said he. "We have the staves sent out in bundles, and we put them together ourselves. Now, you don't see anything particularly sinister about this building, do you?"

I looked round at the high corrugated iron roof, the white wooden walls, and the earthen floor. In one corner lay a mattress and a blanket.

"I see nothing very alarming," said I.

"And yet there's something out of the common, too," he remarked. "You see that bed? Well, I intend to sleep there tonight. I don't want to buck, but I think it's a bit of a test for nerve."

"Why?"

"Oh, there have been some funny goings on. You were talking about the monotony of our lives, but I assure you that they are sometimes quite as exciting as we wish them to be. You'd better come back to the house now, for after sundown we begin to get the fever-fog up from the marshes. There, you can see it coming across the river."

I looked and saw long tentacles of white vapor writhing out from among the thick green underwood and crawling at us over the broad swirling surface of the brown river. At the same time the air turned suddenly dank and cold.

"There's the dinner gong," said the Doctor. "If this matter interests you I'll tell you about it afterwards."

It did interest me very much, for there was something earnest and subdued in his manner as he stood in the empty cooperage which appealed very forcibly to my imagination. He was a big, bluff, hearty man, this Doctor, and yet I had detected a curious expression in his eyes as he glanced about him—an expression which I would not describe as one of fear, but rather that of a man who is alert and on his guard.

"By the way," said I, as we returned to the house, "you have shown me the huts of a good many of your native assistants, but I have not seen any of the natives themselves."

"They sleep in the hulk over yonder," the Doctor answered, pointing over to one of the banks.

"Indeed. I should not have thought in that case that they would need the huts."

"Oh, they used the huts until quite recently. We've put them on the hulk until they recover their confidence a little. They were all half mad with fright, so we let them go, and nobody sleeps on the island except Walker and myself."

"What frightened them?" I asked.

"Well, that brings us back to the same story. I suppose Walker has no objection to your hearing all about it. I don't know why we should make any secret about it, though it is certainly a pretty bad business."

He made no further allusion to it during the excellent dinner which had been prepared in my honor. It appeared that no sooner had the little white topsail of the *Gamecock* shown round Cape Lopez than these kind fellows had begun to prepare their famous pepper pot—which is the pungent stew peculiar to the West Coast—and to boil their yams and sweet potatoes. We sat down to as good a native dinner as one could wish, served by a smart Sierra Leone waiting boy. I was just remarking to myself that he at least had not shared in the general flight when, having laid the dessert and wine upon the table, he raised his hand to his turban.

"Anything else I do, Massa Walker?" he asked.

"No, I think that is all right, Moussa," my host answered. "I am not feeling very well tonight, though, and I should much prefer if you would stay on the island."

I saw a struggle between his fears and his duty upon the swarthy face of the African. His skin had turned of that livid purplish tint which stands for pallor in a negro, and his eyes looked furtively about him.

"No, no, Massa Walker," he cried, at last, "you better come to the hulk with me, sah. Look after you much better in the hulk, sah!"

"That won't do, Moussa. White men don't run away from the posts where they are placed."

Again I saw the passionate struggle in the negro's face, and again his fears prevailed.

"No use, Massa Walker, sah!" he cried. "S'elp me, I can't do it. If it was yesterday or if it was tomorrow, but this is the third night, sah, an' it's more than I can face."

Walker shrugged his shoulders.

"Off with you then!" said he. "When the mail boat comes you can get back to Sierra Leone, for I'll have no servant who deserts me when I need him most. I suppose this is all mystery to you, or has the Doctor told you, Captain Meldrum?"

"I showed Captain Meldrum the cooperage, but I did not tell him anything," said Dr. Severall. "You're looking bad, Walker," he added, glancing at his companion. "You have a strong touch coming on you."

"Yes, I've had the shivers all day, and now my head is like a cannonball. I took ten grains of quinine, and my ears are singing like a kettle. But I want to sleep with you in the cooperage tonight."

"No, no, my dear chap. I won't hear of such a thing. You must get to bed at once, and I am sure Meldrum will excuse you. I shall sleep in the cooperage, and I promise you that I'll be round with your medicine before breakfast."

It was evident that Walker had been struck by one of those sudden and violent attacks of remittent fever which are the curse of the West Coast. His sallow cheeks were flushed and his eyes shining with fever, and suddenly as he sat there he began to croon out a song in the high-pitched voice of delirium.

"Come, come, we must get you to bed, old chap," said the Doctor, and with my aid he led his friend into his bedroom. There we undressed him, and presently, after taking a strong sedative, he settled down into a deep slumber.

"He's right for the night," said the Doctor, as we sat down and filled our glasses once more. "Sometimes it is my turn and sometimes his, but, fortunately, we have never been down together. I should have been sorry to be out of it tonight, for I have a little mystery to unravel. I told you that I intended to sleep in the cooperage."

"Yes, you said so."

"When I said sleep I meant watch, for there will be no sleep for me. We've had such a scare here that no native will stay after sundown, and I mean to find out tonight what the cause of it all may be. It has always been the custom for a native watchman to sleep in the cooperage, to prevent the barrel hoops being stolen. Well, six days ago the fellow who slept there disappeared, and we have never seen a trace of him since. It was certainly singular, for no canoe had been taken, and these waters are too full of crocodiles for any man to swim to shore. What became of the fellow, or how he could have left the island is a complete mystery. Walker and I were merely surprised, but the blacks were badly scared, and queer Voodoo tales began to get about amongst them. But the real stampede broke out three nights ago, when the new watchman in the cooperage also disappeared."

"What became of him?" I asked.

"Well, we not only don't know, but we can't even give a guess which would fit the facts. The niggers swear there is a fiend in the cooperage who claims a man every third night. They wouldn't stay in the island— nothing could persuade them. Even Moussa, who is a faithful boy, enough, would, as you have seen, leave his master in a fever rather than remain for the night. If we are to continue to run this place we must reassure our niggers, and I don't know any better way of doing it than by putting in a night there myself. This is the third night, you see, so I suppose the thing is due, whatever it may be."

"Have you no clue?" I asked. "Was there no mark of violence, no bloodstain, no footprints, nothing to give a hint as to what kind of danger you may have to meet?"

"Absolutely nothing. The man was gone and that was all. Last time it was old Ali, who has been wharf tender here since the place was started. He was always as steady as a rock, and nothing but foul play would take him from his work."

"Well," said I, "I really don't think that this is a one-man job. Your friend is full of laudanum, and come what might he can be of no assistance to you. You must let me stay and put in a night with you at the cooperage."

"Well, now, that's very good of you, Meldrum," said he heartily, shaking my hand across the table. "It's not a thing that I should have ventured to propose, for it is asking a good deal of a casual visitor, but if you really mean it—"

"Certainly I mean it. If you will excuse me a moment, I will hail the *Gamecock* and let them know that they need not expect me."

As we came back from the other end of the little jetty we were both struck by the appearance of the night. A huge blue-black pile of clouds had built itself up upon the landward side, and the wind came from it in little hot pants, which beat upon our faces like the draught from a blast furnace. Under the jetty the river was swirling and hissing, tossing little white spurts of spray over the planking.

"Confound it!" said Doctor Severall. "We are likely to have a flood on the top of all our troubles. That rise in the river means heavy rain up-country, and when it once begins you never know how far it will go. We've had the island nearly covered before now. Well, we'll just go and see that Walker is comfortable, and then if you like we'll settle down in our quarters."

The sick man was sunk in a profound slumber, and we left him with some crushed limes in a glass beside him in case he should awake with the thirst of fever upon him. Then we made our way through the unnatural gloom thrown by that menacing cloud. The river had risen so high that the little bay which I have described at the end of the island had become almost obliterated through the submerging of its flanking peninsula. The great raft of driftwood, with the huge black tree in the middle, was swaying up and down in the swollen current.

"That's one good thing a flood will do for us," said the Doctor. "It carries away all the vegetable stuff which is brought down on the east end of the island. It came down with the freshet the other day, and here it will stay until a flood sweeps it out into the main stream. Well, here's our room, and here are some books, and here is my tobacco pouch, and we must try and put in the night as best we may."

By the light of our single lantern the great lonely room looked very gaunt and dreary. Save for the piles of staves and heaps of hoops there was absolutely nothing in it, with the exception of the mattress for the Doctor, which had been laid in the corner. We made a couple of seats and a table out of the staves, and settled down together for a long vigil. Severall had brought a revolver for me, and was himself armed with a double-barreled shotgun. We loaded our weapons and laid them cocked within reach of our hands. The little circle of light and the black shadows arching over us were so melancholy that he went off to the house, and returned with two candles. One side of the cooperage was pierced, however, by several open windows, and it was only by screening our lights behind staves that we could prevent them from being extinguished.

The Doctor, who appeared to be a man of iron nerves, had settled down to a book, but I observed that every now and then he laid it upon his knee, and took an earnest look all round him. For my part, although I tried once or twice to read, I found it impossible to concentrate my thoughts upon the book. They would always wander back to this great empty silent room, and to the sinister mystery which overshadowed it. I racked my brains for some possible theory which would explain the disappearance of these two men. There was the black fact that they were gone, and not the least tittle of evidence as to why or whither. And here we were waiting in the same place—waiting without an idea as to what we were waiting for. I was right in saying that it was not a one-man job. It was trying enough as it was, but no force upon earth would have kept me there without a comrade.

What an endless, tedious night it was! Outside we heard the lapping and gurgling of the great river, and the soughing of the rising wind. Within save for our breathing, the turning of the Doctor's pages, and the high, shrill ping of an occasional mosquito there was a heavy silence. Once my heart sprang into my mouth as Severall's book suddenly fell to the ground and he sprang to his feet with his eyes on one of the windows.

"Did you see anything, Meldrum?"

"No. Did you?"

"Well, I had a vague sense of movement outside that window." He caught up his gun and approached it. "No, there's nothing to be seen, and yet I could have sworn that something passed slowly across it."

"A palm leaf, perhaps," said I, for the wind was growing stronger every instant.

"Very likely," said he, and settled down to his book again, but his eyes were forever darting little suspicious glances up at the window. I watched it also, but all was quiet outside.

And then suddenly our thoughts were turned into a new direction by the bursting of the storm. A blinding flash was followed by a clap which shook the building. Again and again came the vivid white glare with thunder at the same instant, like the flash and roar of a monstrous piece of artillery. And then down came the tropical rain, crashing and rattling on the corrugated iron roofing of the cooperage. The big hollow room boomed like a drum. From the darkness arose a strange mixture of noises, a gurgling, splashing, tinkling, bubbling, washing, dripping— every liquid sound that nature can produce from the thrashing and swishing of the rain to the deep steady boom of the river. Hour after hour the uproar grew louder and more sustained.

"My word," said Severall, "we are going to have the father of all the floods this time. Well, here's the dawn coming at last and that is a blessing. We've about exploded the third night superstition anyhow."

A gray light was stealing through the room, and there was the day upon us in an instant. The rain had eased off, but the coffee-colored river was roaring past like a waterfall. Its power made me fear for the anchor of the *Gamecock*.

"I must get aboard," said I. "If she drags she'll never be able to beat up the river again."

"The island is as good as a breakwater," the Doctor answered. "I can give you a cup of coffee if you will come up to the house."

I was chilled and miserable, so the suggestion was a welcome one. We left the ill-omened cooperage with its mystery still unsolved, and we splashed our way up to the house.

"There's the spirit lamp," said Severall. "If you would just put a light to it, I will see how Walker feels this morning."

He left me, but was back in an instant with a dreadful face.

"He's gone!" he cried hoarsely.

The words sent a shrill of horror through me. I stood with the lamp in my hand, glaring at him.

"Yes, he's gone!" he repeated. "Come and look!"

I followed him without a word, and the first thing that I saw as I entered the bedroom was Walker himself lying huddled on his bed in the gray flannel sleeping suit in which I had helped to dress him on the night before.

"Not dead, surely!" I gasped.

The Doctor was terribly agitated. His hands were shaking like leaves in the wind.

"He's been dead some hours."

"Was it fever?"

"Fever! Look at his foot!"

I glanced down and a cry of horror burst from my lips. One foot was not merely dislocated but was turned completely round in a most grotesque contortion.

"Good God!" I cried. "What can have done this?"

Severall had laid his hand upon the dead man's chest.

"Feel here," he whispered.

I placed my hand at the same spot. There was no resistance. The body was absolutely soft and limp. It was like pressing a sawdust doll.

"The breastbone is gone," said Severall in the same awed whisper. "He's broken to bits. Thank God that he had the laudanum. You can see by his face that he died in his sleep."

"But who can have done this?"

"I've had about as much as I can stand," said the Doctor, wiping his forehead. "I don't know that I'm a greater coward than my neighbors, but this gets beyond me. If you're going out to the *Gamecock*—"

"Come on!" said I, and off we started. If we did not run it was because each of us wished to keep up the last shadow of his self-respect before the other. It was dangerous in a light canoe on that swollen river, but we never paused to give the matter a thought. He bailing and I paddling we kept her above water, and gained the deck of the yacht. There, with two hundred yards of water between us and this cursed island, we felt that we were our own men once more.

"We'll go back in an hour or so," said he. "But we need a little time to steady ourselves. I wouldn't have had the niggers see me as I was just now for a year's salary."

"I've told the steward to prepare breakfast. Then we shall go back," said I. "But in God's name, Doctor Severall, what do you make of it all."

"It beats me—beats me clean. I've heard of Voodoo devilry, and I've laughed at it with the others. But that poor old Walker, a decent, God-fearing, nineteenth-century, Primrose-League Englishman, should go under like this without a whole bone in his body—it's given me a shake, I won't deny it. But look there, Meldrum, is that hand of yours mad or drunk, or what is it?"

Old Patterson, the oldest man of my crew, and as steady as the Pyramids, had been stationed in the bows with a boathook to fend off the drifting logs which came sweeping down with the current. Now he stood with crooked knees, glaring out in front of him, and one forefinger stabbing furiously at the air.

"Look at it!" he yelled. "Look at it!"

And at the same instant we saw it.

A huge black tree trunk was coming down the river, its broad glistening back just lapped by the water. And in front of it—about three feet in front—arching upwards like the figurehead of a ship, there hung a dreadful face, swaying slowly from side to side. It was flattened, malignant, as large as a small beer barrel, of a faded fungoid color, but the neck which supported it was mottled with a dull yellow and black. As it flew past the *Gamecock* in the swirl of the waters I saw two immense coils roll up out of some great hollow in the tree, and the villainous head rose suddenly to the height of eight or ten feet, looking with dull, skin-covered eyes at the yacht. An instant later the tree had shot past us and was plunging with its horrible passenger towards the Atlantic.

"What was it?" I cried.

"It is our fiend of the cooperage," said Dr. Severall, and he had become in an instant the same bluff, self-confident man that he had been before. "Yes, that is the devil who has been haunting our island. It is the great python of the Gaboon."

I thought of the stories which I had heard all down the coast of the monstrous constrictors of the interior, of the periodical appetite, and of the murderous effects of their deadly squeeze. Then it all took shape in my mind. There had been a freshet the week before. It had brought down this huge hollow tree with its hideous occupant. Who knows from what far distant tropical forest it may have come. It had been stranded on the little east bay of the island. The cooperage had been the nearest house. Twice with the return of its appetite it had carried off the watchman. Last night it had doubtless come again, when Severall had thought he saw something move at the window, but our lights had driven it away. It had writhed onwards and had slain poor Walker in his sleep.

"Why did it not carry him off?" I asked.

"The thunder and lightning must have scared the brute away. There's your steward, Meldrum. The sooner we have breakfast and get back to the island the better, or some of those niggers might think that we had been frightened."

JELLAND'S VOYAGE

"**W**ell," said our Anglo-Jap as we all drew up our chairs round the smoking-room fire, "it's an old tale out yonder, and may have spilt over into print for all I know. I don't want to turn this club room into a chestnut stall, but it is a long way to the Yellow Sea, and it is just as likely that none of you have ever heard of the yawl *Matilda*, and of what happened to Henry Jelland and Willy McEvoy aboard of her.

"The middle of the sixties was a stirring time out in Japan. That was just after the Simonosaki bombardment, and before the Daimio affair. There was a Tory party and there was a Liberal party among the natives, and the question that they were wrangling over was whether the throats of the foreigners should be cut or not. I tell you all, politics have been tame to me since then. If you lived in a treaty port, you were bound to wake up and take an interest in them. And to make it better, the outsider had no way of knowing how the game was going. If the opposition won it would not be a newspaper paragraph that would tell him of it, but a good old Tory in a suit of chain mail, with a sword in each hand, would drop in and let him know all about it in a single upper cut.

"Of course it makes men reckless when they are living on the edge of a volcano like that. Just at first they are very jumpy, and then there comes a time when they learn to enjoy life while they have it. I tell you, there's nothing makes life so beautiful as when the shadow of death begins to fall across it. Time is too precious to be dawdled away then, and a man lives every minute of it. That was the way with us in Yoko-hama. There were many European places of business which had to go on running, and the men who worked them made the place lively for seven nights in the week.

"One of the heads of the European colony was Randolph Moore, the big export merchant. His offices were in Yokohama, but he spent a good deal of his time at his house up in Jeddo, which had only just been opened to the trade. In his absence he used to leave his affairs in the hands of his head clerk, Jelland, whom he knew to be a man of great energy and resolution. But energy and resolution are two-edged things, you know, and when they are used against you you don't appreciate them so much.

"It was gambling that set Jelland wrong. He was a little dark-eyed fellow with black curly hair—more than three-quarters Celt, I should imagine. Every night in the week you would see him in the same place, on the left-hand side of the croupier at Matheson's *rouge et noir* table. For a long time he won, and lived in better style than his employer. And then came a turn of luck, and he began to lose so that at the end of a single week his partner and he were stone broke, without a dollar to their names.

"This partner was a clerk in the employ of the same firm—a tall, straw-haired young Englishman called McEvoy. He was a good boy enough at the start, but he was clay in the hands of Jelland, who fash-ioned him into a kind of weak model of himself. They were forever on the prowl together, but it was Jelland who led and McEvoy who followed. Lynch and I and one or two others tried to show the youngster that he could come to no good along that line, and when we were talking to him we could win him round easily enough, but five minutes of Jelland would swing him back again. It may have been animal magnetism or what you like, but the little man could pull the big one along like a sixty-foot tug in front of a full-rigged ship. Even when they had lost all their money they would still take their places at the table and look on with shining eyes when anyone else was raking in the stamps.

"But one evening they could keep out of it no longer. Red had turned up sixteen times running, and it was more than Jelland could bear. He whispered to McEvoy, and then said a word to the croupier.

" 'Certainly, Mr. Jelland; your cheque is as good as notes,' said he.

"Jelland scribbled a cheque and threw it on the black. The card was the king of hearts, and the croupier raked in the little bit of paper. Jelland grew angry and McEvoy white. Another and a heavier cheque was written and thrown on the table. The card was the nine of diamonds. McEvoy leaned his head upon his hands and looked as if he would faint. 'By God!' growled Jelland, 'I won't be beat,' and he threw on a cheque that covered the other two. The card was the deuce of hearts. A few minutes later they were walking down the Bund, with the cool night air playing upon their fevered faces.

" 'Of course you know what this means,' said Jelland, lighting a cheroot; 'we'll have to transfer some of the office money to our current account. There's no occasion to make a fuss over it. Old Moore won't look over the books before Easter. If we have any luck, we can easily replace it before then.'

" 'But if we have no luck?' faltered McEvoy.

" 'Tut, man, we must take things as they come. You stick to me, and I'll stick to you, and we'll pull through together. You shall sign the cheques tomorrow night, and we shall see if your luck is better than mine.'

"But if anything it was worse. When the pair rose from the table on the following evening, they had spent over £5,000 of their employer's money. But the resolute Jelland was as sanguine as ever.

" 'We have a good nine weeks before us before the books will be examined,' said he. 'We must play the game out, and it will all come straight.'

"McEvoy returned to his rooms that night in an agony of shame and remorse. When he was with Jelland he borrowed strength from him; but alone he recognized the full danger of his position, and the vision of his old white-capped mother in England, who had been so proud when he received his appointment, rose up before him to fill him with loathing and madness. He was still tossing upon his sleepless couch when his Japanese servant entered the bedroom. For an instant McEvoy thought that the long-expected outbreak had come, and plunged for his revolver. Then, with his heart in his mouth, he listened to the message which the servant had brought.

"Jelland was downstairs, and wanted to see him.

"What on earth could he want at that hour of night? McEvoy dressed hurriedly and rushed downstairs. His companion, with a set smile upon his lips, which was belied by the ghastly pallor of his face, was sitting in the dim light of a solitary candle, with a slip of paper in his hands.

" 'Sorry to knock you up, Willy,' said he. 'No eavesdroppers, I suppose?'

"McEvoy shook his head. He could not trust himself to speak.

" 'Well, then, our little game is played out. This note was waiting for me at home. It is from Moore, and says that he will be down on Monday morning for an examination of the books. It leaves us in a tight place.'

" 'Monday!' gasped McEvoy; 'today is Friday.'

" 'Saturday, my son, and 3 a.m. We have not much time to turn round in.'

" 'We are lost!' screamed McEvoy.

" 'We soon will be, if you make such an infernal row,' said Jelland harshly. 'Now do what I tell you, Willy, and we'll pull through yet.'

" 'I will do anything—anything.'

" 'That's better. Where's your whisky? It's a beastly time of the day to have to get your back stiff, but there must be no softness with us, or we are gone. First of all, I think there is something due to our relations, don't you?'

"McEvoy stared.

" 'We must stand or fall together, you know. Now I, for one, don't intend to set my foot inside a felon's dock under any circumstances. D'ye see? I'm ready to swear to that. Are you?'

" 'What d'you mean?' asked McEvoy, shrinking back.

" 'Why, man, we all have to die, and it's only the pressing of a trigger. I swear that I shall never be taken alive. Will you? If you don't I leave you to your fate.'

" 'All right. I'll do whatever you think best.'

" 'You swear it?'

" 'Yes.'

" 'Well, mind, you must be as good as your word. Now we have two clear days to get off in. The yawl *Matilda* is on sale, and she has all her fixings and plenty of tinned stuff aboard. We'll buy the lot tomorrow morning, and whatever we want, and get away in her. But, first, we'll clear all that is left in the office. There are 5,000 sovereigns in the safe. After dark we'll get them aboard the yawl, and take our chance of reaching California. There's no use hesitating, my son, for we have no ghost of a look-in in any other direction. It's that or nothing.'

" 'I'll do what you advise.'

" 'All right; and mind you get a bright face on you tomorrow, for if Moore gets the tip and comes before Monday, then—' He tapped the side pocket of his coat and looked across at his partner with eyes that were full of a sinister meaning.

"All went well with their plans next day. The *Matilda* was bought without difficulty; and, though she was a tiny craft for so long a voyage, had she been larger two men could not have hoped to manage her. She was stocked with water during the day, and after dark the two clerks brought down the money from the office and stowed it in the hold. Before midnight they had collected all their own possessions without exciting suspicion, and at two in the morning they left their moorings and stole quietly out from among the shipping. They were seen, of course, and were set down as keen yachtsmen who were on for a good long Sunday cruise; but there was no one who dreamed that that cruise would only end either on the American coast or at the bottom of the North Pacific Ocean. Straining and hauling, they got their mainsail up and set their foresail and jib. There was a slight breeze from the south-east, and the little craft went dipping along upon her way. Seven miles from land, however, the wind fell away and they lay becalmed, rising and falling on the long swell of a glassy sea. All Sunday they did not make a mile, and in the evening Yokohama still lay along the horizon.

"On Monday morning down came Randolph Moore from Jeddo, and made straight for the offices. He had had the tip from someone that his clerks had been spreading themselves a bit, and that had made him come down out of his usual routine; but when he reached his place and found the three juniors waiting in the street with their hands in their pockets he knew that the matter was serious.

" 'What's this?' he asked. He was a man of action, and a nasty chap to deal with when he had his topmasts lowered.

" 'We can't get in,' said the clerks.

" 'Where is Mr. Jelland?'

" 'He has not come today.'

" 'And Mr. McEvoy?'

" 'He has not come either.'

"Randolph Moore looked serious. 'We must have the door down,' said he.

"They don't build houses very solid in that land of earthquakes, and in a brace of shakes they were all in the office. Of course the thing told its own story. The safe was open, the money gone, and the clerks fled. Their employer lost no time in talk.

" 'Where were they seen last?'

" 'On Saturday they bought the *Matilda* and started for a cruise.'

"Saturday! The matter seemed hopeless if they had got two days' start. But there was still the shadow of a chance. He rushed to the beach and swept the ocean with his glasses.

" 'My God!' he cried. 'There's the *Matilda* out yonder. I know her by the rake of her mast. I have my hand upon the villains after all!'

"But there was a hitch even then. No boat had steam up, and the eager merchant had not patience to wait. Clouds were banking up along the haunch of the hills, and there was every sign of an approaching change of weather. A police boat was ready with ten armed men in her, and Randolph Moore himself took the tiller as she shot out in pursuit of the becalmed yawl.

"Jelland and McEvoy, waiting wearily for the breeze which never came, saw the dark speck which sprang out from the shadow of the land and grew larger with every swish of the oars. As she drew nearer, they could see also that she was packed with men, and the gleam of weapons told what manner of men they were. Jelland stood leaning against the tiller, and he looked at the threatening sky, the limp sails, and the approaching boat.

" 'It's a case with us, Willy,' said he. 'By the Lord, we are two most unlucky devils, for there's wind in that sky, and another hour would have brought it to us.'

"McEvoy groaned.

" 'There's no good softening over it, my lad,' said Jelland. 'It's the police boat right enough, and there's old Moore driving them to row like hell. It'll be a ten-dollar job for every man of them.'

"Willy McEvoy crouched against the side with his knees on the deck. 'My mother! my poor old mother!' he sobbed.

" 'She'll never hear that you have been in the dock anyway,' said Jelland. 'My people never did much for me, but I will do that much for them. It's no good, Mac. We can chuck our hands. God bless you, old man! Here's the pistol!'

"He cocked the revolver and held the butt towards the youngster. But the other shrunk away from it with little gasps and cries. Jelland glanced at the approaching boat. It was not more than a few hundred yards away.

" 'There's no time for nonsense,' said he. 'Damn it! man, what's the use of flinching. You swore it!'

" 'No, no, Jelland!'

" 'Well, anyhow, I swore that neither of us should be taken. Will you do it?'

" 'I can't! I can't!'

" 'Then I will for you.'

"The rowers in the boat saw him lean forwards, they heard two pistol shots, they saw him double himself across the tiller, and then, before the smoke had lifted, they found that they had something else to think of.

"For at that instant the storm broke—one of those short sudden squalls which are common in these seas. The *Matilda* heeled over, her sails bellied out, she plunged her lee rail into a wave, and was off like a frightened deer. Jelland's body had jammed the helm, and she kept a course right before the wind, and fluttered away over the rising sea like a blown piece of paper. The rowers worked frantically, but the yawl still drew ahead, and in five minutes it had plunged into the storm wrack never to be seen again by mortal eye. The boat put back, and reached Yokohama with the water washing halfway up to the thwarts.

"And that was how it came that the yawl *Matilda*, with a cargo of five thousand pounds and a crew of two dead young men, set sail across the Pacific Ocean. What the end of Jelland's voyage may have been no man knows. He may have foundered in that gale, or he may have been picked up by some canny merchantman, who stuck to the bullion and kept his mouth shut, or he may still be cruising in that vast waste of waters, blown north to the Bering Sea, or south to the Malay Islands. It's better to leave it unfinished than to spoil a true story by inventing a tag to it."

B. 24

I told my story when I was taken, and no one would listen to me. Then I told it again at the trial—the whole thing absolutely as it happened, without so much as a word added. I set it all out truly, so help me God, all that Lady Mannering said and did, and then all that I said and done, just as it occurred. And what did I get for it? "The prisoner put forward a rambling and inconsequential statement, incredible in its details and unsupported by any shred of corroborative evidence." That was what one of the London papers said, and others let it pass as if I had made no defense at all. And yet, with my own eyes I saw Lord Mannering murdered, and I am as guiltless of it as any man on the jury that tried me.

Now, sir, you are there to receive the petitions of prisoners. It all lies with you. All I ask is that you read it—just read it—and then that you make an inquiry or two about the private character of this Lady Mannering, if she still keeps the name that she had three years ago, when to my sorrow and ruin I came to meet her. You could use a private inquiry agent or a good lawyer, and you would soon learn enough to show you that my story is the true one. Think of the glory it would be to you to have all the papers saying that there would have been a shocking miscarriage of justice if it had not been for your perseverance and intelligence! That must be your reward, since I am a poor man and can offer you nothing. But if you don't do it, may you never lie easy in your bed again! May no night pass that you are not haunted by the thought of the man

who rots in jail because you have not done the duty which you are paid
to do! But you will do it, sir, I know. Just make one or two inquiries, and
you will soon find which way the wind blows. Remember, also, that the
only person who profited by the crime was herself, since it changed her
from an unhappy wife to a rich young widow. There's the end of the
string in your hand, and you only have to follow it up and see where it
leads to.

Mind you, sir, I make no complaint as far as the burglary goes. I
don't whine about what I have deserved, and so far I have had no more
than I have deserved. Burglary it was, right enough, and my three years
have gone to pay for it. It was shown at the trial that I had had a hand
in the Merton Cross business, and did a year for that, so my story had
the less attention on that account. A man with a previous conviction
never gets a really fair trial. I own to the burglary, but when it comes to
the murder which brought me a lifer—any judge but Sir James might
have given me the gallows—then I tell you that I had nothing to do with
it, and that I am an innocent man. And now I'll take that night, the 13th
of September, 1894, and I'll give you just exactly what occurred, and
may God's hand strike me down if I go one inch over the truth.

I had been at Bristol in the summer looking for work, and then I had
a notion that I might get something at Portsmouth, for I was trained as
a skilled mechanic, so I came tramping my way across the south of
England, and doing odd jobs as I went. I was trying all I knew to keep
off the cross, for I had done a year in Exeter Jail, and I had had enough
of visiting Queen Victoria. But it's cruel hard to get work when once the
black mark is against your name, and it was all I could do to keep soul
and body together. At last, after ten days of woodcutting and stone-
breaking on starvation pay, I found myself near Salisbury with a couple
of shillings in my pocket, and my boots and my patience clean wore out.
There's an ale house called "The Willing Mind," which stands on the
road between Blandford and Salisbury, and it was there that night I
engaged a bed. I was sitting alone in the taproom just about closing
time, when the innkeeper—Allen his name was—came beside me and
began yarning about the neighbors. He was a man that liked to talk and
to have someone to listen to his talk, so I sat there smoking and drinking
a mug of ale which he had stood me; and I took no great interest in
what he said until he began to talk (as the devil would have it) about the
riches of Mannering Hall.

"Meaning the large house on the right before I came to the village?"
said I. "The one that stands in its own park?"

"Exactly," said he—and I am giving all our talk so that you may know that I am telling you the truth and hiding nothing. "The long white house with the pillars," said he. "At the side of the Blandford Road."

Now I had looked at it as I passed, and it had crossed my mind, as such thoughts will, that it was a very easy house to get into with that great row of ground windows and glass doors. I had put the thought away from me, and now here was this landlord bringing it back with his talk about the riches within. I said nothing, but I listened, and as luck would have it, he would always come back to this one subject.

"He was a miser young, so you can think what he is now in his age," said he. "Well, he's had some good out of his money."

"What good can he have had if he does not spend it?" said I.

"Well, it bought him the prettiest wife in England, and that was some good that he got out of it. She thought she would have the spending of it, but she knows the difference now."

"Who was she then?" I asked, just for the sake of something to say.

"She was nobody at all until the old Lord made her his Lady," said he. "She came from up London way, and some said that she had been on the stage there, but nobody knew. The old Lord was away for a year, and when he came home he brought a young wife back with him, and there she has been ever since. Stephens, the butler, did tell me once that she was the light of the house when fust she came, but what with her husband's mean and aggravatin' way, and what with her loneliness—for he hates to see a visitor within his doors; and what with his bitter words—for he has a tongue like a hornet's sting, her life all went out of her, and she became a white, silent creature, moping about the country lanes. Some say that she loved another man, and that it was just the riches of the old Lord which tempted her to be false to her lover, and that now she is eating her heart out because she has lost the one without being any nearer to the other, for she might be the poorest woman in the parish for all the money that she has the handling of."

Well, sir, you can imagine that it did not interest me very much to hear about the quarrels between a Lord and a Lady. What did it matter to me if she hated the sound of his voice, or if he put every indignity upon her in the hope of breaking her spirit, and spoke to her as he would never have dared to speak to one of his servants? The landlord told me of these things, and of many more like them, but they passed out of my mind, for they were no concern of mine. But what I did want to hear was the form in which Lord Mannering kept his riches. Title deeds and stock certificates are but paper, and more danger than profit to the man who takes them. But metal and stones are worth a risk. And then, as if he were answering my very thoughts, the landlord told me of

Lord Mannering's great collection of gold medals, that it was the most valuable in the world, and that it was reckoned that if they were put into a sack the strongest man in the parish would not be able to raise them. Then his wife called him, and he and I went to our beds.

I am not arguing to make out a case for myself, but I beg you, sir, to bear all the facts in your mind, and to ask yourself whether a man could be more sorely tempted than I was. I make bold to say that there are few who could have held out against it. There I lay on my bed that night, a desperate man without hope or work, and with my last shilling in my pocket. I had tried to be honest, and honest folk had turned their backs upon me. They taunted me for theft; and yet they pushed me towards it. I was caught in the stream and could not get out. And then it was such a chance: the great house all lined with windows, the golden medals which could so easily be melted down. It was like putting a loaf before a starving man and expecting him not to eat it. I fought against it for a time, but it was no use. At last I sat up on the side of my bed, and I swore that that night I should either be a rich man and able to give up crime for ever, or that the irons should be on my wrists once more. Then I slipped on my clothes, and, having put a shilling on the table—for the landlord had treated me well, and I did not wish to cheat him—I passed out through the window into the garden of the inn.

There was a high wall round this garden, and I had a job to get over it, but once on the other side it was all plain sailing. I did not meet a soul upon the road, and the iron gate of the avenue was open. No one was moving at the lodge. The moon was shining, and I could see the great house glimmering white through an archway of trees. I walked up it for a quarter of a mile or so, until I was at the edge of the drive, where it ended in a broad, graveled space before the main door. There I stood in the shadow and looked at the long building, with a full moon shining in every window and silvering the high stone front. I crouched there for some time, and I wondered where I should find the easiest entrance. The corner window of the side seemed to be the one which was least overlooked, and a screen of ivy hung heavily over it. My best chance was evidently there. I worked my way under the trees to the back of the house, and then crept along in the black shadow of the building. A dog barked and rattled his chain, but I stood waiting until he was quiet, and then I stole on once more until I came to the window which I had chosen.

It is astonishing how careless they are in the country, in places far removed from large towns, where the thought of burglars never enters their heads. I call it setting temptation in a poor man's way when he puts his hand, meaning no harm, upon a door, and finds it swing open before him. In this case it was not so bad as that, but the window was merely fastened with the ordinary catch, which I opened with a push from the blade of my knife. I pulled up the window as quickly as possible, and then I thrust the knife through the slit in the shutter and pried it open. They were folding shutters, and I shoved them before me and walked into the room.

"Good evening, sir! You are very welcome!" said a voice.

I've had some starts in my life, but never one to come up to that one. There, in the opening of the shutters, within reach of my arm, was standing a woman with a small coil of wax taper burning in her hand. She was tall and straight and slender, with a beautiful white face that might have been cut out of clear marble, but her hair and eyes were as black as night. She was dressed in some sort of white dressing gown which flowed down to her feet, and what with this robe and what with her face, it seemed as if a spirit from above was standing in front of me. My knees knocked together, and I held on to the shutter with one hand to give me support. I should have turned and run away if I had had the strength, but I could only just stand and stare at her.

She soon brought me back to myself once more.

"Don't be frightened!" said she, and they were strange words for the mistress of a house to have to use to a burglar. "I saw you out of my bedroom window when you were hiding under those trees, so I slipped downstairs, and then I heard you at the window. I should have opened it for you if you had waited, but you managed it yourself just as I came up."

I still held in my hand the long clasp knife with which I had opened the shutter. I was unshaven and grimed from a week on the roads. Altogether, there are few people who would have cared to face me alone at one in the morning; but this woman, if I had been her lover meeting her by appointment, could not have looked upon me with a more welcoming eye. She laid her hand upon my sleeve and drew me into the room.

"What's the meaning of this, ma'am? Don't get trying any little games upon me," said I, in my roughest way—and I can put it on rough when I like. "It'll be the worse for you if you play me any trick," I added, showing her my knife.

"I will play you no trick," said she. "On the contrary, I am your friend, and I wish to help you."

"Excuse me, ma'am, but I find it hard to believe that," said I. "Why should you wish to help me?"

"I have my own reasons," said she; and then suddenly, with those black eyes blazing out of her white face : "It's because I hate him, hate him, hate him! Now you understand."

I remembered what the landlord had told me, and I did understand. I looked at her Ladyship's face, and I knew that I could trust her. She wanted to revenge herself upon her husband. She wanted to hit him where it would hurt him most—upon the pocket. She hated him so that she would even lower her pride to take such a man as me into her confidence if she could gain her end by doing so. I've hated some folk in my time, but I don't think I ever understood what hate was until I saw that woman's face in the light of the taper.

"You'll trust me now?" said she, with another coaxing touch upon my sleeve.

"Yes, your Ladyship."

"You know me, then?"

"I can guess who you are."

"I dare say my wrongs are the talk of the county. But what does he care for that? He only cares for one thing in the whole world, and that you can take from him this night. Have you a bag?"

"No, your Ladyship."

"Shut the shutter behind you. Then no one can see the light. You are quite safe. The servants all sleep in the other wing. I can show you where all the most valuable things are. You cannot carry them all, so we must pick the best."

The room in which I found myself was long and low, with many rugs and skins scattered about on a polished wood floor. Small cases stood here and there, and the walls were decorated with spears and swords and paddles, and other things which find their way into museums. There were some queer clothes, too, which had been brought from savage countries, and the lady took down a large leather sack-bag from among them.

"This sleeping-sack will do," said she. "Now come with me and I will show you where the medals are."

It was like a dream to me to think that this tall, white woman was the lady of the house, and that she was lending me a hand to rob her own home. I could have burst out laughing at the thought of it, and yet there was something in that pale face of hers which stopped my laughter and turned me cold and serious. She swept on in front of me like a spirit, with the green taper in her hand, and I walked behind with my sack until we came to a door at the end of this museum. It was locked, but the key was in it, and she led me through.

The room beyond was a small one, hung all round with curtains which had pictures on them. It was the hunting of a deer that was painted on it, as I remember, and in the flicker of that light you'd have sworn that the dogs and the horses were streaming round the walls. The only other thing in the room was a row of cases made of walnut, with brass ornaments. They had glass tops, and beneath this glass I saw the long lines of those gold medals, some of them as big as a plate and half an inch thick, all resting upon red velvet and glowing and gleaming in the darkness. My fingers were just itching to be at them, and I slipped my knife under the lock of one of the cases to wrench it open.

"Wait a moment," said she, laying her hand upon my arm. "You might do better than this."

"I am very well satisfied, ma'am," said I, "and much obliged to your Ladyship for kind assistance."

"You can do better," she repeated. "Would not golden sovereigns be worth more to you than these things?"

"Why, yes," said I. "That's best of all."

"Well," said she, "he sleeps just above our head. It is but one short staircase. There is a tin box with money enough to fill this bag under his bed."

"How can I get it without waking him?"

"What matter if he does wake?" She looked very hard at me as she spoke. "You could keep him from calling out."

"No, no, ma'am, I'll have none of that."

"Just as you like," said she. "I thought you were a stouthearted sort of man by your appearance, but I see that I made a mistake. If you are afraid to run the risk of one old man, then of course you cannot have the gold which is under his bed. You are the best judge of your own business, but I should think that you would do better at some other trade."

"I'll not have murder on my conscience."

"You could overpower him without harming him. I never said anything of murder. The money lies under the bed. But if you are fainthearted, it is better that you should not attempt it."

She worked upon me so, partly with her scorn and partly with this money that she held before my eyes, that I believe I should have yielded and taken my chances upstairs, had it not been that I saw her eyes following the struggle within me in such a crafty, malignant fashion that it was evident she was bent upon making me the tool of her revenge, and that she would leave me no choice but to do the old man an injury or to be captured by him. She felt suddenly that she was giving herself away, and she changed her face to a kindly, friendly smile, but it was too late, for I had had my warning.

"I will not go upstairs," said I. "I have all I want here."

She looked her contempt at me, and there never was a face which could look it plainer.

"Very good. You can take these medals. I should be glad if you would begin at this end. I suppose they will all be the same value when melted down, but these are the ones which are the rarest, and, therefore, the most precious to him. It is not necessary to break the locks. If you press that brass knob you will find that there is a secret spring. So! Take that small one first—it is the very apple of his eye."

She had opened one of the cases, and the beautiful things all lay exposed before me. I had my hand upon the one which she had pointed out, when suddenly a change came over her face, and she held up one finger as a warning. "Hist!" she whispered. "What is that?"

Far away in the silence of the house we heard a low, dragging, shuffling sound, and the distant tread of feet. She closed and fastened the case in an instant.

"It's my husband!" she whispered. "All right. Don't be alarmed. I'll arrange it. Here! Quick, behind the tapestry!"

She pushed me behind the painted curtains upon the wall, my empty leather bag still in my hand. Then she took her taper and walked quickly into the room from which we had come. From where I stood I could see her through the open door.

"Is that you, Robert?" she cried.

The light of a candle shone through the door of the museum, and the shuffling steps came nearer and nearer. Then I saw a face in the doorway, a great, heavy face, all lines and creases, with a huge curving nose, and a pair of gold glasses fixed across it. He had to throw his head back to see through the glasses, and that great nose thrust out in front of him like the beak of some sort of fowl. He was a big man, very tall and burly, so that in his loose dressing gown his figure seemed to fill up the whole doorway. He had a pile of gray, curling hair all round his head, but his face was clean-shaven. His mouth was thin and small and prim, hidden away under his long, masterful nose. He stood there, holding the candle in front of him, and looking at his wife with a queer, malicious gleam in his eyes. It only needed that one look to tell me that he was as fond of her as she was of him.

"How's this?" he asked. "Some new tantrum? What do you mean by wandering about the house? Why don't you go to bed?"

"I could not sleep," she answered. She spoke languidly and wearily.

If she was an actress once, she had not forgotten her calling.

"Might I suggest," said he, in the same mocking kind of voice, "that a good conscience is an excellent aid to sleep?"

"That cannot be true," she answered, "for you sleep very well."

"I have only one thing in my life to be ashamed of," said he, and his hair bristled up with anger until he looked like an old cockatoo. "You know best what that is. It is a mistake which has brought its own punishment with it."

"To me as well as to you. Remember that!"

"You have very little to whine about. It was I who stooped and you who rose."

"Rose!"

"Yes, rose. I suppose you do not deny that it is promotion to exchange the music hall for Mannering Hall. Fool that I was ever to take you out of your true sphere!"

"If you think so, why do you not separate?"

"Because private misery is better than public humiliation. Because it is easier to suffer for a mistake than to own to it. Because also I like to keep you in my sight, and to know that you cannot go back to him."

"You villain! You cowardly villain!"

"Yes, yes, my lady. I know your secret ambition, but it shall never be while I live, and if it happens after my death I will at least take care that you go to him as a beggar. You and dear Edward will never have the satisfaction of squandering my savings, and you may make up your mind to that, my lady. Why are those shutters and the window open?"

"I found the night very close."

"It is not safe. How do you know that some tramp may not be outside? Are you aware that my collection of medals is worth more than any similar collection in the world? You have left the door open also. What is there to prevent anyone from rifling the cases?"

"I was here."

"I know you were. I heard you moving about in the medal room, and that was why I came down. What were you doing?"

"Looking at the medals. What else should I be doing?"

"This curiosity is something new." He looked suspiciously at her and moved on towards the inner room, she walking beside him.

It was at this moment that I saw something which startled me. I had laid my clasp knife open upon the top of one of the cases, and there it lay in full view. She saw it before he did, and with a woman's cunning she held her taper out so that the light of it came between Lord Mannering's eyes and the knife. Then she took it in her left hand and held it

against her gown out of his sight. He looked about from case to case—
I could have put my hand at one time upon his long nose—but there
was nothing to show that the medals had been tampered with, and so,
still snarling and grumbling, he shuffled off into the other room once
more.

And now I have to speak of what I heard rather than of what I saw,
but I swear to you, as I shall stand some day before my Maker, that what
I say is the truth.

When they passed into the outer room I saw him lay his candle upon
the corner of one of the tables, and he sat himself down, but in such a
position that was just out of my sight. She moved behind him, as I could
tell from the fact that the light of her taper threw his long, lumpy shadow
upon the floor in front of him. Then he began talking about this man
whom he called Edward, and every word that he said was like a blistering
drop of vitriol. He spoke low, so that I could not hear it all, but from
what I heard I should guess that she would as soon have been lashed
with a whip. At first she said some hot words in reply, but then she was
silent, and he went on and on in that cold, mocking voice of his, nagging
and insulting and tormenting, until I wondered that she could bear to
stand there in silence and listen to it. Then suddenly I heard him say in
a sharp voice, "Come from behind me! Leave go of my collar! What!
would you dare to strike me?" There was a sound like a blow, just a soft
sort of thud, and then I heard him cry out, "My God, it's blood!" He
shuffled with his feet as if he was getting up, and then I heard another
blow, and he cried out, "Oh, you she-devil!" and was quiet, except for a
dripping and splashing upon the floor.

I ran out from behind my curtain at that, and rushed into the other
room, shaking all over with the horror of it. The old man had slipped
down in the chair, and his dressing gown had rucked up until he looked
as if he had a monstrous hump to his back. His head, with the gold
glasses still fixed on his nose, was lolling over upon one side, and his
little mouth was open just like a dead fish. I could not see where the
blood was coming from, but I could still hear it drumming upon the
floor. She stood behind him with the candle shining full upon her face.
Her lips were pressed together and her eyes shining, and a touch of
color had come into each of her cheeks. It just wanted that to make her
the most beautiful woman I had ever seen in my life.

"You've done it now!" said I.

"Yes," said she, in her quiet way, "I've done it now."

"What are you going to do?" I asked. "They'll have you for murder
as sure as fate."

"Never fear about me. I have nothing to live for, and it does not matter. Give me a hand to set him straight in the chair. It is horrible to see him like this!"

I did so, though it turned me cold all over to touch him. Some of his blood came on my hand and sickened me.

"Now," said she, "you may as well have the medals as anyone else. Take them and go."

"I don't want them. I only want to get away. I was never mixed up with a business like this before."

"Nonsense!" said she. "You came for the medals, and here they are at your mercy. Why should you not have them? There is no one to prevent you."

I held the bag still in my hand. She opened the case, and between us we threw a hundred or so of the medals into it. They were all from the one case, but I could not bring myself to wait for any more. Then I made for the window, for the very air of this house seemed to poison me after what I had seen and heard. As I looked back, I saw her standing there, tall and graceful, with the light in her hand, just as I had seen her first. She waved good-bye, and I waved back at her and sprang out into the gravel drive.

I thank God that I can lay my hand upon my heart and say that I have never done a murder, but perhaps it would be different if I had been able to read that woman's mind and thoughts. There might have been two bodies in the room instead of one if I could have seen behind that last smile of hers. But I thought of nothing but of getting safely away, and it never entered my head how she might be fixing the rope round my neck. I had not taken five steps out from the window skirting down the shadow of the house in the way that I had come, when I heard a scream that might have raised the parish, and then another and another.

"Murder!" she cried, "Murder! Murder! Help!" and her voice rang out in the quiet of the nighttime and sounded over the whole countryside. It went through my head, that dreadful cry. In an instant lights began to move and windows to fly up, not only in the house behind me, but at the lodge and in the stables in front. Like a frightened rabbit I bolted down the drive, but I heard the clang of the gate being shut before I could reach it. Then I hid my bag of medals under some dry fagots, and I tried to get away across the park, but someone saw me in the moonlight, and presently I had half a dozen of them with dogs upon my heels. I crouched down among the brambles, but those dogs were too many for me, and I was glad enough when the men came up and prèvented me from being torn into pieces. They seized me, and dragged me back to the room from which I had come.

"Is this the man, your Ladyship?" asked the oldest of them—the same whom I found out afterwards to be the butler.

She had been bending over the body, with her handkerchief to her eyes, and now she turned upon me with the face of a fury. Oh, what an actress that woman was!

"Yes, yes, it is the very man," she cried. "Oh, you villain, you cruel villain, to treat an old man so!"

There was a man there who seemed to be a village constable. He laid his hand upon my shoulder.

"What do you say to that?" said he.

"It was she who did it," I cried, pointing at the woman, whose eyes never flinched before mine.

"Come! come! Try another!" said the constable, and one of the men-servants struck at me with his fist.

"I tell you that I saw her do it. She stabbed him twice with a knife. She first helped me to rob him, and then she murdered him."

The footman tried to strike me again, but she held up her hand.

"Do not hurt him," said she. "I think that his punishment may safely be left to the law."

"I'll see to that, your Ladyship," said the constable. "Your Ladyship actually saw the crime committed, did you not?"

"Yes, yes, I saw it with my own eyes. It was horrible. We heard the noise and we came down. My poor husband was in front. The man had one of the cases open, and was filling a black leather bag which he held in his hand. He rushed past us, and my husband seized him. There was a struggle, and he stabbed him twice. There you can see the blood upon his hands. If I am not mistaken, his knife is still in Lord Mannering's body."

"Look at the blood upon her hands!" I cried.

"She has been holding up his Lordship's head, you lying rascal," said the butler.

"And here's the very sack her Ladyship spoke of," said the constable, as a groom came in with the one which I had dropped in my flight. "And here are the medals inside it. That's good enough for me. We will keep him safe here tonight, and tomorrow the inspector and I can take him into Salisbury."

"Poor creature," said the woman. "For my own part, I forgive him any injury which he has done me. Who knows what temptation may have driven him to crime? His conscience and the law will give him punishment enough without any reproach of mine rendering it more bitter."

I could not answer—I tell you, sir, I could not answer, so taken aback was I by the assurance of the woman. And so, seeming by my silence to agree to all that she had said, I was dragged away by the butler and the constable into the cellar, in which they locked me for the night.

There, sir, I have told you the whole story of the events which led up to the murder of Lord Mannering by his wife upon the night of September the 14th, in the year 1894. Perhaps you will put my statement on one side as the constable did at Mannering Towers, or the judge afterwards at the county assizes. Or perhaps you will see that there is the ring of truth in what I say, and you will follow it up, and so make your name forever as a man who does not grudge personal trouble where justice is to be done. I have only you to look to, sir, and if you will clear my name of this false accusation, then I will worship you as one man never yet worshiped another. But if you fail me, then I give you my solemn promise that I will rope myself up, this day month, to the bar of my window, and from that time on I will come to plague you in your dreams if ever yet one man was able to come back and to haunt another. What I ask you to do is very simple. Make inquiries about this woman, watch her, learn her past history, find out what use she is making of the money which has come to her, and whether there is not a man Edward as I have stated. If from all this you learn anything which shows you her real character, or which seems to you to corroborate the story which I have told you, then I am sure that I can rely upon your goodness of heart to come to the rescue of an innocent man.

**Other rediscovered classics
by Sir Arthur Conan Doyle
available from Chronicle Books:**

The Lost World & The Poison Belt
The Professor Challenger Adventures: Volume I
Introduction by William Gibson

When the World Screamed & Other Stories
The Professor Challenger Adventures: Volume II